RAVE REVIEWS FOR THE WORK OF DOUGLAS CLEGG!

"If any author is going to usurp the throne of Stephen King, it will be Douglas Clegg."

—*Pulphouse Magazine*

"Every bit as good as the best works of Stephen King, Peter Straub, or Dan Simmons. What is most remarkable is not how well Clegg provides chills, but how quickly he is able to do so."

—*Hellnotes*

"Unforgettable!"

—*The Washington Post*

"Doug Clegg is one of horror's most captivating voices."
—*BookLovers*

"Douglas Clegg's short stories can chill the spine so effectively that the reader should keep paramedics on standby!"

—Dean Koontz

"Douglas Clegg's writing is like a potent drink that goes down with deceptive smoothness—right before it knocks you on your derriere."

—Horroronline

"Clegg's skill at elucidating the psychological lives of his characters in precise, revealing prose makes the emotions more disturbing than the violence itself."

—*Publishers Weekly*

"Clegg has cooler ideas and is much more of a stylist than either Saul or Koontz."

—*Dallas Morning News*

"Reminded me of King and McCammon at their best. I was awestruck."

—*The Scream Factory*

YOU COME WHEN I CALL YOU

DOUGLAS CLEGG

LEISURE BOOKS NEW YORK CITY

A LEISURE BOOK®

March 2000

Published by

Dorchester Publishing Co., Inc.
276 Fifth Avenue
New York, NY 10001

ISBN 0-8439-4695-4

For Linda Marrow.

With the understanding that this is as much for Raul Silva, Sky Nonhoff, Johanna Nielsen, Rich Chizmar, Matt Schwartz, David Silva, John Scoleri, Peter Enfantino, Irwyn Applebaum, Meg Ruley, and every single person at Dorchester Publishing, including but not limited to Don D'Auria, Brooke Borneman, Tim DeYoung, Kelly Bloom, and Kim MacNeill. Thanks to Francoise Hardy for helping me through the final rewrite. So many people lived through this novel with me—all understood what I was doing, no matter how mad it might've seemed at the time. This novel is madness; this novel is part of my blood; this story is something that has been with me for years. Now it's yours.

"You come when I call you."
—what we say to dogs and children and those beyond our control

Interview with the Demon

1

The teenaged boy spoke into the tape machine:

"Here's all I know. We did something terrible. It wasn't us. But we let it in."

His interrogator asked:

"How did you let it in?"

The boy said:

"If I tell you, you won't believe me. If I tell you, you're gonna say we're insane. I'm not stupid. I know what you think. You think, 'Here's this sixteen-year-old who probably killed all these people, and now he doesn't want to have to take the blame so of course he blames it on demons.' But here's the thing: I was there. You weren't. I saw them. I saw her."

"Where?"

"Inside me. I saw her inside me. She's inside all of us. It's too late."

"And where is she now?"

"I don't know. Maybe sleeping. Maybe she's waiting. Maybe . . ."

"Yes?"

"Maybe she wants all of this to be forgotten and then maybe she'll come back, years from now, maybe she'll come back because we hurt her, we wounded her in some way, and she doesn't have as much power. Maybe when she's all healed, she'll come back."

"What did you do to hurt her?"

"Not just me, all of us."

"How did you hurt her?"

"There are rituals. One of us knew how. Maybe he didn't know how. Maybe he lied. You gotta understand it was crazy. It was crazy. Everything was burning. Everyone was dying or dead. It was like this little point of—I don't know—craziness that made total sense. What we did. At the time. It seemed right. It seemed like the only thing. But now it sounds insane. It sounds like something evil. What we did."

A pause on the tape.

The question was repeated.

"We stopped her," the boy finally said.

"You stabbed her with this knife that you mentioned? The one that—"

"Sends people to Hell. That's what it was supposed to do. But, no. We didn't. We should've maybe. You weren't there. It's crazy. What we did."

"What did you do?"

"All of us did it. We all did."

"How can you stop a demon?" the man asked.

2

A girl said into the tape machine:

"I don't remember what happened. You tell me."

The man asked, "You mean you don't remember what happened to your family?"

Silence on the tape for several minutes.

Then: "My grandmother gave me a Bible to read. In it, there are demons, but none seem very real. Do you believe in God?"

"That's the search of life. But yes, I believe in God. Perhaps not the way some people would think of God, but yes."

"I guess if you believe in God, you'd believe in demons, too, wouldn't you?"

"Perhaps."

"I don't believe in demons. It's stupid to believe in demons, isn't it? It's like fairy tales or dreams. It makes no sense. I think it's all a lie. I think one of them did it all. I saw him kill my mother. I saw him kill all of them."

"Where are the bodies?"

"I don't know," she said. "I don't remember. I told you."

Then, after a moment's pause, she added:

"I do remember one thing."

"What?"

"I remember a wall. I remember a shadow on the wall. I remember . . . wings, like bats, in a cave, all around me . . . and seeing a light so blue that it was like a perfect sky and then I saw what looked like a wolf above me lean down and whisper something dreadful to me."

"What did the wolf say?"

"My name. That's all. He called me by name. He knew my name. But it was a dream. It was a nightmare. I'm awake now. It didn't happen."

3

A different boy laughed as the tape whirred. "This is a big fucking contraption," he said.

"I don't like cassettes."

"Yeah, I guess they suck. So, I guess Peter probably told you that completely nuts story about demons and stuff, right? Yeah, I knew he would. He's delusional. There's no way that happened."

"Alison told me that you did it."

A pause.

"Is this for the cops?"

"No, it's for my own research."

"Okay. Well, I didn't do it. It wasn't me anyway, even though I guess my hands did some of it." He laughed again. "All right, I'll tell you the truth. It wasn't demons, it was the Devil, I'm pretty sure, yeah. It was like the Big Bad Guy. Possession and all that bullshit—I mean, I'm not Catholic or anything, but I sort of believe in Hell at this point and I sort of believe in Heaven, and maybe I'm as messed up as all these docs say and maybe I really think I saw the Devil or maybe it was like a movie of the Devil or maybe I really did murder a bunch of people, but hell, find their bodies, okay? Find their fucking bodies. That's what the lawyers said. Find their bodies, and then you can come execute me or whatever they do to kids who kill."

"What did the Devil look like?"

"See, I can tell you don't believe in this shit. That's cool. Most jerk-offs in this world think there's no such thing and that it's all make-believe and stuff, but that's because they never experienced it. They never got touched by it, like we did."

"I've studied cases of demonic possession before."

"Yeah, like *The Exorcist*, right? Shit, a kid in a bedroom spitting pea soup's kind of sweet compared to what we went through."

"Tell me about the Devil."

"Okay. Well, it's not just one thing, is it? It's many. It's goo dripping out of someone's brain and that someone still talking to you and maybe it's got claws and maybe you're just dreaming standing up—and maybe it crawls across your hands like ants and scorpions and then it just looks like maybe a pretty girl. A pretty girl who knows how to get boys. A pretty girl who has things inside her. Well, there was this girl—wait, she was more like a woman—and she was a demon only not like you think of demons, and she could sort of change things, she could bend things, you know? Like a mirror—like a funhouse mirror—and she had this thing where once she had you, you were hers and she made all kinds of things happen . . ." He kept laughing as he spoke, giggling, sniggering. "Like, you know, people would . . . oh shit, I can't even say it, you know I saw all kinds of shit, stuff that you only dream about. It was all in us to begin with. I don't think she could've done what happened without us. I think we were each part of her. But it was all the Devil, you know? It was all this other thing going on, I mean, I got this from the source, I got it from the person who knows. Shit, we're still part of her. She's in us. I tried to stop her. Hell, we all did. I even had this knife—this sort of ritual thing. It was called an athame. It could've sent her to Hell. I know it could've."

"Are you possessed?"

"I don't know, but even when I'm talking to you now, I can see her, over there, calling me. But that's why I'm going into the looney bin, ain't it?"

"Over here? By the window?"

"Yeah. Right there."

"Describe her."

"Well, Christ, she's really pretty and she—wait . . . she's . . ."

"What's she saying to you? Right now?"

"If I was to tell you, she'd kill me. And maybe you, too. I can't tell anyone. It's something that's between her and me. Until the end of time."

The last tape played.

"Who are you?"

A sound like rushing wind on the tape.

"I am that I am."

"Why are you inside him?"

"He has sacrificed to me. He has given his soul to me."

"What do you mean to do with him?"

"What I mean to do with all of them. All of those I have touched. All of those who have partaken of me."

And then, something that sounded like a screeching howl, overlaid with another sound, like hundreds of people whispering secrets in an echoing cavern.

When the sound had finally stopped, the man asked: "Are you a demon?"

"I am the enemy of your kind."

"And your name?"

"Lamia," and even though the voice was still the boy's, it sounded like a woman speaking from within him.

"Why are you here?"

"You called me."

"And why did you come?"

"These children. They have stolen something from me. I will never leave them until I have it again."

"And what is it they have?"

The silence began, and it was a silence that seemed to stretch across twenty years.

BOOK ONE

NOW, TWENTY YEARS LATER
DAYS OF RECKONING

The Heart Is a Lonely Hunter
—the title of a novel by Carson McCullers

PART ONE: OTHERS

Chapter One

Alison, Los Angeles

"I'm crazy," the woman said, blinking. "Right?" She looked from her bandaged wrists to the doctor and then at the bookshelves. She was self-conscious. She would crawl out of her skin if she could.

She had done something terrible once. This much, he knew.

She wore glasses, and her hair was long and light brown. She was obviously very pretty although she had worked to frump herself up by wearing a long shirt and a gold sweater that gave a pallid cast to her olive complexion, as well as emphasizing her short waistline. Somewhere in her life she had taught herself to not be too pretty. Perhaps she rebelled against the pressure of living in the Los Angeles area, where beautiful was the golden mean. Perhaps it was something deeper. Something that made her not want to attract anyone. Made her want to try to disappear within baggy clothes, homely outfits . . .

He knew from reading through her file that she had been in and out of institutions for many years, and now lived with her husband in the Los Feliz section of the city. "I used to be schizo, then just bipolar, and now, Doc, I got to tell you, I'm not so sure." She had learned to be glib, in order to distance herself from the ordeal she had lived through. Continued to live through. He had seen patients similar to this before; similar, but not the same as this one.

She was different.

She was trying to get at the truth of her life.

He knew.

Dr. Diego Correa, sitting across from her at his desk, shook his head. "I think you've been misdiagnosed. Unfortunately, back when you first underwent psychiatric treatment, that label was pretty much given out across the board. Nobody should ever make that kind of pronouncement on a girl of sixteen."

"I don't know, Doc," she said, scanning the books on his shelf, "schizo seemed as good a word as any." She giggled slightly, perhaps aware of her own madness. She shook her head, dismissing a question only she might know.

"I don't believe it," he said. "I've been working with schizophrenics for years, and you don't exactly conform to any of the known behaviors."

She did that thing with her eyes again—blinked twice before she spoke, as if she were still trying to control some inner rage—the clenched fists on the arms of the chair, the blinking eyes, the tight set to her lips. "I was in the Falmouth hospital for six years, Doctor. I know crazy. When I talked to them about demons, the other patients, they told me they'd had visits from demons, too. So, what, you're going to tell me that's not a classic pattern? Delusions, demons, all that stuff. I had it in a big way."

"But you didn't see demons at Falmouth, did you?"

The woman shrugged. "I've seen them before, though."

"I think you saw something, too. Before."

She took a breath. Deep. She must have been a smoker once, for she breathed the air like it should have a taste to it. "I don't remember any of it."

"I believe you do. I believe that somewhere inside you is a key, and with that key, the doorway to a mystery."

"Your colleagues told me you were a bit unorthodox." She actually smiled, and for a moment he thought he saw just a brief image of the girl she must once have been. Before the fear had set in.

The dread.

"Actually, they laugh at me." He grinned, finally. "But I have a reputation, so they laugh and then they send me the ones that don't fit in their pigeonholes."

"Like me."

"Like you."

"Well, I've been through electroshock, and I almost OD'ed on Thorazine before I was twenty. Now I'm mid-thirties, and I'm tired of the meds. I don't want any more drugs. I don't want any more experimental treatments. So, what else you got?"

"It's simpler than that," he said. "Have you ever heard of regression therapy?"

"No, thank you. That sounds . . . well . . . nuts."

"Not as nuts as you think. I'm just going to hypnotize you. Nothing more. I'll ask you questions about your childhood. About that time. I understand from Dr. Hart that you've been having some more problems."

She sighed, and in that one brief exhalation, there was resignation, perhaps even acceptance of something she'd been fighting for years. "Call it what you want. I've been seeing it again."

"What?"

She looked beyond him, through him, as if he were just another in a long line of doctors and psychiatrists and specialists she had seen and would continue to see into eternity—and yet not really *see* at all. It was as if she had told this story a million times and would have to tell it a million times more. "The wall. It's a high, yellow wall—like a garden wall. And there's this shadow on it, only it's made of blood. It's a woman. And it moves. And then my head starts pounding really hard. And I bleed."

"Nosebleeds?"

"Nosebleeds, mouthbleeds, other, more private places."

"You menstruate?"

She hesitated. Less glib about this aspect of her life. Then, almost a whisper, she said, "Yes . . . Not on schedule, either. Maybe it's like Dr. Hart said, maybe it's just stress." Her voice changed, almost imperceptibly, from the wisecracking tone to this core of vulnerability. She was this beautiful child, untouched, somewhere inside the grown woman's body, confused by the world now that she had to live by adult rules and beliefs. "I see this wall. And that's it. I break out in a cold sweat. Something is coming over that wall, or I'm going over it. Something. Something *terrible*."

"Do you remember anything other than the wall?"

"Not really. But it terrifies me. And I know that's what it wants."

"It?"

"The demon. Do you believe in demons?" She jutted her chin out like a willful child.

He liked seeing this spirit in her, just when he'd been worried that her spirit had been broken on the psychoanalytical wheel.

"I'm not sure," he said.

"Well, that's *something*. They put me in Falmouth because of

17

that. Because I told them I knew a demon. Those doctors were positive there were no demons."

"Do you remember how you met this demon?"

"No."

"Would you like to try a session now?"

"Regress?" she asked, then nodded. "Sure. Why not."

"First," he said, "close your eyes."

She said, "All right, but promise me something."

"Of course."

"Promise me you won't do anything to make me afraid."

"I promise."

"It lives on that. Fear. That's why it never died. Because we're still afraid of it."

"Do you think it will come and get you? Is that what you're afraid of?"

"Oh," she said, her smile trembling, "I know it will. As long as we're all alive and safe and afraid, it's going to find us."

"Close your eyes," he said. "Now, tell me your name."

"Alison. Alison Chandler."

"What was your name when you were fifteen?"

"Hunt."

"In the room in your mind, Alison, there's a mirror. I want you to go to it, to look at yourself. I want you to see Alison Hunt when she was seventeen. I want you to tell me what she looks like, and what she's wearing. Can you do that for me?"

"I can't remember."

"All right. Look in the mirror. Alison Hunt is fifteen or sixteen. Can you see her now?"

"Yes," she said, "clearly. I'm sixteen. I'm sixteen. I'm in love. I'm pretty, I guess. I look the way sixteen-year-old's look, except for one thing."

"What's that?"

"The blood. Oh, my God, the blood. Oh, Jesus, look at it, look at all of it."

"On your hands, Alison?"

"No," she whispered, *"on my lips."*

Chapter Two
Sacrament of the Sacred Heart Church

In another part of the city, a man listened for the darkness as it approached.

It moved in a fog of silence. He could feel it. He could hear it. He could smell it.

Like a cold, dripping cave, the smell of dead animals, of warm, damp decay. What waited for him knew his real name, the name of the Beast, the Beast of his soul and heart and mind, for he had a name other than the one he went by. What waited for him would not call him The Face, although that was the name he had chosen to hide within. What waited for him knew his secret name. The Face knew about names, how they would betray you, how they would hold power over you . . .

But he knew what he had been called before, and he knew that someone would come calling for him.

He had hoped to die before it happened.

The man who called himself The Face had been living in the old church for nearly eighteen years. It had once been called *La Infantida,* nearly a century before, and then it was Saint Matthew's, and then, when World War Two broke out, it became known as the Sacrament of the Sacred Heart of the Blessed Virgin. It was a stone structure now, although the church had begun its existence as wood and adobe. It had been added onto until it looked cold and severe and unapproachable. Its dwindling congregation through the past two decades attested to this quality—as if the church, Roman Catholic by design, required abandonment in order to fulfill some architectural destiny. It was, this man thought, more cavern than cathedral, with its burrows beneath the nave, and the low-rent mausoleum below ground; behind it, two small bungalows that had served as church offices and shelters for runaways and the destitute. That had been when there was still a congregation, when there was still a priest. When he had first come, the stern church had been sanctuary to him—he was not Roman Catholic, and he didn't believe or accept the tenets of that faith, but he took comfort in a ritual that seemed to stave off the lonesomeness of his existence. He had performed menial tasks for the priest. He helped with the collection baskets on Sundays. He mopped the floor of the basement before a meeting or a prayer breakfast. He had watched the devout begin to attend services less and less, in favor of other churches, as if this one had acquired an invisible stain since his arrival.

Because of the way he looked.

His appearance was too frightening for anyone but the priest, so he wore a makeshift veil across his face, beneath a baseball cap. The parishioners only knew that he was deformed; they did not know in what way. Although certain children, mischievous, had torn the veil more than once to get a glimpse of the Dog Man, or as some in the neighborhood called him, *el hombre del diablo*. The priest had been kind to The Face, but was a drinker, and a smoker, and succumbed within a few years to disease. Then, when the church had fallen on hard times, and the clergy and congregation both had abandoned it, The Face stayed on, sleeping in one of the old offices. When the rats and the vagrants became too difficult to fight off, he had moved into the church basement, which was small. He left candles around him all day to keep the rats back, and he stayed up every night, waiting. Occasionally, as was the case this night, he had a companion—an old woman who lived mainly on the street, dying of something in her gut, came in and slept when the nights were too cold or the threat of harm from a harsh city were too much. She might moan with pain now and then, but she left him alone even when she sat near him. It was good to have some companionship, even if the two never spoke. The warmth of another human being was enough.

His mind grew dim, but the sense of *It* had grown stronger with the years.

He knew this was because *She* was growing stronger, like a radio signal increasing its wavelength.

The fires were harbingers of her approach—the neighborhood had housefires periodically, and sometimes the dry grass in the old park caught fire, too. It all had meaning.

And the dead girl, left on the steps, a message.

"We are those she touched," someone whispered to him while he *was fighting to stay awake, a whisper like a heartbeat, a whisper like wings moving in a dark cave. "She's within us now."*

The vestibule was lit with votive candles. Their light allowed him to read his books all night long, and when some poor soul came into the church, the candles somehow helped calm and comfort them. Sometimes he burned incense, just to rid the place of the smell of vermin and mildew; the scent of the incense lingered from the previous night.

The Face felt older than years, and as *She* grew stronger, he grew more enfeebled. He passed his hand through his white hair. It was night, and he stood before the space where the old wooden cross had once hung, where his prayers at the altar had gone unanswered. How could there be a kind God when such as those lived? The old woman, homeless and diseased, lifted her head from the front pew. She mouthed a word. He could not understand her.

Passed through the blood like a virus, like a gene, like a throwback to the beginning of the world.

He looked toward the sacristy door. He thought he heard a noise. The people who had set fire to the block two nights before had left the church alone. It would not be them. "Who's there?"

The old woman at the pew lifted her head again, and glanced toward the door.

"Perhaps we have a guest tonight," he said, but did not go to open the dark, wood door. He did not feel fear so much as the acceptance of what was inevitable. Whether this was the thing he dreaded most or not, now, did not matter.

What he dreaded most would come to him.

Would find him.

Then, whatever was there, in that room, pressed the door open.

As it swung wide, The Face whispered, "Is it you?"

He smelled the dry air, the dust, and the meat, like a slaughterhouse.

The old woman, seeing what approached, opened her mouth in a silent scream. A sliver of blood slid from the corner of her lips. The candles extinguished all around, and the sounds of the dark grew deafening.

Chapter Three
Deadrats in New York

Dirty, filthy, said the thing with the red eyes, lurking there in the dark corner like a thief. *Still here, my friend, still waiting, and I can wait a long, long time to be let out. And you will let me out, my boy, you will all let me out because you've been very bad and you need to take your medicine. Look, look where I've gnawed a hole in your heart, in your brain, like cheese, just nibble, nibble, nibble. Just us rats, you and me in here, just us rats.*

All of this was in his mind, and the man who should've been sleeping, for he hadn't in days, kept his eyes wide open. He surveyed the street, and watched as several children stood gawking at him from the sidewalk.

Okay, Deadrats, it's time to drink their blood. You want to do that, don'tcha, huh, don'tcha? Remember how good it tastes to lap at the open sores and the wounds of the dead and the almost-dead? Fucking incredelicious, partner! Make you feel like a kid again. He kept his grip tight on the steering wheel of the taxicab, and brought it over to the curb at Third Avenue. The children just stared at him, and he noticed that their skin all seemed to be rotting, and the flies buzzed around their festering sores. *Taste it don't waste it, Deadrats, my boy.*

"Get out," he told the thing in his head. "Get back in my brain-cave."

Don't it just get that ol' ticker beating hard and fast inside you, my boy, don't it give you a hard-on just like in the olden days when you think of the blood across your mouth, of pulling one of them screaming right down on your face and taking a big ol' chunk out of them right between their ribs?

"Shut up," he said.

A young woman came out from the gathering of children. She was the most beautiful woman he had ever seen, with sparkling hair, and the creamiest skin, but her dress was made out of some kind of animal hide, wrapped tight around her, and near her chest there was a gaping hole, as if someone had just stabbed her. And yet, she approached his taxicab as if she were just fine. She was not much out of her teenage years, and when she smiled, she looked like an absolute angel.

There she is, the thing in the room in his mind said. *Go to her, my boy, she is the love of your life.*

Something about her face, though, like it was melting wax in a burning sun, for the skin dripped across the eyes, obscuring them, and the lips blistered down her chin.

He pushed the door of the cab open, and stumbled out onto the street.

For a second, it didn't look like a woman at all, but something else.

Not what she was underneath.

Your eyes can play tricks on you, kiddo, ya never know in this life, maybe it's a girl, and maybe it ain't. Maybe it's an old man wearing a threadbare gray suit and holding an umbrella in his left hand.

Maybe it ain't.

Lightning struck somewhere above the skyscrapers. The landscape jolted. Manhattan melted down like ice cream, hardening into a sandy crust. He stood in a wasteland, in front of a small, brown tract house that was burning with no one around to stop the fire. He saw the great swarm of bees burst above the fire, and the dead, empty, white sky explode with fireworks and bees and showers of blood like afternoon rain.

And then, Manhattan again, Thirty-third and Third. The smell of grease and rubber and trash and flowers.

A woman with something in her hand, something she was holding out for him as she approached. It was a mass of twisted brown-red, and she said, *"Excuse me, but can you take me?"*

Dirty, filthy, it said in his head.

He grabbed her by the neck—

an old man with a face full of surprise like he had just encountered a nightmare.

And she kept smiling even while he strangled her—

She brought the thing in her hand up to his face and pressed it against his lips like an obscene kiss—

And the children who stood around him, all teenagers with their

23

faces blistering, their skin peeling, continued staring at him until someone off the street came up and pulled him back, socking him in the gut—

And he saw that he had almost killed a man in his early seventies who had, perhaps, just wanted to get a cab, and the girl, and the voice of the bad thing in his head, were gone.

He knew that It would be back, too.

It wasn't a girl or an old man or a swarm of bees, burning.

It was the orgasm of damnation.

It was the torn face of the past.

Peter, he thought, *is this happening to you, too? Is she calling all of us?*

PART TWO:
THE BUNGALOW

Chapter Four
Peter, Los Angeles, and What He Found There

1

After the riots and earthquakes of the previous years, Los Angeles had transformed, not just physically, but as if the city had an emotional life that was no longer vibrant, a life with barely a pulse.

Peter Chandler sought out the dead streets, the parks that looked more like graveyards than playgrounds, the places where the pulse was weakest.

The buildings were empty shells down the two side streets alongside the park. He had watched them burn from the hillside back in the late spring a few years before. After the recent earthquake, there were cracks along the foundations, chainlink fences around the apartments and bungalows, red-tagged by the city as uninhabitable. He knew that this would be the place where he felt most comfortable, the blackened earth, the emptiness, the bits of paper, windblown, across this desolate stretch of the city. There was a beauty to torn brick and broken glass, to bungalows strung end to end like Christmas lights gone out, to the church on the corner of Fuego and Castor Street, the church called the Sacrament of the Sacred Heart, with its boarded windows, its bent and haggard face. It was only another mile to Little Tokyo, and he could go have lunch at Su Hiro for a few dollars, and then walk back up to the park across from the church. He would not have noticed the church except for the riots, when parts of the city were torched and palm trees had exploded as if with napalm on the boulevards. But it was a place, now, for him, that seemed to be the threshold to a memory.

It had been in May that the *L.A. Times* had run the story about Sacred Heart on Fuego, downtown, about how it had been shut down nearly ten years before, and had fallen into disrepair in a neighborhood that had never known repair. How there had been a murder, at the church, on its steps.

Sacred Heart.

No ordinary bullet-to-the-head murder, no knife-to-the-back, no drive-by-shooting.

It was a woman who was killed on the steps of the Sacrament of the Sacred Heart Church, and the police thought it might be the work of a religious group, perhaps a black magic offshoot of *Santeria* or maybe something even as simple as an ex-lover seeking revenge. In blood, the killers had written:

el corazon.

The victim had been operated on, while she was still living, and her heart had been removed.

The murdered girl was only seventeen, the newspaper clippings went, when they had finally identified her. Her face had been burnt beyond recognition, but the rest of her was unmarked.

Except for the wound.

Woman's little wound.

The place where her heart had been taken.

Peter had been sitting at home, on a Friday afternoon, reading the paper, and when he had come to this item, in the Metro section, he had looked up at his wife. She was across the room from him, going to the kitchen for more coffee—in his mind, she froze, time froze, and he wished that he had not seen the paper that day.

2

Oh, yes, the memories came back in a rush like a flooding river, he couldn't spend his life pretending he hadn't done what he had done.

But he could pretend for her.

At least, for his wife, he could pretend that nothing was up, nothing was gnawing at him on such a fine day.

He glanced back down at the newspaper, pushing a more painful memory out of his mind for the moment.

The church.

The dead body on its steps.

Peter had a sudden feeling of displacement, as if all that was around him, the smell of coffee, the newspaper in his hands, the taste of a remembered kiss, all of it was a dream.

3

He went to find the Sacred Heart, and with it, he found the park directly across from the church, and the young people who lived in the empty buildings.

And he watched them.

Weeks passed, and still he went, because he knew: this was the time.

This would be the place.

He wasn't fired from his job until the middle of October, and this freed him to keep his vigil most of the time; he disliked lying to his wife about how he spent his days, but he knew that there was no choice. He was not going to reopen old wounds for her, not if he could protect her from them.

At night, he wrote about his life—not because it interested him, but because he could no longer hold it inside.

He called these writings his "confessions."

4

Peter Chandler Confessions

I never thought I would write down what happened in Palmetto, California, the summer I turned sixteen. I figured it would just blow away like the town itself has, over the years. Maybe I just need to set the record straight after all the lies that were written and taken as the God's honest truth. I guess I thought if we never spoke of it, it might lose some of its power. And then, perhaps, the lie would become more real. We were—all of us—afraid that someone would find out the true story and try to find her through us— and try to bring the pieces together again.

I know it can happen.

I feel it.

I don't think we really killed her, and I don't think she's given up, even after all these years.

She's always in my dreams.

She never lets go.

I dreamt of her last night. I was in a slaughterhouse, filled with the pathetic whimperings of half-dead animals, some just becoming con-

scious of the fate awaiting them. They screamed like human beings—
they had, in the extremity of their tortures, passed the barrier that
divided humans and beasts. Skinless creatures swayed in death throes
from thick, silver hooks. Beneath them, on the turquoise mosaic
floor, rows of buckets overflowed with clotting blood.

She was there.

She was at work on one of the animals. She'd peeled its skin off
with her fingernails. Her face dripped blood. She was uncon-
scionably beautiful with the dark liquid trickling like tears across
her cheeks, down her chin, along her slender neck.

She gave the call.

I felt it rising in my throat when I awoke in a cold sweat to a
dark room—my own bedroom.

"You'll wake up in a cold sweat in the middle of the night,"
she'd said in the dream, "and you won't know where you are. And
no matter where you think you are, you are here, always, with me.
In here."

I got up and went into the bathroom. I looked in the mirror to see
who this person could be.

My face was still there—but inside my face, I saw her, staring
out through my skin, a reflection within a reflection.

I feel like she's here, somewhere. The hallucinations, the
dreams, the telegrams, even the riots.

Even the Sacrament of the Sacred Heart.

I'm going to go there again.

I know she's there.

Waiting.

Chapter Five

Another House of Darkness

1

One dawn, in Los Angeles, in late October, Peter Chandler was sitting with a cup of coffee on a bench in the park. He watched a

teenaged girl through the chain-link fence that marked the boundary of Fuego Park downtown. The sky threatened rain, but one never knew with this sky; the ocean breeze could come down and blow the ash-gray clouds out to sea or across the hills to the valleys. He sniffed the air—the city smelled different, and perhaps it was the promise of rain. *Good. Needs it.*

The girl caught his attention because she was alone.

There were a few other people in the park: vagrants, and a strung-out looking woman with two very young children in tow.

But the girl—she was between fifteen and seventeen, and wore a blue tee shirt and black jeans. Her hair was reddish; she was pale, and appeared to be having some trouble moving. For a moment, he thought she wasn't there at all, and that he had imagined her. But there she was, real. As she walked by him, he felt sure she had seen him. A fear thrummed against his heart, a dread he had forgotten about years ago. But then, she went about her business—she was looking for something, as if she'd lost some money, or left a book, or a jacket, down near the bus stop on the corner. She glanced up and down the street—looking for the bus, or a friend? She wiped at the hair that fell down over her forehead.

She must have sensed his watching, for she turned.

It took his breath away for a moment.

When she did that.

Turned.

Her face was less than beautiful. *Scraggly.* Eyes like pennies. Dark hollows beneath her eyes, and her lips were drawn tight as if someone had taken sewing needles and threaded them together.

He could barely think the name, let alone say it. His tongue was dry in his throat when he called to her, and the worst thing that she could do, she did.

She smiled because somebody knew her name.

2

Peter Chandler/Confessions

I looked at a picture taken of us that summer. Alison, Nathaniel, Sloan, and me. The dog, too. Can't forget the dog. I see, in it, that Charlie is there, too, way in the background, watching from the

Rattlesnake Wash. Probably spying on us, because he was always in love with Alison. There are some people in the world who believe that the soul is captured in a photograph, and I wonder if it's true.

Because she had all of us.

Alison, Nathaniel, Sloan, Peter, Lammie, Charlie.

I got the telegrams this week, too. Some of them said: *something's wrong. don't come. don't return, no matter what. none of you together.*

All unsigned. But one of the telegrams sticks out in my mind.

It says, simply, *you are what you eat.*

3

Peter, watching in the park across from the church, didn't know what he would do with the girl, but he knew he had to stop her. He could not imagine hurting a teenager, but he might have to do something to keep her away from here.

She may be a dream, he thought. *She may be a flashback through memory. She may not exist.*

But part of him felt compelled, even if this was a phantom.

Peter got up, forgetting the book on the bench, and walked in her direction. He thought it curious, this girl all by herself downtown, so assured in her walk, so determined.

Why am I following her? he wondered, hoping he'd come up with an answer. He couldn't say the name again. The name he thought belonged to her, because he was afraid she would smile at him again, and he would have to swallow a scream.

What if he were *right?*

She turned left onto Castor Street, with its remaining bungalows. When he turned the corner, she was out of sight. He looked from house to house, but did not see her hiding in any of the yards, and he did not hear a single door shut.

He was relieved that she had not gone up the church steps.

He walked the block three or four times, but none of the houses seemed right for her.

And then he stopped dead in his tracks.

Down an alleyway, alongside one of the larger houses, was a small bungalow with a partially caved-in, fire-blackened roof. Plywood had been nailed sloppily over the large square windows. Trash had piled up in the yard. *No one lives there*, he thought. Something haunting about it, something that kept him gazing at the rotting house.

It was the graffiti that was spray-painted across the chipped walls that caught his attention. Most of it was about gangs or Jesus, but clearly he saw the words, *NO MAN'S LAND*, sprayed in red, and he felt a jolt as if shaken by a brief and nearly imperceptible earthquake.

Then the world was still.

Peter felt a few tentative drops of water on his face, and he looked away from the bungalow and up to the skies. The smell and feel of rain was not clean at all, but dirty and warm like a child's hands. He closed his eyes and tried not to remember the girl's face. My imagination. Shrinks were all on target—hysteria, drugs, alcohol, trauma, imagination. No demons. No monsters.

"You're It!" someone shouted from the past, a child playing tag. "You're It!"

He opened his eyes upon the bungalow. He walked toward it without really wanting to. He made fake promises to himself: *If I get there and don't see her I will go home and forget this and never go to the park again. If I get there and the girl is there, I will come back another time with a gun to make sure she doesn't hurt me. If I get there and everything is boarded up I will pretend that it's too hard to get in and look around.*

He stepped over coiled barbed wire and leftover cartons from MacDonalds and Burger King. The ground beneath all the yard trash was blackened from fire. Wadded papers rattled as something scuttled through the yard—he assumed rats or squirrels. He was not shocked to see a pile of wispy, blue pigeon's wings, as if torn from dead birds and stacked up on the porch. This was a place of filth. From the porch he could smell the house. The stench assaulted his senses: Human and animal feces, rotting food and garbage. Peter figured the place was full of drug addicts or was a gang hangout, or else nobody was in there at all . . . and something worse than life existed within those walls.

Or someone had died in there, behind that door, in one of those rooms, someone had died and it was the deathsmell.

31

And then he thought of something: the murdered girl . . . on the steps of the church . . .

What if she had been murdered around the corner from the church, and taken to the church steps as the sickest joke in the world?

The sacrament of the sacred heart.

He hadn't noticed until now how much this bungalow resembled the house that he and his family had lived in when he was a boy. The chipping stucco walls, the yard these dimensions, the family room window on his right, the door on his left. Even the trash in the yard—they had lived downwind of the town dump, and papers would sometimes drift into the yard when the winds picked up. Even the disrepair. The house on the desert, and this one in the city. Like a cyclone had lifted it from its foundation and brought it down this alley. *What if she comes to the window? Pressing her nose up against the glass, her breath fogging it up? What if she knows I followed her here? What if she's waiting?*

Just like the ruin of the house in Palmetto.

And the smell.

Even the deathsmell.

He could never describe it well—it was actually sweet and revolting at the same time.

It was the smell of the valley of the shadow.

Peter stood there, shoulders shaking. He managed to wipe the tears and the threat of memory from his eyes. He took several steps back down the alley, refusing to look back at the bungalow. No, he would just not go in there, he would go home. He had no doubt that this was the place where the girl had gone, but he would not go exploring.

"You believe what you can't see, boy?" his father was asking from distant memory.

Peter had no answer then. Still had no answer. He was halfway down the block, on his way back to the park, when he knew that he should go back to the bungalow. Perhaps he had seen wrong. Perhaps the girl was just part of his imagination. So many years ago, and here he was, still believing it. Believing what he couldn't see, and perhaps had never seen.

By the afternoon, Peter Chandler decided to break into the bungalow.

He had tried calling his wife, but she wasn't home—if she had been, perhaps he wouldn't have worked up sufficient nerve to go back there, down that alley, in the rain. *I'll just go in the front. Not like breaking in, anyway.* The porch was rotted out; he had to step over and around holes and broken boards to get to the front entrance. Just as he got up to the door, nailed over with plywood, his left foot broke through a weak spot of the porch floor. He had to grasp the doorframe for balance. Just as he drew his foot back up through the hole, something down below brushed his ankle.

A rat, he thought with a shiver, and brought his foot up.

The plywood on the door was easy to break off in chunks; it, like most of the house, was rotted to a cardboard thinness. Once he had cleared a space large enough to fit through, he tested the floor inside before placing all of his weight over the threshold. The coldness of the interior did not surprise him too much—the nights had been colder than normal lately, and houses like this would retain the temperature. The front hall was dark, and half of it was black and skeletal from a previous fire. It still smelled burnt. *This is where rats come to die.* He wanted to shout hello out of habit, but there didn't seem to be any need. Something about the bungalow silenced him.

It was as if something in the house would awaken if he spoke aloud. The area that had been the living room was shadowy—diffuse light came in from windows that were only half-shuttered with plywood.

He took a step into the room.

Shapes were huddled together in corners, and from them came snores. *Runaways*, he figured, and he was just about to back out of the house and forget the girl who looked like someone he had once known. *Some other day*, he promised, *you'll follow her again. She may not even be here.*

A woman's voice came from the shadows: "Anywhere you like."

Peter glanced about in the gray light. His vision finally adjusted; he could distinguish between the walls and sparse furnishings and the sleeping figures. A young woman, as thin as he had ever seen a young woman be, lay next to a sleeping teenaged boy. The boy was moaning lightly in some dream. The woman raised herself up and leaned back on one elbow. She watched Peter. "Just don't wake my old man," she whispered.

Peter nodded, not knowing what to say.

"You're looking for a girl," the woman said, and Peter felt sweat break out along his neck. She swiftly and silently disentangled herself from her boyfriend and rose from the floor. She went over to Peter, walking as if she were stepping on hot coals, and grabbed him by the wrist. "Tammy," she whispered in introduction. "It ain't much of a house, but it's paid for."

She took him back into what had once been the kitchen. It smelled of grease and something else—dead rats? The light was better; the window above the caved-in sink was only covered with plastic wrap. Tammy's face was drawn and tight; her eyes rested upon blackened smudges. Her hair was shaved on one side, and wild like twisting branches on the other. The word *eat* was tattooed into her scalp just above her right ear. She was bone-thin around the arms, which were studded with welts and bruises and tiny red dots. She wore a tight tee shirt, revealing ribs and collarbone; for shorts, she wore men's boxers. "You got to be real quiet, dude. Hey, you here for Mace? He got the power, dude, he got the juice, but he ain't been here yet, so we don't want no trouble. You got bread on you?"

Peter said, "The girl."

"You got her," Tammy said, doing a clumsy spin around to show off her body, then slapping her hips. She smiled a horrible grin, her teeth yellowed and rotted up through swollen gums. "For the right price, I'm the right girl. You got bread?"

He reached down into his pocket and found a few crumpled bills. He handed the wad to her.

She looked disdainfully at the money. "Shit."

"A particular girl. I think she lives here."

"Dude, we got lotsa girls here, boys, too, you can take your pick, but my old man's gonna want more'n this for even a feel. I'm special."

"The young girl. Seventeen. Red hair. I just want to know where she is. I want to see her."

Tammy wrinkled her nose as if smelling something awful. Her voice was husky and low, and it was obvious that she thought he was the most vile thing she had ever met in her life. "I know who you want," she said.

"She just came through here, I think."

"Yeah, yeah, that's her. You're kinda sick, y'know? We don't like that kinda trade here."

"What's her name?"

She shrugged. "Lives downstairs. Cellar. She got her old man, too. You look kinda straight—she in trouble or something?"

"She reminds me of someone." Peter swallowed hard.

Tammy sighed. "We all do. Dude, I am beat. You want a smoke?" She reached into her shirt, and brought out a crumbly cigarette and a pack of matches from between her breasts. "Hey, don't look at me like that; you *are* straight, it's Marlboro Light."

Peter glanced around, peering through the ruins of the hallway. There only seemed to be this one floor. Bungalows didn't have basements. This was crazy. This was . . . unreal. "Are there stairs down?"

"You gonna go *down* there?" She almost burned her fingers with the match. "Shit, dude, nobody goes down there'n ever comes back. I mean, I seen my old man beat the shit outta one a his girls 'til she was a goner, and I seen more ODs than highs, but what goes on down there ain't nothin' like you never saw."

He wanted to tell her, *I've seen a lot in my time.*

She was tripping over her words, as if she were afraid she wouldn't be able to get them all out of her mouth before someone shut her up. "Shit, he takes 'em down there and they don't *never* see the sun again, and it stinks down there, Jesus, they live offa rats, and my old man says we gonna haveta get ridda that geezer soon. Gives me the fuckin' creeps." She licked her lips.

"What about the girl?"

Tammy stepped closer to him.

Peter felt something, not the sexual heat this woman wanted him to feel, but something more like hunger. *What Sloan must've felt. Incubating. Inside.* She looked at him with her hollow eyes, gazing seductively, like a death's-head mask. Peter disgusted himself, repulsed by the image in his mind.

The face like the inside of a furnace. The consuming fire.

He wanted to shut her up, somehow. *Rip out her heart,* the thought came without his bidding. Didn't she know how she smelled? Like meat. Fresh red meat. Marbled with fat. He broke out in a sweat, but Tammy didn't notice. She smoked her cigarette

35

and glanced out the window. In the thin shaft of daylight she hardly looked real: she looked like a sketch.

But that smell of meat.

Tammy said, "She does okay. He don't hurt her, I guess. But I don't like her. I told Mace he gotta burn those two outta there. We had to burn this other freak out once. We can do it. She got sumpin' in her eyes, you know how you see people in the eyes? Well, she got nothin' there but what's good and rotten. I told Mace she look like a girl but she sumpin' else. What they do down there"—and Peter saw a tear trickle down the side of her face— "to others . . ." Tammy stubbed her cigarette out against the wall; the trace of her tear glistened in the light. "It's worst'n anything I ever hearda. Awful. Just awful. A sin."

Peter found himself asking what he didn't want to ask. "What do they do?" It was hardly a question; he wished he could suck it back into his throat like smoke so she wouldn't hear it. He had lived with the memory of awfulness most of his life. He knew the worst. He remembered nightmares beyond imagining. *You could just take Alison away again. Get as far as possible from what's awful in the world. You've done it before, you've run before, and it found you, finally, it found you.* "What do they do?" he repeated the question.

Tammy barely parted her lips.

"They hurt people," she said, slowly, deliciously. "It pleasures them." Her eyes lit up as she spoke, the tears making them shine, as if she, too, somehow enjoyed hurting people, and there was a madness to her look—he'd seen this before, back in those days when he was a teenager—a madness that was like an animal cunning. "You should hear them sometimes, down there, you should smell what they do, you should hear it, the last sound they make, the last sound. It's nothing, *nothing* like you never heard before. Like dirty little children . . . Like," she closed her eyes, remembering. "Like their hearts are being torn out."

5

Peter left Tammy standing there, tears staining her cheeks, an insane half-smile across her face, and went in the direction of the cellar. The stairs down had been burnt out, but there was a ladder, and he took a step down. *You believe what you can't see, boy?* The smell of animal came up stronger from below him. Urine, feces, rotting meat. At the bottom of the ladder, he stepped into a pile of leaves; as he balanced himself on the floor, he felt the icy chill of water along the soles of his feet. He moved away from the ladder, and the water streamed along his toes, soaking through his shoes. He heard water running as if from a faucet; the holes and cracks in the ceiling made jagged streaks of light through the darkness; the air was filled with motes of dust, floating in lazy spirals; something moved through the shallow water, toward him.

He held his breath, as the thing came into light.

A rat.

But it was dead, drawn by some unseen drain in the middle of the cellar floor, its fur matted and soaked through, its jaws opened in a death rictus. Caught with it, some leaves and twigs, and an old worn sock, as if this were the funerary raft to carry this rat to the halls of the dead.

Something else, too.

Floating slowly with the rat and its barge.

It was only in the brown, dusty light for a moment. But it seemed to stop there, in the shaft of light, as if unwilling to be tugged toward where the water flowed down. If Peter had not had the extra second or two, he might've thought it was an upturned leaf. But it was a human hand, small and perfect. The hand of a young child.

"What kind of son are you, anyway?" his father asked, the hand coming back like a whip, and down, and down, and down.

And then, it was gone, the child's hand, pulled back into the oily, dark waters.

It's not a dream, you're not hallucinating, it's too real. Get out of here, you idiot, he thought, *run up that ladder and burn rubber out of this hole and don't ever look back. You don't ever want to look back, remember? You promised that, you swore it. That night, when you got away, you made the deal, "Don't ever look back." But the calling. How the hell was I to know about the calling? That voice, over and over again through the dreams, "Peter! You got to get me out! Peter!" And how you repeated* "Don't look back or it'll get you, don't look back," *until you didn't hear the screaming anymore, and then you were miles away and you told yourself it was probably over quickly, you told yourself it wouldn't even've hurt it was prob-*

ably so quick, and what were you supposed to do, anyway? After all of it, what were you supposed to do? Don't look back. It gets you when you look back. Nobody should've looked back, but they did, didn't they? They looked back, and look what happened. It's not your fault, so get the hell out of this rat nest and get back in your car and get home to Alison and make sure you never look back.

But something else was moving. He smelled it: Something human, something alive. It was near the source of the dripping faucet. It scraped against a wall.

Peter moved away from the ladder, trying to adjust his eyesight to the darkness. Something brushed his ankles—another rat, but he held his breath to keep from giving himself away. He moved slowly backward, the chill of the water numbing his feet. He met some resistance as he went, trying to avoid the spears of light, staying to the shadows; but he didn't want to find out what he was stepping on, or over, or by. He backed up to a wall. He thought he would try and make his way back to the ladder, when he heard voices coming from the upstairs. "I don't give a fuck," a man said, and Tammy was whining and swearing, and Peter watched in horror as the ladder was pulled up from the cellar.

"You go down there, you take your chances," the man up in the house said.

"We got to burn 'em outta there, I tell you," Tammy said, her voice nervous and crackling.

Shout, damn it. Shout for help. Why can't you shout? Peter felt frozen inside, helpless. *Let out a scream, why don't you scream?* But he knew the answer. He was scared. He tried moving his lips, but only wind came through. No sound.

Someone was splashing water over in a corner.

Peter stood still. *I will die here,* he thought. *I looked back, and now I'm going to die for it. Jesus, you moron, you didn't even bring a weapon. How the hell do you expect to survive? You're going to die here and nobody's even going to know.*

Then it was quiet again. Just the dripping of water.

Maybe she's gone.

After ten minutes had gone by—minutes that seemed like hours to him—Peter moved along the wall, stepping over clumps of fur and leaves. He had noticed basement windows on the outside of the bungalow. Perhaps they were low enough that he could break the glass quickly and get out. Perhaps there was no glass and they were made of boards he could push aside. *Got to try something, Chandler, or you'll go down the drain with the rats.* He stopped every few steps to look through the lighted areas for the girl. *Girl. Who knows what she is?* He felt along the walls, until he thought he felt the edge of a window casing. He patted what he assumed would be the pane, but was merely cardboard. *This won't be hard.* He pushed on the board, and it gave fairly easily. It was slimy with mildew. He stripped the edge off.

Daylight illuminated a triangular patch all around him. The light hit something at his feet. She lay curled in the fetal position, raised above the water level by bundled rags and leaves and clumps of what could only have been dead rats. Her face was upturned in the light, although her eyes remained closed, and the gentle sound of light snores came from her nostrils.

Peter Chandler didn't know what the sound was that came from his throat, but it was like a shiver and a scream and a whisper—and nothing at all.

"Wendy," he said her name, for he recognized the brilliant red of her hair, and the bone-whiteness of her skin, and the turn of her carnelian lips. And he reached down to touch the face, the way a child might reach to touch fire even after he knows it might burn him, because he felt a kind of reckless madness in his blood. *How could she be?*

He heard the loud beating of his own heart.

His fingers, as they grazed the sleeping face, came away with human skin.

He stood over a sleeping girl whose face had come off in his hand like a mask, and beneath it, another face.

A different face, rotting.

We are those she has touched.

"You're here with me, in here, no matter where you are," the face beneath the face said, *"and when I call you, you come."*

"You believe what you can't see, boy?" that voice inside him, so familiar. *"I know you,"* it whispered from the back of his head, like a needle thrust through gray matter. *"I know you, inside and out. All of you."*

And then, omething shimmered across the face, like heat, something rippling beneath the skin.

It was a face that had been torn at by rats, its eye sockets empty.

Its jaw slowly opened, and roaches poured from its mouth as the light from the window fell across them.

Peter backed away, and tore at the cardboard along the window. He heard liquid movement surrounding him, as if there were others in the darkness with him. He smelled something different—*gasoline?*

"Burn those fuckers outta there!" a man upstairs shouted. As Peter looked up to the cellar door above him, he saw Tammy and a man with wild white hair and a ragged face dropping wads of burning newspaper down into a pile until there was a bonfire reaching almost up to them. The fire lit up most of the cellar, a fire that floated unnaturally on leaves and newspaper over dark water, and Peter now could see what he was surrounded by.

It looked like a smokehouse.

A slaughterhouse.

Human torsos strung from the ceiling, and ribcages stacked knee-deep in the water. And the shadows of other body parts cast, flickering in the growing flames.

And the smell.

The smell of it.

Fresh meat.

But the greatest obscenity of all was up against the wall on the other side of the fire.

Another man might've thought these were simply masks or dried paper lanterns, but Peter had seen too much in his life not to recognize these for what they were: faces of women and men and children that had been skinned and dried.

They formed one great tapestry of human suffering and carnage.

The fire caught there, too, and spread along the faces, flaring briefly, before dying out.

The smell was like a barbeque—

a town on the desert, burning.

And there was something there, with the shadows of the tortured, hiding its face.

A movement.

He ripped the rest of the window open, and looked back.

The light illuminated the cellar, and there, against the far wall, beyond the hanging bodies, was an old man with his arms spread wide apart at shoulder-height, his legs corded together.

You Come When I Call You

His face was long and twisted along the jaw line, and his skull seemed too narrow to be human. If Peter were to specify a creature which this human face most resembled, it would be that of a skinned dog.

And yet, Peter recognized the face. Sloan. Kevin Sloan.

Crucified.

The man's jaw worked silently.

Peter moved as if in slow motion around the burning refuse, through the muddy water, toward the man with his wrists spiked into the wall. The face was twisted and elongated, his eyes all but extinguished of life. He began bleating like a sheep about to be slaughtered.

Peter reached him, just as the fire burnt itself out, and only a square of light from the casement window shone through the room.

"My God," Peter said, and while he could no longer see the face of the man, he could feel his breath on his cheek as he got nearer to him. "My God." Light from the window illuminated his torso.

"Nah," the man whispered, "nah."

Tattooed on the man's chest was an image. It was a sketchy drawing of a heart rising off a thorned stem, as if the heart were a rose, and through the heart of the heart, several knives. Tattooed beneath it, in pale blue letters: *el corazon.*

Scars ran along his ribcage—healed bullet wounds.

"You're already dead," Peter whispered. "I killed you. I know I did."

The crucified man whispered, his breath rank as if what was in his mouth and down in his gut was putrid and steamy, "Who can kill a nightmare?" Then, he laughed, like a mad man, only softly, and his eyes stared at nothing.

And then, Peter felt no breath at all.

He felt a strong chill wind go through him, a bloodmemory.

The skin of the crucified man's face turned hard, and crinkled like parchment, folding in on itself, as if he had been dead for months and only now allowed to decay.

Peter was not sure if he was capable of movement. Then something animal in him took over, something beyond his thought process, beyond his logical mind. He raced for the open window, climbing out, scraping his sides on broken glass, *just anything to get out of there*, because he felt it, something else in there, moving across the shallow water and filth, something not quite human. His heart was beating so fast he could barely catch his breath when he stood up in the daylight world.

Behind the bungalow, the back entrance to the dilapidated church.

Sacrament of the Sacred Heart.

The house was on fire. He stood there, watching it as if he were still unsure whether or not this was a waking dream.

6

Yes, of course: sacrament of the sacred heart.

That's what it had been, some part of him whispered.

A sacrament.

What you did.

What happened in Palmetto, back when you were all young and innocent.

That night, Peter turned on the microcassette recorder and began:

It's in all of us, I'm sure of it. Delusions, waking dreams, hallucinations, and some that are very real. Our nightmares are flesh; our flesh is nightmare; she is coming again. We all feel her, still with us, her howling madness, the taste of her, and now, just as we knew it would happen, she's calling again in her own way, calling and drawing us, wanting us.

And we have what she wants.

BOOK TWO

THEN,
PALMETTO CALIFORNIA, TWENTY YEARS BEFORE

"Oh, Whistle, and I'll Come to You, My Lad"
—the title of a story by M. R. James

PART ONE: THE SOURCE

Chapter Six

When It First Arrived

1

It came to the high desert of California at the onset of summer with the dying of the dried-blossom Joshua trees, with the deflowering of the desert, in the form of a man. He had once been called Michael Southey, although he hadn't used that name for ten years, not since he'd caught it at his father's tent revival in some desert shitdust town. It had been passed to Michael by a little girl whose mother claimed she was possessed by demons, a child who swore with such passion, screamed the vilest obscenities, barked like a dog, even tried to bite, and from whose very fingertips fire spat. In those days, Michael had himself believed that the girl was inhabited by a nest of demons. It was the late 1960s, and he knew that devil worshippers were everywhere: in the growing hippie communes and the LSD psychedelic culture. It was the Devil's time. He was sure. He had laid his hands on the girl to cast out her demons, and cast them out he did.

When Jesus cast out demons, he sent them into swine, and sent the swine to their deaths.

But the demons Michael Southey cast from this girl came into himself: she bit him on the arm as he laid the flat of his palm against her forehead.

He became the vessel.

Michael Southey learned that what had gotten inside him was a glimpse of the Eternal. He thirsted for the knowledge God had bestowed upon him. As it took hold and became part of him, he acquired a new name through its baptism.

He called himself The Juicer.

The man stood five-foot, eight-inches and wore a smile across his face like Alfred E. Neuman, with the gap right in the middle. His eyes were yellow with disease; a brownish, scaly crust had already begun to seal them half-shut around the lids. His face was the color of summer squash, and seemed to have dried out as much from lack of spirit as from the desert air which he had been living in for the past six months. When he smiled that *What, me worry?* grin, he didn't seem to have any lips at all, just deep red gums engulfing gray teeth. He wore the clothes he'd torn from his fourth victim—torn those clothes off with his bare hands while the terrified man stood paralyzed with fear. Stood there, waiting for what was to come. What he knew would be his destiny.

'Cause I am a fucking celebrity, the man on the highway giggled to himself. *And that dumbass bastard was just waiting for me to give him The Squeeze.*

The clothes were filthy. They'd been that way since the day he'd taken them, almost a year and a half ago. But the man with the gap-toothed grin loved the smell of them: those folks he'd squeezed like an orange, their pungent odor when they brushed against his shirt, against the crotch of his pants.

Dried blood caked the Polo shirt until it had gone from a pale lavender to a brown, blotchy shade.

His slacks, once a bleached-khaki color, now were tie-dyed with blood and yellow urine stains. Sometimes the material chafed him down around his crotch; a rash had spread out along his legs from his testicles down.

It made him feel more alive than he'd felt in years.

He scratched his balls just thinking about that warm, itchy feeling. He remembered the woman's face from last winter, after he had pulled her out of the hot tub, when she realized who he was.

I am The Juicer, bitch, and God has sent me to squeeze his harvest, the grapes of wrath, bitch, make wine out of human blood and turn flesh into bread, for this is your body and your blood which is given for me, eat, drink, and be merry, bitch, we gonna make juice of you, we gonna make the freshest fucking blood juice and then I'm gonna sit down and have a pitcher of fresh-squeezed bitch, yowzah!

The woman looked like she was about to scream, so he grabbed her by the lips and stretched them across her face. She still screamed, but it sounded funny. He even laughed when he tore her lower lip right off.

And then he Juiced her.

He liked that part best.

He was damn strong. The strength of God pulsed through his veins. God was in him, and the Holy Ghost, too, and no man alive could stop him. *Her eyes were the best part, the way they kept watching even after all the blood had been hosed out of her, her baby blues turning to pink when the end came. Juicy bitch, she was.*

But then, after her, the last one, God had done what He always did: He left The Juicer to his own devices, to let the demons eat away at him from the inside.

That's just the way inspiration works, the Breath of God gets in you for a time and then blows out your ass like a Santa Ana wind. My Daddy told me there'd be times when God would leave, but not to feel beat, oh, no, 'cause God abideth in the Soul of Man even when he sleeps, yowzah. When Daddy healed the sinners, he gave 'em God in a handslap, a squeeze on the shoulder, and they came from their wastelands to Daddy's tent for that squeeze. But even then, God could be cruel, leaving Daddy to die in a drunk tank. But Daddy's soul flew on, he got Juiced by the Holy Ghost and got drunk by his Heavenly Maker. So the Piece of God that passeth understanding, that one Piece that gets in me and gives me the power to Juice, it comes and goes. When it goes, oh, Lordy, when it goes it don't leave nothing behind.

So he'd spent the rest of the winter and spring hibernating here in the desert canyons, eating jack rabbit and rattler. He didn't Juice them, because it wasn't time. God had not come back into him. Even Jesus had his time without God in the wilderness, tempted by the Devil, and The Juicer was beyond that, because he knew that God and the Devil were two sides of the same coin, the greater your torment and suffering, the finer the redemption, and The Juicer's demons helped send souls onto God, and now God lay sleeping. The Juicer accepted this, but prayed nightly for God to shoot back into his veins.

He was walking along the highway at four in the morning. The One Who Called Him Home, the Chosen Vessel of God, led him in

47

this hour of darkness, called him back in these empty days. He hadn't seen the child since the first time it was sent into him, since the first day he'd truly accepted God in his life, the Dark God who willed him to Juice.

And the girl. Her face would be different now.

She would be older.

But there was still a squeeze or two left in him, God willing, before he would return the gift she'd given him.

The Holy Motherfucking Gift.

The Juicer could feel the Piece of God throbbing in his groin, and the need to Juice boiling inside him. *Oh, road, take me to a sinner's home that I might Juice, and send her soul to the Lord Almighty who is above and below, that she might be saved from eternal fucking damnation, and that I might take on her sins, the Sins of the World, that through her Juice I might do the Lord's work and turn her blood to wine and break this her body and eat it for this is the bread of the covenant, yowzah!*

He glanced at the green sign at the highway's edge.

NARANJA CANYON had been crossed out with spray paint.

Written in its place: NITRO.

Beneath this, PALMETTO, ¾ MILE.

And there was God, like cocaine up his nostrils until he could feel the blood trickling down through his nose; he poked his tongue out of his mouth and slathered it on his upper lip to catch God's blood as it dripped down.

God said to him, *Juicer, my man, you will find a shitload of sinners in there, just waiting for redemption. Send 'em to heaven, baby, and take on their sins. Your God is a jealous God, Juicer, and a thirsty one, too, so let's get the vineyard pouring, 'cause this is the vineyard for fresh-squeezed souls.*

A lonely wind blew across the desert landscape.

A musky, sexual scent mixed with dust came to him.

He glanced over in the direction of the scent—shadows of trailers out along a yellow mesa, backed by rocks formed from ancient volcanoes. The canyon was sketched in purple and red. Sharp dawn sunlight slashed an arrow between the trailers, and God illuminated his work for him.

The Juicer, feeling the Word of God blocking his sinuses, turned off onto the gravel road toward the canyon.

You Come When I Call You

He knew that this would be the last day of his life in the flesh.

Ah, he thought, *the freedom of having no skin, no jail of bones, only the wind across the filth of life, and the sweet fire of darkness exploding across the desolation!*

2

From the summit of the Naranja Pass, the road descended, briefly and sharply, into an area that could not properly be called a valley. It was more of a bowl with a crack in its side. This was the Rattlesnake Wash, which ran between the two sections of Palmetto: the town itself going northwest on Highway 4, and Naranja Canyon, or Nitro as it was more popularly known, which sat upon the edge of the crack. Before 1953 there was nothing here other than the Boniface Ranch and Well, but beginning in the fifties, a man named Gib Urquart begat a vision which begat a tract housing development which, ultimately, begat a town and several fast-food joints along the section of the highway known as The Strip. Urquart had a dream, then, that this would be a commuter town for those who worked down in the Springs, or over in San Berdoo, and briefly, the dream had flared, and then, like all misbegotten dreams, died, leaving these houses peppered across the high desert, having created a town that was dying before it could even be born.

There was an old man who slept, as often as not, at the edge of the Wash, within the circular pipe that was thrust beneath the cracked and potholed highway as it crossed over this point. He had a blanket and a pillow and an old gas lantern. He was not exactly homeless, for he had a ramshackle spread up in the hills beyond town, but he was what you might call crazy, and what he might himself call "afeared." His name was Lucas Boniface, and his grandfather had officially settled this area in the way back, but few people in town knew him by his real name, he was mainly called Bonyface, or sometimes, simply, The Bone, and he had adapted quite well to this moniker.

And as Bonyface lay there, dreaming his scorpion dreams, as the sun's first light cut through the purple dark, he sensed it, for he had, as they say, the *nose* for it, and felt something churning in his gut that made him wish he'd never been born.

As he awoke, he said to the tabby cat that slept beside him, "They always come back, Isaac."

He looked out of the hole, into the wine-dark light of morning, and saw the high, yellow wall of the big house that was called Garden of Eden to the right, and the trumpet flowers that grew from snaking vines over its edge; he heard the bees, too, for the Beekeeper still lived there and had boxes of them in the garden of the great house. And the damn roses, the beloved and accursed roses, their brambles clinging to the walls of the house, like in *Sleeping Beauty*, ready to scratch the eyes out of anyone who dared enter that castle. Every morning when the old man awoke, he looked at the yellow wall, its snaky roses along its top, and cursed the name of the Beekeeper and all who had taken the land from his own family.

But this morning, he cursed no one, and held his breath. He took a sofa cushion that someone had dumped by the highway, and covered his ears with it so he could block out the annoying buzzing of the bees. "Demons," he muttered. "Lord of the flies come back, dammit."

The sun would come up in a coppery blast shortly, but for now, the landscape was almost lunar, veiled in a purple-blue, with a thin, white spear of sunlight thrusting out from the eastern mountains.

To the inhabitants of the town called Palmetto, this time of the morning, before seven, before the rush of the day, before the heat became unbearable, was a soft time, a lazy waking hour of coolness and taking a moment to reflect and plan and to look at the beauty of the purple and blue and yellow desert. The morning temperature could almost be described as a goosebump chill; before the sun was completely up, the heat would bleach bones through skin. This was the desert, as summer approached, as spring died.

This was pre-dawn.

Some called it the Magic Hour.

3

But the man who called himself The Juicer, moving on up the road, did not notice the dawn or the encroaching light, nor was he aware of the man who tried to go back to sleep beneath the curve in the road.

Something called to him, like a longing, like an ache.

Like home.

He could smell it through the air. When he heard the truck approach, he moved quickly to hide so he wouldn't be seen from the road.

The driver of the truck was a woman. He took a deep breath of air and held it within his lungs: barely a woman. *A girl, really.*

And it was time to do the ultimate Juicing.

4

Wendy Swan had beautiful red hair down to her shoulders. She wore a tee shirt and jeans and a scarf around her neck as if to off-set her casual appearance. She parked her truck alongside the highway, in front of the big house. A jet-black pit bull sat up in the truck bed, tethered with a chain. She got out of the truck, and walked over to the gate of the house. She looked as if she were about to beat on the door, for she raised her fists up, and then let them fall to her sides again. If you were watching her, you would think that there was something within those walls surrounding that house that this girl wanted badly.

You could smell her, though, if your senses were strong enough, if you were The Juicer, and you were sniffing for just this one girl, how pretty she was,

how something within you knew her scent, had it almost genetically inside you, her chemistry somehow mixed with your own,

how you knew that she had brought you to this desolate land-scape,

called you in some inexplicable way.

And somehow, she knew you would come to this place at this time, and the final juicing of the flesh harvest would begin.

If you were watching her, you would notice that she turned her head to the left, as if she could sense you were there.

The girl looked at the man who had come from the road.

A stranger.

The feeble light of dawn cast a cold streak of pink down the side of his face.

At first, she thought she knew him, and was about to say something. Before she could, he grabbed her around the shoulder. She opened her mouth to scream, but he covered her lips with the palm of his hand. What she saw of him was a face that looked as if half of it had been burned, the other half mildly deformed like wax left too long in the sun. There were things moving on his face, things that reminded her of worms caught on hooks, but it was too dark, and he was moving his face rapidly from side to side so it blurred. Pain, too, along her ribs and back, and she thought she heard something snap. He began squeezing her so tight that she felt like she was going to burst at any minute, and she wondered, as she grew faint and could no longer struggle, why no one was coming out to help her.

5

"For you," The Juicer slobbered into her ear, his tongue mopping across her cheek, "for you, I give my—"

The Juicer opened his mouth impossibly wide, and the girl thought she saw something else down there, in his throat, something moving swiftly up to his mouth.

Something that burned.

The last thing she heard was the pit bull in the truck, snapping and snarling, breaking free of its chain.

A word, too, and she wondered if it were the voice of Death, for she was fairly sure that she was dying now, but thankfully the pain had stopped and she was numb.

The voice, familiar and tickling, whispered her name.

The old warmth spread through her, and she was no longer afraid.

6

The house called the Garden of Eden was of Moorish design, with its high walls making all but its fake minarets invisible to the outside world. It was built in the 1920s, and then restored again in the 1950s when the current owner bought it. But now, more than two decades after restoration, its beauty was fading, and it had more the look of a prison than a mansion. The garden had overtaken the yard, the roses had clutched the walls for so long that they were less wall than vine and thorn. The Beekeeper was up early, at six, withdrawing the thin drawers of the boxed hive, and pouring the honey into a gallon jar. The Beekeeper, for that was the only name that the kids in town knew for the house's owner, wore a pith helmet with long white netting around it, and thick leather gloves, while carrying no other special equipment. White slacks, and boots, all protective from stings, gave the Beekeeper a certain anonymity in the community—some said the Beekeeper never ate anything other than honey. Some said the Beekeeper's face was swollen and deformed from too many stings. Some kids thought it was like the Invisible Man, with nothing beneath the pure-white clothes—even some of the grownups in town had never seen an inch of the Beekeeper's skin. The bees flourished in the air; but the Beekeeper ignored them, and went about the morning's business.

By the time the sun had risen, the Beekeeper noticed something lying by the road, beyond the thin iron gate in the wall.

Saw something else, there, too. Lying on the edge of the highway.

It was a girl's scarf, red, damp, torn.

Beside it, a human hand.

Chapter Seven
Dog Days

1

News item from the Palmetto (CA) Tribune
June 18, 1980

KILLER IDENTIFIED: "TELLTALE TEETH"
The man known to most of Southern California as "The Juicer" because of his bizarre habit of crushing his victims to death, was positively identified yesterday as the victim of a wild animal attack on Highway 4.

His real name was Michael Southey, and he began his reign of terror in October, 1975, killing some seven people in the Southern California area, with possible links to three murders in Taos, New Mexico. His final victim, Dina Lockhart, died in Cathedral City in November of last year. Although Lockhart was found dead in her winter home, she was the only of his victims to bear teeth marks on her arms and along her neck.

"The Juicer," in his frenzy, left those indentations as a calling card, which later led to the identification of his body. Southey's body was found scattered in pieces along the two-mile stretch of highway just south of Palmetto and the Naranja Canyon exit.

An investigator on the case told this reporter that Mr. Southey, a drifter from Santa Fe, New Mexico, had evidently been wandering toward Palmetto, perhaps looking for another murder victim when some wild animal must have attacked him.

"We were picking up bits of him with shovels and dumping them into wash buckets," said one member of the Yucca Valley Police Department, who preferred not to be identified. "It was a grisly sight. Reminded me of that old Jim Croce song, you know where he says the guy looked like a jigsaw puzzle with a couple of pieces gone. That's what this guy looked like—a couple of pieces gone, and what was left wasn't pretty. We were all pretty nauseated—is that the right word? Yeah, very nauseated, but now that I hear it was this Juicer guy I think he got what was coming to him. Makes you think there *is* a God."

Wade Franklin of the Animal Control Board confirmed the opinion held by the police, that the animal that attacked and killed Michael Southey was probably a sick wolf that wandered out of the mountains. "It was the fires up in the hills. Drives them down into the canyons," he said. "But we're on the lookout now for this animal, which might pose a threat to our communities."

2

Peter Chandler Confessions

I saved the article from the local paper about The Juicer getting killed, because I know that's how it all started in the past.

Imagine the world that I'm almost two decades away from, and yet a world I am convinced, were I to climb in a machine and go back to that year, that summer, I would not understand the language, I would not be able to breathe the air. And yet, I do go back there, in memory, often, to try and make sense out of what happened to me, to the town of Palmetto, California, to Naranja Canyon, to the Rattlesnake Wash. But most of it seems like static on the radio: I pick up the vaguest idea of that year, the pop songs, the TV shows, world politics. All the things that I've used to block Palmetto, to block *those* signals, especially what happened there with Kevin Sloan and the others, out of my mind, off my wavelength.

And her, the girl of my dreams, the girl of all our dreams.

I was fifteen—a no good age. I wouldn't turn sixteen 'til the Fourth of July, a few weeks away. You couldn't drink, or smoke, or see R-rated movies; you couldn't drive by yourself, you couldn't vote. Except for voting, every fifteen-year-old in Palmetto, California, had, of course, done all these things: what was stopping us?

But by the end of that summer, I had done much more than I ever thought possible. By the time I turned sixteen, I had committed the most atrocious act imaginable.

Who knows what the human heart is capable of?

You couldn't live in Palmetto, California, for more than twenty minutes without running into one of the Campusky clan. The mailbox in front of the cinderblocked Campusky compound read, *Campus Family*, but they were Campuskys and everyone called them Campusky from little Lollie who was two, all the way up to Hank and Greg, the twins, who were almost twenty-three. Twenty-three years Mrs. Campusky had spent bearing little Campuskys like a queen ant living out her years in the linoleum darkness of her kitchen and bedroom, barefoot, pregnant, and strangely, happy, if you can imagine it. At least she was always jolly. But twenty-three years! Pampers, Huggies, Gerber's Blueberry Buckle! Fights over television shows multiplied by ten! Flu viruses that must've seemed eternal! Twenty-three years of refrigerators being ransacked after midnight by those hungry, devouring creatures! Twenty-three years of Snickers, Devil Dogs, Twinkies, Little Debbies, Charm's Pops, and chicken potpies! They ate so much food out of the can, the jar, the tinfoil, the box, that the youngest thought her mother's name was Sara Lee.

And Than was the forgotten Campusky in all that. His mother

was always dragging little ones around like burgeoning balls-and-chains at her ankles, and his father was wise enough and cruel enough to be home only long enough for the next conception, then off on the road again with his truck. It was said that Mrs. Campusky's ovaries were like popcorn poppers and the desert heat kept her puffing up with a never-ending pregnancy. Who's to question such a rumor? She hadn't had a period since 1964.

Who could then have time for a boy like Than? His brothers and sisters were off in their own worlds of gluttony and sloth and summer reruns. Than was bigger than they were: he out-Campuskyed the Campuskys.

For all that, underneath the fat you could see a nice guy, albeit a perennial reject, struggling like a moth in a cocoon to emerge whole and shining and adult. He had clear blue eyes, high, almost aristocratic cheekbones over which jowls hung like heavy velvet curtains. His jet-black hair shone like dark onyx in the sun and was always greasy and stringy. His shoulders were actually broader than his hips, if that was humanly possible. He had huge hips, which had apparently earned him the nickname "Thunder Thighs." Even in my own moments of adolescent cruelty, that seemed *too* cruel. His better physical qualities were hidden for the most part beneath the fat and the twin curses of zits and tits. The pimples were endemic at our age; Than referred to them as "facial hemorrhoids." His chest on the other hand was unique in that it was larger than any girl's in town.

I had only been in Palmetto two days when this overweight kid introduced himself to me as Than Campusky, the boy with the fartistic temperament. I remember thinking, *Oh, sweet Jesus, the rejects are already seeking me out.* Than was fat, nearsighted, zit-peppered, and he saved his farts for special occasions.

Still, one summer night, when he persuaded me to meet him at the one form of real entertainment the town offered, he could be a good friend.

In Palmetto, in 1980, what passed for real entertainment turned out to be the pit bull fights.

3

The hot, dry air of the summer night sucked at the back of Peter's throat as he gasped, cooling down from his run. He had had to

sneak out the back window of his house and hightail it. His dad
had been drinking so *he* wouldn't notice. His little sister Annie
would squeal on him if she so much as heard a floorboard creak
after ten at night. He didn't like jogging much. He wasn't all that
athletic, and had, in fact, run all the way from home in topsiders. It
felt like he had blisters all around his toes.

He searched the shadowy crowd of faces along the edge of the
Wash, across men the size of boulders, in red tee shirts, checked
flannels, three-day old beards, red-rimmed eyes, baseball caps,
long greasy hair; a few women in the crowd, too, skinny, hungry-
looking women with long blond hair, breasts standing straight up
as if aimed skyward, tight jeans and tee shirts, even tighter skin.
Headlights from cars and trucks provided the only illumination
besides the pinpoint light of stars. Peter heard the sound of a dog
growling, and almost jumped as he passed a silver-white pit bull in
a chicken wire cage that sat in the back of an open Jeep. The dog
began gnashing its teeth and foaming. A few of the men laughed.
The air was thick with smoke and a swampy smell of beer—but
above all of it, was the pungent stink of dog and man mixed like
poison.

Than whistled for Peter from one of the cars parked along the
gravel road. He was sitting in the back of a flatbed Ford truck,
drinking Dos Equis beer out of the bottle. He had a Big Mac, too,
that he was just finishing off between beer gulps.

"What took you so long?" Than asked when Peter approached
him, out of breath. Than held his hand out for money.

"I only have ten bucks," Peter said, reaching into his pocket and
pulling out a wad of bills.

"I don't know, man, you know, it's supposed to be more."

"Yeah, well, how much did *you* pay for the privilege?"

"Yeah, but I know people. See that guy over there?" Than raised
his eyebrows and Peter looked back over his shoulder. A short,
broad-shouldered, paunch-bellied man in a red sweatshirt and
white slacks stood in the midst of the other men; he was taking
money from all of them. "He's Pepe, and he's my friend. You can
talk to him about the money, but he's a tough son of a bitch, I'll tell
you."

"Campusky, I think the other ten bucks was to buy your way in."

"No *duh*, man, no shit, Sherlock, and that calls for more suds,"

Than said, tossing his empty bottle back into the truck. It rolled noisily across the metal, hitting something in the back with a soft thud.

"Hey!" A woman's voice came from beneath a black tarp that was bunched up, and, now that Peter looked at it, was rippling in the back of the truck; it shimmered like water when a fish surfaces.

Than grabbed Peter by the neck and brought him closer so he could whisper, "Someone's humping someone back there."

Peter smelled beer breath fizzing against his ear.

Than let go and grabbed another bottle out of the ice-filled trash can.

"Some sleazy setup," Peter said. "How many beers you have so far?"

Than shrugged. "Four? Six?"

"What if cops show up?"

Than belched. "They won't. It's not like I'm smoking grass." He made a feeble attempt to twist the cap off the bottle, groaning with the effort. "That's the Big What If, isn't it? *Guy,* Chandler, that's one of your least attractive qualities, always worrying about the What Ifs of the world. What If someone catches us, What If you go blind from it, What If What If What If," he hiccupped.

Peter reached into the trash can, grabbing a fistful of ice. He flung most of it to the ground, but sucked on a couple of ice cubes. "What if you're wrong?"

"Hey, I been wrong before, I'll be wrong again."

Peter turned and walked back into the circle of men. Their whispered exclamations sounded like an auction with the volume turned down; every one of them looked like a down-on-his-luck pirate, bandanas or baseball caps on their heads, dark, greasy features shining in headlights, ripped shirts, torn jeans, wild eyes, all of them fanning themselves with paper money, talking about killing: "Rip you to shreds, mofo," "Gonna take you apart, sucker," "You got a wusshound, man, I'm gon' bite your head clean off."

The man in the center was the only silent one. Pepe Alvarado. He just kept taking the cash, folding it neatly as it was passed to him. Some he thrust into his back left pocket, some into his back right, some down into his breast pocket.

"You Pepe?" Peter asked as he approached. Someone in the crowd turned a flashlight on him, and then, just as quickly, the light went dead. The flash blinded Peter for a few seconds, and when he looked back at the man called Pepe, he seemed to be enveloped in a shining aura.

Pepe squinted at him, looking like a wild animal cautiously sizing up its prey within the camouflage of desert brush; he pushed one of the other men aside. His face was sharp and long like a coyote's, with the same mixture of fear and curiosity and balls in his small dark eyes. Then Pepe's face transformed: he had, in a split second, sized Peter up and now he looked at Peter the way a butcher does a skinny animal, to see where the knife would dig in with the least resistance. "You Nathaniel's amigo?"

Peter nodded.

"Who you on?" Pepe's voice was low and barely audible. He stood there, his sharp chin thrust out, arms crossed over his chest, like he owned everyone and everything within his sight.

Peter didn't understand.

"I mean, who you puttin' money on?" Peppy grew quickly impatient. "Ain't no slow train here, boy. We got the fight in five, so who you on?"

Peter held up the wad of bills. He stared at it dumbly as if expecting it would speak. His face was turning red.

One of the men in a baseball cap grabbed the money from Peter's hand. "Silver Molly, put it on Silver Molly!"

Pepe held his hand out and the man passed him the money. He counted it out, one bill at a time. "Ten bucks, boy, not enough to piss on. I told Nathaniel to get in he got to bring in least double this. Ten lousy bucks!" he shouted, and the crowd let out a stream of profanities the way a tent revival congregation might burst forth with "Amens" and "Hallelujahs!"

Pepe tossed the money down on the ground. The other men parted away from it like it was poison. "You and Nathaniel, you want to be big gamblers, you need to take the stakes higher, boy. Bigger risk, better game."

Peter muttered under his breath; Pepe Alvarado was laughing at him.

Peter went to his knees and began gathering up the bills. A couple of them had fluttered down to the edge of the Wash.

Than waited cautiously by the truck until all the men had moved away from Peter. "I told you twenty."

"Nice crowd you know, Campusky."

Than broke out in an ear-to-ear grin, "Yeah, but you're in now. Peppy let it go—I've seen him toss people out on their asses if they weren't in. You passed, man. You're in."

"I didn't want to *bet* on the dogs."

"Don't attack *me*. This is the most exciting thing going. I did this as a favor to you, be grateful."

"Why are we friends? What do we possibly have in common?"

Than turned pensive for a moment. "Nobody else wants to be friends with us?"

Peppy shouted out, "Sloan! Hey! Any you guys see Sloan? Where the fuck is Sloan and that bitch of his? Somebody wantin' to go get 'em? You boys know we don't get no show on no road 'less we got his bitch."

A few of the drunken men volunteered for the mission, and dust rose from their Jeeps and trucks as they swerved out the dirt road to the highway.

"Who's Sloan?" Peter asked Than.

"*Sloan.*" Than whispered the name like it was an occult invocation. "He and his girlfriend: white trash city. They Neanderfuck. They do. He's a Neanderfucking caveman. He's a mean one, and his dog's meaner than he is. Somebody even said that he . . . his dog." Than made a gesture with his fingers to simulate sexual intercourse: his forefinger thrust through a hole created by the thumb and forefinger of his other hand.

Chapter Eight
Nitro

1

Nitro slouched beneath the shadow of the canyon like a bum sleeping off a three-day drunk in a ditch. It had no gas stations, no big name fast-food joints the way Palmetto did. There was a taco stand (*Paco's Tacos*) at the edge of the highway just at the turn off to the Naranja Canyon Mobile Home Park. There was a saloon, *Coyote Cantina*, with an enormous parking lot that was never quite full up even on a Saturday night. On the front of the cantina was a picture of Wile E. Coyote chasing the Roadrunner, with the words "Beep! Beep!" in dark letters above the bird's head. A large movie-style marquee proclaimed: BINGO—THURS THRU SAT IN CACTUS LOUNGE/LADIES NITE WED/LIVE ENTMENT FRISATSUN/DARK MON.

Other than these two commercial ventures, Nitro was a grave-yard of trailer parks: six of them in a five-mile stretch, Naranja Canyon Mobile Home Park, Sun Dial Trailer Park, Joshua Tree Gardens, Ed and Inez "Home on the Range" Park, Quail Motor Homes, and the more simply named, "Park."

Right now, at ten minutes after midnight, most of the elderly res-idents of Nitro were asleep. Others sat up in their beds watching tel-evision, some played cards with their buddies on card tables erected beneath green-striped plastic awnings in front of their mobile homes, lamps plugged into outdoor sockets. But some of the men and a few of the women were down at the Wash, placing bets on one of Nitro's most popular summertime sports: the dog fights.

Fights in the Wash usually didn't get going until twenty minutes after the hour, and on this particular Saturday night, it would be 12:30 before they began because one dog had yet to show up.

2

Outside Kevin Sloan's trailer at the Sun Dial Trailer Park, a truck and two Jeeps pulled up, headlights hitting the dark pitbull that was sitting in front. The dog scampered beneath its home.

A man leaped from the back of the pickup truck. He was drunk. He wore what appeared to be the uniform of the evening: a red baseball cap, tee shirt, jeans, and beergut. He yelled, "Get your ass out here, Sloan, we gonna howl tonight!"

"Hell, man, they're fucking like bunnies in there," the driver of the Jeep said. He'd slid out from behind the wheel and was now standing on his tiptoes, peering through the back window of the trailer. "Let's just take Lammie and leave him to his fun. No man wants to get caught with his dick hangin' out."

The first man crouched down on his hands and knees and looked beneath the trailer. His gaze was met by two flaring red eyes staring back at him.

The dog growled at him from her shadowy hiding place. She'd dug a shallow ditch there beneath the trailer and was curled up in it.

The man stuck his hand near her muzzle.

She snapped her jaws, and he jerked his hand back just in time to avoid getting his fingers chomped off.

"She tried to kill me," he said, clutching his hand against his chest like it was a wounded bird.

The other man came around and swatted at his cowering buddy. "Get out of there, Junior, let me show you what a *real* man can do here."

"You're full of it, Fisher."

The man from the Jeep went down on his knees. The dog's red eyes flashed out at him. The growl. "You got to know Lammie, now, you got to appeal to the woman in her. Come on, sweetcakes, we gonna take you for little ride in my car."

This was Nitro at night in the summer.

3

"Hey, Alison!" Charlie Urquart shouted.

He was in the backseat of his father's Mustang convertible, drunk off his ass. *Fuck Dad for telling me I can't go out tonight, fuck him—the old fart can go to hell for all I care.* The voice inside Charlie's head that spoke those words didn't seem to be Charlie's at all, at least not to *him*; it was something that just got loose inside him sometimes, a kind of wildness that turned off the regular Charlie most of the other kids knew. It was like automatic pilot, and it usually came on after his father gave him a talking-to. *That's one*, Charlie thought, knocking back the last of his Budweiser. He waved the can around, crushing it in a fist. He was wearing his letterman's jacket, and was drenched with either sweat or beer or both—a senior from Yucca Valley, Billy Simpson was driving the car (he was only half-drunk), while Terry Boyd, who had once streaked across the gym floor during one of the girls' basketball tournaments, rode shotgun and splashed beer indiscriminately around the upholstery.

They were parked in the circular driveway of a small, gray

stucco house. Although the front porch and driveway were lit up, the house was dark.

"Nobody's home," Terry said. "Let's go."

"Dickhead, she's in there, she's in there, I can *smell* her," Charlie snarled. "Don't you think I fucking know her smell by now? Shit, it's like a tuna factory."

When Terry glanced back at his buddy, well, it didn't look like Charlie Urquart at all, and both Terry and Billy knew that when Charlie was like this, drunk and zoned out, his personality became like sharp, jabbing glass, to the point that even *they* didn't want to be around him.

"She dumped you, man," Billy said, slapping him on the shoulder, " 'member?"

"Dumped you like shit," Terry added.

Charlie's eyes were like glinting steel. "No, my friends. She didn't dump me. She just made me want her more."

4

Life sucks and then you die, Alison Hunt considered as she looked out the living room window, trying to keep her head low so the boys in the Mustang wouldn't see her. She'd been watching *Saturday Night Live*, enjoying her evening of having the house to herself—her mother and father had driven to Redlands to have dinner with her Aunt Jenny, and her brothers were down at the garage working on some project they were keeping to themselves (although Ed Junior kept slipping up and mentioning her recent birthday, so she thought they must be fixing up the old T-Bird for her)—and then she'd heard the shouting from the driveway.

"I love ya, Alison!" Charlie shouted. His voice sounded like he was chewing gravel and spitting it out. "I want to shoot you full of my love bullets!"

Terry and Billy were laughing and making pig noises.

"We know you're home!" Billy shouted.

"Yeah, come on, baby, we just want to make you feel more like a girl!" Charlie said, leaping uncertainly out of the back of the car, scratching a line down its side. He landed on his hands and knees on the driveway. His beer can clattered into the low juniper bushes, spraying beer as it rolled. He sprang up in the air like a jack-in-the-box, touching down on the balls of his feet, wobbling. He was grinning as he walked toward the front porch. "Alison, come on, you know I'm the only guy for you, sweetmeat. I know you're somewhat confused about us. But you're all woman to me, babe. Terry— wasn't I just telling you that pretty little thing shouldn't be a grease monkey or playing basketball? Wasn't I?" He grinned like he was going to split his face open with his teeth. "You should be on your knees, bitchkin."

"Hey, man, what ya doin'?" Terry asked, sloshing beer over his shoulder. "We're gonna miss the Big One, and like what if her mom's home or—"

"Her mama ain't home, birdshit, and you can bite the big one for all I care."

Alison had kept her head low, to the left of the drapes, but she moved for a second, and his eyes followed the motion.

He saw her now.

He waved.

Alison shut her eyes tightly, so tight it hurt. *Just go away, just go away.*

As if to answer her, the doorbell rang. There was a pause. Then another *ding-dong*, and another and another, and she thought he would never stop.

She arose from her hiding place and pulled the drapes aside. Charlie stood directly beneath the front porch light. He was the kind of high-school-handsome that made her sick: almost too pretty with his red lips, dark eyelashes, and dark penetrating eyes. A shock of dark, thick hair fell over his forehead, fanning down around his eyebrows. And yet, she had been his girlfriend for almost a year.

You stupid moron, she recognized now.

In the year she had dated him, her reputation had been shot to hell, and she had only found this out when Than had told her to her face. *"I know it's not true, but he's making up stories, like that you're peanut butter 'cause you spread so easy and stuff."*

And then it had taken her another three months to dump the jerk.

Charlie saw himself as the Big Man On Campus, and when other kids liked him, it usually was because of his being handsome and warped simultaneously: he had a thing for torturing small mammals, and he wasn't too bad at mind-fucking his fellow students.

But Alison had liked him for another reason.

Pathetic, she thought now.

Although, at the time, when he had opened up to her, *really* opened up, and told her his deepest, darkest secret in the whole world, she had felt he was good, at least *at heart*.

They had that as a bond.

But no more.

"What do you want?" Alison asked, rolling open one of the smaller windows alongside the picture window. But she knew what he wanted.

He wanted to terrorize her.

5

Charlie licked his lips as he glanced toward Alison, staring at him from her living room window. "I see you, Alison. I SEE YOU."

"Get in the car, Urqu!" Billy called out. "It's probably already started!"

Without turning back to his friends, Charlie flipped the bird to them.

"Hurry it up, willya, Urqu?" Billy gunned the motor.

"Just give me a sec so I can piss on her door—it's the way dogs mark their territories and I wanna make sure no other dog gets to her first, I want her all to myself," Charlie said, unzipping his jeans. He wobbled back and forth on the balls of his feet while he fiddled with his underwear. "I want her, man, she's my girl."

"We're leaving," Terry said, no longer laughing.

"Pussies."

But Billy did not drive off.

Alison shouted, "My brothers'll get you for this!"

Charlie Urquart cackled. "You gonna send the retard after me, Al? what's he gonna do, drool me to death? Or is it gonna be the faggot, and I guess we all know what *he'd* try to do. Tell me, sweetmeat, if I was to rape you, would you let me, or just *try and beat me off?*"

6

Although Alison could not quite see what Charlie was doing because he had positioned himself so close to the front door, she heard the steady hissing stream as he urinated.

She turned and ran down the front hallway toward her bedroom, hoping he would not leave until she returned.

7

When Charlie finished peeing, spraying some last drops of urine on his shoes and hands (he wiped his hands on his red letterman's jacket), he heard the bolt click in the front door. Then the door opened slightly. The chain was off. The door opened wider.

The first thing he saw was the thing pointing directly at his balls, which still hung out of his fly.

An arrow with a sharp metal tip.

Alison stood there in a white tank top and blue shorts, barefoot, her blond hair pushed behind her ears. Her blue eyes gleamed with the tears she was fighting. She had a bow and arrow in her hands; her hands trembled; the bow was stretched tight. In another second she might let go of the string, and the arrow would lodge somewhere either in his right testicle or his left, although she might be able to skewer both of them shishkebab style, if she gave a little twist to her wrist when she shot the arrow. Her lips curled back in anger.

"I am less than a foot away from you, Charlie. Now you know my aim is pretty good, 'cause you've seen me hit targets out at the dump. Of course, sometimes I have been known to miss the bull's-eye, but I can tell you, this is one time I won't miss. If you want to take the chance that I will, well, be my guest. Now, get off my porch, and you and your boyfriends can go and do what you little boys do without your girlfriends on a Saturday evening."

Charlie grinned, nodding. "Very good. You're bluffing, Hunt, but I'm not gonna to let you win this round."

"Get the fuck off my property," Alison snarled.

Charlie looked her directly in the eyes. "I will tell everyone I know. Unless you come out tonight."

She hesitated a moment, closing her eyes. *I will not cry, I am not weak, he can't hurt me anymore.*

"I mean it," he said, almost softly. "Baby, you know how much I love you, but I mean what I'm saying. We're good together, you know it. That girl in Yucca Valley didn't mean a thing. It's you, babe, always you."

Slowly, she lowered the bow and arrow.

66

"Good girl," he said, "that's my good girl."

"Bastard," Alison whispered.

Charlie went back and climbed over the side of the car, falling into the back. The Mustang backfired.

As he revved the engine, Billy said, "I'm sure we missed the fight."

Alison came out of her house, turned to lock the door, and then, without saying a word, got into the Mustang next to Charlie. She looked like some part of her had died within just a few minutes.

He put his arm around her and whispered the most vile obscenity she could imagine in her ear.

"Good girl," he murmured so close to her ear it was like a yellow jacket buzzing there. "It was only four months along, anyway, and nobody's gonna know but me as long as you behave yourself."

But she had already blocked out the pain she was feeling, and pretended that this wasn't really her life at all. She had become good at that, because everything in life since she'd become a teenager seemed like nothing but pain.

8

Back at the Rattlesnake Wash, some of the men had gone to get Sloan's pitbull, and within ten minutes, the fight had already begun.

"Jesus Christ," Peter gasped, flattening himself against the side of the truck. Than had convinced him to drink a beer ("You'll be less pissed off at me," he'd said with typical Campusky logic, over Peter's protests—and Campusky logic won out). Peter was feeling buzzed, it was his first beer ever and he had become suddenly paranoid that the cops were going to bust him.

"Right, Chandler, they'll bust you," Than said, grinning, his eyes widening with glee. "Then they fingerprint you, then they put you in The Cell. And then . . . then"—he rubbed the palms of his hands together—"*then* you're in with five hardened criminals for a long hot night. And one of them, the one who smells like sweaty underarms and looks like a Sherman tank looks at you and says, 'You're kinda purty.' "

Peter stared over the bed of the truck and thought he recognized the voice of someone shouting, flickering lights moved in off the highway.

"What is it?" Than looked over the truck to see if someone was coming their way. The fight had only been going for a few minutes. Some of the men showed up with a large growling pit bull in the back of another truck. Peter couldn't see the dog clearly: it was as dark as the inside of a cave, and looked to him like a demon with its ears pointing straight up, its eyes reflecting red in the glare of headlights. There were about sixteen men standing around the edges of the Wash looking down into it, swearing, waving their cash in the air like fans, alternately goading and coaxing the two dogs down in the fight. And then, there was the endless growling and snapping of dogs.

Neither Than nor Peter had been able to bring himself to look down into the Wash at the damage the dogs were doing to each other. Beyond the group of men, two headlights had just turned down the dirt road to the Wash.

"Campusky, Jesus Christ," Peter whispered a third time. "Why didn't you tell me *he* was going to be here?"

"Who he?" Than asked, but then saw who Peter meant.

"Charlie Urquart."

Or not quite Charlie, but his father's red Mustang convertible, kicking up gravel and dust as it turned off the highway and onto the ridge overlooking the Wash. Looked like one of Charlie's Unholy Trio, Billy, was driving—and Than made out Alison Hunt sitting in the backseat next to Charlie.

"We could run," Than blurted out.

"Not a bright idea, the only direction is out there," Peter nodded toward the endless canyons blossoming beyond where they stood. "I don't even know why I turn spineless around that guy. It's my wimp factor coming through."

"I think when you deal with a kid who uses switchblades to make a point, we can safely assume fear," Than said. "But he's probably not interested in bothering us tonight. And if he is, it's probably gonna be you who gets it. Seems to me he *owes* you one."

"All right, bitch, stay in the car for all I care," Charlie spat. "Just be here when I get back."

Charlie Urquart slammed the car door shut; the noise reverberated in the canyon, above the buzz of the gambling men, above the snapping of the dogs in the Wash. The air carried the acrid scent of cigarette and marijuana smoke, the smells of beer and Brut aftershave. Charlie glanced down at the dogs.

The dark one they called Lammie had Silver Molly by her throat and was shaking her mercilessly. Then Molly tore herself free, bleeding beneath her collar, blood spotting her muzzle, and rose up on her hind legs, coming down against her opponent with all her weight. Lammie was momentarily crushed beneath the larger dog. She rolled over; Silver Molly went for her stomach, sharp teeth flashing in the headlights from cars above them; Lammie rolled out from under her and spun around to face Molly. Jaws snapping like steel bear traps, dripping with foam, muzzles bloody and wrinkling. Lammie went down on her forequarter and leaped for Silver Molly's throat again. Her jaws slammed together, teeth almost touching through Molly's fur and skin as she shook the dog mercilessly.

From the edge of the Wash, above the dogs, Charlie slapped Pepe Alvarado on the back. "Hey, Pepperoni, how's it hangin', mimigo?"

"Too late, Charlie, we already got two dogs—no need for you, too." Pepe didn't turn away from the fight.

"Hey-hey, good one, wasn't that a good one?"

Billy Simpson and Terry Boyd passed the joint they'd been smoking back and forth, but Charlie waved it away. They grinned stupidly at their leader.

Charlie Urquart reached into his back pocket. His hand came out with a wad of cash. "Fifty bucks, my man, count 'em, fifty." He waved the money in front of Pepe's face. "I bet you could buy a lot of poon with this."

"Also too late for your bet—we got Lammie up against Silver Molly. No second fight tonight."

"Now that is a pity, my friend. Isn't that a pity, boys?"

"Really," Terry coughed, sucking on the joint.

"Sure enough is," Billy added.

"Maybe," Charlie shouted, and a few men turned to his voice, "one of your illegals would want fifty bucks to fight one of those dogs. Need some real entertainment here, *comprende*?"

"Maybe you should get the *chinga* out of here," Pepe spat out.

"Translate, William," Charlie said, turning to Billy.

"I think it's their word for 'fuck,' man, yeah, I'm sure."

"Chinga, chinga, chinga," Charlie said, "that's cool, Pep, that's cool."

"You boys excuse me," Pepe said, brushing Charlie to one side, "I got to get back to the fight."

"Hey—" Terry started after Pepe, but Charlie socked him in the shoulder.

"Leave Señor Avocado to his fight. I spy something that has more possibilities for fun . . . give me that," he said, grabbing the dwindling joint from Billy's fingers, "you been bogarting it too long." As he took a long drag on the joint, Charlie waved toward the truck where Than and Peter stood.

10

Peter Chandler/Confessions

All it took was my first sip of beer, and instead of the proverbial bravado alcohol is supposed to give you, I became a shriveling wimp. I was fifteen, but inside I felt about seven years old. All because of Charlie Urquart, pointing at me and Than over by the truck.

I completely understood what Charlie had against me, but I think if we had met under different circumstances he might not be at my throat so much—perhaps if we lived in a town where there was more to do on a Saturday night than bet on dogs. Not that I would've liked Charlie very much: he was a sadistic son of a bitch, but one thing I learned from constantly being uprooted is that you can get along with a lot of different kinds of people if you put your mind to it, sons of bitches included. But we'd met in March, at school, about the same time Than Campusky and I were getting to know each other, soon after I'd moved to Palmetto. And I guess, as

Charlie himself would say, he "owed me one" after our introduction to each other.

New kids are always easy targets.

You couldn't be Charlie Urquart, quarterback, heartthrob, son of the man who developed Palmetto into the middle-class slums it had become by 1980, you couldn't be Charlie Urquart, brown-noser extraordinaire, without wanting to mutilate poodles and pummel a few kids senseless. It came with the territory. Charlie always "owed" somebody "one," because the one thing everyone pretty much knew about Charlie was that his old man beat him up and otherwise terrorized him on a regular basis, and I guess Charlie was just giving back to the world a little of what he got. He and I actually had a lot in common, come to think of it, only I handled my end of things in a different way—or not at all.

Charlie, he lashed out. It was rumored that he popped Black Beauties like they were going out of style, too, and in his letterman's jacket pocket he usually carried a paperback Satanist's bible.

What had endeared me to Charlie in March occurred, as do all bad memories of high school, in the locker room after gym.

I was coming in from intramurals when I heard some boys yelling, "Squeal like a peeg!" Students passed around *Deliverance* that year in the library, along with *Portnoy's Complaint, The Happy Hooker*, and *Fear of Flying*, reading only the dog-eared passages (so the only novel anyone read straight through was the Xaviera Hollander opus). Some of us managed to see the movie of *Deliverance*, too, with that scene where Ned Beatty is about to be raped by the weird backwoodsmen—so I recognized the "pig" line when I heard it. From the steamy yellow-tiled locker room came the sounds of a struggle, the clang-banging of locker doors slamming, the wet snaps of rat-tailed towels hitting someone's backside, and finally a boy's weak tenor squeaking, "Oink, oink, ree-ree-ree!"

I went to the back of the room, through the mists of the showers, the graveyard smell of dirty socks and greasy jockstraps digging up into my nostrils like fingers. There, pushed up against the mildewed tile walls, just inside the shower was the fat kid I'd spoken with in Geometry class: Nathaniel Campus, aka Than Campusky.

He stood there naked, his eyes open wide with practiced fear, his gym shorts pulled down around his ankles, his tee shirt tossed on the slippery floor. The only modesty alowed him was an athletic supporter. Four naked boys, clutching their white towels, twisting them into rat-tails, surrounded him.

One of those boys had a switchblade, blade out, circling Than's right nipple with the blade.

This was Charlie Urquart, a junior.

He and his cronies had pinned Than in that position.

Charlie drew a thin red line of blood across Than's chest, between his nipples like connect-the-dots. "You put Raquel to shame," Charlie laughed, while Than continued to oink. "What do you think? You think maybe Campusky's tits are bigger than Alison's? What do you take, Campustule, a 44-triple-E?"

"He's gonna squirt milk in a second, remember that movie about the giant tit?" one of the other boys said.

"You my two-ton-fun-bun, Porky?" Charlie asked.

Before Than could answer, I said, "Leave him alone, assholes."

Charlie turned around for a second, looked right through me as if I was not there.

Then he smacked Than across his chest. "It's a rite of passage, Campustule, isn't that right? You've got to be *branded* by my blade."

Then he turned back to me. "Every boy in this school gets branded. Even you, geek."

"Listen," I said, "just because your life is shit doesn't mean you have to make everybody else live it."

Charlie drew the blade back in. The other boys grinned stupidly, and followed Charlie as he stepped back out of the shower area into the locker room.

But before Charlie was completely out of sight, he glanced back at me again, as if he were mentally taking a picture of me, to keep for future reference. I knew then that he owed me one for that, because Charlie Urquart was not the kind of guy to get back at you on *your* time. He had his own schedule, he liked his revenge cold, when you didn't expect it.

Maybe when you'd forgotten he owed you one.

11

"So, Chandler," Charlie said, lifting the smouldering joint, "you want a drag?"

Peter held up his beer bottle. "Already got this, thanks."

"Pretty neat fight, huh?" Than asked nervously; his jowls trembled.

"Yeah, it's cool," Charlie inhaled the sweet smoke. His eyes were bloodshot and became glazed over as he held his breath, and then exhaled the smoke. "But all these wetbacks standing around—doesn't it make you feel like putting in a call to Immigration or something?"

"That's a good one," Campusky chortled. "Yeah, that's a real good one, Charlie."

Urquart did not take his eyes off Peter.

"You think it's funny, Chandler?"

"Not half as funny as you are," Peter said.

"I think *you're* funny, Chandler, I think you're a regular laugh riot."

"I'm glad I can provide you with entertainment." And Peter wondered drunkenly, *Did I really just say that?*

"You and me, Chandler, we're like those dogs down there, it looks like we're at each other's throats, out for blood, but really, we're just playing a game."

"A game."

"Yeah, that's right, you know, boys will be boys, dogs will be dogs."

"God," Than said drunkenly, "this reminds me of this show I saw on Tuesday where this guy—"

"Shut your face or I'm gonna have to break it, Campustule," Charlie said.

Than belched.

Charlie stepped closer to Peter, just a few inches from his face. Peter could smell his own breath, thrown back to him through the marijuana smoke that Charlie exhaled.

Charlie stepped forward.

Peter moved back.

Charlie took another step forward, and as if in a dance, Peter went back another step.

"We're missing the fight," Charlie said. "Don't you want to see how it turns out?"

From behind him, Peter heard the dogs, growling and pounding against each other in the Wash.

Below him.

Charlie took another step.

Close again to Peter.

Peter's head began to spin with the beer, the stars and the world spun with him. He did not step backward.

Charlie said, "You sure you don't want to puff on this?" He held out the joint to Peter.

Behind and beneath Peter, the sound of snapping steel jaws, barking, gnashing teeth.

Charlie reached out and tapped lightly on Peter's shoulders. Then he drew something from his jacket pocket. Steel shone in the feeble light. "Don't you think it's about time I branded you, Chandler?"

The switchblade popped out, inches from Peter's neck.

"I could cut your heart out with this, boy," Charlie whispered, "and stuff it down your throat while you die."

"Shit!" Peter cried out, "you're psycho, Urquart," stepping back, feeling his ankle turn as he fell down the side of the Wash.

Chapter Nine
Valley of the Fallen

1

Peter rolled onto his back, and then sat up. His side hurt, and something was wrong with his right ankle. He looked up to the lights around the Wash, and then down again, hearing the growling of the dogs. He guessed that the dark dog had smelled the blood on his elbows and his right knee. Lammie, the midnight-black pit bull who was the victor and had managed to sustain no wounds, smelled his blood from as far away as she was—the opposite end of the Wash, closer to the highway. She growled, raising wobblingly up onto her haunches to sit and sniff the air; then on all fours as she moved toward him, her head bobbing toward the ground to sniff; growling between sniffs.

The dog looked like a demon from the wrong side of the tracks in Hell.

On his knees, his shirt ripped, his right ankle aching and swelling for all he knew, Peter let out a cry for help that came out of his mouth in a gasp of wind. His throat was desert dry; he had no voice in him. He tried to stand, but his ankle hurt so much he fell down again before he'd even risen; started to crawl back to the wall of sand and gravel that rose up to form a side of the Wash.

Above him, Peter heard these two men laughing drunkenly, still betting on the fight. The one that was about to occur between the fallen kid and the pit bull. *Jesus, they're betting against me.*

Than, with that half-moon grin cutting across his round pudgy face, his jowls starting to flap like a lizard's dewlap in its mating ritual, shouted something unintelligible down at him. Charlie Urquart, stoned out of his mind, was laughing with his buddies.

And the dog was getting closer; its thick saliva dribbled down its throat; it was hungry and flush with its recent victory.

Peter finally found his voice: "Get me the fuck outta here!" He crawled like a crab, but with every movement, his ankle felt like it was on fire—he screamed on the inside as well as the outside of his body.

Then, the sound of a gunshot, nearby.

The men up on the rim of the Wash scattered, shouting curses, dropping their liquor bottles, dragging their women and their dogs off with them, even the bloodied silver dog in the Wash that hadn't moved from the place where it lay bleeding—a big, muscular guy leaped down into the Wash and grabbed his loser dog while one of his buddies drove their Jeep over the road, down into the gulley beside him. The silver-white dog groaned, and the muscleman threw the wounded animal in the back of the Jeep and hopped in himself while the vehicle continued moving slowly down the Wash. Peter looked up to the edge of the Wash—all he could see was the red lights of retreating trucks, even Charlie Urquart's Mustang coughing up dust as it sped out to the highway, even Than Campusky had vanished—*that wimp.*

The other pit bull, Lammie, watched the rim of the Wash.

Dead silence after the gunshot, after the Jeeps and trucks and broken down redneckmobiles hightailed it for the road.

Then, the crunching of gravel as someone—no, *two* people approached.

They stepped into the light from the floodlamps that bedecked the outer walls of the Garden of Eden.

A guy who looked like he was eighteen with a long, brooding face, dark shadows beneath his eyebrows, and a clump of prematurely gray hair on his scarecrow head, glared down into the Wash. In spite of his slender frame, he seemed hulking, dominant, as if he imagined himself to be a impenetrable fortress dressed in human skin. He was closed, locked, unreadable, unfathomable. His dark gaze was terrible, his shadow eyes fixed on the dog. A handgun trembled in his hand; he crushed his white-knuckled fist around it as if to keep it still, to keep it from shooting again. A puff of smoke lingered about the gun's barrel.

Then a girl sidled up next to him, practically bumping him with her hips, a tall, slender redheaded *woman*, actually, and she was pretty. Younger and older at the same time. Her hips, pressed against the man's, were perfectly curved horseshoes, her breasts small and high, her shoulders slung back in invitation. Her tight jeans hugging her hips, her blouse sheer like a diaphanous curtain partially blown back by a breeze. She was the kind of woman who inspired countless adolescent wet dreams.

Her hair, like fire, cooled by something in her face, a void there in her eyes looking to be filled. She looked like a woman waiting for inspiration.

The man said, "Lammie. Come."

The pit bull moved to the edge of the Wash, hunkering down, shivering as if she'd been sprayed with ice water.

The man with the gun said, "Fuck him for stealing her like this."

The woman said, "You'll get your money."

Then she noticed Peter, shining a Flashlight his direction. "You hurt, boy?"

Peter kept looking back to the gun in the man's hand.

"Sloan," she said, "he may be hurt. We should do something."

The man called Sloan grinned, turning his attention away from the dog. He shook the gun in his hand, pointing it at Peter. He said, "Maybe we should put the boy out of his misery."

Sloan and his girlfriend introduced themselves: Kevin Sloan, Peter Chandler, Peter Chandler, Wendy Swan, as they helped him into the truck, his ankle hurting. Wendy examined it.

"It's only bruised," she said. "And bleeding. If you'd sprained it it would be a balloon." She massaged it with her warm fingers, and Peter soon forgot about any pain. Peter sat between them in the truck, and she massaged; Sloan smoked a cigarette and turned back to pet his dog through the sliding glass window between the front of the truck and the back.

"The Grubman's bound to come along after that shot," he said, referring to the local policeman, named Chip Grubb but known universally as the Grubman. Sloan passed his cigarette to Peter, who took a lungful and then passed it to Wendy.

Almost scared and almost thrilled, Peter said: "I've never smoked that stuff before," waiting for the thrill of getting high to come over him.

"What? *Camels*?" Sloan said, and Peter felt stupid: *of course, it was just plain tobacco*.

Wendy stopped massaging his foot as she smoked the cigarette; she kept glancing in the side mirror, looking back; Sloan passed a beer over; Peter drank it and felt terrified to be with these people and happy that at last he had found some escape from the abyss of summer.

Wendy was the first to see the flashing red lights of the police car as it turned off the highway onto the gravel. "You were right about Grubman," she said. Her face was a shadowy silhouette. The smell in the truck was stale beer and cigarette ash; empty cans knocked each other on the floor. In the back of the truck, the black dog barked, and when Sloan turned to say something to Wendy, his breath was whisky and beer.

Sloan said, "It's that prick, all right."

"Just gonna sit here?" she said. For Peter, it was like sitting between two rednecks, their accents Southwestern and emphasizing every other word as if not comprehending their own speech. Than had been right—*white trash city*.

Sloan flipped off his truck's lights. He turned the key in the ignition. "Beer's under the seat, boy."

Taking the orders, Peter reached down and brought out a tall can of Pabst Blue Ribbon. It was warm and sweaty. He popped the tab and took a swig. It tasted like spit; it tasted great.

"Gonna wait 'til he's right on my ass," Sloan said "Gimme a beer, boy."

"You only live once," Wendy whispered, looking back at the slowly approaching police car. Wendy was getting tense—she slid her left hand down Peter's right arm from his elbow to his wrist. Her fingernails felt like they were digging into his flesh. She turned and whispered something specifically to him; her breath was almost unbearably sweet, like orange blossoms: "He's like this"; but her words were less important than the fact that while her fingers dug into his pulse, she *knew* what effect she was having on him. He felt it. She knew that just her touch had aroused him. Even her painful touch.

Sloan heaved his foot against the accelerator. The truck sped down the dark Wash, blindly, chased by flashing red lights and the smell of beer and orange blossoms all around, and those fingernails digging into Peter's wrist. Sloan turned up his cassette of Bruce Springsteen's *The Wild, The Innocent, and the E Street Shuffle*, and Peter Chandler felt like he was on the wildest ride in the world.

3

"You was shittin' bricks back there," Sloan said to him a half-hour later.

The cop had given up the chase as Sloan pulled into an arroyo, turning the engine off. The truck smelled like burnt rubber and grease. They watched the police car spraying dust as it drove on, swerving around, turning back up to Highway 4. Peter's heart was beating fast. He was drunk and embarrassed, and there was nothing but darkness like a deep cave around the truck. How many Blue Ribbon cans had he finished off? Six? Seven? After the truck's motor died, he had somehow been transported to the bed of the vehicle. Sloan and Wendy glanced back at him.

Peter's mind blurred like a frost-covered window. He saw things, but they didn't quite register on his brain: where was he? Who were these people? Had he been drinking? Was he getting sick? Would his dad kill him when he returned home? He was in a truck with two strangers, a pit bull, and a handgun. He might as well have crossed into another dimension, this was so far removed from the suburbanity of his life. This was outlaw country.

Somewhere in that night, Sloan said to him, "You ever kill anyone, kid?"

"Huh?" Peter asked.

"Nothin'. Forget it."

The moonless but clear night spread out like a thick army of ants, it went on forever in constant motion, jittery stars between the blackness—like his insides, jostling, quivering and empty. Drunk, he saw mosquitoes where there were none, he felt his teeth with his tongue, it felt like they would drop out of his mouth. Sloan's Ford pickup had searched out the rocks and bumps of the wavy desert landscape, and with each lurch of the truck, a corresponding leap threatened to erupt from his stomach. They had traveled across a lunar territory, craters abounding, accompanied by a silence as if the world had ended.

Lammie, the monster dog, who had promised Peter a flesh-rending death down in that Wash, a demon from Nitro Hell, now lay, subdued, in its collapsible wire cage, as friendly as any dopey puppy, perhaps goofier. It whimpered. When he glanced at it, between sips of beer, she wagged her tail and grinned—if a dog can grin, if a pit bull fresh from its gladiatorial bloodfest can grin like a nerdy kid who has just discovered love or chocolate or dirty jokes. She now looked like the lovable pup from the "Our Gang" comedies. When he petted her, he found that her stomach seemed full—her nipples hanging down. He was about to say, "Hey, I think your dog's pregnant," but when he opened his mouth, a series of hiccups interrupted his words.

Then Peter vomited over the truck's side, *ralphing* as Campusky would say, ralphing his guts out; then he was standing beside the truck in a cold sweat, listening to coyotes.

And then, who knows how many drunken moments later, he watched the shadows of this redneck couple thrust against each other—Campusky had been right, they were Neanderfucking for all he knew, and he listened to the music: the radio played in the truck, a country singer was singing about bad times and bad women. Before he passed out—thinking, you're just like your old man, *born to be a drunk and a derelict and amount to nothing*, the dog licking his hand—Peter was about to say something aloud when he heard the shadows whisper obscenities and grunt and moan. The moonless night filled with the yips of jealous coyotes.

4

That night, for the first time in two years, Peter Chandler did not have the nightmare in which his father beat his mother to death.

Instead, it was Peter himself who was raising his bloodied fists over his mother's face.

Chapter Ten
Morning Rituals

1

Mornings always began with darkness.

In Nitro, within a trailer, Wendy Swan stirred in her sleep, her eyes moist with tears.

The sound of the dog's whining awoke her.

Her eyes opened suddenly, as if shocked from sleep.

She had been dreaming about that other woman again, *the face in profile, the anger flashing in the eyes, the head turning, bearing down . . .*

Her mother.

She stretched her arms over her head; the bed creaked. She heard the sounds of trucks passing on the highway, horns blowing.

"Sloan," she whispered. She lay next to him in the bed he'd fashioned from an old table and two mattresses piled one atop the other. Her head pushed in an uncomfortable position against the window of the trailer; whenever she slept with him the back of her neck always seemed cold from being pressed against the window. There was a chill for her that had nothing to do with the external temperature: it had to do with an emptiness she felt inside, whenever she awoke suddenly, a feeling of not being connected to the world to which she was waking.

Instinctively, she reached up and touched the beaded scar around her neck, just beneath her chin. "*Looks like somebody give you one helluva case of hickeys*," he'd said the night they'd met last year. He had kissed along the ridge of the scar when they made love that night, and when she saw the approaching climax in his eyes she pressed her neck against his lips and he had lapped hungrily at the scar as if he were some animal trying to reopen a wound.

Someone trying to reopen the wound—and within each wound, a world.

She didn't bother trying to wake him again. From his congested snoring she knew he was still too drunk. Sloan hadn't even bothered to take the baseball cap off; its rim poked up from beneath the yellowed sheet, his nostrils shaped like almonds, flexing with each snore.

She turned awkwardly in the small bed.

Out the window, the Sun Dial Trailer Park's lights were like those in a football stadium, creating an artificial day long before sunrise. The other trailers were still; no doors slamming, no other dogs barking. Beyond them there was a hint of lavendar that might've been dawn just stretching from the east, but it might've been the glare from the trailer park's lights.

She glanced at the Budweiser clock that Sloan had stolen from the Coyote Cantina: 4:20 A.M. It was two hours off; the damn thing never kept good time. But she knew the time. She felt time passing, and wasn't sure why, as if a memory were repressed within her.

Carefully, she slid the sheet off her body. Her skin should've been smooth; she'd turned seventeen last December. But she felt old, and the desert had made her dry.

She slid to the end of the bed. Sloan sniffled and the baseball cap fell backward off his head. His eyes opened briefly, fluttering, not seeming to recognize her, and then closed again. His peppered hair was matted against his scalp.

Sloan, in bed, made hawking noises in the back of his throat. He shook his head dreamily, opening his eyes. His slate-gray eyes were outlined with red, bordered by dark circles.

"Hamster eyes," she whispered softly.

"What was—did you hear something?" he coughed, clearing the back of his throat.

"You were dreaming," she said, "sweet little hamster eyes."

"Oh." He closed his eyes, sliding his arm out from beneath the covers and patting the empty space next to him. "Back to bed."

"In a minute."

"Sleepy."

"Sweet little hamster eyes."

He turned, drifting off to sleep, murmuring her name. "Wendy. Miss Swan. Miss Wendy Swan the love of my life. My mate." He was used to her getting up this early, going for a drive in the truck. Once, he had followed her out, and watched the truck kick up dust out to the road. She had parked alongside the gulley near the Garden of Eden, and had just gotten out of the truck and stood there, watching the old house as if she were trying to memorize something about it.

He stretched his arms across his face, and his mouth opened slightly.

Later, after the enormity of sunrise was upon the town, Wendy Swan stood on the small stoop of cinderblocks that Sloan had erected beneath the narrow front door of the trailer. She shivered from the cool morning air, covering herself with her white terry cloth robe. The doors of other trailers and mobile homes creaked and grated as people awoke. She wondered what they all did— what did people do in the world, anyway? What was the purpose that kept them waking up in the morning, what made them take that first step? The thin wind coughed carbon monoxide from cars starting up, mingled with the odor of instant coffee. The hills and canyons were pale blue, the sky, dead empty. Beer trucks, Coca-Cola trucks, Arrowhead Water trucks, trucks loaded with oranges and avocadoes rolled and bumped along the pass over the Rattlesnake Wash on their ways through to Palmetto.

When Wendy went back inside the showed him the chewed-through leather muzzle, Kevin Sloan was sitting in his jockey shorts at the breakfast table; he rubbed his white-socked feet together where the fleas had bitten in the night.

"I heard something earlier," Wendy told him. "But by the time I got out, she was gone."

"Damn dog," Sloan said. But Sloan was always like this before he had his morning Ovaltine and cigarette. She set the leather muzzle down in front of him and went to the cupboard by the sink.

He lifted the torn muzzle up in front of his eyes as if it were an expensive diamond necklace. "I shoulda known she was gonna do this. But I guess it means she's a fighter, don't it?"

"She ran off somewhere." Wendy sniffed at the quart of milk; it was partially soured. He might not notice if he'd already started smoking. She mixed it in a glass with Ovaltine. Then she reached into her robe's pockets, withdrawing a couple of cigarettes. She slipped these between her lips and lit them both. She inhaled. She took the cigarettes out of her mouth. She bent down over Sloan, kissing him deeply, exhaling smoke into his mouth.

He coughed, "Whew," pulling his mouth free of her exploring tongue. "Wendy, honey, I think we both got a case of the zacklies. Musta been the beers last night—zacklies is when your mouth tastes 'zackly like your ass."

She felt his hand rubbing her leg, searching for the gap in her bathrobe. When his hand found it, Wendy stepped away from him. She thrust one of the cigarettes into his mouth. She puffed on the other.

Sloan took a drag on the cigarette. He said, "I love you, Wendy. And I know you don't love me. I know about you."

"Oh, you do?"

"Yep, I know all about you and your mysterious past. Nothing but secrets."

She said nothing.

"Yep," Sloan hacked, but continued puffing on the cigarette. "You didn't run away from no home in Bakersfield, that's the truth. You're from here, right here. I know. I know about the way you go and look at the Beekeeper's place. He your daddy or something?"

"Not my daddy," she said, and then grinned, sweetly. "You're so smart, baby."

"Where'd you come from, then?"

"Oh," she said, "a very dark place. A very cold dark place."

"Tell me," he whined.

"If you want to know," she said, leaning back against the small range, putting her half-smoked cigarette out in a bowl of leftover Kelloggs Corn Flakes, letting her robe fall open, "it's all there. Inside me. Do you want that? Boy? Do you want that?"

"Yes," he gasped, coughing into his glass of Ovaltine and practically falling back in his chair, "Jesus God yes."

"Show me how much you want it," she said, leaning farther back, reaching for the barbed wire that she kept for such occasions in the cabinet above the sink.

2

An hour later at the Sun Dial Trailer Park, four men sat on a concrete deck outside a double mobile home. Another hot Sunday morning, none of them wearing shirts, with their beerguts hanging down proudly across their laps. They were hungover, still sleepy. Their women had sent them out of the trailers early; they wore sunglasses to hide the sleepiness; one man flexed the tattoo on his biceps; the man on the end spat a wad of brown chewing tobacco every few seconds.

Wendy Swan walked by, carrying an open umbrella.

"Ain't no rain likely," the tattooed man said.

She didn't look their way. She wore a pair of aviator's dark glasses which gave her face a vaguely comic look. She wasn't smiling. She seemed to be heading somewhere, although there was nowhere to go in the trailer park but to the desolate highway.

"Lookit her."

"All you ever gonna get to do's look."

"Bet she's been had by the best and the worst," another said.

Spit. "Sloan may be the worst. Bet he's had her every which way."

"Thinks he's hot shit fresh out of the cow's ass."

"He beats her. See those bruises about two weeks back?"

"I'd treat her sweet if she was mine, that's all I'm saying. He hits that pretty thing?"

"She was all bleeding one morning. Ginger told me about it—said she saw her getting out of her truck one morning, and she was all torn and bruised. Son of a bitch."

Spit. "Jesus, God, it's gonna be a hot one today."

The tattooed man whispered, mostly to himself, "Pretty little thing like that. Oughta report it to somebody, 'bout him hittin' her and all, 'fore he kills her."

Another shook his head, "He ain't gonna do nothin' worse'n break her heart."

3

Charlie Urquart awoke that morning one of his favorite ways: a boner in one hand, a beer in the other. The beer was a leftover from the previous night, but the boner was new and shiny (at least to him) and there was a name attached to it, and it was the name of that white trash girl he'd seen out at the Wash, the one with that redneck, Sloan.

Wendy something, that's who she was.

He had seen her once before, in Nitro, he and Billy and Terry had gone trolling through the trailer park once or twice to get some drunk-ass idiot to start a fight so the boys could clobber him—

when Charlie had caught a glimpse of her, through the trailer window—

naked—

fresh from the shower—

he noticed her white thigh—

where someone had branded her.

Jesus, it got him hard just thinking about it. Hadn't had sex for almost five months, ever since Alison's little mishap, and now he wondered how he was going to get any satisfaction—

her pale white thigh, the scar tissue around the brand, the glow of her face . . .

Charlie resumed his second favorite activity (next to torture).

4

Anyone who has ever lived up on the desert will tell you: no one goes to live in towns like Palmetto unless they're hiding from something.

They hide under rocks and in houses and in shady bars, waiting for the day to pass.

And pass it does, slowly, into the afternoon, a Sunday when the streets are empty and the churches are full and night will not descend for several hours.

Chapter Eleven
Secrets of the Bone

1

The town was originally called Boniface Wells. Back in 1897, a good twenty years after the mining disaster of the El Corazon Mine, Norton Boniface decided that the natural springs beneath the ground were curative, and attracted a following as a preacher and healer who finally succumbed to a bad case of lockjaw in 1927, having refused all medication that might have easily remedied his condition. His widow raised their four children, although only one survived into adulthood, named Lucas, who then went and took a wife at the ripe age of forty. This woman was bad—everyone said it though few ever met her—and married Lucas because she needed the solitude he took for granted. But Lucas was land-rich and cash-poor, and his wife was then given to certain extravagant habits, so when Gib Urquart came along and offered him twenty-five thousand dollars for land that was basically shit-dust, he took it, and kept the land around the Rattlesnake Wash as well as the miniature castle his father had called, in his extreme vanity, the Garden of Eden. The story was, Lucas's wife left him, after she lost a child at birth, but there were enough Fundamentalists in Palmetto to spread the story that she worshipped the Devil, and was insane, and never turned toward the true light. These were the founders' families, and their stories.

After his woman ran off, Lucas Boniface fell apart. Someone else took over the big house, and Boniface himself just went to seed. Gib Urquart then took the ball, and ran with it, building nearly four hundred ramshackle development houses, all looking mostly alike; he brought in investors, and soon there were burger joints along the narrow highway. Naranja Canyon, transforming into Nitro, sprung up fullblown across the Wash, as soon as the trailers had parked across the rocky soil. Gib Urquart was a man with vision and drive, both rarities up on the high desert, and soon he actually had the place incorporated and was, himself, running the subatomic particles of the local political machine and having a grand old time.

And then, for no reason other than the difficulty with which anything is grown at such altitudes and in such heat, the town died, and Gib Urquart's fortunes declined, and although they still had the annual Chili Cookoff on Grubstake Days in July, and still had a small outpost for civic and legal matters, Palmetto, and its sister, Nitro, barely even made the local maps.

There it is. History of a small place. Nice and neat.

But anyone who has ever lived up on the desert will tell you. There's more. If you dig.

2

It was the beginning of the week, or maybe toward the middle—the man that lived beneath the road didn't have much use for a calendar. He awoke, stretched, smelling the dirt of the Wash. Someone was burning something nearby, something that stank, along with mesquite. *Who the hell would be lighting a fire in the morning? Holy moly.* He looked at the Rolex that he had hanging around his cat's neck: it was closer to noon than he'd like to admit to. "Demons are here, Isaac. I got the juice, but it ain't enough. They been tryin' make a nest here since back before I remember."

Isaac, the tabby, snarled at something, the hair on his back rising straight up, his ears going back. Something was down the other end of the corrugated steel cylinder that supported the road and provided a roof over the old man's head.

He picked up the flashlight near his pillow and shined it down to the dark end.

The light hit two small red eyes.

Fierce eyes.

Demon eyes.

"The Lord is with me, Evil One," the man gasped, using his free hand to reach for a bottle of hootch. It was Thunderbird, and even though he had the money for better stuff, his tastes were simple. "Yea, though I walk through the valley of death, still I don't fear

87

evil." He took a good long swig, and felt sweat break out across his forehead. He could smell his armpits stinking with fear.

Isaac hissed, moving toward the Dark Thing with the Red Eyes.

"I knew you come back," he said, "I knew it. I smelled you out there on the road that day. I found what you left behind. But I ain't scared o' you. Nossah. As in the last days, ye shall reap what ye sow, and what you gonna reap ain't gonna be my soul. I know how to stop you."

He set the bottle down, and reached beneath the serape upon which he slept.

He drew out a large knife, almost a buck knife, but fancier.

He shined the flashlight on the blade. "Looky here, demon, I got the one thing you scared of, the one thing turns you to chickenshit on a shingle. You know where this is gonna send you? Straight to Hell, you 'bomination. And this . . ." he said, remembering the thing in the handkerchief.

What he had found.

He redirected the light back to the demon eyes, and the Thing moved closer, well into the light.

Before the old man could see what it was, he smelled it.

The cat backed away, yowling.

"Shit," the old man said, because it wasn't a demon odor at all, but the stink of a skunk. Sure enough, the polecat started running straight for him, and he and his cat both backed out of that cylinder as fast as they could. He ran out into the Wash, stinking to high heaven, with a little skunk, its tail raised high, running off in another direction.

This was a typical morning for him, and as he stood there, shirtless, catching his breath a few moments later, he saw two boys out on the road and waved to them because he was friendly and lonely and crazy.

And because someone had to warn people of what was to come.

3

Than Campusky said, "There's the Bone. Old Bonyface. See him?"

He pointed to an area up along the thorny brush on the other side of the highway. Peter saw nothing other than the endless

You Come When I Call You

Joshua trees and the crumbling adobe arch that was the beginning of the old Boniface graveyard beyond. They'd been walking through the Rattlesnake Wash by way of a shortcut from Nitro, where most of the fast-food joints were, back home to Palmetto. Peter still had a bit of a limp where his right ankle had twisted, but he endured the pain somewhat quietly, only moaning when he wanted sympathy. They were out looking for summer jobs—and barely speaking to each other, because the heat was getting to them, and they were angry and tired. They had only been able to fill out one application, at Paco's Tacos, because they weren't quite sixteen. Sixteen was the magic age, and Peter would turn in just a couple of weeks, but Than wouldn't get there for five more months.

"Hey, you're not still mad about last night," Than said, lip-farting. "Give me a break. What was I supposed to do? Jump down in there and fight off the dogs? Jesus, somebody shot a *gun!* So I was either gonna get shot or get my balls chomped. My mom'd kill me if she knew I was down there!" Than was always a little too excitable.

"Forget it." But it was all Peter could think of—not his anger at Than, but the excitement of riding with those two—Sloan and Wendy—of being drunk for the first time. Of knowing that he didn't have to be the good kid anymore who obeyed the rules and did what was expected of him. He was almost sixteen. He could do anything he wanted.

He could practically taste freedom in the dusty air.

Even sneaking in through his bedroom window at three A.M. and for the first time in his life, not getting caught and punished—even that was something.

"Wonder what the Bone's up to." Than pointed again toward the opposite side of the highway.

Peter saw something moving, but it didn't seem to be quite a man. Low, down along the scrub, between thatches of tumbleweed, the crusted-over old lizard wriggled. Peter had heard about Bony-face now and then at school, but had never actually experienced a sighting. It was as good as seeing a UFO because the Bone was supposed to be like a chameleon, able to blend in with the desert perfectly. Actual sightings were rare and somewhat suspect. The only evidence of him, they said, were the Thunderbird bottles strewn along the Wash.

89

"He sees everything that goes on in this hellhole," Than said. "I bet he watched you fall into the pit last night. I bet he sat there and laughed and drank his Thunderbird. I bet he knows what everybody does in this town. C'mon." Than tugged at Peter's dirty tee shirt. "Let's check him out. He's good for a laugh." Than hobbled ahead of Peter, not bothering to look both ways as he crossed the road. The sun was burning. It turned the land into a griddle, and the heat seemed to seep right through Peter's sandals. His ankle still hurt where he'd twisted it, and he was still a little cotton-mouthed from a bitch of a hangover. His dad had hauled him out of bed by nine and told him to get his ass out and find a job, Jesus Christ it was almost fucking July and he hadn't earned a penny, what kind of goddamned lazy-ass pussy kind of son was he raising, anyway? His mother grabbed Annie and had gone off to church—the Baptist Church over in Upperville, where she could speak in tongues and avoid reality for at least one day. Life as usual. It was a pissant hot day and he was sick of this one-horse town; somehow, he knew his life had to change, one way of another, because right now, it was just frying.

"Peter!" Than turned, raising his hand, waving him on through the shimmering heat that rose and curved off the bitter highway. "C'mon, we can have fun with the Bone!"

4

"Boyz," Bonyface said, covering his face with his leather venous hands, "you leave the old Bone alone, now, you hear? Leave him alone. I know who sent you, that Devil, torment the Bone, but gitalong outta here now." He kicked his feet out, shooing up flies and small pebbles. He was barefoot, and Peter noticed that there were thorns and burrs and foxtails stuck in the flesh along his toes and soles. A mangy-looking, gray tabby cat followed alongside him, rubbing up against his ankles. Seeing that the boys weren't going away, the Bone dropped his hands from his face and settled down.

"Jesus," Peter gasped, on seeing his face. It was studded with what appeared to be small silvery thumbtacks. Through his lips, a chain ran all the way up to his left nostril; along his ears, several small gold crosses pierced the lobes.

Than apparently knew what the Bone looked like—this didn't

surprise him. "He's into body piercing or something. He's like a human dartboard."

Bonyface, watching the disgust on Peter's face almost evaporate, kept it alive by saying, "Look here, boyz."

He grinned, his mouth open wide. There were small fishhooks thrust into his gums around his teeth, and two through his tongue. The old man reached in and, carefully, as if he were working a splinter, drew a tiny hook from the pink, receding flesh of his gum, and held it before them. "It don't hurt, boyz, it don't hurt. It's atonement for my sins—atonement ain't about hurtin', it's more 'bout sufferin'. You wanna know about sin? Ask that godless Beekeeper in the big house. That's a soul knows all about sin. My hooks, they ain't bad. It feels good, as a matter o' fact, it feels damn good. Wanna see something more? Something real special? Something you ain't never seen before?"

"Yeah," Than said, grinning.

Peter took a step back. "I better get home," he said.

"Chicken," Than said.

"Yeah." Bonyface nodded. "Chicken. Bwawk-bok-bwawk!" He folded his elbows up and flapped them. His skin was pale-worm-white around the armpits, and like burnt steak on the forearms and up by the shoulders. "You don't want to know 'bout no devils in this town, but the Bone, he sees 'em. They been here before, in that devil girl, and the Beekeeper called 'em back, that one did. Can't help it, no sah. You can try to kill all your babies, but if one lives, it's bound to its nature, just like a scorpion's bound to its stinger, and a rattler to its poison spit, a dog to its bite—you follow? But I know how to stop her, boyz, and none of yous is gonna listen to the Old Bone, is ya? Demon's back. Only way to stop her is divide it up and serve it raw and ripe."

Than said, "I don't believe in demons, Bone. I don't think I do. Not really."

Bonyface laughed, and slapped his thigh, turned to his cat and said, "Hear that, Isaac? This boy don't believe in what's all around us. You want to talk demons, boyz, you come see the Bone sometime. I got lotsa books with pitchers."

Peter tapped Than on the shoulder. "Let's go, Than."

"You go," Than said. "See if I care."

"C'mon, Than, this is too weird."

"Looky looky," the Bone said, and brought a handkerchief from his back pocket.

"C'mon," Peter said, but even saying this he wanted to see what the weirdo had to show.

The Bone delicately unwrapped the handkerchief, a trail of spittle hanging at the edge of his studded mouth. "The Beekeeper wanted this, but Bone was watching, and Bone run up and git it 'fore the Beekeeper got to it. Looky looky."

The handkerchief was spread backward, and Peter thought that what was in the middle of it was a small, curled starfish, or perhaps a large, dead tarantula.

"Holy shit," Than said. "It's a *hand!*"

Peter lip-farted. "Nah. It's fake." He reached over and touched it, and then withdrew his fingers as if he'd just touched a live wire. He rubbed his fingers together.

Bonyface had a lopsided grin, and when he opened his mouth, it was pure 100 proof. "Hush now, boyz, Bone don't want nobody comin' over and takin' it. It ain't just a hand, boyz, it's a Hand of Glory, a murderer's hand, it's got bad magic all around it, it crawls inside you and stays there. I seen it, I seen it all, what the wild thing did to him, tore him limb from limb, I saw the demon come outta him, I saw the wild thing drink the demon juice, too much at one draft, I saw the dark thing crawl into her, passed back to her after all these years—all it wanted to do was get home, its home, its nest. I saw it with these two eyes, and I got me a souvenir. Looky," he said, and with his free hand, plucked a fishhook from his skin and jabbed it into the center of the curled Hand of Glory.

The finger twitched. "It's powerful, boyz, you get near it, it's like fire, gives off heat, burns into your brains, into your *dreams.*"

Peter and Than almost jumped back, but the old man laughed, and covered the hand up again. He smacked his lips. "Only protection from the Devil's if you drink the demon juice, best from the heart, that'll stop it for sure." His nose wrinkled up like he was smelling something bad. "Don't like demons, no sir, but just some blood is good, only not too much or you get 'fected with it yourself. You go like this . . ." He lifted the hand up to his mouth, nipping the edge of the thumb.

And sucked.

By the time he stopped to take a breath, blood on his lips, the two boys were gone.

5

"Jeez," Than said, after he and Peter got out of there. "Holy mother. Creepy, huh?"

"That man is insane," Peter said. "My dad's always talking about the feebs in this town . . . I *touched* that thing."

"Maybe you'll get some disease. The Bone disease."

Peter looked at his left hand, the one that touched the hand. He brought it up to his nose. Sniffed it.

"What's it smell like?"

Peter thrust his hand under Than's nose. Than jumped back. "Holy shit!"

"Smells like a dead animal," Peter said. "God, Than, I just want to get it off me." He wiped his hand on the side of his shirt, and then brought it back up to his face. "I can still smell it. Yuck."

Than looked about the mournful highway, to the south, the trailer parks, but they were too far and they'd just come from there. To the north, was the beginning of Palmetto, and the Magnificent Diner was over on the other side of the road.

Then, there was the Garden of Eden, with its yellow walls.

"Let's go to the diner," Than said. "I'm kinda hungry, and you can go wash up."

But Peter had spotted, not twenty feet away, a spigot on one of Eden's walls, and began walking toward it. The gate to the great house was slightly ajar, and Peter walked right up to it. He bent over the spigot, and turned the rusty lever until brown water came out. It turned clear, and he thrust his hand under it. It was warm. He squatted down and rubbed his hand in the soil, and then under the running water again. The spigot squealed as the water came out. He shut the water off. He sniffed his hand. "Pretty much gone." He turned around to look for his friend, but Than was standing a ways back by the road. He had to shield his eyes with his hands in order to see him through the glare of the sun. "What's the matter?"

Than said nothing, but watched the house. He rubbed his left ankle over his right.

Peter got up, wiping his wet hands on his shorts. He heard a sound, and turned to look over the iron gate. Inside, there was a garden, growing wild, vines snaking across vines, flowers blooming almost unnaturally, and between the plants, gray wooden box upon box upon box, all stacked against the walls, with a thin path to the front door. Above some of the flowering plants were pink bed sheets, spread like tents, no doubt to provide shade for the more delicate specimens. A bee flew past his head, over the gate, and down into the garden. Peter noticed that other bees flew about, flower to flower, in and out of the boxes.

They must waste a hell of a lot of water to grow all those flowers up here.

He had never seen a garden like it on the desert, anywhere. Oh, there was the retired colonel out on Canyon Road, with his drought-resistant garden, and there were some cactus gardens in the back of some of the tract houses. Nothing could compare with what was within this garden.

What amazed him most of all were the squat trees—three of them, beneath the narrow windows of the house: orange trees. There were small, round, green oranges hanging from the branches; the dull yellow and orange ones had already dropped to the ground. Peter stood on his toes to see further into the garden. It was so beautiful; he had no idea that anything was this beautiful in this wasteland. Closed his eyes—smelled lemon, honeysuckle, orange blossom, and a rich fertile stink, as if the earth itself within those walls was one huge mulch pile giving forth seedlings. The sound of the bees surrounded him, and he pushed the gate a bit. It opened further.

He took a step forward.

"Peter!" Than called out. "C'mon!"

Peter glanced back. Than was waving wildly, like he had to go to the bathroom or something.

He looked at the garden again.

Eden.

There were roses on latticework, climbing up the walls of the house, the sand-yellow walls, cracked from time. *Just like Gramma's garden in Cook Country, the rose vines, and the wysteria, before Gramma died, before Dad began drinking so much, before Mom lost it.* He had been nine when his grandmother had died, and it was one of the worst things in his life because she had been his protector, and seemed to keep Mom safe, too. She would sit with him in her garden for hours reading stories about knights and dragons and rescuing fair damsels from high towers. It was like this place, a sanctuary. He wondered, for a second, if the oranges tasted good. There were still, small, white blossoms on the trees, and the bees circled the branches like jeweled bracelets.

Then he noticed something else.

From one of the long windows, a face.

At first, he thought it was an infant's face, staring out from a dark room, and he felt a chill run along his spine.

But when it moved—for whoever was there noticed him—he saw not a baby—it was a woman staring out at him.

6

"Get away from here," Than said, grabbing him by the shoulder. "Peter, come on, man."

Peter felt as if something had slipped beneath the surface of his skin, and he almost jumped when Than touched him.

"I thought you said it was locked," Peter said.

"It used to be. A kid went in there a buncha years ago," Than said. "And almost got stung to death. By a gazillion bees. He just got over the walls, and he fell into one of those boxes. The County Health Department came out and tried to get the Beekeeper to get rid of them, but they couldn't do it. The kid was trespassing. The kid knew the bees were there. The kid was allergic to bees. That was the story. He was eight years old, man. But I heard something else." Than's voice dropped to a whisper, as if he were afraid of being overheard by something in the house. "But it's all bullshit, I guess."

Peter listened intently, glancing back and forth to the stacks of boxes, the vines, and the pale green leaves.

"C'mon, I hate this place. Whoever lives in there doesn't want kids around, believe you me. And anyway, I'm hungry. Let's go to Trudy's."

"You're always hungry."

"Hey, I'm a growing boy. You comin' or ain'tcha?"

Chapter Twelve

The Magnificent Diner, Love at First Sight, and Joe Chandler

1

Trudy Virtue ran the Magnificent Diner just the Palmetto side of the highway. It was a brief walk in searing heat that made it seem like a mile. Once the boys got inside the chrome-and-wood diner car, the air conditioning was going full blast. Than picked out a dark wood booth, part of the diner add-on, and sat down. Out the window, you could see Hunt's Garage, and, just the other end of the diner, the beginning of the fountain of Palmetto goods and services: the All-Nite Rx and Sundries, a Baskin-Robbins, the Shoe Brothers Laundromat, and a Christian Science Reading Room. The diner was lit like a hospital ward—too quiet, pale green, and smelling of rubbing alcohol, because Trudy kept it so damn clean. Three men sat up at the counter, while a woman and her little girl sat at the small round table. The juke box wasn't even playing; Peter dropped a quarter in the selector at his table, but nothing played, and the quarter came back out. The one bald man sitting opposite Peter and Than had to put his back on his head because the shine from his scalp was too much for Trudy Virtue, the giantess with bad eyesight. Her booming voice ripped through the silence like a cannon. "Can't see in my own place, mister, you should go work for Edison, make some real money. Now, where the hell is my waitress? Anybody seen the girl who's supposed to be working here?" She was larger than life, with a head the size of a melon, and big liver lips, and eyes like a fish. She wore an old-fashioned waitress uniform that was too small for her, and she turned to Than and Peter and snapped, "What'll it be?"

"Pie," Than said immediately. "Boysenberry pie."

"Out. Ran out of it this morning, ten A.M.," she said, then, looking at Peter. "You gonna eat, kid, or just watch my tits?"

"I wasn't—" he said.

She waved her stubby pencil in front of him like it was a magic wand. "You was, you was. We got specials, we got ham steak, we got liver and onions, we got homemade guacamole and carnitas, we got apple pie."

"Apple," Than corrected his order. "With ice cream."

"You want cheese with it, not ice cream, Nathaniel. Apple pie without cheese is like a kiss without a squeeze." She grinned, showing six perfectly yellowed teeth on the top, with gold fillings back to the hinterlands of her throat.

"Ice cream," he insisted. "Vanilla."

"You?" she turned back to Peter.

"Just a Coke."

"Just a Coke," she said flatly, and walked back to the kitchen, shouting, "Coke, pie with, and where the hell is my waitress?"

And then, for Peter, one of the wonders of existence, the mystery of all human mysteries, showed its face for once in his life.

For, coming out of the back of the diner, was the most beautiful girl he had ever seen. Each time he saw her, he tried to deny that, but it was like denying breath, or denying heartbeat. She wasn't the most beautiful girl in existence, he knew that, but something about her overtook him, captured him, and he didn't think he would ever quite feel that. She wore a blue-checkered dress, with a grease-stained apron; her hair was drawn back in a ponytail, although a stray shock of it had come loose and hung down over her forehead; her eyes were the darkest brown, and her nervous smile seemed to lift the entire diner out of its doldrums. He had even seen her before in school, but never like this, and he realized that the diner truly *was* Magnificent. She stood there while Trudy bawled her out ("You sneak cigarettes, you do it on your own time, honey," "I wasn't. I was just . . ." "Just go take this out. Booth two."), and all Peter saw was that she was sweeter and more lovely now in this setting, slightly beleaguered, with just a touch of rebellion to those lips, than when he'd noticed her at school. *Alison Hunt.*

"It's Urqu's girl," Than said.

"I wish she were mine."

She approached the table, with the Coke in her left hand, a glass of ice water in her right. Peter noticed that she had a locket around her neck, in the shape of a heart. Slow motion, she came to him, carefully balancing her burdens, not yet noticing who she was waiting on; she seemed flustered and a little lost. *Alison Wonderland*. She wasn't like Wendy, although Peter compared the two for a moment in his head: Wendy was rough and wild and trashy, but Alison, Alison Hunt was sweet and had kindness in her eyes. He felt something that possibly only fifteen-year-old boys feel, that fleeting moment of wanting to marry her and have children with her and grow old with her. There were other, more hormonally encouraged thoughts, too. But God, she was pretty. Without wanting to, he sighed as she set the Coke down.

"Hi," she said.

He knew then.

He knew the way you know that things will work out, or won't work out.

He knew the way he could tell when something felt comfortable.

He knew, but he wasn't sure. What if he let this pass by? What if they would never run into each other again? What if she knew right then that it was love at first sight, but because he didn't pick up the signals, it would be another Great Lost Love and he would end up in one of those awful marriages like his folks had and he'd be a drinker and a wifebeater and a creep?

He couldn't let it pass.

"Hey, Alison. I thought you'd be at your dad's garage."

Alison shook her head slightly. "Not this summer. Mom thinks it's unladylike for me to be a grease monkey, so I'm stuck slinging hash in this dive. Who has the Coke?"

Peter grinned. She set it down. She set the ice water in front of Than.

"So, how's Charlie?" Than asked, picking up the glass and sipping the water.

Alison didn't take her eyes off Peter; her look wasn't dreamy, it was curious. She said, "I guess he's fine. After last night, I don't think I'll be seeing much of him."

"You two broke up?" Peter asked.

"A long time ago. Almost a month."

Peter didn't hesitate. "You want to go out sometime?"

"I don't know."

For a moment, he was plunged into the despair of human existence, and his heart sank.

Then, she said, "Okay. Maybe to the movies. Sometime before

the weekend. My shift on Monday to Thursday is ten to four. I can drive—I got my license in April, and I've got the car. The rest is up to you. But I want a real date—you call me, you take me out, and don't expect me to do anything on a date your sister wouldn't do."

"My sister's nine."

She grinned. "Well, you know what I mean. You call me tonight, okay? If you don't call, forget it. I don't wait by the phone." Then she walked off to take the bald man's order.

Peter closed his eyes; opened them; tasted his Coke.

"You look like Polly-fucking-Anna," Than said. "Hullo, Peter, hullo in there." He waved his right hand in front of Peter's face.

"She seems pretty nice. I've never really spoken to her before."

"There's a lot of stories about her, but nice isn't one of them. She's a slut. She's Urqu's girl."

"Shut up. Don't talk about her like that," Peter snapped. "You heard her. They broke up." He scratched the back of his scalp, and wiped his hands across his face as if trying to take the silly idiotic feeling of a crush off his skin.

"Maybe according to her. You don't know Charlie Urquart all that well, do you?"

"Well enough to know he's a jerk. Who cares about him? Did you see her smile? She's got a great smile. She's supposed to be smart, too—I mean, she seems smart. I sound like a two-year-old," he said, finally relenting. "It's only a date. Maybe she wants me to call her just so she can laugh at me." But he didn't believe it even when he said it.

"All I'm saying is, you go out with her, you're asking for trouble. But"—Than arched his eyebrows—"she does have her driver's license—I see that as a major plus in her favor."

Peter flicked the top of Than's forehead with his thumb and forefinger. "I'm beginning to think that you're the one who fell into the beehive, Campusky." He looked at his watch. "Damn it, my dad's gonna be pissed off. I'm supposed to be home for supper by now."

2

It took almost a half-hour for Peter to make it home, limping most of the way, and he knew he was in for it.

"Peter!" Joe Chandler bellowed from the back bedroom. "Goddamn it, Peter!"

Peter had barely just gotten inside the house; the door shut behind him. His little sister Annie was staring, transfixed, at the television, although it wasn't even turned on. He saw the back of her head, the light brown curls going down her neck, the white dress she always wore to church on Sundays. He knew his mother would be sleeping—she was either in church or asleep or reading in order to avoid confrontations. If she were asleep, she would've taken some sleeping pills, and would be dead to the world.

He heard the kitchen clock ticking, and somebody's dog, out in the trash dump that was a quarter-mile behind the house, howling and barking, maybe chasing a jack rabbit.

His sister was moving her head slightly, back and forth, back and forth, the way she had when she was three and they'd called her autistic, even though he knew she wasn't. She was just doing what his mom did, too: *avoiding.*

She was crying, only she didn't have tears in her, just the dry heaves of weeping.

"Goddamn it!" his father roared, and then Peter knew he was coming, because he could hear the clomp of the heavy feet, like bull's hooves on the carpet, and the scraping of his hands down the narrow hallway. Joe Chandler was a big man, six-four, and nearly as broad. When he was mad he looked just like a mad bull with his nostrils flaring, and his eyes going all red and fiery, and his skin, too, turning color, almost blue as if he were so angry that he had to hold his breath so as not to let all the rage out at once. "Damn God damn!" he shouted, coming around the corner.

Peter just stood there.

The late afternoon light, through the curtains, was orange and white, spilling across his father's features. The Mad Bull was out of the pen. His hands were curled.

"You missed supper, your mother was worried, we don't know what kind of people live around here. And just where the hell have you been?" his father demanded. When his father spoke, Peter smelled the whiskey. Brown liquor always seemed to change his father from an ordinary jerk into the Mad Bull from Hell.

"Looking for a job."

"I mean last night, you pussy."

"I went to see Than."

"Where? Where'd you go?"

"No place. Around."

"I was down at the Cantina, boy, and I heard from some god-damn barflies that you been down to the dogfights. Hanging out with rednecks, Christ, Peter, you're just like your mother's family, all trash. You don't hang around with these people. They're common, and I won't have a son of mine becoming some trash hound, you hear me? You hear me?" His father came closer, and seemed to calm down the more he spoke. He had small eyes, no longer fiery, now dark and beady. He hadn't shaved, and the stubble looked like mold along his chin.

Peter hung his head. He was furious, but he knew better than to show it. He'd spent most of his life learning how to hide his true feelings from the one person who knew how to stomp on them the hardest. "Yes, sir."

"I am not gonna have a son of mine become some common white trash fuckup, Christ Almighty, some candy-ass hick. You're gonna end up some goddamned feebleminded—you don't mix with these people, boy, you're just gonna mess things up for me again, aren't you, just like you did in San Diego, you goddamn . . ." And his father came at him, and knocked him back against the door. "You're gonna tell the whole goddamn world a pack of lies because you want everyone to feel sorry for you, don't you? Don't you? Open your mouth, goddamn it, and say something!"

Peter crumpled down and stayed still. He knew how to play this. His father would take a few more hits at him, and then stop.

"C'mon, pussy, c'mon, fight back, you damn weak—" But his father only gave him one swat on his head, and then stopped. "Jesus, you're not even worth fighting, are you? I wish I'd never had a son."

What happened next, Peter thought only happened in his head.

He didn't realize that he was actually saying the words.

"Up yours, asshole," he muttered.

"What? What the hell did you just say to me?"

Peter knew it was too late.

So, he repeated it. "I said, 'Up yours, asshole.' " It was suicide, he knew, but he was getting sick of sitting back and taking it all the time. His dad was just like Charlie Urquart, only grown up, and he was sick and tired of putting up with it, of his mother for putting up with it, of just about everything. He thought: *you come near me again, and I kill you, Dad.*

Joe Chandler looked at his son, as if he could not believe the words. For Peter, those words, *up yours, asshole*, seemed to hang in the air like a fine mist. He smelled his father's breath. His father's nostrils weren't flaring. His father's hands unclenched.

His father wasn't going to hit him after all.

Joe wore a grin on half of his face like the other half was dead. "Well, you're not totally spineless, are you? Come on, get up, son." His father reached a hand out to him.

Peter hesitated. He looked at his father's hand. It was smooth, uncalloused. His father would never condescend to do any common labor. It was Peter and his mother who had always had to do the house and lawn and garage work. Joe Chandler had been raised in a good family, not like his mother's, but a good upper-middle-class home and he had been sent to the best schools, and should've been a doctor or a lawyer. His hands, Peter's grandmother used to say, were the hands of a surgeon, or a writer. Nothing as common as the working class jobs of towns like Palmetto. The only things that even approached common labor that his father knew about were hunting and fishing, and Peter was convinced it was because his father liked to shoot and kill things.

Remember Jaspar? Tail wagging, happy to see just about anyone, and within six months with his father, the dog was turned into a snapping, sniveling basketcase, until finally the dog got kicked one two many times by Dad, and then went berserk and ran. Peter knew about running. He had run away from home five times since he was ten, but each time he came back because he didn't know how to survive, and he was tied, somehow, to his hatred for his father.

His father's smooth, white hand.

Peter took it, and his father grabbed Peter and yanked him hard to a standing position. "You idiot," Joe Chandler said. "Did you really think you were gonna get away with calling me that? What do you think your old man is, boy, a horse's ass? You kids, you goddamn kids, think you know everything, don't you?"

And his father threw him across the room.

Chapter Thirteen
Come Sundown

1

Here's what happened in town before sundown:

Trudy Virtue bawled out Alison Hunt for not wiping the tables thoroughly enough. She took Alison table by table and showed her the proper way to do it. Then Trudy told Alison that if she didn't shape up, she would be looking for work: "Because I can't take none of that teenage laziness in my diner, missy; I have a reputation to protect." Afterward, Trudy went home to her trailer at the Ed and Inez Trailer Park, and put her feet in a bucket of warm water with Palmolive and Epsom salts, and watched *60 Minutes*.

Alison waited outside the Magnificent Diner for her brother Harv to come pick her up. She didn't like the wait, because Charlie sometimes came by—he worked at the All-Nite Rx and Sundries, which his dad owned. She was hoping that she wouldn't ever have to see him again, although she knew that in a town the size of Palmetto, it was inevitable. *Can't fight fate or it fights back.*

2

Than got home in time for supper and played his older sister's cassette stereo—she only had an old Jackson Browne tape called *Late For The Sky*, and Led Zeppelin's *Stairway to Heaven*. She owned about twenty others, but they were in her car, and she was in Yucca Valley seeing her boyfriend. So he played them both, and ate beanie-weenies with brown bread. He listened to the noise outside his sister's bedroom—there was always noise at the Campusky Compound, and he was fairly used to it, although he never tired of family sounds. He was pretty happy at the moment, too, because he had Peter Chandler as a best friend, he had a pretty nice family, and even if the Bone had scared him a little, and that house, that awful house, had scared him a lot, life was okay sometimes.

But that house.

Hate that place.

He knew he shouldn't have lied when he had told the story of the house to Peter, but he just didn't want Peter to go in there.

He knew he should've told Peter the truth.

After all, Peter was his best friend.

After all, Peter had told *him* his deepest darkest secret. The one about how his dad hit him and his mom and sister all the time. He felt pretty bad for Peter, if it was true. Than sometimes made up stories about things, so he was never sure if other kids didn't do the same thing. But he was *pretty* sure that Peter was on the level.

It was me, Peter, me.

I was the one who fell into the bees and got stung.

But somebody else was with me.

Somebody who kinda changed afterward.

We both know and hate him.

Charlie the Irk Urquart.

Only he didn't just get stung, no, sir. He went down into the house, through the basement door.

He saw something down there.

Charlie used to be a nice kid, most of the time. Not that much different than you, Peter.

But he changed after that.

He changed like nobody's business.

3

Bonyface got back into his tunnel with his cat Isaac and finished off a bottle of T-Bird, and then he got his flashlight out and flicked it on. He opened a book and began reading in the dark of his cylinder. It was a book on demonology, and he read and read and read.

4

The Daughters of the Western Star had just put up the *Pioneer and Grubstake Days* banner, strung from the one-room school-

house that was now the Palmetto Chamber of Commerce building, all the way across Highway 4—two lanes as it went through
town—to the Golgotha Free Ordained Church. Actually, the
Daughters themselves, composed, in Palmetto, of seven elderly
ladies who were also quite good shots with a rifle, did not put the
banner up. It was Than's older brother Greg and a nineteen-year-
old named Phil Philbrick. When they were done they went and
looked at the banner, realized it was upside down and swore to
high heaven because now Greg had to climb back up to the
steeple to swing it around. Hy Griffin, the preacher who ran the
church, looked out his small office window at the boys and
wished to God the young men in town weren't so damned attractive. The services that day had been long and painful, and there'd
been much speaking in tongues and calling down the Holy Ghost,
so he was ready for a big night out, maybe, just maybe he'd take
a drive down the hill to Palm Springs, or maybe he'd brave the
three hours to Los Angeles where nobody could possibly recognize him.

5

Kevin Sloan was out with his pit bull, Lammie, trying to get her to
run, but something was wrong with her, and when he checked,
kind of mad that the bitch wasn't doing what he wanted, he felt her
stomach and saw that her nipples were all puffed up, and he realized that she was going to have puppies and he hadn't even known
it. *That's why she run off,* he thought.

"Who the hell knocked you up, girl? Better not've been some
poodle. Can't make no money selling pit poodles, 'cept maybe to
some biddy ass." But, for once, he actually showed the animal
some tenderness, took her back to his truck, and set her up in the
bed, covering her with blankets. He had a gun in the truck, and he
went and got it. He sat with his dog, and pointed the gun at rocks
and shot at birds and jackrabbits, but hit nothing.

He couldn't stand Wendy anymore, and had spent most of the
day in the middle of nowhere, by the caves of No Man's Land, the
old mines, because he just wanted to be as far away from her as he
could get.

It was the feeling she gave him.

In the dark.

He had fallen for her because there was so much mystery to her, she was such a babe.

But in the dark.

Something else.

Something had changed about her. Just in the past week or so. Something had come over her, but he didn't know what.

And when they'd played their games with the barbed wire and the handcuffs, and he had been at her mercy, he felt her skin, and it wasn't what he thought it should feel like.

It was rough.

It was like a snake.

He was scared, but thought he might be going crazy like everyone else in his family had.

'Cause he knew he was bound to go crazy someday. It was just like his ma had always said, "You're just like your Pa, that lying, son of a bitch psycho from Hell."

As he watched the sun move westward, and the shadows lengthen, he didn't know whether to keep shooting at the tweetbirds or just put the gun to his own head and do what he'd been trying to do for the past three years.

6

What do dogs dream of? When their legs kick the dust, and they growl as they chase something down in the twisting avenues of their brains, what do they run after? The dark pit bull, Lammie, lay sleeping beneath Sloan's trailer. The cries and the slapping sounds that had been coming from inside the trailer had not kept the dog up. The dog basically viewed her master's life with a curious sniff, but did not appear surprised by any of it.

But in the dog's belly, something moved, something hit her in the gut, and this woke her. Her puppies. It was almost time. To pretend to know what an animal such as this dog was thinking would be foolish, but it would not be hard to guess her motivation as she began digging in the soft, dry earth beneath the trailer, not if you knew what had happened with her last litter, how they'd all been pulled away from her almost as they were born and sold to evil-looking men who had no love in their eyes.

Lammie was going to dig herself a safe place in which to have her litter, a place that even her master would not easily be able to get to.

By sunrise, perhaps, she would rest again.

7

Here's what their fathers and mothers did:

Alison's mother was reading a romance novel, and her father was looking at the dirty magazines he kept out in the gas station and garage that he ran—while her mother's book was called *Love's Tender Triumph*, her father's magazine was called simply *Jugs*. Alison's mother was reading in bed—at the Motel 20 with Chip Grubb, also known as the Grubman. Chip snored, while Alison's mother, reading her romance, wondered how to disentangle herself from the life she had been leading.

Peter Chandler's mother pretended to be asleep, because she was sick of all the fighting. If the truth were to be known, she valued peace and harmony above all things, which is why she kept a small, airport-miniature bottle of Jack Daniels beneath her bed, along with a vial of pills that helped her pretend to sleep. If she took all these, she lost the will to fight back against her husband. Her husband Joe had gone out again, for a drive, because he was so angry at his wussy-ass son.

Than Campusky's mother was cooking, which, given the number of children she had, lasted all day and all night. His father was on the road with his truck, but would be coming back through town at about four in the morning.

Charlie Urquart's father, Gib, watched Laurette Montgomery, the Healer Lady, on TV who believed that if the Spirit is Strong, Anything Can Happen, All is Possible. Charlie's mom, Gladys, was out playing cards with three other ladies. "Playing cards" was another way of saying "getting plowed, getting faced, getting plastered," but nice ladies in Palmetto who wanted to climb out of the wasteland never called it that. Playing cards was good enough, and around about eleven, she would drive home somewhat shakily, perhaps taking a turn just a mite too fast, and if she were lucky, she might avoid hitting small animals.

8

Wendy Swan's mother lay down in darkness.

9

Others, too, finished suppers and watched television or went for early evening walks, for the temperature dropped to a good seventy degrees as the sun itself dropped.

Few stores stayed open past six on a Sunday in the Palmetto-Nitro area, although the All-Nite Rx and Sundries was open 'til nine, with none other than Charlie Urquart behind the counter.

10

"Well, hey, sweetheart," Charlie Urquart said, a big, old shit-eating grin plastered on his face like he just got laid. He put down the *Playboy* magazine he was ogling and nodded to Wendy Swan. "You look about as out of place in a drugstore as I do."

She didn't smile. Her sunglasses seemed impenetrable. "You look like you fit right in like a pack of Trojans," she said.

"Lambskins or ribbed?" It was almost closing time. Charlie hated this damned summer job business, but his dad practically handed him this one, seeing as how the Old Man owned the All-Nite Rx and Sundries, and even though it was billed as All-Nite it hadn't been since 1973, a month after it had opened. Only a bunch of old biddies coming in for Sominex and Epsom salts since he opened at ten that morning—Mike Frost, the pharmacist was off on Sundays—and damn, he hated wasting his summer behind the counter.

"What are you looking at, boy?" she asked.

"Something that looks good enough to eat."

"I'm afraid I've got to get back to my boyfriend," she said, but didn't move. "We're going out tonight."

"Way I figure it, it's a good four hours or more 'til night."

She finally smiled. "Is that what you want?"

"What—I—want?"

"Is that what you want? My body?"

He gulped, finishing the last of the Ice Cold Cherry Gushee, setting down the *Playboy* and the paper cup. "Yeah, sure," his voice was a whisper.

"If I give you what you want," she said, "will you do me a favor?"

"Anything," he gasped, and felt more like a little boy than he ever had in his entire life. *Damn Alison for dumping me, anyway.* Charlie Urquart was going to get some tonight.

"Where can we go?"

"My place."

"I need somewhere dark. I want to do things to you in the dark."

"I know where," Charlie said, and all of it was forgotten later—how he closed up shop, how they got in his car, how they moved from the living room to the garage because she said she wanted to feel him there, dirty, greasy, cold.

In the dark.

11

"Don't touch me," Wendy said. "Not like that."

White light shone through the cracks in the garage door—the headlights to his mother's car. But Charlie knew his mother wouldn't open the garage door, not if she'd been out playing cards. She usually left the Cadillac in the driveway; sometimes she forgot to turn off the headlights.

He hated his mother. He heard the door of her car creak open, and then the uncertain steps of her heels on the walk. She had forgotten to shut the door. Then, the clatter as she tried to wrestle her keys from her purse; then the sound of the front door opening.

The shards of light that penetrated the cracks in the garage door and outlined the objects around them in white shadow: a bicycle hanging from above, a small car—his dad's Mustang—draped with a cloth, cans of paint jutting out from the edges of shelves, two plastic trash barrels, like sentries guarding the door into the house.

His own shadow, melding with hers. His breath was all Pabst Blue Ribbon and Certs, with a touch of Listerine, because he'd gargled just before he'd shut the All-Nite Rx and Sundries down. He wanted to kiss her, but she hadn't allowed him that privilege.

Douglas Clegg

He brought his fingers around her shoulders, but she pushed him away, holding him back. His desire weakened him—he wanted to hold her, to have her, to screw her.

"You're night and day, you know that?" His voice was scratchy, almost disappointed. "I thought we were gonna have some fun. Hell, we coulda done it at the drugstore. But you wanted to do it in my old man's garage."

"I want to do it in your old man's bed."

"Kinky," he said, not thinking she was serious. "But he's in it."

"You boys are easy," she said. "You promised me you'd do me a favor."

"I meant it. But you promised something, too, and you better deliver."

"Little boys like you," she said, her hands sliding down his waist until he shivered because he was so damn horny, "so easy."

"Is *this* a little boy's?" He grabbed her wrist and cupped it over his crotch, deftly unzipping his pants with his free hand.

"I said, don't touch me," she spat the words at him, wriggling free of his grasp. She wiped her hand against her stomach. "I'm the one doing the touching," she warned him. "If you touch me again, when I don't want it, that's it, I slice it off."

Given the tone of her voice, Charlie Urquart believed her like he had never believed anyone ever before.

She calmed down. "Tell me what you want. Not what you're used to getting, but what you really want."

He couldn't bring himself to say it, not because he was too embarrassed, because very little ever embarrassed Charlie the Irk Urquart, but because it was something he'd been dreaming of since he'd been a little boy, something that would feel like a humid velvet curtain drawn across his nerve-endings, something beyond what other people expected.

"Tell me," she said.

He almost had tears in his eyes when he asked for it—he, Charlie Urquart Scourge of Seven Palms High, Quarterback in Training, Stud, The Thruster—tears and fear and even a little terror.

"I . . . I . . ." he stuttered, "want it."

"What is it?"

"The big one. The Big O. The Big O. Please."

Then, like night and day, she changed, her mood, her hands, her

110

caresses, because he had told her what he wanted from her. She came to him.

She gave him what he craved.

12

But afterward, he felt *different*.

Chapter Fourteen
Charlie Urquart and the Big O

1

The truth about Charlie Urquart was he would've given his right ball for the Big O. It was something all the guys talked about in school. The mind-blowing orgasm at the end of the universe. That's how Campusky had put it. "The place where your pecker meets nirvana head-on, and boldly goes where no man has gone before." As if Campusky knew.

Charlie knew there was something to what Campusky said. Somewhere out there the Big O was waiting for them all, all boys as they went into manhood. Had his father ever experienced the Big O? Or could you only get to that state of orgasmic grace with a woman so wild, so uninhibited, like the women in *Penthouse*? Charlie's ex-girlfriend, Alison Hunt, she only put out under intense pressure, and he knew what she had really wanted to do: force him into marriage, when that was the last thing that Charlie was ever going to do. There were too many nice girls in Palmetto, anyway. He had watched Wendy for the weeks following the end of the school year. Never seen her before that, but Jesus H, when she sidled up to him, what else could he do but pop a boner? A guy couldn't spend the rest of his life living on a diet of porno mags just because one bitch dumped him, could he? Wendy Swan was the kind of girl who took care of the needs of guys like Charlie, he was sure of it.

Sex was weird with her, but even more of a turnon than normal because of it: she wanted total darkness as if she were ashamed of her body. She had told him to imagine that she was any girl he wanted her to be. She made him lean back and then climbed on top of him, rocking back and forth, breathing in a way that was demanding, wanting, and he lost himself in the sensations. At first, it was her, Wendy, riding him. Then he let his mind go, and he was making it with Alison doggy style while she protested, and then he was choking Mrs. Gaffney, the school nurse who was ugly as a cow with two heads. He imagined fiddling with her innards until she starting singing—then, it was Alison again, he was pumping Alison (*what she did to me, the look of superiority in her eyes when her family was nothing but trash, what would that bitch look like moaning on top of him, under him, begging for it, deeper, deeper . . .*).

For just a second, a blink, a shiver, it was *in the cellar of the house, he was eight years old, he was looking at a face, something so deformed that it had no mouth at all just skin and scar tissue beneath the nose, but its eyes staring at him, and the sound, the whatifwhatifwhatifwhatif, like giant wings beating, and he looked up, because whatever was there was coming down for him, and he called out, "CAMPUSKY!" but no one was there to save him, or help him, and when the thing above him grabbed him, he looked at the mouthless face and was sure he heard a scream come from it, although it must've been in his head.*

Then, it was Wendy in the dark, shuddering on top of him.

He was sure if there were a Big O out there, this was the woman to take him to that peak, to push him over that edge.

Afterward, Charlie Urquart felt like he'd been up two weeks in a row, drinking coffee and popping speed down the back of his throat. He felt twitching in his face, his eyebrows, his cheeks, his nose, muscle spasms running the length of his neck, tugging at his Adam's apple, and down, rippling through his chest, across his shoulders. He felt like he'd run a marathon: he was sore all over, and his muscles were cramping up on him. But he also felt more alive than he ever thought he would feel, he felt like he could do anything he wanted to, he was the Desolation Angel he had dreamed of becoming, he was a fucking destroyer.

So this was it, the Big O, holy shit! He was stronger now, that's how he'd changed, his battery was recharged. He was a man, he could take on the universe. How had she done it? How had she sent him *there?*

He combed his fingers back through his dark greasy hair; bit his own lower lip until he drew blood; he could feel his skin glowing with the difference. The change.

"I feel like I'm a god or something," he said.

He was answered by the dark night, by the sound of a howling dog, by the woman lying naked next to him, her right leg draped over his thigh. Wendy Swan said, "Now you're mine."

They lay there entwined for what seemed like hours while Charlie felt blood pumping through him like it was gasoline and he was revving his engine up. It burnt and it tasted sour in the back of his throat, but he felt as if he'd been injected with heroin or something, and even while he wanted to leap up and race down the streets into town, raising hell, his flesh seemed paralyzed, unable to move: the signals in his brain weren't connecting to his nerves. Even though he felt like hot shit he couldn't bend one lousy finger.

Now when he asked her, there was a tremor in his voice: "What did you do to me?"

"You got what you came for. And so did I."

It was as if he'd been under anesthesia, because he could recall the moments of building, like a rocket launch, the ten-nine-eight-seven-six of countdown, the sweaty, sucking slaps her thighs made as she rode him. But the moment of orgasm was forgotten, a blank, as if he'd gone from hard to soft with no fireworks in between.

Where had his mind flown in that millisecond?

Where had she taken him?

2

As they lay there, together, he felt something different about her.

Her skin.

It was slick, almost oily.

She whispered in his ear, "Now you have to do what I ask."

"Okay."

She pressed a hammer into his hand.

Just then, he heard footsteps coming to the door that led into the kitchen.

The door opened.

His father stood there, staring into the shadows of the garage.

Flicked the light up.

When the light flooded the garage, Charlie saw that he was lying there, naked.

Hammer in his hand.

"What in the name of God are you doing, Charlie?" His father demanded.

Charlie sat up, and hefted the hammer. It was a good-sized hammer, one he had used to drive in stakes around the property before they'd put the fencing up. Something in his head hurt, real bad. Like there was an animal in there, scratching at his skull. It was a big headache coming on, and his father was yelling at him while the headache grew and grew, a big balloon of a headache, with some wild animal in there trying to pop it.

"Charlie," his father said. "That's one. Now you get inside and explain to me what's going on here."

But in his head, a galloping fever, a scratching claw, a gnawing like he had a tumor growing and this animal this this—

deadrats

deadrats behind the refrigerator

was trying to claw its way through him.

"GET OUT OF MY HEAD!" Charlie shrieked. He was about to slam the hammer into his ear just to stop the pain, but his father rushed down the steps and held his hand down, trying to peel his fingers off the handle.

"Give me the hammer, Charlie," his father said. "Charlie, obey me, son, now that's *two*."

For a moment, the noise in his head stopped.

Charlie sighed.

His father's face was red. When his father got angry, his father got very angry and did the one, two, three routine. *"That's one,"* his father would say, and if Charlie didn't stop what he was doing it became, "that's two," and if he STILL didn't stop, it turned into, "that's three," and the punishment became unbearable.

Now, if Gib Urquart had stopped there, Charlie figured, perhaps things would've turned out different.

Perhaps Charlie would've just lied his way out of this situation, gone to bed, heard the end of it. His father would've gone to bed, his mother would've woken up the next morning to make scrambled eggs, bacon, and toast with chicory coffee, and life would've just greased on the way it always had in the past. If Gib Urquart had just let it go, maybe Charlie would've, too.

But he didn't.

"That's three, son, now give me the hammer, put your pants on and get inside the house this minute."

Deadrats said, "Dirty, filthy, naughty man, you want the hammer? You want the HAMMER?"

Gib Urquart looked at his son strangely, as if he were seeing him for the first time. Funny what you notice about people you've known all your life, because when Charlie looked up at his father he saw a paunchy middle-aged Emperor Wannabe with Grecian-Formula'ed rust-gray hair, a round, pink multiveined nose, a lipless mouth, and yellow teeth that needed some polishing to make them shine. But he wasn't scared of his old man anymore, nosiree.

Not with Deadrats out of the braincave.

"Yes, Charles, I'd like the hammer."

"Say please."

"Give me the hammer."

Charlie obliged.

It was just like hammering the stakes into the ground, one by one. The first blow knocked his father out, and then the next made a cracking sound just behind his ear.

Charlie went for the nails that his father kept in a Mason jar near one of the paint cans. There were thirty nails or so in it, and he took one out. He returned to his father who was still breathing.

The nail was long and slender, and Charlie positioned it just above his father's left ear.

And he hammered.

And he hammered.

And he hammered.

3

When a boy works that hard, hammering away, there's bound to be some noise, and even when someone, say, his mother, has been drinking and then falls asleep on the couch in the living room, even

115

then, that person will hear the noise and call out to see what the ruckus is about.

And when that person, say the boy's mother, goes out to investigate, smiling drunkenly, why, that boy may see that he's got to stop her from screaming because it hurts his head too much, and the Thing in his head doesn't like it.

Oh, but he doesn't need a hammer anymore.

Oh, no.

Now he feels the claws in his fingers.

He feels the snarls in his throat.

He smells the meat.

The walls, coated with blood, look like the entrance to some red forest full of red birds, their red red feathers flying.

"Yes!" he shouts at the walls, and he thinks he will yell about how he feels so fucking good—at the top of his lungs—but all that comes up from his throat is a shriek that might be the howling of a wolf.

Chapter Fifteen
Summer Days and Nights

1

"Why the face?" Than Campusky's mother asked him. Gretel Campusky was overweight, but not uncomfortable-looking, with her hair up in pink foam curlers for the night, and her green sateen robe wrapped tight around her breasts and thighs. He looked down at her—he was now, at five-foot-three, taller than his mother. She seemed to be the only person shorter in all of Palmetto. He mumbled something about a glass of water.

"I figured you were up for water, Thaniel, but why the face?"

"I'm tired. Can't seem to sleep."

"Poor baby," his mother said in mock sympathy, and padded on down the hallway. It was nearly three A.M., and the baby would be crying for milk soon. He watched his mother turn left, back toward her bedroom. The baby started crying, and the coyotes began yipping out on the mesa.

He went and poured some water, went and peed, and passed his mother again in the hallway. She had the baby up to her breast, but had covered it well with the robe. "So why don't you tell me why you can't sleep?"

"Oh," he sighed, "I don't know. I don't feel so great about things."

"You did fine in school last year. You do your chores. You have your friends. That's life."

"I know Mom."

"Is it something about a girl?"

"What?"

"I have raised three teenaged boys before you, Thaniel, and I know what boys your age think about. Girls, girls, and more girls."

"It's not about girls. It's about me. I'm fat and I'm ugly. I hate myself."

"So when did this delightful mood come over you?"

"I don't know. I went around with Peter all day. And there's this girl who's sort of pretty, and she only looked at him. Girls never look at me. I don't blame them, either. Peter's gonna have a girlfriend soon, and I'll be friendless forever. I'll go live in some dark cave and eat bats and grow old alone and die and nobody will care."

"Let me play the world's smallest violin and weep while you tell me your sad and pathetic fate." His mother shook her head. "Well, you have an overactive imagination, Thaniel, and a lazy-butt brain. You're not fat, you're just growing. And you can't be ugly. All my children are beautiful and smart, a genius each and every one."

"Yeah, Mom. Sure."

"And another thing, if you lose a friend because he got a girlfriend, you didn't have a friend to begin with. You read me?"

"Goodnight, Ma."

"Nighty," she said, holding the baby close.

He went back to the room he shared with two of his brothers, and climbed into the bottom bunk. His small bedside lamp was still switched on. His brother Greg, who had the top bunk, was snoring away; Les, in the bed across the room, was silent. Than opened up one of his *Mad* magazines, and munched on some graham crackers, wondering if he was going to get any sleep at all.

2

Than had left the light on, so, half-asleep, he reached up and switched it off.

He glanced at the window because he'd caught some movement out of the corner of his eye. *Could be an earthquake, way the windowpane's rattling.* Whenever there was any shaking at all, earthquake or no, he always wondered if this were the Big One about to send California out to Hawaii. Would the upper bunk with Fat-Ass Greg sleeping in it protect him from being buried alive beneath the rubble, or would it smother him right away like the way the bed in the horror movie *Thirteen Ghosts* came down on Martin Milner in the end? Than had watched so many horror movies in his life, including *Earthquake*, that he looked upon very ordinary objects as potential instruments of death. His biggest fear in the event of the Big One was never instant death from the walls falling on him. It was living burial that bothered him. Having to claw at the unyielding walls of some makeshift tomb. Or starving to death and hearing people outside trying to rescue him, but knowing the situation was hopeless. *If this is the Big One,* he thought while the window rattled, *will I be buried with Greg and Les, and will we end up drawing straws to see who eats who? Will Greg's porky arm taste good, or will it taste as bad as he looks? Will I have to eat my toes one by one, like Vienna sausages?*

He thought this fear out extensively. He mapped it in his imagination, and as irrational and unlikely as it seemed, Than held the theory that human beings could only fear what was inevitable— that if the thought arrived in his brain it was only because it was bound to happen sooner or later.

So, as he awoke, he sat upright. Then he felt paralyzed with the kind of fear one can only feel in the dark, at four A.M., before eyes can adjust to the darkness.

He watched the rattling windowpane.

A face burst across it just as if someone had shoved it against the glass.

But the window didn't shatter.

Than felt his heart freeze.

The glass began to mold itself around the shape of the face, stretching toward Than's bed.

Only a dream. Than was sure now.

Than couldn't find his tongue anywhere in his mouth; his blood became a frozen river; his heart no longer pumped.

The man's white hair flew long and wild behind his high forehead. His skin was darkened with dirt and scum. He looked as if he'd just crawled out of the earth. Small silver fishhooks pinned his eyelids back against his brow. Where his nose should've been was a gaping hole, a running sore beside it. The man grinned, for it could not be helped—his lips were peeled back with more tiny hooks. His entire face was studded with hooks connected to thin nylon lines that tugged at him, trying to hold him back in the darkness on the other side of the window. The man's clenched teeth flew open, his lower jaw dislocating, dropping into the back of his throat, lodging farther down near his Adam's apple. The man was trying to scream, the same way that Than was trying to scream: Than's mouth opened wide, but nothing came out.

He had no breath.

Oh my God help me scream you idiot, I can smell his breath, he smells . . . dead.

The man behind the molten glass struggled to break through it, but like strands of a spiderweb, the more he pushed and pressed to break free, the more the glass clung to him. Then, the nylon threads that held him became taut—something was pulling him. The hooks in his face tugged at the doughy skin, his scalp stretched backward. Still, the man pushed outward with his hand, pleading for Than to grasp it and pull him through. His fingernails were long and curled, and carved through the liquid glass.

The glass shattered around his hand, shards of glass slicing into his wrist, digging down.

Sawing.

The hand was cut clean from the wrist.

The wriggling hand flew toward Than just as whatever mad pup-peteer controlling this phantom pulled hard on the fishing lines. The face, the body, the arms were gone, drawn back into the deep waters of night.

As if it had only been a few seconds, Than reached for the bed-side lamp and turned it on.

The window was still. Unbroken.

I was *dreaming.*

No glass, no hand, no face out in the night. His brother Greg was snoring in the upper bunk, smelly feet hanging over the end; Les was in his bed, too, swaddled in sheets, lying on his stomach.

Even though Than Campusky knew it was only a dream, he woke both of his brothers up a good two hours before they had to get out of bed, just so he wouldn't be the only one watching the window at four-thirty in the morning.

He remembered Bonyface's words only after he'd calmed down.

"It's powerful, boyz, you get near it, it's like fire, gives off heat, burns into your brains,.into your dreams."

Than Campusky was a young man who believed in such things.

3

Alison Hunt woke up at six, just before her alarm was about to go off. She set the alarm, even in summer, because she wanted to try and remember her dreams. She had even bought a notebook just for the purpose of remembering dreams. She had read an entire book, *Freud's Dream Analysis,* both because she wanted to maybe be a psychologist one day (or a veterinarian), and because she would try just about anything to inducing dreaming. She awoke staring at the ceiling, trying to put together the puzzle of whatever she'd just been dreaming.

She wrote in her diary: *Parents are shadows. My mother is heav-ily involved in the Chili Cookoff celebration for Grabstake Days, and she keeps telling me that I should starve myself so that a nice boy will want me after my shame with Charlie U. Lighter notes. Peter C. said he'd call. Didn't. Don't know why high school boys think it's their right to just do what they want and expect us to go along with it. I think, if he does end up calling, I'll punish him by not being available for a few days. I hate Charlie, too, so maybe I should just apply that hatred to all men. I hate Charlie. Hate him. What he made me do. What I made myself do.*

4

Alison had kept a diary since she was eleven, although until this past year, her life had been recorded with such scrawls as: *hate Rita Saunders. Had my first period, yuck.* Then, at thirteen, she'd read the *Diary of Anne Frank*, and had begun writing as if she were trapped in a silent house with the Nazis tapping on the walls. Or *Harriet the Spy* crossed with *Nancy Drew*, discovering the secrets of the human heart by spying on her friends. Her diary had grown to several volumes, and she found that it became her obsession at times. The previous spring, she'd written twenty times:

I'M IN LOVE WITH CHARLIE URQUART.

Then, in September, all she wrote was: *oh shit.*

She chronicled their breakup in excruciating detail, but there was the one major event that she could not bring herself to record in her diary, but she knew she didn't have to, because it would be remembered until the day she died.

The abortion.

Charlie's and hers.

How did I ever let that happen? She had asked herself the same question a thousand times. She had no real answer, nothing that worked for her. The only thing she knew was she had to get away from home, and Charlie had done that trick for her while they were dating—she'd never been home.

At least Charlie said he loved me, even if he doesn't know what it really means to love someone.

In her diary, she wrote:

Peter Chandler is asking me out to the movies. He says he's going to, but I know boys. We'll have to see about this. He seems okay. I don't know. Who needs a boyfriend anyway? He's nicer than Charlie, but once he gets to know me, he'll probably dump me. Once Charlie has told all the stories about me he wants to, making me out to be a slut, then nobody's going to want me.

Then I'll never get out of this house.

5

Time passed—that's the best one can say about summer on the high desert. It passes slow, it passes hot, and sometime accidents happen. Teenagers went to their summer jobs at the stands and stores, while their parents planned trips or planned new air conditioners; a few people paid the exorbitant price for Betamaxes and VHS players so they could watch movies at home, only they had to drive all the way to Palm Springs for the nearest video store; some still went to the Drive-In in Yucca Valley; others managed to forget that they lived on the desert and stayed inside most days and just watched network television, as cable TV was only for the big cities and had not yet snaked into Palmetto. A kid named Rory Wallace fell down one of the old mines out in No Man's Land, but only broke his arm; when the fire marshal from over in Yucca brought him out of the hole, he laughed and told Rory's mom that the kid was unbreakable; Alison Hunt, in her souped-up T-Bird almost got in a wreck with Ernie Alvarado, Pepe's cousin, out on the highway, but she managed to bring her car off-road and avoid a collision; the Nevilles, a fairly new family to Palmetto who had moved to a small three-bedroom with a big three-baby family just after Peter's family had moved to the area, began alienating their neighbors left and right because they wanted to put up a nine-foot-tall fence all around their property; Than began staying away from people, for his nightmares seemed to real, their property; Than began staying away from people, for his nightmares seemed too real, and Peter no longer hung out with him mid-week; Ginny and Boz Wimberger began a lawsuit with the County Water Authority over problems of pipes and lack of good drinking water on their property, but they knew they wouldn't win; Pepe Alvarado decided there'd be no more pit bull fights for a good three weeks until the cops laid off him; Than sought out Bonyface to ask him questions about his dreams; people went to work just like anywhere else, some in town, and some far away, and some stayed home and collected disability and unemployment; neighbors began asking Charlie Urquart about his father's trip, for Charlie had already begun a story that his dad and mom had flown off one night on a second honeymoon and would not be back until after the Fourth; the Daughters of the Western Star were all at home most nights working on their chili recipes because this year's Grubstake Days—a desert variation on Founder's Day—would no doubt be the toughest competition of all; the Grubman shot a coyote up in the hills because he claimed some of them had been eating one too many cats lately; part of Highway 4 grew a big crack or two just as it always did over the course of the years, and yes, people like Vince Davis and Chase McQuail complained to no end about how the county needed to spend a little tax money on road repairs even if Palmetto was not as valued as Yucca Valley, and probably if Gib Urquart had not taken off on his impromptu vacation, he'd have gotten some roadworkers out there even if the temperature had risen above 100 degrees; and then that pit bull, Lammie, felt the stirrings within her, and her master, Sloan, wanted to ask somebody if it was usual for a bitch to give birth just a week or two after being pregnant, but he was drowning in the cheapest whiskey he could find and pissed off because Wendy still hadn't told him where she went at night, and something about her had changed, and he didn't really have the balls to find out exactly what went on with her or with the damn dog; and then, something happened that became legendary for a good day or two in the boredom of summer heat, and it woke everyone up for a moment from their dreams of reality.

A truck crashed at the Rattlesnake Wash.

But there was more to it than that.

6

His name was Orson Ledbetter and he drove trucks for the Sunny Mountain Springs Company. He was not meant for Palmetto or Nitro, but in those days, you could cut across the mountains a little faster by going through Highway 4, particularly if you'd had a few beers at the Coyote Cantina in the late afternoon and maybe if you had a girl up there that your wife didn't know about, a girl of thirty-three who lived at the trailers and still believed that married men left their wives when it felt like true love—but then, in her thirties, she still believed that she was a girl as new to love as any sixteen-year-old. Orson had two hours to get back down the hills and out to San Bernardino, and after a quickie and those brewskies, he wasn't quite sure if he'd arrive in time to get water that amounted to the same thing as what came out of the tap to all those impatient and thirsty people in the valley. So he might've just hit his accelerator a little too hard, or he might've just lost control of the wheel when he hit one of the newer bulging cracks on the highway.

That's what they said later, mainly because Orson didn't survive.

What Orson knew in that millisecond before he also knew that he might not survive the crash was that something nightmarish had touched him.

What he didn't know was how it had gotten onto the hood of his truck.

It didn't quite look like a dog, and it didn't quite look like a man, and it didn't quite look like anything that he'd ever seen before, but when the second one burst through his open window, and he saw what he knew to be a demon from Hell, but with a face very much like a face that had only recently been in the news—

But he couldn't quite remember the news story or why he knew that face—

He screamed, and then he swerved, and then before he knew it, the world was on fire all around him.

Orson Ledbetter didn't die just yet, but lay upside down while a fire spread from his truck and covered all he saw, including the two animals that might've just been large puppies, and their human faces screamed, echoing his own, as they burned, too.

The fire flashed, and Orson was no more.

7

It was a big to-do out at the Wash, what with a truck on fire.

Everyone turned out to see it, and the firetrucks came over from Yucca Valley to make sure it was contained.

This event brought the Beekeeper out of the Garden of Eden in full white uniform, netting over her face as she stood at her gate watching. Peter was there with Alison, and Wendy Swan, too, standing by herself, away from the crowd, with the late afternoon sun casting copper across her features. Charlie sat on the hood of his father's Mustang, and his friends kept their distance from him.

But the accident was forgotten in days.

The heat picked up, and July was merciless as it arrived.

Peter began to forget about friends, and even stopped calling Alison. Something had happened, that's what Than thought, but Peter wasn't talking.

And no one asked Bonyface his opinion about any of this, although if they had, he would've told them the time of demons was upon them.

8

Kevin Sloan remained drunk for three solid days, and his neighbors at the Sun Dial Trailer Park were kept awake at all hours by his curses and his screeches. He slept in his jeans and Western shirt the whole time, too, and marched around his trailer slamming his fists into the wall. "Women and fucking dogs!" he'd shout, the room shaking as if from an earthquake. "Well, fuck you, fuck everyone of you! Unnatural, disgusting things! I don't know what you done, but you done it to her and you made me—made me hear all these things and see them things—you made me want to—Wendy get out of my head! Get out!"

He had seen the puppies as they had crawled from the hole in the ground, just as the sun had been moving to the West, just before the truck had crashed less than a mile away, he had seen them and had run to get his gun to kill them as soon as they had come out of Lammie, but they were gone when he returned.

And while the truck had burned, he had pointed his gun to the side of his beloved dog's skull and wept bitter tears as he killed her.

And doing it, he had lost what little mind he had left.

He didn't even remember fighting with Peter Chandler.

Chapter Sixteen
True Confessions

Written and then destroyed by Peter Chandler

I can recount every little thing I've done wrong in my life before I was sixteen, from the time I cheated my sister out of a dollar owed her from a bet when I was thirteen, or the moment when I knew I despised my father and would lie to him every chance I could, or even the time I cheated on my third-grade history test. But the summer I turned sixteen, everything was wrong and nothing would be right ever again.

I had begun dating Alison, just a movie here and there and some making out in the back of her car, but nothing too heavy even though I knew she was "the One" even then. Al, Ali, Alison, there are things I've never told you from that time, things I've wanted you to forget, things I wish I could burn out of my own memory. I suppose I should go back and forgive that teenager named Peter, but I don't feel much removed from him.

I knew what I was doing.

I knew it was wrong.

I let it happen.

I went out to see Sloan after the truckfire in the Wash, but all I found was a man standing beside a dead dog—the pit bull called Lammie. Her head had been torn apart by a bullet, and there he stood laughing over the dog's body. He began babbling incoherently—and perhaps if I'd listened, I would've begun to understand what was to come, but all I knew was the asshole had killed a dog and was laughing about it.

"Her babies, Peter," he gibbered, drool slipping from his lips. "I saw them. There was two! Two! They almost looked like dogs, but shit, they had these faces, Peter, and they had these bodies, bigger than any damn puppies I ever saw. Unnatural monsters! Seriously,

126

Pete, I ain't shittin' you! It's Wendy, Peter, she brought it here, I saw their faces, man, I saw their fuckin' faces, and she knew, my poor, poor Lammie got it in her somehow, but she knew, Wendy knew, she's not a woman, nope, I seen her in the dark, in the dark, Peter, when she climbs on me now, something's changed, something gotten into her, she's a fuckin alien or something!" Rage and laughter mixed in his voice with whiskey that permeated the space around him, and without knowing why I went right up to him and raised my fist. I barely remember the fight, but afterward, I was hurting in every place a boy can hurt, and he was still laughing and pointing to the dead dog. I went and threw up behind the trailer, and that's when Wendy slipped her arm around me, offering me water, wiping my lips with a towel and whispering, "He's gone mad, Peter. I need your help. Please."

And perhaps if I had just left her there, things would be different.

If I had just gotten her to the police or to some other place.

If I had not felt aroused by her need. If it had not made me feel more like a man, bruised as I was, taking her into the truck and getting her the keys from her, and driving her out onto the desert, out to No Man's Land, where the hills rose sharply, where we drank some beers and where she wept, telling me stories of his abuse, of how he'd threatened to shoot her like the dog. And then, in my arms, weeping, she looked up into my face, and I knew she would kiss me.

And I wanted her to kiss me.

And I thought of Alison while she kissed me and then, late, night came on, and we had done more than kiss. She whispered, "I need you, Peter, I need all of you."

"All of . . . us?"

"All of you."

The night and that weird aura of the desert seemed to change the way she looked—she seemed to glow in the gathering darkness. For a moment, I thought I saw something in her eyes like shiny glass.

And then for a second I saw what was beneath her skin.

Something oily and coated with slime. If I closed my eyes it was as if I were embracing a large, wriggling eel with spines along its back.

I had the sensation of being within a nightmare, of having dreamed the entire day, and I felt my skin break out in goose bumps as she licked my ear. "All of you," she repeated.

I tried to struggle from her arms, but it was as if some creature had locked tentacles around my back. "Who are you? Who the hell are you? Are you even human?"

Wendy, placing a kiss on my lips, a kiss so hot as to burn, with a tongue of wet fire pressing into my mouth said words that seemed to appear in my mind without coming from her lips—"I am all you want now."

I tasted the blood from the back of her mouth.

And then my body betrayed me.

And I was no longer where I thought I had been.

And she had me.

I can still recall, years later, the feeling of entering her body. It was as if my skin were being slowly ripped from my flesh.

And the shivering, erotic intensity of the pleasure, there, in the dark, by the caves.

The intensity was what I began to crave.

Chapter Seventeen
The Tapes and a Confession

1

The interview with the boy named Peter continues

"The authorities all believe that you were insane. There was a history of abuse in your family. They dug up records in San Diego."

"Abuse. Sure. My dad liked to hit. So did Charlie's dad. For all I know, all dads like to hit. And drink. And wish their sons had never been born. And move up to the high desert to get away from everything. But, no, I wasn't some victim of abuse who suddenly got together with my friends and decided to . . . do what we did."

"Why won't you tell me more about her?"

"Why do you think?"

"Because it keeps her alive?"

"You're the smart one, you tell me."

"Because you've seen something that most human beings never encounter."

"Lucky me."

"Tell me about the others. Alison. Why did her grandmother pull her away?"

"She had nothing to do with it."

"I spoke with her."

"Alison?"

"No, her. Wendy."

"That's not possible. No way. Not after what we did. Even what she became . . ."

Silence for several minutes.

Then, the boy says:

"Well, then, you'll bring her here, to us, won't you? We stopped what happened. But you're going to bring it back again, aren't you? You don't even know what she is. You can't even imagine."

He catches his breath.

"That's it. No more interviews. What are they going to do to me?"

"Not as much as you'd think. You'll probably undergo more tests."

"I mean, after all that. Prison?"

"Charlie confessed. You'll probably go to relatives or foster homes. You might get emancipation status so you can work and support yourself, I guess. If that's what you want."

"Charlie?"

"I doubt he'll serve time. Might end up in a boy's camp-type situation. A boy can confess to anything he wants, but unless his fingerprints are there, it's tough to prove anything. Claw marks don't cut it. And the bodies? Where are they?"

"I bet they're still up there, somewhere. I bet the Devil has a way of hiding his work. You can send cops and investigators and FBI to Hell and back and I bet they'd never find a single campfire."

"It was the Devil?"

"No. I don't know. It was . . . I guess demons are no good excuse for what happened. I don't have words for what I saw. Maybe I'm too stupid. Demons is the best I can do."

"I believe you, Peter."

"Then . . . help us. Help me. Help Charlie."

"All right. I'll do what I can."

A momentary silence. Then, "Thank you."

2

Taped interview with Alison, continued

"Who am I speaking with now?"

"One of the thousands who occupy this bitch."

"Devils?"

"Fuck you."

"What do you want from her?"

"We want to be born."

"But you already exist. Why be born?"

"Because we must come through."

3

Taped interview with Charlie, continued

"That's an interesting knife."

"Yeah. You read Latin?"

"Yes, I do."

"What's it say?"

"It says that this is an athame. It's a ceremonial blade. It's rather fantastical."

"Does it mention demons?"

"A particular one, yes. It calls her Lamia, Goddess, Mother, Fertile One, Mistress of Howling Night. And then it has one other word. Translates as 'oblivion.' "

"Hell," the boy said.

"Perhaps."

"You believe now? I mean, I told you where to find the knife. I want it back, too. I know you can't give it to me now, but I want you to promise you'll keep it safe and locked up and then you'll give it back to me when I'm through. If I survive whatever fucking looney bin I get shipped off to."

"I promise."

"Good."

"It's at least a thousand or more years old. Did you know that?"

"No. I think it's older. I think someone with a lot of power created it to stop her before. They just didn't."

"Sending demons to Hell," the man said. "You kids out there, fighting this thing. Believing. Charlie, why don't you just retract what you told the police? You won't be dealt with so harshly. After all, you weren't the only one."

"I have a lot to make up for."

"If it was a demon—"

"I don't think you get it, Doc. Nobody does. Not even me. I do and I don't. I guess nobody does until they're right in the shit middle of it."

"Fair enough. But why you? Why you and Peter and Alison?"

"I don't know. I guess 'cause we were there. I guess 'cause we were ready. Maybe because we could be had. Why does anybody get hit by a car? Or end up on the one jet that crashes? Why does someone fall off the same cliff that a hundred other jerks have been hiking around for years?"

"And what about her mother? Who was she?"

"She's dead, too. We killed her. She was nobody. She was the mother of a demon. That's all."

"All right. And her father?"

4

Peter Chandler/Confessions

Portrait of Palemetto, California, in the summer of 1980. It was the beginning of the terror. Charlie was the first to kill. Didn't know who lived in that Garden of Eden, not until after Charlie had killed his folks, and before the rest happened.

What Wendy had inside her.

It's calling.

Who's left, I wonder? Who will hear the call?

BOOK THREE

TWENTY YEARS LATER
NOW
THE CALL

"The devil resides in the heart."
—old Welsh saying

PART ONE: LOS ANGELES

Chapter Eighteen
The Interrogator

1

Diego Correa owned a muddy-green Mustang that he'd had since 1974, and although the seats had been falling apart for years, he enjoyed the symbolism of the car. It had been bought with the royalties of his first book, *The Rain Dwellers*, and although it was in terrible shape and was in the garage two days out of three, to Diego, symbols were *all*. But it was raining—sprinkling, really—and one of the tires was bald, and the brakes weren't in the best of shape. Still, if he drove carefully, slowly, he would not have to worry about sliding. "Oh, Teresa, but I will never get used to this traffic," he said aloud to his nonexistent passenger as he fiddled with the radio.

As he turned left into the parking lot, he saw three of his female students standing in wait for him, and he cringed. *You are sixty-two, why would those college girls even pretend to be entertained by your old stories? They should get out there and* live, *not listen to some old man tell of his adventures!*

"Dr. Correa!" one of the women called out, a young woman he did not recognize from his classes, and he pretended to be deaf as he got out of his car and walked swiftly toward his office.

2

After class, Diego went back to his office just to smoke a cigar and relax. He enjoyed the corridor the most when everyone was gone. He could sit and read with the office door open until one or two in the morning; he was working his way through Jung again, as he always did in the fall. When Teresa had died—*at least left the earth, who knows where her essence has gone on to*—he hadn't enjoyed being home. Although his housekeeper, Mrs.

135

Warhola, kept the place tidy and cooked dinner for him, she had her own family to care for, too, and she wasn't interested in talking, particularly about mythology or religious experience. Teresa had gone very quickly, while he had been away; he had only heard she had pneumonia one day, and then the next that she was dead. It had been just like her to do that, to go so quickly. She had done it to him before, in smaller ways. She had gotten tired of the Andes, when he was doing his research on human sacrifice, and had just gone out to get a cup of coffee. The next he knew, she was calling from Los Angeles to say she missed the house and had work to do in the garden, and couldn't he come home soon? Another time, in Nepal, she'd taken off for a weekend with her sister to Bangkok and only breathlessly told him an hour before she was to board a plane. He admired her for it: neither of them had grown up with such independent parents. In his household, his father had been master and his mother had been servant, and he'd always felt a great sense of shame for the role his mother had had to play, given that she was the more creative of the two. Once he had asked his mother why she was content with such a situation, and she had told him, "I'm not. I've never been happy with it." But his mother had been on the cusp of the old ways; Teresa had just caught the tide of the new. It was why he still loved her, still felt her beside him. She had taught him so many things that he would never have learned on his own. "It is because of my cold heart, Teresa," he said, speaking as if she were hovering nearby. He leaned back in his cushioned chair, settling in to read. "You warmed it for awhile, but you had to take off in another direction, didn't you? And leave this old man to teach like a used-up bit of gray matter."

Diego almost jumped out of his chair when he glanced up from his book and saw a woman standing in the doorway. He glanced at his watch; it was only eight A.M. Perhaps she was the woman applying for the new secretarial position. "Hello?"

"I'm looking for Dr. Correa," she said. She lingered in the doorway, as if stepping in his office were tantamount to dropping off the edge of a cliff.

"You found him."

And that had been a red-letter day for Diego Correa, because it was the first day of treatment with Alison Chandler, a woman he had met and spoken with briefly when she had been just a girl.

That had, for him, reopened the dream of his life: to get to the root of what had happened in Palmetto, California, in 1980.

A town that burned, that was abandoned, around which legends had arisen, and what could've happened to a town on the high desert in which its occupants disappeared?

Demons, is what the children had said.

No one had listened; no one except for Correa and some of the tabloids. Even the authorities had abandoned their search for bodies, as if something up there in that place had convinced them that there was no answer.

Correa began to meet with Alison Chandler twice a week, to help her find what had been denied both of them for too long.

The day that Peter Chandler saw something in the basement of a bungalow was the date of the sixth session that Diego and Alison had together, and it was the first in which she mentioned the town of Palmetto, California, directly.

3

"The case. 1980. I know you studied it in detail," Alison said. "I've read a few of your books. The one called *The Secrets of Childhood, The Mysteries of Youth.* You devoted three whole chapters to it. Palmetto—the vanishing of a town."

"There was little to study, but I spoke with two of the boys. And a girl."

She smiled. "One was my husband."

"And you were the girl."

The smile vanished. "I don't remember."

"I know. Your husband . . ."

"Please, I feel like I'm betraying him by just being here," she said, looking directly into his eyes for the first time. Before she spoke he felt his heart skip a beat because in her eyes was a softness, an understanding he had only found with one other woman, and it terrified him with its suggestion of intimacy. Then it was gone, that light in her eyes. *Is it my imagination?* he wondered. "My husband lied to you. Who can blame him? We were hounded by doctors and reporters. Anyone would've lied just to be left alone. They thought he was crazy, you know. But he lied to protect me."

Diego took a sip of coffee. "The original story they gave was about another girl. And a monster. And demons. And a dog. But neither boy agreed on what happened. Do you know what happened?"

"I don't remember . . . I told you. I want you to take me back there. I'm ready."

"You're sure? You weren't ready before. Something always held you back, even when you were under. And I can't promise much," Diego said. "It probably won't be pleasant, because whatever happened there was extremely traumatic for you."

"I want to go back there," she said, and he did not need to look into her eyes again to know that she was weeping. "I lost all that time. All the memories."

Diego Correa nodded. "All right. Let's put you under." He spoke the words he had used before to help ease her into a relaxed state of mind. He placed his hand over hers to calm her.

Then the woman's eyes glazed over, as if he'd keyed into some mantra with the simple phrase: *what if*. Her hands, cold a moment before, began to warm, and she would not let go of his hand. Her own hand felt so hot to him it was as if her blood were boiling beneath the surface of her skin, and he was afraid that they would both burst into flame if he did not let go of her hand.

"I saw a man eating his own skin," she said, but her voice was different. It was the voice of an adolescent girl. A very different young girl who was more confident than this woman sitting before him. "Peter," she said, her eyes moving rapidly in their sockets as if she were dreaming with them wide open. "I can't go back there. Don't make me go back there *ever*. Promise. Promise."

4

When the session was finished, he waited while she slowly awoke. "Shall I replay the tape for you?" he asked.

"Did I say anything bad?"

"You're not a little girl; you're allowed to say a few bad things."

She grinned, covering her face as if trying to hide the fact that she was blushing. "I say far too many bad things as it is."

You Come When I Call You

Because the session had left him perspiring, just hearing what she'd said while she'd been under, he opened his top desk drawer and took out a pack of Salems. "Do you smoke? I do, I hope you don't mind. I didn't start 'til I was sixty, and then only because I had dreamed all my life of smoking and had put it off because of the health hazards, until finally I thought: what are you waiting for? But I only smoke when I'm onto something, which isn't often." Diego shook his head as he lit the cigarette. "My dear, I feel like I'm on the threshold of something absolutely illuminating."

Why has she bewitched you, abuelo? Is this young woman the key to the door you wish to unlock? Or are you deluding yourself yet again, chasing down a phantom that only exists in the imagination? Her hands were so pale and smooth. He wanted to touch her hands, in friendship and comfort, but when he had held them before, ah, the heat they had generated. "I will tell you what happened. I said two words that triggered something, perhaps a memory. And then from there, you were out and quite amenable to answering whatever question I could think of. Let me play the tape for you and you will not be so worried about your sanity." He reached across his desk and pressed the play button on his Sony. "I wasn't quick enough to press the record button at first, so it begins in the middle."

The voice on the tape sounded different, younger, more confident than the woman who sat in front of him.

5

"*. . . Ever. Not ever. Promise me, we don't have to go back there.*"

"*Are you talking to your husband?*"

"*Peter.*"

"*And your name is?*"

"*Alison. Alison Hunt.*"

"*And, Alison, are you scared?*"

"*The scared Alison is gone. Really gone. I killed her. I made sure she died. Peter helped bury her. I don't ever want to go back there, understand?*"

"*What was Alison scared of?*"

"*Demons.*"

"*Demons? But there aren't any, are there?*"

"*Yes. There are.*"

"You saw them?"

"No. But not everything is visible. Some things you see and some things you don't. I didn't see any demons, not the way demons are in pictures, but I saw a girl eating something terrible. Something bleeding all over her hands. She ate as much of it as she could."

"Why did she do that?"

Silence.

"Alison? Why did she do that?"

She paused, and then said slyly, *"Because she liked the taste."*

6

Alison reached across the desk and shut the tape machine off. "I don't want to hear the rest. Not now. Maybe never. I don't need to hear it. But maybe you can tell me about it. About what's wrong with me."

Diego leaned over the desk to her. "You are either insane or blessed, and let me tell you, it maybe the same thing. Don't be afraid," he said. "You're not crazy just because something happened to you a long time ago."

"Have to go," she said, standing up abruptly, almost knocking her chair over.

He nodded. There would be other days; there would be time. *You must not let your excitement scare her away. She has been through so much.* "I am here. You call me if you want to. I would like to speak with you some more. I think I can help you. I don't think you're in any kind of trouble. But I would like to help you. Here. . . ." He reached for a pen, and tore off a piece of paper from the calendar on his blotter. "My home number." He began writing the phone number down for her.

"Look, I think I was wrong to come here," Alison said.

When he looked up from his desk, she had already left his office; he heard her footsteps as she hurried down the hallway.

7

Diego listened to the rest of the tape. When it was done playing, he rewound it and played it again. At first, Alison was speaking in that youthful, confident voice, but as she continued speaking, her sentences broke down into fragments that he hadn't understood: *"demon sky cold is is not snake skin red flower dog dog dog what if big what green rat house wall wall wall . . ."* And then, even the language had shredded, until she was making noises in the back of her throat as if she had somehow forgotten how to form words.

Diego stood, stretched, and went to his file cabinets. He opened the middle drawer. Dust blew out from the crush of yellowed papers. The interviews with the children. One of the two boys he'd spoken to would grow up to be Alison's husband. *You will be up all night, old man, reading about it again. About the demons he had spoken of, too, but back when no one believed him. Not even you. Back when you thought there might be nothing more than a boy's imagination.* He found the notebook he was looking for. It was marked PETER C., JANUARY, 1981.

How that boy kept her safe all these years, and how wrong he was to do it, how wrong and how understandable. Diego opened the notebook to the first page, and chuckled, because he remembered how this one boy had changed his story three times, *three times*, and never admitted to lying at all.

It would be several days before he would see Alison Chandler again.

8

Early one evening, Diego Correa leaned back in his chair, opening his *Alison* notebook, where he'd left off scribbling the night before. The final page read: *. . . but what real progress do we make, she and I? I get the jumble, the clutter of non sequiturs, and she seems more confused with every session. Must speak with husband, he's got the connecting tissue. Only he can help open up her mind and help her grow. What kind of a man would want to dwarf her life like this? She is so innocent, so terrified, and yet so strong. Strong, but breakable, like a spider's thread. Abuelo, how have you come this far and gone nowhere? How many years of this must you document before you find that illumination? Mention possibility of brain hemorrhage, fever. Is she seeing some physician?* He barely noticed Alison's entrance. He looked at his watch. She was early. "I didn't expect you for another hour."

"I know. I'm beginning to think I'm using our sessions like a

141

drug. Leave it to me," she plopped down in the chair opposite him. She seemed to be getting more nervous as the sessions wore on. He wondered if he was only doing damage to this woman, or if some good would come of his explorations of her subconscious.

"You seem to be a quick study. It's amazing to me that the doctors you've seen in the past wouldn't try to regress you. My guess is you were too smart for them." He watched as she blushed—she didn't take compliments easily. "That's the upside. The downside is you seem rather young to have had a stroke. You did have some sort of stroke, didn't you? When you were younger?"

She heaved a great breath, as if a tremendous load were taken off her. "What do you—how do you know—about it?"

"Your voice, your *language*. You have worked on your voice. You have had to learn your voice over again, haven't you? You lost words or comprehension at some point."

Alison was finally trusting him, opening a little more. She stood and went to pour herself a cup of coffee from the pot by the window. "My husband taught me. It took six years, and every day he had to sit down with me and the alphabet, and records, and times tables, but I finally relearned things. And then school. I officially graduated from high school at my grandmother's in San Francisco, but it was Peter who cheated for me so I'd get by. I'm not sure if I can do anything by myself."

"Yet you project a great deal of confidence."

She laughed, sipping from the Styrofoam cup. "I can fake anything for about an hour. It's having to talk with other people and things. That's half the reason I work with animals. I, um, get along fine with animals, and, like I said, with people I can fake it."

"What's the other half?"

"Excuse me?"

"Why you work there? You implied there's another reason besides not dealing well with people."

"Did I say that? That's funny. Maybe there's no other reason. I have a hard time keeping most jobs I've tried. Sometimes I say these things . . ."

"But there's another reason. Something about dogs."

"I can't think what. I just like animals."

"Why do you like them?"

She considered this question a minute. "You're going to find this strange, and I've never even told my husband this. But it's something about the smells. The way animals smell. It makes me feel—I don't know—*safe* or something." Alison went back to the desk and sat down. She began combing her fingers through her hair.

Diego turned his tape recorder on. "I'm going to put you out now."

"You are? But we've done it twice this week. I thought you said it wasn't a good idea to keep at this thing." There was a worried note in her voice. "You said that a couple of times a week was enough."

"I think it's reached a crisis, Alison. I think we can make some real progress."

"Oh." She seemed to calm just a bit. She closed her eyes. "All right."

"Feel all the tension melting from your body. Think of darkness. Cool darkness. And in that cool darkness, what if there is a dog, what if you know that dog, what if . . ."

She whispered, "Dog blood dog Peter Wendy Sloan Charlie."

Chapter Nineteen
Confessions

Peter opened his notebook computer and began typing:

I am scared shitless. The bungalow. Hallucination? Madness? Seeing him down there, after all these years. Crucified. The basement like the Corazon. The bodies. The faces. The fire. I have been wrong. She will not give up. She will not let us alone. Twenty years have not bought us freedom.

She is within us.

She is back.

She wants what we took from her.

Chapter Twenty

Alison Runs a Fever

1

Alison opened her eyes. She didn't recognize the older man at first. Consciousness returned slowly—and she realized she was lying back in the lounge chair in the office of the mythologist and writer, Dr. Diego Correa. She felt something hard and thin, like a glass straw, stuck beneath her tongue. She tried talking, but the straw was in the way. Diego leaned over her and plucked it from her mouth. *A thermometer?* She couldn't remember it going into her mouth. Just a few seconds before he'd told her he was putting her out.

"You've been running a fever," he said, his voice full of concern.

"Don't—nothing—understand," she said, trying to sew the words together correctly from the jumble of language in her mind.

"You were out quite awhile—three hours—and one thing I've noticed is your body starts, well, *overheating*, for lack of a better expression, when you start this trance state. So I took your temperature every half hour, and you got as high as 104, and then dropped down in the last forty minutes. Usually, in a trance, the body cools off a bit."

"Am I sick?"

"Perhaps you should get a physical."

"Did I talk the entire three hours?"

"Give or take a few minutes for the thermometer, yes. I'd like to talk to your husband if I could."

"No. I don't think so. He doesn't even know I'm here right now."

"Do you think what we're doing here is bad?"

"I almost feel like I'm cheating on him, or something."

"Why is that?"

"Private reasons. If I'm going to work through this, it's going to be *without* Peter knowing. That's it."

"Fair enough. Would you like to hear the tape?"

"Should I?"

"You repeated one phrase the entire time. Nothing monumental, although I'm certain you'll know what it means. You said: *fire skin cold light blood*. I stopped the tape an hour ago. I asked you questions about it, but it's all you said. There's another word you've been saying for the past four sessions, and when I ask about it, you go back to that phrase."

"What was it?"

"*Lamia*. Do you know what that means?"

She shook her head and almost grinned. "That is one word I've never run into." She was afraid her voice was sounding too stressed-out; her head was beginning to throb, and there was something about that word that made her wish she'd never heard it. *I'm crazy. The whole problem is I'm crazy and Peter's just been too good a man to tell me. Maybe coming to Dr. Correa was all wrong. Maybe it's unsafe.*

Correa smiled, too, but something in his dark eyes made her think that he knew how scared she was beneath the surface. "Lamia. Well, while I haven't had much experience with them, I have seen cultures that worshipped or feared such things under various guises. The feminine personification of the darkness of the universe, somewhat related to vampires as well as serpents—and even wolves. The shapeshifter. In myth, her children were murdered and she roams the night stealing the children of others. When the Judeo-Christian-Islamic world took hold, she became, as did all good fallen gods, a demon. When I interviewed your husband, when he was in his teens, he mentioned her, too. He also spoke of the territory of demons, a place called no man's land. What does that mean to you?"

But she drew a blank, and what was finally emerging in her mind continued to hurt, a hammering away at her brain and skull from the inside. Could he tell how much she hurt, or was she hiding it well enough? He looked at her so knowingly. It was a headache she recognized, one she had with increasing frequency, one that she'd been having whenever she hit the wall in her mind. The yellow wall that came up without warning most times. When it had first happened, in her early twenties, she'd been afraid that it was a tumor, or a sign of some kind of depression, or even a seizure. She hadn't gone to see a doctor. As time went on, she got used to the headaches. They were like hammers on her skull, but she got used to them. She would go and lie down in a cool, dark place and rest and tell her coworkers it was just a killer migraine. But always there was the leaning of memory, of the clicks and buzzes in her brain as if the computer were checking its files, certain words that she did not understand, holdovers from relearning the language, as if Peter hadn't taught her every word again, as if he'd withheld some. Alison closed her eyes, trying to will the headache away. The words formed an image, the wall.

And over the wall, what?

The man reached across his desk and pressed down on the play button of the tape player. "I want you to listen for a minute. Something you said."

Alison barely recognized her own voice on the tape.

"We are those she touched."

"How were you touched?"

"We saw her face. Her real face. We saw what she was. And it touched us."

"What was she?"

And then, Alison heard a noise from the tape that made her shiver, like she was listening to someone being tortured. Not a scream, and not a moan, and not a laugh, but all of these. Pure human pain.

Diego Correa reached back to switch the machine off, but she shook her head. She wanted to hear the rest.

She listened as her voice on the tape growled. Then the sound of what seemed like a wolf's howl came, but within her voice, other voices, as if several people were crying out at once.

"Stop it!" Alison stood up. "Shut it off! Turn it off!" She clapped her hands over her ears; tears burst from her eyes; she began shivering.

Correa turned the tape machine off.

She sat back down in the chair, covering her face with her hands. "Jesus Christ, I know those people. Jesus."

"Who are they?"

"Oh, Jesus," she began weeping uncontrollably, and it took

nearly ten minutes for her to calm down enough to tell him that they were her brothers and mother and father.

2

Alison felt a presence in the parking lot that night. This didn't seem terribly unusual to her: she was always feeling some sort of presence, and she attributed it to her childhood trauma, that part of her adolescence that had been wiped clean, the part of her that finally required seeing Diego Correa—and still she didn't feel she'd made any real progress. All she felt was guilt and stupidity because something in her mind was keeping her from knowing herself as well as she should. *Instead I hit a wall and sit there wondering why I can't see around it. So I feel weird things in parking lots at night. Terrific.*

So why are you so scared?

She'd come out of Diego's office just after ten, feeling exhausted and a little weak; she wondered what new excuse she'd give Peter when she arrived home late again. She hated confrontation more than she hated certain unremembering parts of herself. *How do you love someone,* she wondered, *when he keeps something this important from you?* And yet she knew: Peter had brought her into life. The past, the town on the high desert—it had all been a nightmare. She was one of the few survivors, and whenever she read an account of it, she hit the wall and could go no further. It *hurt* to hit the wall; the fever rose beneath her skin and her brain chewed on itself until she was popping Advils like they were M&M's. She knew she should see a physician, but doctors scared her; and she was so worried about the possibility of a tumor in her brain that she didn't *want* to find out. *Does that make sense?* she'd asked herself, as she walked. *Does anything I do make sense?*

And then the parking lot.

She didn't feel the chill of the night air until she was halfway across the parking lot. It was almost empty. The lamplight shone metallic off the hoods of the few cars still scattered throughout it. Her Honda Civic (bought in 1986 for four thousand dollars, and it looked it with its bashed in back fender and expired registration and bald tires) seemed miles from the other cars, and another end of the world from the guard booth. The guard was there, though, sipping coffee in his booth, clipboard in his hands, and she smiled and waved, but he did not look up to see her.

Nothing bad happens to you if security's around. Naturally in the parking lot after ten at night you're going to freak over nothing, especially after talking demons with Diego Correa, the man who believes that myth has reality, that the unseen exists. Demons, Ali, do you really buy that?

The autumn days could be in the high seventies, but after dark the temperature could drop severely to an uncomfortable chill. Alison Chandler tugged her blue cotton sweater down, stretching it almost to the pockets of her jeans.

In the pit of her stomach she felt the need to go seek out someone, maybe the guard, maybe Diego. She felt watched. *But then, Alison, you're certifiably mental, haven't you always known that? Haven't you known that since you learned to talk again, learned to think again? If it hadn't been for Peter you would've been either stuck in some state institution or forced to live with the grandmother from hell.*

She walked across the lot, hearing the echoing steps of her own shoes. She reached her car and took a deep breath. Checked the backseat to make sure no madman with an ax was hiding there. *All clear.* Alison caught her breath, trying to hold it in silence while she slipped the key in the door to unlock it: she glanced around the lot. *Animals do this*, she told herself, *they sniff the wind for predators, they sense things without seeing them.* She smelled nothing but her own cologne. When she climbed into the Honda, she rechecked the backseat. "Nobody's in here with me," she said to the car's interior, and pulled out a stick of Juicy Fruit gum from the glove compartment.

Alison locked the door; checked the other door to make sure it, too, was locked; strapped herself in with the seat belt; turned the key in the ignition; pumped the accelerator; turned on the headlights.

When she put the car in reverse, she glanced up to the windshield.

On the other side of the chain-link fence surrounding the lot, she saw the man watching her.

The man's features were bleached a flat white in the brilliant headlights. His chalk-white hands clutched the fence. His face, pressed against it. He wore a sweatshirt, but the hood was pulled up, obscuring most of his face.

He opened his mouth wide.

Something in the emptiness of that shadowed face terrified her.

Just a shadow.

But a shadow she had seen.

Before.

I'm hitting the wall, a small voice rose up within her.

Her whole body began shaking uncontrollably, and tears rolled down her cheeks. The pain in her head was enormous. She didn't even realize that her nose had begun bleeding.

3

In her head, she was not staring out the windshield at all, but *speeding like a rocket, moving toward a wall that was moving just as recklessly toward her—and she was sure she would smash against it like a fly on a windshield.*

She heard a boy say, "Alison, you are gonna regret this."

The blood silhouette of a woman pressed against a high yellow wall met her head on. And the blood moved in liquid down the edge of the wall, and the blood cried out to her, "You are always here with me. In here. In darkness. Come to me. When I call."

4

Alison awoke, gasping. She felt cold. She saw curved, smooth forms, a landscape of circles and lines. Her scalp felt raw, as if someone had torn her hair out. The ache behind her eyes was rhythmic and painfully slow. Eyes hurt. Throat filled; taste of blood. She tried to form a word, but could not come up with one. A thought. No thought.

Finally, a thought and a word, *dying*.

5

But that thought was replaced with another one: *Oh, hell, I'm only alive and suffering, damn it.*

Her head rested against the steering wheel. She heard the sound of a distant train, a horn, *car horn*, blasting from far away, and then coming closer and getting louder, until, as she lifted her head carefully from the wheel, it was suddenly silenced.

Tapping at the window. She saw the man standing there. It was hard to focus on anything, and her eyes felt like they were filled with sand. Then her vision became clearer: the man looked concerned. Had on a uniform. The security guard. It seemed like hours before she finally rolled the window down and lied. "Sorry. I have a blood sugar problem and just fainted, but it's okay now, I had some crackers." *Would he buy it?*

The guard was in his twenties, probably a full-time student, and obviously not experienced in the world of bad blood sugar levels. He had a face like a donkey—long and dumb. "Okay, lady." He walked away.

Alison sat for another ten minutes in the car. Just breathing, wiping her eyes, wishing she had a Diet Pepsi to nurse. *And Advil. A ton of Advil. And a glass of brandy. A hot bath. And a coma. One coma to go.*

What had she seen? She couldn't remember. Just the wall. *Ouch.* A man and a girl on the other side of the fence. Their silhouettes flashed in her mind like lightning. She scanned the fence again, but did not see anyone there. Her head throbbed. Pain like needles pinching all along her scalp. She adjusted the rearview mirror—bloodstains around her nose and upper lip. She wiped at them and sniffed. *Maybe you should see a doctor, maybe it* is *a tumor.*

Maybe you've waited too long.

Chapter Twenty-one
The Angel of Desolation

1

The hooded man grinned as he watched Alison Chandler drive off. *Angel will find you, Angel knows where you sleep at night, knows you sleep naked, knows you sleep with him who denies his true nature, his calling.*

He licked his lips; his stomach growled. He needed the blood and sometimes even the fatty tissue to survive. He had lived off fat during most of his time with his mistress. But this city, alive, so very alive with vessels of blood.

Hungry. Need some, some warmth, some . . .

Love.

There was a house, the one he'd been staying in, whose owners had fled sometime back. Fire had damaged the kitchen and dining room, but that had not kept the runaways from invading it and sleeping on its bare floors, covered with newspapers for warmth. The windows had been broken, and the kids had taped cardboard from boxes up against them—it was always dark there. And the basement. It was the perfect place for him to sleep, absolute darkness, darkness where he would find her, and warmth, so much warmth from their young bodies pressed up against his while he slept, for they, too, were night creatures.

He had had to kill a few of them, the temptation had been so strong. How much better were living and breathing bodies than those that were already dead.

He felt stirrings in his loins when he thought of the children, his children, sleeping with him in that house. How they looked up to him, or feared him, for it was all the same; and he held them when they shivered from withdrawal, or kissed them when their veins burned with the liquid fire of heroin they kept there. And they came to him, they saw in him their release into bliss.

The night was like the voice of his mistress, like ice melting against warm skin. He felt his heart beating faster. He tried to calm himself. He could've taken her, right then. *Alison.* They had been on the same frequency for those precious seconds, and he thought he'd heard her skin ripping. Heart beating too fast. He brought his hands up to his chest and felt the pulse of his life. *Those who betrayed*, he promised, *will come home*. Getting into the car he'd stolen, he closed his eyes, thinking of her. Then he opened his eyes, glancing into the backseat where the dead woman lay. She had provided him with sustenance. But now he

151

needed more. He needed to bring home all the children who had abandoned their beloved.

His beloved.

He turned the key in the ignition. He loved all the children of the world. All those who had once been children, all who would become children, all who had betrayed him.

His love was savage and endless.

Alison and Peter, he grinned. *Alison and Peter. My friends.*

The night, the smells.

Beckoning.

The thought of juice in the back of his throat, burning and cool. He had to go find sustenance, the fatty tissue and the skin and the blood, all would give him strength to bring the children home again.

2

Within an hour, on a dark street in downtown Los Angeles, a woman lay sprawled behind a dumpster, and he leaned over her, feeding. The wall of the bank building behind him had a stain from a tower of blood that had shot up as if to the sky—

Before three A.M., three teenagers's bodies would be found torn as if by dogs—

By sunrise, the police would already be gathered around what looked like the most brutal slaying since the Black Dahlia murder in the 1940s, a woman with red hair, her skin all but stripped from her bones, and human teeth marks deep into her torso—

3

Dawn would be coming—he could smell it in the sky, in the chill that was burning off. Still he was unsated.

He was tired, but the drive was still there: he wanted to find her, the girl, the right girl, who could take away the nightmares of that empty place inside him, the girl whom She could come into, could possess for that one moment between life and death. The freshness of flesh.

The driving force within him would be his appetite.

Chapter Twenty-two

The Trials of Marriage

1

Alison slid into bed, and whenever she did it, she knew Peter would wake up. She hated waking him up. Peter was always so sweet asleep, so calm. Sometimes, the nightmares, sure. But not all the time. Not most of the time. *How can you love somebody so much and lie to them?* She could answer so few of her own questions in life. She felt sticky with sweat and freezing cold; she pulled the sheet up around her shoulders. "You awake?"

"I guess I am now." As he said this, she saw the shadow of his arm stretching for the bedside lamp, hesitate, and then drop down to the bed again. "How was class?"

Her eyes adjusted to the dark. She couldn't tell if his eyes were opened or closed. His voice was strange, like he'd been lying in bed pretending to sleep for her benefit. He didn't sound sleepy. *Maybe he suspects. Jesus, what's he going to say when he finds out I've been seeing Correa?* Her head still echoed a hammer beating down on a spike. *Four little Advils later and one glass of cheap wine from the fridge, and it keeps on ticking.* "Ali?" He said.

The head-banging continued unabated, and she began to worry that she would start screaming at him for no reason at all. *Like having a full year of periods at once.* The palm of his hand rested on her forehead; his hand was like ice.

"You're burning up."

She tried to sound fine. "*Peter.*" She reached over and scruffed his hair up. "Just a touch of fever. Maybe I should sleep on the couch so you don't catch anything. Maybe it's the flu."

"No, stay here, okay?"

"I'm all achy."

He wrapped his arms around her. It made her feel uncomfortable. "If it's the flu . . ."

153

"No, I was kidding, I'm fine. I'm just overheated. Like a car. I was studying so hard it made my brain hurt, if you can believe it. I think I'll take a bath," she said, disentangling herself from his arms. "You sleep, I'll be in later. Oh, damn and double damn," she said, rising, throwing off the sheet. "I forgot to take my contacts out. God, I was so keyed up today, I always end up keeping you up, and you've got to get up so early." She was almost in tears from the pain and she didn't want him to know it, because she wouldn't have an explanation. Walking across the carpet barefoot seemed like stepping on nails. It was the headache, it was the damn wall in her mind, making every part of her body sensitive as if she were all nerve endings.

"No problem—I wasn't really asleep, anyway," he said, switching on the light. His dirty-blond hair hung over his eyes. He watched her in the mirror as she set her contacts in solution. "How was work?"

She sighed. Work was years ago in the morning, before her session with Diego. Handling cats and dogs. "Same old same old. Had to help put a sixteen-year-old spaniel to sleep, and I couldn't stop crying. Isn't that stupid? You work with animals, it's what happens. You see anybody?"

He didn't reply.

2

In the bathroom, Alison turned the water on in the tub as hot as she could get it. The bathroom was steamed up when she finally got into the water. She sat down in the tub and let the hot water pour over her. It felt right.

The hooded man on the other side of the chain-link fence at the parking lot. The headache. The blackout. The nosebleed. The worst part of remembering it was that it wasn't an awful feeling. It was a feeling of being alive. Not being made of stone.

She closed her eyes and inhaled the steam of the bath.

She saw: *a boy, dark-haired and handsome, a teenager;* tried to open her eyes but they were sewn shut, *"Alison?"* the boy asked, and then another boy screamed, *"ALISON? HELP ME! ALISON? OH MY GOD, IT'S IN HERE, IT'S COMING FOR*

*ME! ALISON? HELP ME JESUS GOD SOMEBODY HELP ME
DON'T LEAVE ME!"* And then the boy who stood over her said,
*"Don't cry, it's a dream you're having, a bad dream, it's not real,
I don't hear anything, honest to God, you don't have to hear it,
either,"* and he brought his fist down to the side of her face. And
she turned to look away, but she didn't feel anything, he didn't hit
her, after all. Her head was pounding but it didn't hurt, and she
saw a wall. Bright lights like sheets of lightning. She was moving
fast, crying out, "Mom! Where are you? Mom!" And she was seeing the walls move, walls covered with framed pictures, and with
windows that looked out on crosses, and shining tabletops
pushed against the walls. The dark stain outline of a human
being, a woman, mom.*

Alison turned her head back to the boy and opened her eyes and
said, "Charlie?"

She heard water splashing and felt heat and saw fog.

She was in the tub. The steam cleared.

"Ali?" Peter asked from the doorway.

Alison saw the bathroom door opening. Hands parted the glass
partition. Peter stood there in his white jockey shorts, tall and
lanky like a shy farm boy. His ribs stuck out—he wasn't eating
enough; he looked weary.

"I couldn't get back to sleep," he said. He reached down and
slipped his underwear off, kicking it across the bathroom floor. He
had a tan line up to his thighs, and another just below his navel.
"Mind if I join you in the waterfall?"

Hanging onto the metal soap carrier and one side of the tub,
he slid in alongside her, facing her. He grasped the white soap
and rubbed it along her neck and shoulders. He leaned over,
stretching his neck, his jaw moving forward to kiss her; her
shoulders slumped; she leaned toward him, kissing him. His
lips and tongue were smooth and she felt, in the spray, as if she
had never been touched before. She felt his hands slip down
along her breasts, sliding along her ribs; he nestled into her; she
leaned back, raising herself up slightly as she groped with her
feet around his waist until she had her knees pressed against his
sides, her feet flat on the warm tub floor behind him. She
rubbed soap across his chest and nipples, tickling his belly

slightly, curling her fingers into the hair on his stomach, pluck-
ing it back. "Al, Ali, Alison," he whispered, kissing her chin,
her cheeks, her ear, the back of her neck as he pulled in close to
her. They fit together with difficulty, like two pieces of different
puzzles. Making love always involved a level of tension and
discomfort before the pleasure kicked in, even after all these
years—just when they fit together, just when he entered her, it
would take her so long each time to enjoy it, she would try
meeting him with each thrust, but found herself pulling back,
sliding along the tub floor. Why were things always easier in
the imagination than in the act of doing? Why did the mechan-
ics always seem to get in the way with Peter? It had taken
twelve times with Peter before she'd even started enjoying it,
but she thought that was normal. She'd been a teenager then.
The idea of having this large *thing* inside you while you positioned yourself at this awkward angle, in a way you'd been told
all your life was somehow bad and not what nice people did,
while this boy seemed to be jabbing all over the place when you
were wishing he'd just lie still for a few moments so you could
adjust some, while all your life you'd been taught that no one
should ever get the upper hand with you, and here you were ful-
filling a natural calling, and it involved penetration of your
body: well, she hadn't expected the first few times to be fun and
games, there was too much baggage attached with it. But after
all these years together. Loving each other so much. Knowing
so much about each other . . .

Always, with Peter, she felt it wasn't her he desired, but some
other girl, and the blockade came not from within Alison's
body, but from Peter's, as if he were holding something back
when he entered her, keeping something for that other girl. He
curled his mouth slightly when he was inside her, and she
always expected him to call out for someone. For *her*. The girl
of his dreams.

When Peter entered her here, on the tub floor, her hands reached
behind him, her fingers stroking the light hair on his back; pressing, she tried to bring him all the way into her so there was no difference between their bodies.

But as she felt his thrusts become more rapid, as she pressed
her head into his neck, her lips against his chin, as she felt

something within herself spark like a live wire thrown into the tub with them, *she was again with some teenaged boy whose mouth and tongue were everywhere across her pale skin, rough and dry and unrelenting. And he pressed her up against a stained wall.*

Chapter Twenty-three
The Day of Reckoning Is Upon Us

1

The Angel of the Desolation wanted Her so badly, and she would not enter into him, he had not found her. He felt like he'd stepped into Hell without Her. *Wendy. Beloved.*

No sleep.

The Angel of Desolation turned his face upward. Sunlight like drops of whiskey sprayed over him. It stung and it tasted of old memories, he got drunk on the light, and his head throbbed. His neck felt swollen, and the sweatshirt was so tight against his skin. *No sleep, no sleep, give me strength.*

It had been years since he'd seen the sun, since he'd been out where the light was. He'd sat on a hillside overlooking the San Fernando Valley while the fiery ball emerged from the mountains in the east, as if sent by Her to him as a message. The morning brought the shakes upon him, and he became nervous and afraid. He could now be seen. He pulled the hood down farther over his head. He sat in the stolen Buick, parked along the roadside and watched the light shower over the Valley, and then the sun moved to find him, to make him drunk and mad with the memory of the other life he'd led, before She had changed him.

She had rescued him, and had taken him from one darkness into another darkness. It was as if he had died then, those years ago. Endless hours and minutes and days and weeks and seconds underground, pressed there with stones and bricks. Dirt and filth clogging his throat, his nostrils layered with dust, his mouth so

*filled with pebbles that he was afraid that if he screamed for help
he would choke to death before he'd made a sound. How much
time had gone by since they'd buried him there? And who was
there left to come for him? In that eternity he'd felt the stinging of
fire ants across his arms and legs; welts rose where the insects tres-
passed, and with them, fever, and he began praying for death,
praying for release, praying to whomever might be out there to
hear him.*

And it was Her. She would answer his prayers.

*"You belong to me," She said, bringing him forth from the tomb,
hugging him to Her while tears sprouted from his swollen eyelids.*

2

He would waste no more time.

They would pay for their great sin.

Now.

3

This is what happened. These were the first four words of his con-
fessional notebook. Later, too, Peter would think that. *This is how
it happened and I did nothing to stop it until it was all over. Like I
wanted it to happen.*

But when the day was just beginning, and Peter woke up to the
ringing phone, he didn't think these things. He had even managed
to put what he'd seen in the bungalow cellar out of his mind.
He'd hallucinated before, why wouldn't he again? Hadn't he
been convinced by enough medical "experts" that he had some
kind of damage to his cerebral cortex so that he might have the
equivalent of acid flashbacks and start seeing what his imagination was manufacturing? *But it ain't nothing, folks, why you follow a girl who looks like a girl you used to know down a ladder
and then you see a woman's face, and underneath it, another, but
you know it's just a little teeny-tiny bit of brain damage, so
you're supposed to calm down and take a couple of aspirin when
it happens and reassure yourself that nothing's a-coming for to
carry you home. Just a trick of the mind. Now you see it, now you
don't. You believe what you can't see, boy? Not if you can't*

believe what you do see, boy. Every now and then, over the years, you've thought you've seen her, too, in a crowd, just a face, but hers, and then gone. A face. A face peeled back from the skull. Her eyes like onyx. No iris or pupil or white, just onyx. Black translucent stone. Why don't you tell Alison? Why can't you tell her? Every time you are about to, you can't. What kind of a monster doesn't tell his wife the truth?

These were currents in his river of thoughts, and he hadn't slept at all that night, so the river had been running since he'd made love with Alison in the bathtub; the river had been running since he'd run from the bungalow the day before; the river ran time and space together, so that he never knew if he had imagined things or if they were real, and if they were in fact real, what did it matter, then? What did it matter if he was insane, and Alison was insane, and he had visions of things from Hell, and what did life matter?

And then, before he knew it, it started that morning with a ringing phone.

This is how it happened, he thought later, when he could wonder how the hell he had lain there in bed and not held her so tight that no one could possibly take her away from him ever.

4

"Hello," Peter held the phone to his ear.

"I'd like to speak with Mrs. Chandler," a man said. Old man, Peter figured. Maybe someone from the vet's office. Or a professor.

"Mrs. Chandler," he said, nudging Alison, who sleepily whispered back, "Just a few more minutes."

He kissed her on her neck. "It's for you."

She murmured, "Message. Call back later. Too sleepy."

As she turned into her pillow, he looked over her shoulder to the alarm clock. It was only seven. *Who the hell would call at seven in the morning?*

"She's sleeping. If it's an emergency I can get her up, otherwise . . ."

"It's an emergency," the man said.

"Who is this?"

"Is this Peter Chandler?"

159

"Yes, it is. Who is this?"

"We've met before. Years ago. My name is Diego Correa."

The name cut through him like a hacksaw. The only thing he could think to say into the phone was, "You finally got to her, you son of a bitch, you finally got to her. Stay the hell out of our lives."

The man on the line said, "Tell her she—"

Peter hung up the phone. He reached over to the phone cord and snapped it from the wall.

"What was that all about?" Alison murmured, turning over and putting her arms around Peter's waist. She smelled like vanilla and soap from last night's bath. "Peter?"

His entire body was tensed as if ready to spring. "Diego Correa."

"Oh," she said, and her voice had dropped; he could tell she had awakened with the mention of that name. "What did he want?"

For the longest time, Peter was silent. He lay there and listened to the sound of her breathing against his chest. Then he whispered, barely able to get it out, "You didn't tell me about him."

"I knew you'd get mad. I went to him for help. Peter," she began sobbing uncontrollably, and he held her tightly against his body. "I . . . can't . . . function . . . anymore. I need to know things about myself . . . you don't understand."

He gently stroked her back. "I do. I love you. I just don't want people like Correa to touch us." But as the words left his mouth, he could practically *hear* Alison suppressing emotion. *I promised you, Ali, I promised you I would never bring it back and I would never make you look back there, I promised, and even if you hate me I won't break that promise.*

She pushed away from him. "I'm just so . . . tired . . . of all of it. I don't know why it's such a secret. I've read those books, I know what happened that summer. What else is there that's so awful?"

"Al, Ali, I love you. You don't know what these people put me through, what they tried to do to you, how they were vultures, just feeding, feeding, feeding, never leaving me alone. It just pushes every button I have."

"I just want to know what happened."

"I told you," he said. He turned away from her, burying his head in the pillow.

"God. Peter, you're not being fair. I know what you told me, but I want it from *inside* me. I want to remember it *myself*. I know you took care of me, I know you taught me how to speak again and how to read, but I want to remember. For myself."

His voice was muffled against the pillow. "What if it hurts you? What if, Alison?"

He heard her voice, strange and wonderful, so much like it had been when she'd been a teenager, and he turned to face her. "*Peter don't make me go back there. Peter, please, don't ever make me go back there, promise me,*" she said. Her eyes were open and he was afraid to touch her because it scared him when this happened; it made him think she would have to be institutionalized again, and this time he wouldn't be able to get her out.

He had heard it before, whenever he said those words without thinking, *what if*. Something about the words that cracked her for a certain period of time, put her in a trance. How many times had they called him from her job to tell him that she had zoned out again, and was she on any medication? She could hide it sometimes, but how much of her life would be spent dreading two words frequently used together?

I only know that I have to keep protecting you. Even if it means with my life.

5

Just as if she were sucked into darkness, Alison was no longer in the room but in an endless corridor of night. The whispering voices batted the air around her. She struggled against the dark, but it held her.

Something freezing-cold breathed against her face, and she heard the whispering voices, *what if what if what if what if.*

6

Peter wiped her forehead with a cool, damp washcloth. "You were burning up."

She opened her eyes to his voice. He was sitting up on the bed, with her head resting in his lap. "I'm worn out," Alison said,

"Maybe it *is* the flu. You should rest today."

"No," she said resolutely and sat up quickly, then leaned back against him. "Work. I'll be better when I take a shower."

"The North Hollywood Animal Clinic will run perfectly fine without you for one day. You can call them," he reached across the bed and plugged the phone back into the wall. Then he handed her the receiver.

"I'm going to work," she said and pushed up off the bed. She held his hand while she steadied herself. "Little dizzy. Coffee?"

"Ali."

"Peter, I am just a little under the weather. I'm going to work. If I feel sick, I'll call you and you can come get me, deal?"

"Are you going to talk to Correa?"

She looked away. "Probably."

"All right, then. If you want to see him, see him. But be careful. He told me he was helping me, too, and all he did back then was pick my brains for the things he was looking for. And he was after you, then, too. No matter what he says now, he knew that you'd had the worst of it, and he wanted to examine you. And if he had, Al, you might've never recovered. Once you went under medical and psychological testing, you would've been dead. They didn't want you to get better. They only wanted to hook you up to machines and record your responses."

"That's all in the past now. Peter, we were sixteen. You can't say for sure that's what would've happened. He's not a bad man. He's good. I can feel it from him."

"Just be careful, then. He broke promises to me. I don't trust him. And it was you he wanted, and he's waited all these years. As I recall, he made a lot of money on that book of his. All on the tragedy of kids and what happened. You would've been his prize. Now he's found you."

"You've got it wrong," she said as she went into the bathroom. "He didn't find me. I found to him."

7

After she'd gone off to work, and after he lied and promised to follow up on a recent job interview, Peter Chandler rose and walked into the kitchen, flipping on the Krupps coffeemaker. He swung the refrigerator door open.

This day, he would try and clean off his desk. He would be late getting out to look for work, but he would clean things up a bit. *Hell, maybe I'll clean out the fridge, too*, he thought, peering into the dead, white light, beyond the front row of Dannon yogurt.

The refrigerator had an old ham that needed to be tossed; some squash and bell peppers, chicken breasts on the top shelf, next to the skim milk, three Diet Cokes and a six-pack of Corona. *Not exactly a hearty breakfast here.* Behind the milk carton he found some packets of Quaker instant oatmeal. Leaning against the refrigerator door, reaching in to grasp one of the packets with his left hand, Peter felt something in his stomach as if his bowels were loosening, his intestines uncoiling beneath his stomach, his knees giving out, his lungs not finding breath, his spinal cord wavering.

Jesus, this better not be the flu. Alison and me both getting sick right now's lousy timing.

And then, Peter *fell back into his body* like he was going down buckled into the seat of a 747.

As he caught himself against the refrigerator door, holding on for support, something came out of Peter's mouth, a noise that he could not identify at first.

As he regained feeling in his arms and legs, pinpricks beneath the skin, he knew what the sound was.

A howl.

The flu, yeah, dream on, Chandler.

You know *what this is.*

You've known this was coming for a long time.

She'd been coming for him for a long time, and in his dreams. Her hair a tangle of rust-colored rattlesnakes, writhing across her scalp, her eyes shiny and black like beetle shells, her face a blood-streaked skull. And then it would all shimmer, the vision in his dream as if he were crying in his sleep, and she would be restored: beautiful and cruel and pale. The Lamia, that's what she was, a she-devil, death's mistress: all those names that required some kind of superstitious belief, and yet hadn't he believed when he heard his blood singing with her voice? Stella knew, that's why she was sending the telegrams and letters. But Peter had ignored it until it could no longer be ignored. The disease had been in the blood, and they had tasted the blood, and now it was Peter's turn.

They all had done the Awful Thing.

What it had done to all of them.

Oh, God, Al, Ali, Alison, don't look back there. Only demons. Only deathsmell. Only what you can't see. Now, within his own body, he heard the call.

She had been growing strong again, after all these years.

She had been waiting for the right time.

She had wanted it to grow within them.

8

Diego Correa tried calling Alison's apartment again six times before he gave up.

He'd been up all night, in his office, listening to the old tapes of interviews with two boys, because he'd wanted to catch every single thing they'd said, not just what he had used in his book. The tapes playing continually through; rewinding, playing, the voices of children spinning the unbelievable story, and the part they were leaving out was about *her*, Alison. The children weren't lying about what had ravaged the town on the high desert, but they were lying about the girl, and if only he'd *understood*, if only he'd had *insight* back in 1981 when the interviews took place. How they'd protected her with their lies, but how, in the end, there was no real protection.

On the old tape:

"What about your friend?"

Peter said, *"She's sick, but she'll get better."*

"Can I talk to her?"

"Don't."

"Is she badly hurt?"

"Cut it out. I'm tired. She's just sick and she's gonna get better. She doesn't know any of this. She just got attacked is all. It wasn't after her anyway, it just wanted to kill. She got in its way."

"Why don't you want me to speak with your friend? Are you trying to protect her?"

"*She's sick. You already talked to her. Her grandmother won't let you talk to her, anyway. Maybe when she's better. I'm tired. Can I go now?*"

"*Peter, do you love her?*"

The boy, on tape, did not respond.

And Peter, at sixteen, had given him one key, and it was only now he knew how to use it. But it was only one key to a door with many locks.

Peter, on tape, had said, "*It's a turning, don't you get it? It's not like he was himself one minute and the next minute this monster, it was like he turned, like it was not something from the outside, but from inside, like he was shedding skin, just like that, shedding skin, and he turned. But I knew it was him. It was him all along. Only turned. I know it's crazy-sounding. He became what he really was, on the inside. Maybe just the bad part of him. Maybe there was a good part, too. But it was the bad that came to the surface. And the Awful Thing. Turning, not like what you said, but like when milk turns, or when a dog turns. It's still the dog, right? It's still the dog? Only, if the dog turns, you got to shoot it anyway, even though it's still the dog . . .*"

From Diego's studies of the rain forest peoples, he had come across a concept different from the European idea of metamorphosis, of something changing into something else. This other version of change, what Peter called *turning*, was more closely akin to manifestation, the Bringing Forth—an infestation within the skin, rising to the surface. And it was what Diego had been up all night with, trying to figure out, trying to put together, listening to the tapes of the two boys, what was *infesting* them. And the girl, she'd had it worse than the boys, she was (it was then rumored) not going to make it, and her grandmother was of a religious conviction that precluded medical attention for the girl. The grandmother, as Diego remembered from repeated phone calls to her house in San Francisco in the spring of 1981, was a religious fundamentalist who believed her grandchild was a sinner of the darkest sort and in need of multiple baptisms to restore her soul to the Godly path. Alison had gone through hell back then. But now, he knew . . .

He'd been wrong.

Why did I not see? The fever, the trances, the words, he'd been bringing it to the surface himself, he was helping to bring it forth. *I am the instrument of her turning. Peter was right to try and protect her from it.*

The demon needed fertility . . .

Teenaged boys and a girl. A demon who wanted to become more than its own monstrosity. A demon who was held at bay. A nest on the high desert: a town called Palmetto. Boys just reaching adolescence, just coming into their sexual beings; and Alison, a girl who was both beautiful and . . .

Pregnant.

That was the sin her grandmother had been upset about. That was what these boys had hidden all these years.

But she was not pregnant with an ordinary child.

Whatever it was that had gotten into her was within her. A piece of it.

Like a time bomb.

In the flesh.

9

After Alison left her apartment, she drove south on the freeway and was almost to work, when she decided to take a sick day. She pulled over at a twenty-four-hour Mini-Mart and called in to the animal hospital. She felt the smallest ache in her head, but when she had some coffee (her fourth cup of the morning) it apparently vanished. A cute man in his early twenties was pumping gas and asked her directions, but she could tell he wasn't really lost, only pretending to be so he could flirt. The coffee was good—in fact, it seemed like the best cup of coffee she'd ever had. Perhaps she was feeling better, after all. It had felt good to finally admit to Peter that she'd been seeing Diego. She slipped more change in the phone and dialed his office.

"Dr. Correa? Diego?"

"Reception," the woman on the other end said. "Dr. Correa stepped out for just a minute. Would you like to leave a message?"

Alison thought for a moment, then said, "I'm just returning his call. My name is Alison Chandler. Tell him . . . tell him I'll call him back in a bit."

She glanced over at the young man who had flirted with her. He was getting into his car.

The car itself made her shiver.

10

Peter went driving, and found himself by the park again, where he'd first seen the girl that looked like Wendy. He drove past the Sacrament of the Sacred Heart Church, and turned the corner to see the bungalow, but it had been badly burned, and most of the first floor was gone. He could not even imagine, in the abstract, a house fitting down that small alley; the burnt hull seemed more real than the bungalow had been. An old man sat on his stoop nearby and called out to Peter, "It was a sight, I'll tell you, a regular sight!"

Peter parked the car, and got out. He walked over to the old-timer. The old man was wrinkled and small, and his face could not have contained smaller eyes or a more surly-looking mouth.

"When did it burn?" Peter asked.

"That place is always on fire. Might as well be hell's gate. Burned again last night, my friend, Halloween, buncha kids set fire to what was left of it. Somebody or other been tryin' to burn that old place down for years and years, I'll tell you, yes. Beautiful sight, fire like that, almost went all the way up, I say *almost*, to the top of that palm tree. Big fire, but that place was ripe to burn, yes, I'll tell you, yes, ripe to burn for a long time."

"I hope nobody was hurt."

The old man looked queer, like he didn't know if he should tell anybody this part. "Well, I'll tell you." His voice became quieter. "Yes, didn't nobody come outta there. Girls and boys just hollerin' and whoopin'. You'da think they coulda jumped out with all the windows just off, but didn't none of them, yes, not a one. Strange thing, that young folks'd burn than breathe. But"—and the old guy chuckled and wheezed—"I s'pose it's a close call sometimes with some folks, a damn close call. Some a them's better off."

11

Alison surveyed the traffic. Normally, in non-rush hour it might only take her twenty minutes maximum to drive to Diego's office,

Douglas Clegg

but there was some accident on the freeway, so it would be at least an hour.

The freeway was packed and moving slowly, and her headache had begun pounding. Spasms of pain jabbed her in the groin, along her thighs, at the back of her ribs; she checked the mirror because her eyes hurt and she wondered if something was the matter with her contact lens. *Killer headache.* Her Honda sputtered and clunked along up the hillside, and she felt a pressure on her bladder and wondered which exit she could turn off at and find a rest room. The cars moved slowly, like a funeral procession. She was at the end of her rope; she wanted to scream at every single driver.

At the Mini-Mart, with the man flirting with her, she'd remembered something, and had hit the wall again. It was the young man's car: a Thunderbird, completely rundown, rusted out, but it brought back the silver of a memory to her: *she saw it parked on a desolate and empty road in the pre-dawn hours, packed with people, sitting upright, sitting still.*

Dead.

A Thunderbird full of dead bodies.

And then the car had begun moving.

Driven by a woman who could not possibly have been turning the steering wheel.

Bloodstain of a woman on a high yellow wall.

But this time, when Alison smacked against the wall, she'd chipped at it, just a mote of light shooting from it. She looked through the small opening to the other side, and the Thunderbird was there, its cargo of the dead, its driver trying to grin even while the skin fell from her face. The driver backed the car up in the dirt and then, in drive, floored it for the wall, heading right to where Alison peered through.

When the car hit the wall, it shattered into darkness.

Alison's head was bashing within itself full-throttle, like a tidal wave of blood crashing against her skull. Her nose dribbled with blood, and she even felt a sudden release of blood from between her legs. *What the hell is my body doing to me?*

But I remembered it, she said, *I remembered it. I broke the wall.*

What she remembered: she sat among the dead bodies of the Thunderbird and heard the whispering voices of the dead,

168

"whatifwhatifwhatifwhatif," and their reptilian wings beating against her face, and the sound of a dog panting above her in a dark cave.

On the packed freeway, heading into the city, Alison glanced up in the rearview mirror to see if her nose had stopped bleeding. It hadn't, but that's not what made her almost smash into the car in front of her.

It was her eyes.

She was shedding tears.

Tears of blood.

12

While Alison, her body wracked with pain, had the sense to pull off the freeway and turn around to drive home and take the sick day in bed and just maybe finally call a doctor or get Peter to take her to an emergency room, her husband had found the office of Diego Correa.

Diego had just returned from the bathroom down the hall, when the new secretary said, "A man barged in here. Should I call security?"

Diego went inside his office, and recognized Peter immediately. "Mr. Chandler," he said. "It's been many years, but you don't look substantially different. I'm glad you came by."

Peter was sitting at his desk, with the tape machine playing.

The voice of the past on the tape said, *"I didn't say demon, I said it was someone who thought he was possessed."*

Peter leaned back in the chair. "What is it you want?"

The voice on tape said, *"Do you believe in demons, Peter?"*

Diego walked over to his window and raised the blinds. The sun washed over the silver and gray landscape beyond. "I've been up all night, Peter. Your wife is in serious danger. I'm afraid I aided it, too."

The man's voice on the tape repeated, *"Do you believe in demons?"*

The boy's voice on the tape said, *"No."*

"But you do believe," Diego said. "You lied to me then, didn't you?"

Peter didn't respond.

"You lied to protect her."

Peter said nothing.

The voice on the tape said, *"Do you believe in the supernatural, Peter?"*

On tape, the boy said nothing.

Peter, at the desk, shut the tape off. "I want you to leave her alone. That's all."

"What was it that happened to her, Peter? The year after Palmetto. Something about her body, the breakdown of language and memory. It wasn't just witnessing the murders, was it? It was something else."

"If I tell you, will you get out of our lives?"

Diego turned away from the window. "Before I make any promises, did you know about her fevers? How severe they are? She's lied to me about seeing doctors—I can tell. She's not a very good liar. Why is she so scared of doctors? What is it about her body that she is so terrified of? Because it's her life you need to protect, Peter, not her fears. If the fevers go any higher she could suffer brain damage. Is that how you want to protect her, by letting her go mad or killing every chance she has for a happy life?"

Peter was silent. Diego could hear the ticking of the clock down the hall.

Finally, Peter said, "If I tell you, you have to swear that you will not use it for a book or hurt her with it in any way. You will have to swear that if you stick your nose into this that you won't go on some stupid talk show and yap about it just to hawk books."

"I am past doing that. I won't hurt her, I promise. I swear."

"No," Peter said, "I can't—can't trust you. She'd be *dead* if . . ."

"I won't hurt her," Diego reaffirmed, "but it's already begun."

Peter glanced up at him.

"She's turning, Peter, turning fast. The body inside her is rejecting her body. It's like cancer, isn't it? It takes over cell by cell. You've got it, too, don't you? Peter, I do believe in demons, I do believe in what you told me when you were sixteen. I have driven up to that town on my own several times, and I saw what was left of it. Whatever force could do that to a town, do you think you could stop it by pretending it never happened? Somehow you and Alison and the other boy, Charlie, were immune to it to some extent. But you know why, don't you? You know why you're here and the rest of that town is not, don't you?"

"I thought this wouldn't happen, it was supposed to stop it, what we did."

"What did you do?"

"The Awful Thing," Peter whispered. He sounded like a little boy. As if beneath his skin, there lurked that sixteen-year-old, only so scared, he might as well have been four.

"What was the awful thing?"

Peter looked him in the eyes. "Than had told us about it. About what would happen if we didn't. How it would keep going, and not just in Palmetto, but everywhere. Old Bonyface, he knew about demons, and the job wasn't done until we took the Awful Thing from her."

"What was it?" Diego asked. "What did you do that was so terrible?"

Peter bit the edge of his lower lip. He mumbled something.

"You what?" Diego asked, leaning forward.

13

Alison had to sit in her car for half an hour on the off-ramp of the Ventura Freeway before she had worked up the strength to drive the surface streets the rest of the way home. She was alternately freezing and boiling up, and she was too scared to look in the rearview mirror again to see if her eyes had stopped bleeding. Her hands slid along the steering wheel with the sweat just pouring out of her skin. Finally, she parked alongside her apartment complex and, using what little strength she had, managed to get from the car to her apartment without falling down. Her stomach hurt terribly, and her menstrual flow had not stopped. *God, just let me die*. She dropped her keys three times before finally holding them steady enough to unlock the door. She didn't even have the energy to call out for Peter, although, in her out-of-focus vision, she thought he was standing there in the living room waiting for her. He was dressed in a sweatshirt and jeans, which would've struck her as odd if she didn't have the jabbing pains and the crunching headache. She was too dizzy—she needed to get to a chair quickly or she'd fall, she was sure, she'd faint, it was that bad—

Peter approached her; she realized it *wasn't* Peter at all, but someone else from beyond her wall, and the man in the sweatshirt said, "Where is it?" while she fell to the foor. She saw his face and tried to scream as loud as she could but nothing came from her throat.

PART TWO: WAKING DREAMS IN NEW YORK CITY

Chapter Twenty-four
Deadrats

1

Dirty, filthy, said the thing with the red eyes, lurking there in the dark corner. *Still here, my friend, still waiting, and I can wait a long, long time to be let out. And you will let me out, my boy, you will let me out because you've been very bad and you need to take your medicine. Look, look where I've gnawed a hole in your heart, in your brain, like cheese, just, nibble, nibble, nibble. Just us rats, you and me, just us rats.*

It was a dream, but it wasn't, and the man who should've been sleeping had his eyes wide open.

His name was Charlie Urquart.

2

"Just look at him," Paula whispered as if the man lying on the mattress on the other side of the two-way mirror could hear her. There were wires running all along his hands and face and chest, but she was not even watching the EEG. Nothing to watch. What fascinated her were his eyes: open and staring blankly. He might've been dead. No alpha or beta activity, no nothing. She hadn't believed it when she'd seen it before, and she still could not comprehend what it might mean. Not just to science or to mankind, but to her.

Her associate, Megan Richmond, chuckled, "Everytime I do look at him, I think of how big that grant's getting."

Douglas Clegg

"No jokes, come on, but have you ever seen this before? It defies everything I was ever taught in graduate school. It's practically living proof of the Jett-Gerrish Hypothesis—and everybody thought *that* was off the wall." Paula tried to keep the excitement out of her voice: she was twenty-six and didn't figure on completing her graduate studies in sleep research for a few more years. This would be just the boost she needed. The Jett-Gerrish Hypothesis had been considered science-fiction, or at best, an imaginative outgrowth of the field of parapsychology. Jett-Gerrish had studied an entire group of survivors from the death camps of Germany who had apparently stopped sleeping for all intents and purposes for four years, but whose hallucinations took them back into the camp even when they were free—so that they had never really escaped, at least not in their minds. Seven of the group committed suicide, and the rest gradually regained their abilities to sleep and dream normally. But Jett-Gerrish hypothesized that, given certain traumas from the past, a human being will go beyond waking life and live as if in a dream, with no need to use sleep as a bridge to get to that dream. It was a survival mechanism.

But this one, this man.

He was a one in a trillion find. Even if he couldn't prove Jett-Gerrish, that hypothesis might be a jumping-off point into whole new areas of dream and sleep studies.

She kept her face taut, professional, no goofy grin that longed to emerge. More than anything in the world, she wanted the money and the time for research on her own terms.

This man lying on the table was going to give that to her without even being aware of it. "He doesn't know it," Paula said. "But he's going to make history."

"Is that what you see in him?" Megan asked.

"I don't get you."

"Ph.D awarded to the Nobel prize winner Paula Quinn?"

"Cheap shot," Paula said, but it was partially true. How often would a graduate student come across this kind of case? She could've gone her whole life without coming across an individual who defied every rule in the book. It had been what Paula called her "spy network" that had helped her find this man. A friend from her undergrad years at Fordham, Griff Hornaby, had called her directly from court to tell her about this pro bono case that she might find interesting. The guy had assaulted an old man on the street, but had been in some kind of a psychotic seizure. The old man dropped the charges soon enough, and Paula had come across the most unique case of sleep deprivation she had ever encountered. She knew from that first meeting that this was her way of getting beyond years of dues-paying to the academic establishment. She would, at best, begin a career of fascinating research, and at worst, get a book out of the experience.

Megan clucked her tongue. "Maybe Ackerman's jealous because you'll get his tenure. You are now unofficially a threat to the assholes-that-be."

But Paula couldn't keep her eyes off her subject. *What had been going on behind those eyes?* "Just look," she said, nodding toward the glass.

"I'm looking, I'm looking. It's something. I just don't know what. How long ago did you interview him?"

"Ten minutes. Another Ken Russell movie. Lots of breasts and penises and acid flashbacks and no sense whatsoever. But there're things emerging—in the dreams. Like the blank spot. The girl. Some girl. I knew there'd be a pattern if I interviewed him often enough. That trauma to his head—he was in an accident as a teenager. So it's some kind of seizure, the scar showed up on the scan, but it's like he's always dreaming."

Megan looked at her with skepticism. "Dreaming? Or hallucinating? You sure there's no history of drug abuse?"

Paula shrugged. "I believe him when he says no. Marijuana and speed in his teens, and beer now and then. I think he's being honest with me, too. I think he's trying to fill in the blanks. Think of what this could mean. Think of it."

"Yeah, now millions of people can lose more sleep."

"You heard the tape. It's like he dreams when he's awake and when he closes his eyes . . ."

"Nothing."

"Nothing, but how can there be nothing? No brain waves, no REM. It's like downtime on a computer. He just isn't there, but it's not sleep . . ."

"And it's not insomnia. And it has nothing to do with Jett-Gerrish, you ask me."

"No, it does, and it *is* some kind of insomnia. You don't just shut *down* to go to sleep."

"Maybe some people do, and nobody's slept with them enough to know it."

Paula felt her face go red. "Thanks. Thanks a lot. And I *haven't*, not that it's any of your business, anyway."

"I just want to prepare you for what they're already starting to say behind your back. And if I were you, I wouldn't keep throwing around Jett-Gerrish, because she was a nut and they'll lump you in there, too. You're swimming with sharks now."

"As if I care," Paula said. "This guy is all mine, and I'm going to show Ackerman and his goons for the stuffed shirts they are. This guy's dreams are going to make mine come true."

3

Transcript from the taped interview Subject 08, SR—36, Paula Quinn

Q: Describe for me what you're seeing now.

A: Lizards running, they've got paws like a lion's . . . and great cones and pyramids rising out of bubbling mudpots, the sky is so yellow, and smoky, like a sulphur fog, and there's a house over there, just beyond that ridge, a hand, a hand is coming up from the swampy ground, pushing through these wriggling masses of . . . what? Mosquito larvae? Frog's eggs? I can't tell, but the fingers are coming up. But the swamp—frozen—it's frozen solid, a sheet of ice, all around me, ice, and the fingers still groping, trying to break the ice, and children are skating over there beyond the trees, but the running lizards have them, grasping the kids as they try to skate away, and they're not lizards anymore, they're, oh, my God, dragons, and they're devouring the kids. But no, they're not, I can't see them now because the fingers keep wriggling.

Q: Can you smell anything?

A: Rotten eggs. Like it just rained rotten eggs.

Q: You see rotten eggs?

A: No, I just smell them. It's like a bad fart.

Here's how it works:

Each package will carry a FREE 10-DAY EXAMINATION privilege. At the end of that time, if you decide to keep your books, simply pay the low invoice price of $11.25, no shipping or handling charges added. HOME DELIVERY IS ALWAYS FREE! There's no minimum number of books to buy, and you may cancel at any time.

AND AS A CHARTER MEMBER, YOUR FIRST THREE-BOOK SHIPMENT IS TOTALLY FREE! IT'S A BARGAIN YOU CAN'T BEAT!

✂ CUT HERE

Q: Great. Can you touch anything?

A: No. It's more like a movie.

Q:Does the hand frighten you?

A: Not really. It's disgusting, with all that gunky stuff hanging from the fingers.

Q: What do you make of what you're seeing?

A: It's just a dream.

Q: Do you believe that?

A: Why not? I know it's crazy. I'm surprised you haven't locked me up yet.

Q: You mean for what you did?

A: Well, I attacked the guy.

Q: He wasn't hurt too badly.

A: Lady, you must have a pretty darn good lawyer.

Q: Best in town.

A: Well, dream's over. Is that recorder on?

Q: Does it bother you?

A: I guess not. It can't be used as evidence, can it?

Q: No.

A: And you're not a doctor so you can't put me away.

Q: Right.

A: You got plans for tonight?

Q: No, Charles, I don't.

A: Charles sounds snooty. My friends call me Charlie. You up for maybe dinner or something?

Q: Now who's asking the questions?

4

Charlie Urquart at thirty-six was almost completely bald, but had a disarming smile and deep blue eyes that were both compelling and distant—a lethal combination for Paula Quinn. *You always go for men who are enigmas*, she thought the evening when she sat across from him at Cafe Bonnelle.

He drank hot chocolate, rubbing his hands against the warm mug. "I love cocoa," he told her. "Always have. This chocolate truffle cake is a killer. You sure you've got enough money for this?"

177

"Yes, Charlie." Paula had trouble looking him in the eyes—he had such a direct gaze. She felt self-conscious, and wondered if she'd crossed the border between helping a patient and using him. The table was a small square of bleached wood; her side was neat and tidy, and his side already had a thin layer of crumbs and spilled cocoa over it. The waitresses wanted to close up the place—it was getting late—but they would have to wait. Paula wanted to see if he would open up to her on his own.

He smiled. His whole face lit up with that smile, so that he looked almost like a kid getting his first car. "Well, I mean, it's been an expensive evening. I don't usually go to nice restaurants, and I never go somewhere else for dessert. Pardon me for saying it, but you've got nice legs. I know that some women don't like getting that kind of compliment, but I've got to say it. I see women get in and out of my cab all day and night, and I notice things like legs."

Paula blushed. She returned her glance to the crumbs around his plate; she was afraid he'd be able to see right through her, and she wasn't even sure what she was feeling. Ten minutes before, she might've confessed that she was going to develop a friendship with this man in order to study him, but now she wondered if she didn't just *like* him. She was so bad at making friends—they had only come through work. "How long have you been driving your taxi?"

He dropped his fork onto the plate, startling her. But he didn't sound angry when he said, "More interview. Why don't I ask you some things. Okay?"

She nodded. "Fair enough."

"Is this your usual technique? Look at me, please?"

Paula steeled herself for his intense gaze. It frightened her a little, because there was so much power behind those eyes. But when she looked at him, he was grinning like a puppy. She giggled nervously, *"What?"*

He rubbed the palms of his hands together just like he was scheming. "Well, okay, you know, here's this guy, a cabbie, beats some old man up on the corner of Thirty-third and Third, lands in court, you come down and psychoanalyze him and then take him out on a date, and then you both end up right around the corner from, as they say, the scene of the crime. If there're things you want to know, just be direct. Okay?"

You Come When I Call You

"Oh, Charlie," she sighed, wondering if he could read her thoughts as well as it seemed. "I'm not really psychoanalyzing you, but otherwise I guess you've summed me up." She took a sip of cappuccino. She put the cup down nervously, certain that he would notice that her hand was shaking ever-so-slightly.

He saw the shiver in her hand, and reached over to steady it. His hands were warm. "I won't hurt you."

"I'm not afraid of that." She felt his warmth. She was more afraid of herself than she was of him.

"I still can't believe I hurt that old guy. I mean, I knew I was doing it, but I thought it was a dream." He took his hand off hers and wiped perspiration from his forehead. "Maybe I need a shrink, I don't know. Don't get me wrong. It's okay what you're doing. All this interview garbage . . . I don't exactly have a full schedule."

"You sure?"

"Yeah. Why, you want to take notes or something? Got that tape recorder?" He peered around the table. "Got a video camera in that monstrous purse of yours?"

"No cameras. But I could jot some thing down. If it's all right with you?"

"Whatever."

She reached into her purse and pulled out a notepad and pen. She flipped back the cover of the pad and jotted down the date. "What would you usually do on a Tuesday night?"

"Back to the interview. Okay. Well, usually I would just drive around all night, you know, for fares. I read, too."

"Like what?"

"Like 'read any good ones lately?' Okay. Let's see, I read a little Nietzsche last night."

"Now you're making fun of me."

"Huh? No—what do you—you think a cab driver in New York's going to be illiterate? I don't have the best education in the world, but I've been making sure I read a book a week for at least, oh, the last ten, twelve years."

"Did you really read Nietzsche?"

"You bet. I think a lot of what he says is crap, but it's got its fascination for me. Like horror stories."

"Why horror stories?"

179

He sighed, exasperated. Paula wondered if she was being tedious. Was she treating him like an idiot? "Well, you know, the old ones like *Dracula*. It's got what you'd call a 'hidden agenda.' At least for me. It's about fighting the unknown. Like if Dracula was cancer and I had cancer, its about fighting cancer. But it's also about wondering if cancer is all that unnatural a thing. Is cancer, or Dracula, really evil? Sounds crazy, and I know I'm not saying exactly what I mean to say—it's the chocolate rush. And don't look at me funny, because I don't have cancer. No wait, I don't mean that. It's like my theory about Adam and Eve, you know how in the Garden they're not supposed to eat of the fruit of the Tree of Knowledge, and they go for it. Well, most people, whether they look at that story symbolically or literally—most people agree it's about this act that explains why, you know, say the world isn't always a great place to be. But the way I see it— and this may sound crazy—what the story is telling you is that definite boundaries of good and evil exist for us only when we chomp down on that fruit, but the real thing is that things are things, they are what they are, they aren't evil or good, they just are. It's Popeye saying 'I yam what I yam,' and it's like none of us has to bite into that apple, but when we do, expect the world to go haywire. God, how the hell do I bring this back around to *Dracula*?"

"Maybe by saying that vampires aren't evil?"

"I don't quite mean that. I mean, I guess, that like Popeye, they are what they are. In *Dracula*, the vampire's the enemy, but one of the women in it *becomes* the enemy, and then her friends have to kill her. Because, you know, she's not one of our crowd, anymore, she doesn't play by our rules. She's just changed, she's just gone from one form of existence into another—that is if you haven't bitten into that apple, to mess some metaphors together. Hey, I'm just a cabbie, so what the hell do I know?" Charlie grinned broadly and glanced around the cafe to make sure he hadn't been speaking too loudly.

Paula grinned, too. "Usually when I have dinner with a man, we don't end up talking about Dracula and the Garden of Eden and Nietzsche."

"What do you end up doing?" His gaze came back and locked into hers, and was so direct and honest, it made her flinch. He had asked it as if he were quite innocent about what went on between men and women.

Paula had to look down at her cup again. "So you read and you drive. Do you have family around here?"

"No, but you know what they say: Manhattan is the island of orphans."

"Your parents are dead?"

He closed his eyes, tensing, then opened them again. "I should never have mentioned your legs; the conversation's gotten way too personal. So you want me for your study? You've got me on tape and I've seen that sloppy notebook of yours. Is that really a professional sleep researcher's yellow pad?"

"These are my rough notes, I filter them through academic and scientific sensibilities only after I've figured them out for my own satisfaction. Sounds like good BS, doesn't it? Look, I won't make you do anything you don't want, it's only if you're interested. I think you'd benefit, too."

"So you want to turn me into a lab rat. Do I get paid?"

"Until a grant comes through I don't have a lot, just what my family'll help out with. If I can convince someone in the department, maybe . . ."

"I was joking. I don't need to get paid. I can still drive? Good. There's something about driving around New York all night long that makes me feel glad to be alive. You think you'll cure me?"

"Do you think you're ill, Charlie?"

He looked down at the table. Like he was collecting his thoughts. Like he was withdrawing from the real world. "No," he said. "I don't think I'm ill. But I do know what I am."

"Quit being so harsh on yourself, whatever this disorder is, it probably can be worked out."

"I know what I am," Charlie Urquart repeated. "I'm cursed."

5

Paula Quinn/Notes on Charles Geoffrey Urquart, III

Two weeks and already great strides. No biological irregularities, nothing organic to indicate tissue damage. Sleep center completely destroyed? Is this a hoax just to get out of an assault charge? But

Douglas Clegg

how the hell does someone stay up for six days in a row and then shut down for four hours with no REM, none of the usual phenomena associated with sleep, and then go on for another four days before shutting down again? No stimulants. Boredom not even a factor. Is he beyond psychotic? Am I in over my head? If I can just keep this a secret from Ackerman and Milton, and if Megan'll keep her mouth shut, maybe I can come up with something. This may be out of my league. Like I'm blindfolded, but I can't let the department in on this completely. Fudged some reports, but what did Ackerman ever do for me? He would take this over and take all the credit like every other academic in this place. Already changed advisers twice, never get my Ph.D before I'm thirty if I don't get this show on the road. Come on, Charlie, let's get to the bottom of this! Subject responds to affection, simple kindness, like he'd never received it before. Rode with him in his cab last night and he said nothing the whole time. Ended up in the Village, through Hell's Kitchen, all these places, but no talk. Has something in his money box, talks about it, but won't show me. Must be a gun— talks about his protection. But not much. Scared me a little, but I don't think, if he has a gun, that it's loaded. Started (finally!) talking nonstop from 2 AM to 7 PM—manic? Rambles on and on about books and theories about existence. Concerned with mortality, thoughts always turning to death, illness and cures, laying on of hands, casting out demons, forms of existence. Sex, too, but not as sex, per se, but as a cataclysm, as a destroyer of personality. Joked about the Big Orgasm at the end of the universe. The way teenagers talk. Conflict between good and evil—doesn't think there's a difference, he says, because it is all relative. Something is only evil to us (humans) if it puts us lower on the food chain, but, he asks, is it really evil? Is disease evil? or death? or man-eating sharks? or demons? (Why demons? why does he keep saying demons, and yet he also professes that he doesn't believe in them?) Waking dreams, his hallucinations while he's conscious (but this study may turn our normal thoughts on consciousness upside down), seem to be heavily influenced by surrealistic art and poetry. Yeats, even a Prufrockism (the scuttling crab in the dream of 10–11—see dreamnotes, as well as the singing mermaids) so Eliot gets thrown in, Goya's witches, Dali's melting watches and ants crawling, some Lewis Carroll (dreamnotes 10–13: baby turning into pig), some classical literature (dreamnotes 10–16: Dido's self-immolation before Aeneas, although maybe I'm reading too much into it). Sexuality heavily emphasized, as evidenced by his physiological response to the waking dreams (rapid heartbeat, facial blushing, penile tumescence). Horny for hours immediately after dreams. God, if Ackerman ever got a hold of these he'd have my head. Teenage boys figure in these dreams, too, as well as humiliation before group like some fraternity initiation. Blind spot in his dreams—unwilling to tell me everything he's seeing. Something there. Maybe an area of his brain destroyed, but undetected by current testing procedures. What is the blind spot? What is he not telling me from the waking dreams?

6

Charles Urquart in his own words, on tape

Paula, so I brought this thing home and now I'm talking into it. I'm not currently dreaming. You want to know more about me. Fine. I came to New York when I was twenty-three. I had gotten involved in some things out West when I was a teenager that I'm not too proud of, and I ended up in a sort of work camp and then a detention home and then a foster home and finally just moved on, and then I decided to get as far away from all that as possible as soon as I could. Don't ask me about that time, I don't even pretend it was real. Hitchhiked across country, doing odd jobs on the road, and sleeping in horse-trailers—it was better than the foster home I'd been in. Arrived in Port Authority with about ten bucks, slept in the streets that summer, but was smart enough to go to the Upper West side, where people threw couches out onto the sidewalks. Had my driver's license, and started working for this guy with a gypsy cab outfit. New York's the right place for me, most of the time. I guess you could say I was shell-shocked and I wanted to be somewhere where everything was controlled and artificial and manmade, and what better place than here?

What else? How in heck am I going to fill up an entire tape with this? So after I came to New York, cabbed it, put some money aside—lived in Jersey City for the first four years. I got this other job driving a truck for Nabisco, paid the rent and got into the city as much as possible. Usually took the PATH to the Village and just wandered around. I felt pretty good, and safe, too, just walking around alone but surrounded by all these people. It was so different than the place I used to live, where you know just about everybody and they know everything about you. In Manhattan, just blocks full of people of all types wandering around. I guess you could say I became a peoplewatcher. It was great, also I started reading, too. I got hold of a place in Hell's Kitchen—luckily my rent's stayed low. And then landed with a more legitimate outfit, cabbing. A guy I knew who was some opera singer—he hung out in the Polish place I used to eat at—was quitting driving because he had gotten on at some company for the season, and he sort of got me in through the backdoor with his friends, and that's it. A bona fide New York driver. I tended to meet a lot of hookers as a driver, and I actually dated one of them and tried to change her evil ways but to no avail. Nice time trying, though. You live in New York long enough, you realize no one in the world is normal anymore, at least it doesn't seem that way, and nobody ever really changes. Not really. They just become more of themselves.

The waking dreams, they started a couple of days ago—at least the really vivid ones, I mean, it's not like I never had nightmares or nothing. I've had this strange sleep pattern for awhile, but I'm not sure how long. Maybe since I've been driving. Maybe earlier. My memory of the last ten years or so is sort of skewered, because my days and nights have been all fouled up for awhile. The waking dreams don't really scare me much. I guess it's like what a drug addict might call an acid flashback, except I didn't ever drop any acid in my time, although I used to smoke dope and take Black Beauties sometimes and I know they find out stuff about that everyday. Usually it feels like I just step off the end of the world and land in another one, although I notice if I'm driving and have one of these dreams, my body takes over and pulls the cab to the curb so I never end up killing myself—although a few passengers have jumped ship at that point. It's like there's some kind of thin skin draped over the world, or in front of my eyes and I can see the dream, and I can see *through* the dream to the rest of the world. Beating up the guy at Thirty-third and Third was something else— I thought it was in the dream I was doing that. Usually, like I said, my physical body does its usual shtick. But in this waking dream I'm fighting a monster, although . . . um . . . can't remember what this monster looks like, and the next thing I know I'm clobbering this old guy out in front of a market. I felt bad, which is why it was me who called the cops and the ambulance. Enough said. I'm happy he dropped the charges. Thanks, Paula for that. Saved my neck. Sleep hits me differently than the dreams, I just conk out. It's like anesthesia, though, because I conk out and then come to and I don't feel like there's been a passage of more than maybe two seconds, like I blinked. I worried for awhile that maybe I've got a tumor, but I think I know the reason.

Because in one of the waking dreams, Paula, it came to me, it came for me, it called out to me.

It . . .

Subject switched off tape recorder at this point.

7

Dreamnotes/subject: Urquart/October

10-22

7 AM/Subject dreamed while walking down Park Avenue/dream: being chased by dogs into an open grave, lying in grave, dogs above foaming and gnashing teeth, subject saw his mother throwing a Tupperware party, and dogs were invited and bought plastic bowls and played games, subject's mother eaten by dogs, then dogs pretend to be subject's mother/duration: over in ten minutes or so.

6:30 PM/Subject dreamed while at traffic light on Hudson/world was ocean, cabs were *crabs*, mermaids singing from rocks, moray eels grabbing fish. Mention of something seen that subject can't describe, white space, a blind spot/duration: approx. three minutes.

10 PM/Subject says sky becomes curtain, draping down, then circus tent, and a magician is on stage at circus and calls subject up to be assistant. Magician smells like urine. Magician has hypnotized woman on stage, woman begins floating. Subject watches as audience claps. Magician begins to wave wand over audience, audience begins screaming, metamorphosing into animals, squealing, bark-

185

Douglas Clegg

ing, mewling, running wild. Magician has cages at all exits. Subject's arms become wings, and to escape, subject flies upward but is caught in circus tent, and down below him the floating woman is not floating but is being lowered into a grave (a very long grave) and subject is standing above ground, holding his mother's hand, only it's not his mother, but again, the blind spot/duration: twenty minutes or more.

10-25

Between 2–3 AM/subject watched woman give birth at street corner, baby that came out was piglet, squealing, man came by— butcher—with butcher knife to cut umbilical cord, but butchered squealing pig in front of onlookers, sky yellow, ground tippled like earthquake/duration:?

10 AM/subject surrounded by gang in alley, each gang member had wings (like birds? angels?), razors in hand, approaching, then strong wind blows them away, and dropped razors become serpents slashing each other, smells of orange blossoms, smells of gasoline. Ants crawling across "trees" made out of body parts— hands, feet, noses, and yes, even penises. One tree with a large hole in center, and some animal living in hole although subject doesn't explain further. Again, perhaps blind spot/duration: 2 minutes.

8 PM/subject sees groups of witches, naked, old hags, dancing around a man with an enormous penis between his legs and horns on his head, and the man is pouring juice (why juice? Subject says he doesn't know why, but just knows it was juice) on all the hags "anointing" them, and then in the midst of all this, here comes that trusty old blind spot. What is it he's not telling? Does he really not remember what it is, what moves in the center of these visions?/duration:?

10-26

Noon/subject watches beautiful woman about to jump off third floor of building, flying in midair, lover down below ready to catch her, sees she is flying, turns back on her, woman's arms catches fire, spreads down and across her body until she is completely burning, still her lover doesn't turn, she is screaming, burning in midair/subject watches until woman turns to ashes and the ashes float down around him like snow, and the ashes build up into heaps and drifts and cars wreck in black snowdrifts, while teenagers (all boys) chase after something down the road which becomes an empty hole/duration: perhaps half an hour(!)

9 PM/subject sees a man walking his dog, dog has same face as man, then looks back to man's face, and it is dog's face, and it is a dog (a Shar-Pei?) walking a man on a leash, subject doesn't see humor at all/duration: less than a minute.

11:30 PM/subject in bar drinking, sees skeletons "through the skins" of all the patrons, skeletons moving, skulls decayed, again crawling ants (red ants) all over skeletons, ants coming out of drinks, pouring from bottles. Then skeletons completely taken over (eaten?) by ants and ants make up "bridges" around skeletons. A man with hands for feet comes in from outside and says, "We have found you," and subjects sees that he too is made up completely of ants/duration: four minutes.

10-27

No dreams, no black out "rests." Subject irritable, restless.

Dreamnotes becoming useless—subject is tired of telling them. Becoming very guarded in his words. Pressure must be lessened.

Cool it, Paula, let him come to you with this stuff, don't always be pumping for information.

8

Paula Quinn/Notes on Charles Geoffrey Urquart, III

Tonight I'm going over to Hell's Kitchen to see Charlie.

I've been trying to finagle an invitation for weeks, but that's the one part of his life he's been keeping pretty private. I don't blame him, but I still think it would help to see how *he* organizes his world. I think I'm going to do something completely against myself, although he's been coming on to me since the sessions began so I know he won't be unhappy. I actually think he's falling in love with me. Ackerman would roast my ass if he found out, but I think I can handle this so there's no unpleasantness. I wouldn't want to hurt Charlie, either. Maybe I won't go through with it. Maybe I'll chicken out, or he won't even be interested. If I could only figure out a way of getting to him.

Chapter Twenty-five
Charlie's Living Room

1

"Paula," Charlie said, opening the door to his apartment, "I didn't think you'd drop by."

She stood there, feeling as if she were shivering in the rain. She hadn't expected to feel dread at the threshold of his apartment. "Sorry. I tried calling you, but your line's been busy. May I . . . come in?"

"It's a wreck," he said, shrugging. "But it's my own wreck."

The apartment was a one-room studio, and it *was* a wreck: dirty laundry in clumps around the floor, dishes piled high in the sink, the kitchen itself a disaster area with the shower stall across from the sink and an actual water closet next to the shower. "Combination kitchen/bathroom, no real aesthetic sense, but each floor of this building used to be one long continuous apartment, so when they were all divided, ratholes like this one became dispensable."

But the living area, with his small single bed pushed up into the window alcove, newspapers tossed on the floor as if by a wind, and books stacked one atop the other (she noticed that most of them were library books that had never been returned), empty bottles along the windowsill, some stacked between books on a low shelf—none of this was as bizarre as what was on the walls.

"Did you do all this?" she asked, and before he could answer, she added, "It's beautiful."

But she was thinking: *No wonder he is so plagued by waking dreams. Who could sleep in this prison?*

Charlie Urquart had papered the walls with posters and magazine cutouts, a collage of human beings, all staring at him. Rock stars, models, the President of the United States, the Queen of England, naked women from the pages of *Playboy* and *Penthouse*, naked couples from even more lurid pornographic magazines, men and women from L. L. Bean catalogs, from Neiman-Marcus catalogs, covers from hardcover novels, a poster of Caravaggio's *Eros*, a print of Botticelli's *Primavera*, several prints of Madonnas and babies—*all* intertwined on the wall, looking over each other's shoulders, watching Charlie, and now watching her, too.

Her first impulse was to run out of the room, down the five flights of narrow staircase, back to the street, and scream for a cab.

But Paula Quinn rarely acted on impulse.

2

They ended up in bed.

Paula Quinn had no way of justifying this to anyone, let alone herself, except that it might further her research, as well as allow Charlie to trust her. She genuinely liked him, as a person, in spite of the oddities, but then, any man she'd ever gone out with in Manhattan had come with a disproportionate share of weirdness. She thought Charlie was attractive in a rather ordinary way; she was lonely, and he was certainly alone. The ramifications of sleeping with him scared her, aside from the ethical impurity it represented. Charlie was, in some way, insane, and as Megan Richmond had been telling her for the past three weeks, she was playing with fire if she thought she could handle Charlie Urquart. She *was* out of her league on this case.

After basic small talk, a couple of drinks straight from a bottle of bourbon, and the usual walking around the issue, they were in each other's arms and it had all begun. Perhaps it had been the two martinis she'd had before she arrived—to work her courage up. Perhaps it was a feeling of needing this. Perhaps it was just something she had trouble admitting to herself:

She was falling for one of her subjects.

Paula Quinn was attracted to Charlie Urquart despite his strangeness, his total lack of charm, his messy apartment, and perhaps most importantly to her, the feeling of dread she got when she was close to him. She both wanted him and wanted to run from him.

Instead, she got in bed with him, and it began.

3

Sex was enjoyable if mechanical, but she didn't expect to enjoy it—all those pictures on the wall watching her as she disrobed clumsily seemed to whisper that this was a public event, not a private one. She felt that at any moment one of the people in the photos would start whistling and clapping. Charlie seemed pretty eager to get her clothes off, and then sighed as he looked at her naked.

"I'm naked but you're not," she said. "That doesn't seem terribly fair."

"I'm a little self-conscious," he chuckled.

"You could turn the light down."

"No, I like having the lights on." He grinned like a little boy, and then kissed her left breast. "You know I've got scars."

"I didn't know."

"The major one's on my left leg, above the knee. I got bit once."

He undid his pants, stepping out of them. She probably wouldn't have noticed the marks on his thigh if he hadn't told her, or she would've thought nothing of them. Skin had been grafted just above the knee. "What bit you?"

"Mad dog."

"That must've hurt."

"It's hard to remember pain. Sometimes I try, but it doesn't seem as bad as, say, the last time I came down with the flu."

"What's that?" she asked, pointing to another scar, just below his knee—it was less a scar than an indentation.

"Oh, I always forget that one, it was so long ago, it's practically a birthmark. I was about twelve. Maybe eleven. I was playing around my father's workshop and he got mad and wanted to teach me how dangerous his power tools were. He was a smart man. He taught me all right. I learned all about power tools that day."

"You used one the wrong way and cut yourself?"

"No, nothing like that. To teach me the lesson, my father put his chainsaw against my leg and just turned it on for a second. Funny, huh? He had an entire routine. See, I'd do something, wrong, in this case, fool around with his work tools. The first time he'd say, 'That's *one*,' and the second time, 'That's *two*,' and finally, you know, '*That's three*,' and that's when he'd get down to business. So he took this chainsaw and put it on my leg, switched it on—for just a second—made this cut, I screamed, and he told me, you know, 'See what you get for messing with things you don't know about,' and 'I gave you two chances before this.' Good old Pop."

She didn't mention the small round scars on his chest and arms, but he saw her looking at them as he took his shirt off.

Sometimes I think I hear him whenever I screw up, saying, 'That's *one*.' "

He kissed each of her breasts.

4

"They bother me." She said this after the great act itself was over, and they both lay there, looking at anything but each other.

"The . . . scars."

"No, the walls."

He glanced around his room. "Oh."

"Don't you think it's even slightly creepy?"

"I guess so. Nothing drives me crazier, though, than a blank wall."

"Do you think there's a correlation between your waking dreams and the pictures?"

"I think," he said, leaning back on his elbows, scanning the faces on the wall, "the pictures keep her away."

"Who?"

"The woman who took away my sleep."

"Is she real?"

"You mean, is she in my dreams or did I know her? Both. And she's *not* my mother."

"I'm not trying to psychoanalyze you, Charlie. Just curious. Just want to know what you're thinking about."

"What do you think of during sex?"

Paula blinked. "I don't know. I guess I don't think a lot during sex."

"I think about *her*. No matter who I do it with, I'm always doing it with *her*."

"Thanks."

"I can't help it. I don't try to think of her, it just turns out that way."

191

"Who is she?"

"She's someone I was . . . involved with. That, as they say, accounts for my troubled youth. I tried to kill her."

"You *tried*? Did you?"

"Kill her? No. That would've been too easy. You look relieved."

"Well, I mean, the thought of sleeping with a murderer isn't high on my list of things to do."

Charlie smiled. "I guess not. I guess I should call a cab for you, ho-ho."

"I can't spend the night?"

"You want to?"

"Sure."

"You're crazier than I am. You some kind of masochist? Wait—I know, you don't believe me, do you?"

"I believe you, Charlie, I'm just tired and I like you."

"I like you, too, Paula."

"If I fall asleep, will you lie here with me and pretend to sleep?"

"You bet," he whispered, nuzzling against her.

Looking up at the Madonna and child on the ceiling, she said, "And protect me from them, too, will you?"

5

She awoke an hour or two later. He watched her. He had intense blue eyes that both disturbed her and entranced her. He was beautiful and ugly at the same time, and for a moment she felt like he was enchanted, the way the Beast was in Beauty and the Beast. He was enchanted and cursed and wild . . .

She was about to say something, but realized by the way his eyes moved that he was experiencing a waking dream. *Damn and double damn, why didn't I bring my tape recorder?* His face had gone chalk-white, his eyes twitching rapidly. He rose up and stood over her, his hands in tight fists. Drool spattered across her face—it dribbled on her neck. She wiped it away.

"Where are you, Charlie?" she asked. "What are you seeing?"

Maybe I can get to my purse, I've got my notebook there, I can jot some of what he says down and then sit down with him later for more recall. She sat up, slipping her legs to the floor.

He pushed her back onto the bed.

"You cunt," Charlie Urquart growled. "What do you want from me?"

Chapter Twenty-six
That's One

1

Charlie awoke suddenly, and found that he was behind the steering wheel of his cab. He slapped himself awake, and then downed a Coke to make sure he wouldn't fall asleep at the wheel again any time soon. It was 4 A.M., and he was driving on the Upper West Side without stopping for fares. Without destination. He just needed to clear his head. The early morning was good for that, not much traffic, at least down side streets, half the city was a graveyard of enormous buildings, hissing wind, the occasional hooker, and other cabs; streetlights so white they washed out the colors of the markets and apartments and bars they guarded. He would avoid the Village, which was the convenience store of town, open all night; he would drive around the park, through the park, enjoying the silent darkness, the sound of his wheels on the road, his engine muttering to itself, the voices of invisible drivers on the radio.

He remembered Paula.

Did I kill her?

The thought of Paula, lying there on his bed. He winced, flashes of the night coming back to him. Why had he done it? What had possessed him? Why had she toyed with him like that? Hadn't enough already happened? Wasn't his torture complete?

He patted the cigar box that doubled as his spare-change carrier. The sound of coins tinkling against metal comforted him. *The best defense is a good offense*, he thought, remembering a cheer from his high school football days.

The dream had begun without too many bumps, even with Paula lying right there. Just like a damp skin spread out to dry over the world: his bedroom, the pictures on the wall, the lovely woman in his bed.

All right, he had thought, *I'm going to sit back and enjoy this. Got my trusty sleep researcher with me, got my human walls watching over us both, got the entire city of New York just a scream away—canyons made of concrete. Nothing's going to get to me, nothing's going to be too bizarre.*

He thought, stupidly and superstitiously, he could keep Wendy away from his dreams if he brought the dreams out into the open, if he made them known so he wouldn't just sit and go crazy inside his own head. It was just something in his brain replaying pictures, spiced up with a few dreams of his own. It was like television. Just pictures. He hadn't told Paula about the dreams that dealt exclusively with Wendy; he wasn't able to, as if he didn't know the right language for it. So he'd told Paula that on those days he had no waking dreams whatsoever.

The clear blue eyes of a born liar, just like people used to say. When Wendy came to him, she was as beautiful as he remembered, and as tempting. She came in a dry wind, her hair blown back away from her forehead, her eyes intelligent and bright, her shoulders slung back in such a way that meant *confidence*, her chin thrust forward, her mouth set in a half-smile—she knew that she would get what she wanted.

"You have what it takes," she said.

"You belong to me," she said.

"Come, now," she said.

"There is much to be done," she said.

And each time she came to him, he wanted her badly; he wanted to recapture something from his adolescence, a feeling of belonging, a connection with something big, as if with her he had been plugged into the wiring of eternity. He'd been running on low voltage ever since.

He'd watched Paula fall asleep—so tenderly, with her hands cupped as if in prayer beside her cheek, her adult personality exhaled with each sleepy breath, and left behind was this little girl, innocent to the darker side of existence. She studied sleep patterns and dreams as if there were a cure for things like this, as if there were some chemical or some therapy that could reach inside him and kill the waking dreams and let him sleep normally again. To live in such a blissful state and to not see this skin stretching across the room, to not see an apartment full of papers and books and bottles and pictures suddenly peel back, and another landscape bleed through: a country of yellow skies and brown hills. And she was there, she was laughing at him, she was telling him what she was going to do with these women with whom he slept.

"Just bones inside a sack of skin, we will tear them, you and I, we will draw those bones out through their cunts." Wendy sat there, near him. He tried to see through her, through the curtain she'd drawn over his apartment. But he could not. She sat there covered with crawling red ants, she was beautiful and she was terrifying, and the ants crawled inside her mouth when she laughed.

"What do you want from me?"

But before she could answer him, he pushed her backward so that she almost fell (and still she was laughing as fire ants poured from her mouth and nostrils) and then he hit her.

As he hit her, she screamed, but her mouth was laughing at him, and he looked at his arm when he felt a stinging pain there: several fire ants had leapt onto him and the back of his hand was burning.

"What are you doing to me?"

"Charlie?" Wendy asked, but her mouth was laughing as the red ants began digging into her neck along the ring of small scars she had.

Charlie?

Wendy was laughing even as her head began to open up, tearing skin in that ring around her neck where the ants were busily working, prying up bits of flesh in their elongated mandibles, and as Wendy's head fell completely backward, clinging to her body by a thin bridge of skin and several dozen red ants, something began emerging from the blood-gurgling stump of her neck.

"Charlie?"

"Paula?" he asked, and the animal's head was emerging from inside Wendy's neck. It had a long, square snout, its lips curled back in a snarl, its eyes milky red.

Something behind it.

"Charlie?"

Charlie Urquart thought he saw Paula Quinn, holding her hands up to defend herself from him, but he wasn't sure it was her (*where does the dream end?*) and he had to make sure the thing that was

195

slithering up from Wendy Swan's innards was not what he thought it was going to be so he grabbed the headless corpse, ants and all, and began shaking it. When it started screaming he threw the woman's body hard against the yellow sky and it struck against the Virgin Mary, who protected her baby from the blow. The baby she held in her hands began growling, and the Virgin Mary undid her robe and offered her five breasts so that her little one could nurse, and somewhere behind the Madonna, Paula Quinn lay very still.

Charlie Urquart had been about to break through the waking dream; about to come back to his senses, back to his apartment; about to make sure he didn't harm Paula the way he'd hurt the old man at Thirty-third and Third.

And when Charlie called out to Paula through his dream what came out of his mouth was halfway between a word and a howl.

2

Did I kill her? Charlie wondered as he pulled his cab over to the curb near Columbus Circle.

The air outside the cab was cold and biting. Two young people passed in front of the cab, clinging to each other, their faces bright and happy—they'd been to a party, or they were newly in love, or they were on their ways to meet friends. Charlie listened to the static on his radio, and the faraway-sounding voices of other drivers getting their assignments. His car smelled like a musty closet. He lit a cigarette using the car lighter, watching its circular orange glow, remembering his father's use for the car lighter (*"That's three"*) and the subsequent burns on his arm above the elbow. *"That'll teach you to keep from resetting my radio," his father said, his face a map of tiny, red blood vessels, his eyes blue like Charlie's own, his mouth curled slightly in that eternal* what have I done to deserve a kid like this *look. And that long-suffering tone of voice, as if a father had to teach his son lessons like this one—as the car lighter engraved a circle in his flesh—if the son was ever going to amount to anything.*

Yeah, Pop, I've gone far in life, now I'm beating up on people. Charlie tapped his fingers on the steering wheel as he sucked on the cigarette, enjoying the hot tickling feeling of the smoke as it went down the back of his throat to his lungs. He thought of opening up the cigar box that lay on the seat beside him: it was his place for keeping valuables while he drove; there was never enough money in there for anyone to bother stealing.

And if worse ever comes to worse . . .

Why the hell does my mind always return to Wendy Swan?

Then the dream came, like an extra set of eyelids coming down, and she was there.

Wendy.

Her body was clothed in skins.

Human skin.

Wrapped tight like a straitjacket at her shoulders, across her waist, barely covering her upper thighs; the skin of human hands hung down like tassles along her pubic area; faces torn off their skulls leered from her breasts. In her clenched fists she held writhing rattlesnakes, twisting backward to bite themselves.

Her beauty was cruel and unforgiving.

Then, as he gazed at the skins she wore, studying their patterns, he began discerning the images they held as if they were tattoos, and the images became the former possessors of the skins. Her body was drawn with their faces screaming, faces of people he knew, faces of all those sent to hell by her.

And there, along her ribs, was his face: Charlie Urquart at sixteen, young and handsome, like a young stallion before the race had begun. Charlie Urquart, his blue eyes bright, his jaws stretched so far apart they looked as if they would split through the skin.

Screaming louder than the rest, the voice higher and more youthful than he remembered.

And then Charlie moved toward her, as they all cried out in pain and remorse for what they had done, for the sin they had committed.

Charlie's teenaged image shouted obscenities at him, rattlesnakes struck at his arms as he reached up and began strangling her; he felt the deep punctures from the snakes; the faces she wore began biting him as he pressed his body to hers; the faces chewed his flesh; she was screaming too as his hands closed tighter around her neck, but her voice wasn't what he expected, it was gruffer; deeper, and then her head elongated and shimmered.

His own body was changing, too, it was all that chewing those faces were doing, and the snake bites, it was changing him, his skin was getting white and tough like leather, his shoulders began to hunch forward (his hands as they closed around her neck became curled and gnarled with a sudden arthritis, as his fingernails grew longer, slicing into her neck), he heard and felt the pain as his spinal cord cracked like a whip.

The dream ended, and Charlie Urquart was still in New York. In a cab. Stopped at a light.

But Paula.

How could he do something like that to her? How could he knowingly let her get that close to him? Of course, Wendy would find a way to destroy him, and this had been it. She had sent his soul to hell, that he was sure of, and his body and mind were now hers. *How did I ever think I could get away from her?*

"You on call or something?"

Charlie looked in his rearview mirror. An overweight, middle-aged man in a business suit was scooting into the backseat. Charlie did a double take. *Okay, the guy's not a mugger. Nobody wearing a suit is gonna do anything other than maybe stab you in the back as Pop used to say in his more lucid moments.*

"You hear me?" the man asked.

"Yeah, I heard you. It's kind of late is all, I didn't expect a fare this time of night."

"I need to get to Thirty-third and Third."

"Excuse me?"

"Thirty-third and Third, is there a problem?"

"No."

Charlie started his cab up, making a U-turn. "No problem, that just seems to be a popular spot these days."

"Your meter running?"

Charlie flipped the meter on. "Yeah."

"I'm glad I found you."

"This time of night, like I said, you're lucky."

"No, I mean I'm glad I found *you*."

Charlie didn't quite understand, and glanced again in the rearview mirror.

His father sat there. Of course it was his father, the suit was one of his father's sweatstained gray suits that no one in their right mind on the desert in California would wear—except Charles "Gib" Urquart II.

The head was bashed in, as if with a hammer.

It was a hammer, Charlie remembered.

Charlie kept driving.

"So she can do this without even warning me."

"I don't get you, son."

"She can make me dream without my even knowing it. How much of any of this is a dream?"

"Life," his father said pulling a stogie out of his breast pocket, "is but a dream. Charles, would you mind reaching over and punching in the lighter? I need something to set the homefires burning."

3

"Why don't you pull over so we can talk?"

"No fucking way, Pop, I'm going to keep driving. If I stop something's going to happen, and it probably won't be good."

"The years haven't exactly brought wisdom, have they?"

"Sure, Pop." Charlie laughed as soon as he said this. "Christ, I'm talking to a dead man."

"Nothing dies, Charles, we're living in the asshole of eternity, even as we speak. Big wheel just keep on *toinin'*. I guess you're never going to punch that lighter in for me."

"I learned my lesson on that."

"I taught you well. But I think it's time for one final lesson."

"Do dreams kill people?" Then Charlie, in the crazy logic of the moment, thought, *Dreams don't kill people. People kill people.*

"Maybe it would be more to the point to ask, is this a dream?"

"Look, why don't we just *get* to the point. She's not going to leave me alone until I'm dead, right?"

"You never listen."

"Pop?"

"That's *one*."

199

Chapter Twenty-seven
That's two

1

"To answer an earlier question, Charles, you did kill her."

"Paula?"

"None other. And rather messily, too. I suppose you weren't used to your transformation, and rather than the clean kill, which would've been more sportsmanlike, you dragged it out for a good ten minutes. Ten minutes is nothing in terms of real time, but when we're talking eternity . . . well, it goes on forever. The look in her *eyes*" . . . His father began chuckling as if over some minor embarrassment. Charlie did not look back.

Charlie dropped his right hand from the steering wheel and patted the top of the cigar box, drawing it closer to his hip.

His father continued jabbering. "A real man would've made it a clean kill—that business about popping her breasts as if they were pimples, not really the proper course of action. You should go for the *heart* first, it's the kindest way, then they may only have a few seconds to experience it, always the *heart*, although ripping the throat out is good, too, but as you saw yourself, a woman can hang in there for a while even with a chunk missing from beneath her jaw. I suppose I should've taught you more of the manly art of butchering. But I did take you hunting, so I can't blame myself. I did take you to your grandfather's in Minnesota those times and showed you how to do it. Always remember: a clean kill is the only way to keep blood off yourself."

Charlie looked down at his sweater; at his hands; he glanced at his own face in the mirror. "I don't have any blood on me. You're lying. I didn't kill her."

"Oh, Charles, don't you remember washing up? In that closet you call a shower, you were scrubbing at your skin for ages. You certainly still have a selective memory."

"I didn't kill her," Charlie repeated, uncertainly this time.

"That's *two*," his father said from the backseat.

2

Charlie Urquart pressed his lips against Paula's neck, his tongue lapping the soft curve of her throat, pressing down on a vein, feeling her pulse. Sweet, she tasted sweet, and he would've continued lapping, faster and faster as if her throat were a bowl of cream, except he was hungry, too.

He drove his teeth down into her warm skin.

As he did this, his eyes went up to his walls. The Virgin watched him and blessed him; the President of the United States nodded his approval, too; beautiful women smoking cigarettes, or wearing expensive furs, or holding up breakfast cereal in their hands, all blew him kisses; men wearing camel's hair jackets, or Rolexes, or jogging in Nikes, all gave him the high sign. They watched him and murmured among themselves like an audience full of old friends, on hand only for him, for this moment.

His teeth met with no resistance, sinking into her skin with an embarrassing sucking sound.

Blood burst into his mouth as if he were eating a ripe tomato, sweet like a ripe cherry tomato bursting inside his mouth.

He drew back from her, smacking his lips, his stomach growling just as he swallowed. Her eyes gazed up at him, twitching in their sockets.

He reached down to her breasts.

His hands were curled into mitts, and from each finger, a long, black fingernail protruded. He pawed the air.

Her breasts lay flattened above her ribs. He grasped the nipple on the left. His claws circled the aureole. He squeezed.

3

"You missed your turn," his father said, tapping Charlie on the shoulder. The cab was now filled with the smothering odor of his cigar, which Charles Urquart II had managed to light without the benefit of the car lighter.

Charlie glanced from the road up to the rearview mirror. His father looked bored and weary. His eyes were puffy, the way they used to be when business was bad and he hadn't been getting any sleep. *No rest for the wicked.*

"I *said* you missed your turn."

"Did I? I guess I was thinking about Paula."

"Well, it's all coming back, is it? Good. Now we're getting somewhere. She would've screamed and brought down the house, too, but you were wise enough to do a little creative surgery on her vocal cords. Sloppy, but creative—I don't think I've ever seen it done quite like that, like boning a live chicken with a dull knife. If it had been me, you understand, I would've had it over with quickly, but I suppose I don't need to keep telling you that."

"No, you don't."

"But you did have a way with her, what you did there between her legs. The unkindest cut of all. She herself would probably tell you (if poor Paula could return from the dead) that what you were doing with that bit of genital mutilation was getting back at your mother for ever bringing you into the world. *That* showed a certain flair."

"Shut up. I didn't do that. I don't believe it. This is a dream."

Charlie tried to block the mental image that was coming to him: *her legs, his claws scratching her legs, everything dark red, the human walls watching him, waiting for him to finish what he had begun, to do what his father would've wanted him to do, to teach her a lesson.*

His father interrupted his thoughts. "Don't you tell me to shut up. That's—"

Paula's eyes milky red, her mouth moving silently like a fish brought out of its lake, its lips opening and closing, opening and closing.

"Shut up shut up shut up!"

The people in the wall pictures, their mouths opening and closing, opening and closing.

His father said, "That's—"

Paula's fingers opening and closing, opening and closing.

"Shut the hell—"

Her trembling lips.

"That's *three*," his father said, and Charlie knew he meant business.

Chapter Twenty-eight
That's Three

1

"Charles, now it's time for your lesson. You have something that doesn't belong to you, and you must give it back. Pull over here, now."

"Pop," Charlie said, fighting tears that made no sense to him. But like a dutiful son, he brought his cab to rest curbside. He kept the engine idling. He kept his foot on the brake, but lightly.

"You've got it, don't you?"

"Got what?"

"You know what. Don't play games with me, son, this is your father you're talking to, not some grad student with her brain where the sun don't shine. *Got what?* God, you're whiny. If I'd had a lick of sense I would've made sure your mother had her diaphragm in place so you'd've just slid down her leg rather than up into her womb. *Got what?*"

Charlie thought: *Just a dream, just a dream.* He felt a fever break inside him, sweat along his forehead, his bladder giving way, his teeth chattering. *Merrily, merrily, merrily, merrily.*

"*Got what?*"

Merrily, merrily, merrily, merrily.

"*Got what?*"

Life is but a dream.

"You know goddamn well what! The knife, you worthless whelp, the knife! We know you have it. We know you've kept it all these years!" His father leaned forward. Charlie felt an arm go around his neck. In the rearview mirror Charlie could see that it was not his father leaning forward, his red eyes glaring back at him, it was something big and gray and smelly.

Behind the refrigerator.

Dead rats behind the refrigerator.

It had a long snout curled back into a snarl as it bared its sharp, dripping, yellow teeth. It smelled musty and cold, and Charlie knew both the smell and the face of this particular rat because once upon a time it had burrowed like a chigger beneath his skin.

Deadrats.

Charlie Urquart reached to his right for his cigar box.

He lifted the lid.

Deadrats.

Reached inside it.

Coins jangling as his fingers combed through them.

Lifted a cloth.

Clutched the knife.

Charlie Urquart pressed his foot hard on the accelerator.

"Want it?" Charlie asked.

His left hand twisted the wheel sharply to the left.

Did I kill Paula? Dear God, Wendy, what did you do to me? Are the others like this, too? Or are they in asylums, are they telling their crazy stories about the girl of their dreams, are they talking to dogs as if the dogs understand, are they howling at the moon?

2

The taxicab sailed into the opposite lane, and if it had not been for the quickness of another driver, would've crashed head-on into a bus, but instead spun a three-sixty before coming to a screeching halt.

Charlie began laughing.

3

Later when the sun was up, he called Paula at his apartment.

"You're alive," he said, relieved.

"Charlie? Are you all right? You started freaking out and—"

"I know," he said. "Listen, I need to go West for a week."

Then he hung up the phone.

He could no longer distinguish between reality and dream.

PART THREE: THE QUEEN OF HEAVEN CATHEDRAL CITY, CALIFORNIA

Chapter Twenty-nine
Nessie and Queenie

1

"Forgive me, Father, for I have sinned," the old woman said, glancing around the bus because she realized she was speaking aloud again.

The man across from her stared, but no one else seemed to have paid any attention to her. Would they see the papers she had in her hands? Would they know she'd stolen them and was scribbling notes on them? No one seemed to be aware of it. *They are pretending,* she thought, *because they want to humor me. But they could be spies, couldn't they? She could've sent them from the canyons, they could be some of her army, couldn't they? She can send them anywhere, into anyone, she could easily have chosen one of them to follow me. She's tried before. She will stop at nothing, and only one thing can stop her. Who has it? Does Peter? Will he answer my prayer?*

The man who had been staring at her looked away, out the window of the bus. The old woman eyed him suspiciously awhile longer before realizing she'd missed her stop.

2

"If you keep these goddamn windows closed," Nessie Wilcox said between coughs, "You're going to drive even the flies away. God Almighty, it smells like it rained piss."

She moved over to the shades, drawing them apart. Her hands bothered her—not just arthritis; she'd handled arthritis for twenty-eight years, but now it was just that her bones were old. That was it. Old bones. The cough wasn't exactly fun and games, either, but you live long enough, eventually everything goes. *Should've been wilder when I was a girl and I wouldn't've lived so dang long.* And she had to care for a woman a good six years younger than she. As far as Nessie could tell, her boarder was as able-bodied as they come at seventy. But the woman spent too much time in bed, as if she were an invalid—just like Nessie's husband, Cove, who Nessie'd had the smarts to move across the street from to avoid waiting on the man hand and foot day and night. *So instead I do the same thing for Queenie, except at least with the Queen I get paid.* "Two things, Queenie. First, you get out in the fresh air now and then, and two, open a window now and again. Wouldn't smell like piss so much in here."

"I would not have expected even you to be so common," the woman sitting up in bed said over her newspaper. "I suppose your husband could just not tolerate it. Perhaps there are still things to learn in life after all." When she spoke, her voice always sounded strained, unnatural—she hid behind it as much as anything else. Nessie only took to people if they were upfront about themselves. Nessie divided the world into two kinds of people: first, those who pretended to be something they weren't (like Queenie, although this was the broadest category in her definition and Nessie could place entire cities inside it), and second, those people who divided the world into two kinds of people, like herself.

"That's right, Queenie, I'm an old desert rat, common and coarse and vulgar and rude and crude and socially unacceptable," Nessie growled. *She's so high and mighty, no wonder her other boarders had nicknamed this one "Queenie." Her name was Stella Swan, and she was anything but—she was just one old ugly duckling. How the hell did somebody live to her age acting like that? Somebody would've shot her by now.* "You'd do well to get out and about now and again."

The dry rattle of the newspaper.

"Summer's gone, you need to get some cool air in here, make you feel glad to be alive."

The woman called Queenie dropped the paper to the side. Everything she did was melodramatic. Queenie said, mocking and tough, "If the room seems particularly redolent with urine, it is a result of your little mongrel running through here. I think I pay you enough at this flophouse for you to keep comments of a personal nature to yourself."

Nessie Wilcox muttered as she turned back toward the door.

"Excuse me, Mrs. W?"

"I was just saying a prayer, Queenie, just a prayer's all."

"I can well imagine."

"Do you some good if you said a few yourself."

The woman in bed opened the silver cigarette case beside her bed, withdrawing a cigarette. After she'd lit it, she said, "I go to church. I do what I can."

"A good prayer now and then's not only for your trips to church, you know. And two things, Queenie. First: I booted Cove out of here, not vice versa. And number two," Nessie said, closing the door, "my little Gretchen would not pee anywhere near your highness. And one more thing, you know the rules, no more smokes in my house. You want to kill yourself, you go outside with those filthy things." She coughed in punctuation, closing the door behind her.

3

Nessie Wilcox had bought the house back from her husband when the divorce was final, but had run herself so far into debt back in 1985 that she had to take in paying boarders just to make ends meet—and even then she barely scraped by. Her kids would send her cash to help out, but Cove needed it more than she did—that man could squander in the most original ways: he fancied himself a sort of Grandpa Moses with a dash of bad Picasso thrown in, and he dropped thousands of dollars on canvas, paints, and gallery shows for paintings that to Nessie looked like they'd do better on black velvet. Cove felt his artistic urges pulling him toward nude studies, which of course accounted for more wild spending, because anywhere within a two hundred mile radius of Los Angeles you could find young girls to take their clothes off for cash, even for an old man whose teeth had gone the way of the dinosaur. Sometimes in the morning she'd look out her window and see him there in front of his little one-bedroom bungalow, with his paints and brushes, a felt beret balanced jauntily on his shiny scalp, blue, red, yellow, and white splotches all over his smocklike shirt, pretending to prepare for the day's work. Nessie had moments when she wished her bedroom window didn't face the road, but sometimes it gave her a good laugh.

"You old fart," she might say as she watched him strut like a headless rooster in front of his model-of-the-day, "just give her three days with you hovering over her like a vulture and your mindless chatter and she'll start looking for a cliff to jump from. Make that two days."

Her four boarders were better company than Cove had ever been, but that bit of knowledge had come forty years too late. Mr. Evans was an old lech at times, but every now and then Nessie appreciated an old lech (and he was only in his sixties, so she still calculated that when she was fifteen he was newly born, so that made him a *young* lech). Ab Speck helped out around the house, being the youngest boarder at forty, and where Ab was ugly to a point that seemed humanly impossible, he had enthusiasm that in anyone over the age of twenty-six you couldn't buy for all the bank accounts in Switzerland. Ab also was the only person in the entire house who shared Nessie's wicked sense of humor.

The two ladies, nicknamed Queenie and Cleo, were generally more problem than they were worth—except they were both worth a lot and their money helped keep Nessie in clean sheets and Cove in naked models (as much as she despised him for borrowing money from her, Nessie was just happy to pay him to leave her alone). Queenie had the room with the "northern light," which her highness needed for her rest and recuperation (as Ab Speck would say, "*Read: alcoholism*"); Cleo lived in the smallest room, just above the parlor, and not only could you smell her coming a mile away (*"Shalimar an inch thick like pond scum on her"*) but she outlined her face with dark eye makeup, her lips were deep red, her yellowing skin dusted with heavy powder. Cleo and Queenie were roughly contemporaries, although Cleo (short for Cleopatra) claimed that "a lady never admits to being more than twenty-five," to which Nessie would reply gruffly, "Ain't no ladies in spitting distance 'round here."

The only lady she was sure of at all was Gretchen, her Scotty, who was one of the few folks in the free world who would listen to what she said. So that was her life. She had raised four children, who had scattered to the four corners of the earth as far as she was concerned (New York, Austin, Seattle, Chicago), she had tossed her husband out on his behind (unfortunately she had been only strong enough to send him about forty feet), and this was the life she had chosen. She sometimes wondered what would happen if any of her boarders came down sick—they all had medical insurance, they all had some money to keep them going, but they needed something more than dollar bills stuffed into their mattresses. All four of them were people who had gotten by with luck and some cleverness, but those things never lasted. The one thing that scared Nessie the most was the question of what would happen to them if *she* died. Who would scold them, who would make sure they got fresh air, who would make them Christmas cookies? Who would chide them for being lazy? Who would get them out of themselves and their petty jealousies, their illusions of grandeur, their angry silences across the dinner table, all those things that kept folks from just having a good time and enjoying a few things before the light goes out?

Nessie Wilcox wouldn't normally be one to dwell on her own death. She actually got a little kick out of watching her body wrinkle up on her like a prune, although she wasn't too fond of the small bald spot at the very back of her white hair—it had taken her until she was seventy-two to start appreciating how a body goes (*still got most of my teeth, too*), how you start fixing arms and legs and gall bladders and eyes and ears and kneecaps the way you'd overhaul a car, how you rock on chairs on the porch because the movement takes away the thought of arthritis for a good ten minutes, how you look in the mirror for the girl's face you grew up with and to your surprise you find it even when other people can't. All that was a hoot, once you accepted the basic premise: that it all goes, all of it, the skin, the hair, the teeth, and finally, somewhere in there, you go, too. *When you see death just up the turn in the road, it looks a lot like a friend waiting for you.*

Just maybe not the friend you wanted to make, but a friend nonetheless.

These thoughts had been occupying Nessie for the past eight months.

Ever since the doctor who had come to see Queenie had suggested that Nessie get a checkup, too.

Ever since she found out about the lung cancer.

"Never put a cigarette to these lips in all my days, Doc," she'd told him, "but I sure as hell been around smokers since I was nineteen."

"That might be all it takes," he told her.

"So that explains the cough," she said.

"Let me tell you what can be done," he told her.

"I know what can be done," Nessie said, but the doctor wasn't listening to her.

4

The pain didn't manifest itself very often, but when it did, it was like a knife driving through her chest, from the inside out. She pretended she was being tortured by the Nazis, or that the Inquisition was breaking her on the wheel. She pretended that the pain, the growing cancer, was perfectly natural, simply the beginning of another incarnation, one that would flower within her and eventually ask her to leave. *You live long enough and something's bound to get you.* She thought of all her old friends who had died over the years, some at forty, some in their fifties, most in their seventies, and how she now envied them their having crossed that border. Their pain was over; hers was just beginning. She didn't tell the doctor about the pain, because she knew once she admitted to someone else that the pain existed then there would be no turning back. She would be playing into the doctor's hands, and she wanted to stave that off as long as possible. She thought of animals that, when sick, would go off by themselves and die in solitude and she wondered, with her boarders, if she could turn her back on them to go into the wilderness where no one could hear her coughs and cries.

One day, she would do that. She would go into the wilderness. As always she would be master of her fate. If Death was there, then she would face it and go to it with love and courage the way she had always wanted to go to a lover but had never found one suitable enough. In her last days, Nessie Wilcox knew she would learn to compromise.

5

She had coughed a lot the afternoon she had to go down to the local Catholic church, a summons from one of the nuns.

"Not again," Nessie said after she'd gotten off the phone. She called Ab downstairs to drive her out, and she arrived to the church feeling as if she were back in grade school about to be punished for some minor offense. She was dressed in her usual uniform: a pumpkin-colored sweater with baggy sleeves, polyester double-knit slacks and sneakers. She'd been dressing up all her life for other people and she was damn sick of it. It didn't matter that it *was* a church she was standing in; she didn't think God wanted fashion plates in heaven anyway. Ab Speck, his flattop rising as his eyebrows dueled across his high forehead, kept his mouth shut.

Sister Agnes Joseph was nothing if not hip in a short blue skirt, her hair cut short but free of the wimple Nessie was used to seeing on nuns. But Nessie knew that Sister Agnes Joseph was a wolf in sheep's clothing: the woman was a ballbuster, and if she had not had the vocation to marry Christ, Nessie was certain she would've answered an ad looking for a dominatrix.

"It's not the paper itself, you understand," the sister said.

"Because she will pay for the stationery," Nessie added.

"Her contributions to the church are sufficiently generous" Sister Agnes Joseph smiled grimly. "The problem is one of *purpose*, Mrs. Wilcox. I believe she is forging my own signature and sending letters off to points unknown."

"Harmless. If I went through her dresser drawers I'm sure I would come up with every letter she's written."

But the sister had ammunition. From the pocket of her skirt she produced one such letter, handing it to Nessie. "This was returned to us because of insufficient postage. Of course, we never sent it. I was addressed to a man in Los Angeles named Peter Chandler."

Nessie read the letter.

6

Dear Mr. Chandler,

You have not responded to our recent inquiry, and I wondered if you received our correspondence to you. We feel that your presence now with regards to Stella is urgently required. It is not a question of money, I assure you, it is one of salvation, Mr. Chandler, the salvation of a human soul.

Yours in Christ,
Sister Agnes Joseph
The Queen of Heaven Catholic Church.

7

"Not my handwriting at all," Sister Agnes Joseph said.

Nessie scanned the letter. "No, it's definitely hers, but this defies everything I've known about her. She swears she has no living relatives, isn't that right, Ab?"

Ab nodded. "Far as I know. Keeps to herself."

"What a mystery for us all, sister. I'll of course mention this to her immediately. Although it doesn't seem to be cause for alarm, does it? It's just paper, and she will stop."

"In the past we've had at least one case of a parishioner soliciting money under the banner of the church."

"I doubt that she's interested in money." Nessie coughed as she said this.

"Perhaps if you were to find out exactly what she *is* interested in, then the mystery would be solved. She won't talk to me and you know she is not interested in confession."

8

After the sister left, turning abruptly, her blockish shoes clopping down the cold stone hall, Nessie nodded to Ab and said, "She's just mad because Queenie's paid for half this church. Well, you foot the bill at a hotel, least they let you do is take some towels home with you."

9

Later, Nessie stood in the open doorway of Queenie's room. "Can I talk to you?"

"If it's more nonsense about the paper I allegedly stole . . ." Queenie was standing at the window. She was looking out the window, but it was dark outside. The window mirrored the woman gazing at it. Nessie could imagine the wicked queen in *Snow White* asking the mirror who was the fairest of them all. Queenie wore her silk dressing robe. Her skin seemed a coral pink from light reflected off the shiny red of the robe.

"No, Queenie, I don't care about the paper. It's just curiosity on my part. The paper, the telegrams, all of it. If we had a computer here, you'd be sending email, wouldn't you?" Nessie swallowed a cough.

"Not as nefarious as it sounds. I've only written a few. I'm lonely, it's some harmless fun. Well?"

"Is this Mr. Chandler a relative?"

"You've come in here without knocking to invade my privacy."

"Don't bark at me unless I bark first, Queenie. I don't give a twig for your privacy. If privacy's what you're after you certainly have the gold to lock yourself up in Fort Knox."

"You have a way with words."

"Three brothers, all lawyers, taught me to speak up."

"Well, I won't shroud this in secrecy any longer. Mr. Chandler is an old suitor, and he and I write back and forth to each other now and again as a kind of joke. I imagine he laughed his head off when he saw the letterhead: Queen of Heaven Catholic Church, and then the signature."

"I raised four children in my time, and let me tell you, Queenie, you lie worse than all four of them put together."

"How dare you—"

"You've been going down to Western Union on Tuesdays and sending messages to this Mr. Chandler every week since you've been here." Nessie detected the strong scent of whiskey. *She's drunk, and she's popping pills. Hell, what kind of a place am I running?*

"Damn you for coming in here!" Queenie yelled in a rage. "You have no right!"

She had not turned from the dark mirror window.

It was as if she were ragging at her own reflection.

10

When six came around on Sunday night, her majesty did not deign to join the rabble at dinner.

"She's sulking," Nessie said when Mr. Evans asked about her.

"Poor delicate butterfly," Mr. Evans said. "Perhaps I should take something up to her."

"You will do no such thing, you masher."

Ab said, "If she's not having her potatoes . . ."

213

Nessie waved her hand wearily, and Ab reached for Queenie's cooling plate to scrape off some of her food. "Can't see them going to waste."

Cleo leaned back in her chair, creaking (and Nessie wasn't sure if it was the chair or Cleo making the noise). "She's always prattling on about her great sin. She's insane. She'll set fire to this place with those cigarettes of hers."

Cove grinned, his teeth like rows of irregular tombstones. "Great sins require great sinners."

"Great foolishness requires great fools, and don't look like you know anything, old man, because you don't," Nessie said. "And if I catch you in front of the TV after dinner I will make sure you're kissing a cactus before midnight."

"Queenie's a sinner?" Mr. Evans asked with some interest.

Cleo nodded, enjoying her moment in the spotlight. "This man she writes to, she's sent him telegrams. I think they have a daughter. She's told me things . . ."

"Enough," Nessie said. "No more gossip."

But Cleo continued undaunted, "I think perhaps this man she writes to murdered their daughter."

The one thing Nessie Wilcox's hacking cough was good for was to disrupt the dinner table, and she pulled it out of her lungs now, coughing and coughing until the subject finally changed to more pleasant matters.

11

The cough often got out of control, and Nessie prayed sometimes that bits of her lungs would just crumble up and come up her throat to choke her. Coughing until she cried, covering her face with a pillow, somewhere in the back of her mind would be the thought: *if I just push a little harder it would be over in seconds, smothering under a pillow would be a nice, soft, dreamy way to go.*

But she'd end up casting her pillow to the floor, gasping in great heaving breaths that brought the cough right back again.

12

Then one day she'd had enough, one day the pain was too much, the knife in her chest, beneath her breasts, seemed to be poking up through the skin.

Nessie Wilcox considered herself less a religious person than a spiritual person; she was a fallen Seventh-Day Adventist. But she knew that her religious beliefs could not be contained in any one Christian tradition: she believed that all things could be forgiven except one, despair.

And second, she believed that suicide for someone her age would be a perfectly suitable way of saying "Up yours" to nature and society.

Anything, she thought constantly, *anything to end the pain*.

Chapter Thirty
The Death of Nessie and the Life of Queenie

1

"Who's there?" Queenie asked the darkness, but knew the answer.
At the window looking in.
Who opened the curtains again? I always close the curtains.
At the window, the face pressed against the glass.
"Rudy?" she asked.
But there was no face at the window.
"Wendy?"
And again, she would lose another night's sleep.

2

"Forgive me, Father, for I have sinned," she said to the window. "I have done those things which I ought not to have done, and I have left undone those things . . . yea, though I walk through the valley

215

of the shadow of death I will fear no evil. Forgive me, Father, for I have sinned."

I have lain with the devil himself, I have made myself a vessel for hell's minions.

I have brought into the world a demon.

3

Her name was not Queenie, but Stella. Stella's skin along her arms and sides was mottled with purplish-yellow marks like tiny stars, the result of pinching herself to try to wake up. The dream was constant, and the dream involved this boardinghouse and these other people and this window through which she saw the other side of the dream almost all the way to reality the way a fish must see the sunlit world when it heads to the surface of a lake. The biblical phrase "through a glass darkly" came to her often: she was chockful of biblical phrases. She had been saved nine times in the past twenty years, first by the Baptists, then the Mormons, then the Episcopalians, the Lutherans, the Jehovah's Witnesses, and then by a string of fundamentalist and/or charismatic organizations including the Jews for Jesus. But they, too, were all part of the dream. Finally, through years of searching for an awakening, she decided to give up. She attended the Queen of Heaven Catholic Church every few Sundays with the other residents, but she mainly went because she had enjoyed the idea of a mother who actually brought a holy child into the world as opposed to an unholy one. It was an idea that amused her. It was the part of the dream that was a joke on her. It was the part of the dream that mocked her, and she, in return, could laugh at herself during Mass.

But she had to break through it, she had to tear the fabric of the dream. She had to find the others, get in touch with the others, because they needed to wake themselves up before Wendy awoke them.

Stella Swan had begun seeing through the dream to the real world, distorted through her bedroom window, coming down from the hills to the northwest.

And on this particular night she saw something else in her window.

She saw Nessie Wilcox running a steaming bath and settling

into it with some grim determination. The water burned her skin. But Nessie didn't seem to mind.

The bathwater slowly began turning red as Nessie's eyes closed, as she smiled.

4

Gretchen, the Scotty, was scratching at the bathroom door as Stella came down the hallway. The dog sniffed and whined and looked up at her.

Stella had developed a fear of dogs over the years. Whenever she came across Gretchen, as harmless as the dog seemed, the animal sensed her fear and usually played upon it by snapping at her heels or growling.

But Gretchen's attention was fixed solely on the bathroom door.

Stella tried the door.

Locked.

She tapped on it. All she heard was the sound of water running.

Gretchen whined.

Water running.

"Mrs. W?"

Gretchen began wagging her tail, trying to thrust her paws beneath the door.

"Mrs. W?"

Rudy was behind her, stroking her belly as she stood there.

Stella shook the vision, the feeling, off. Rudy was not touching her. Rudy had been dead for years.

A thought occurred to her, something from the past, something her mother had once said, *"Nothing truly healthy ever happened in a bathroom."* But her mother had been referring to Rudy's always taking forever in the toilet in the Santa Monica house. *"What does that boy do in there?"*

"Mrs. W?"

The water stopped running. Stella heard someone squeaking it off. She imagined Nessie's hands turning the water off.

Gretchen scratched.

Stella knocked again on the door.

"Occupied!" came the response.

"Mrs. W? Are you all right in there?"

When the woman inside the bathroom responded, Stella knew that it must be Nessie Wilcox because Nessie had announced "Occupied!" just moments before, but the voice that answered her was her half-brother's, Rudy, and he asked, *"Why don't you come in and do my back, Star? Door's open."*

Stella turned the handle of the door involuntarily and it was, after all, unlocked, tugging against her fingers in an effort to open even while she tried with all her might to keep the door closed.

5

Rudy sat on the edge of the tub smoking a cigarette. As skinny as he was, his behind was flabby and bunched up, leading up to his pear-shaped middle and narrow chest and shoulders. He leaned on one hand, splashing water with the other. His body was completely hairless except for a reddish triangle down around his penis, hidden for the the most part by his crossed legs. At twenty, he had deep lines like walnut shells around his eyes, his skin was shiny and sallow, his hair was thin and greased back exposing his large ears. He spoke with his sophisticated nasal accent as he splashed water up with his foot. "Mother's gone down to Ensenada for one of her weekends again, and I can't scrub my back without her. Would you mind terribly?"

He reached into the steamy water and brought out a fat yellow sponge, squeezing it: soap foam spurted from its craters. He stood up and then eased himself down into the water. The girl Stella had once been crouched down beside the bathtub. He handed her his cigarette. She put it in her mouth. He bent forward. His back was ridged like a dinosaur, his ribs stuck out, his back muscles formed a narrow V. She took the sponge up and scraped it across his back. The sponge glided smoothly along his shoulders.

"Very good, Star, I did train you well."

She dropped the sponge in the water.

"Done so soon?" He leaned back, lying down in the tub, his face floating just above the water. "Do you want to scrub my front now?"

And she had reached in with both hands and pushed his face down under the water. He fought her, and as always, he was stronger, he would win, she would not be able to drown her half-

brother, and she knew that when he had managed to rise up from the bathtub, he would grab both her wrists and say to her, "Is this what you really want from me, Star, my baby doll, is this what you really want?"

6

But Stella was standing outside the bathroom door; Gretchen looked up at her, wagging her tail; Nessie Wilcox said, "Go away, I'm all right, just go away."

Stella remembered the vision of Nessie in the red water.

She drew her housekey from her robe. Any key could unlock any door in the house. She put it into the keyhole and opened the bathroom door. Gretchen went in ahead of her.

"Get out," Nessie's voice came to her through the steam. "Please."

Stella could barely see through the whiteness of mist. She went to the tub.

The blood was just beginning to seep out of Nessie's wrists, coloring the water around her.

"Please, Queenie," Nessie said. "Just leave me in peace."

"Let's get you out of there and cleaned up," Stella said, and reached down, touching both of Nessie's wrists. "My real name is Stella," Queenie said as she bandaged each wrist in turn. "But I think I like Queenie better."

7

They sat side by side in the twin rockers on the front porch several hours later. The view from the porch was not lovely: six one-bedroom bungalows that had once been part of a motel, now individual apartments. It would be morning in a few hours, and it was cold, but both women needed the cold. Stella kept a blanket tucked up around her neck, stretched down to her toes. Nessie had neither wanted nor needed a blanket. Nessie swore she was willing to freeze to death, although she did accept a cup of Lipton tea.

"If you mention doctors again I'll throw this at you," Nessie said, holding the teacup to her lips with both bandaged hands. "All a doctor's going to do is want to cut me and shoot me full of chemicals and hit me with a ton of radiation until I'm glowing like the aurora borealis."

"Killing yourself in a bathtub seems more glamorous, I'll grant you that," Stella said, not even bothering to conceal her sarcasm.

"You'll grant me? Hell, Queenie, I didn't think you had a sense of humor and now when I'm opening my wounds in front of you, you're a barrel of monkeys."

Stella wiped her hands across her face as if she were washing herself. Then she looked at her hands. She did not look up. A smile stole across her face as if she'd just told herself the funniest joke she knew. "It's because I've been there."

Nessie softened a bit, and wanted to reach out and at least pat the other woman on her hand for comfort. She sighed, and looked over the rooftops to the stars. "You've had cancer? You never told me that, Queenie."

"I mean I've attempted suicide. Several times."

"You seem like the type who would've succeeded by now."

"Well, I have always had someone watching out for me."

"This Mr. Chandler?"

"No. Not Mr. Chandler. In a way I have spent the past several years watching out for *him*."

"He's not an old beau."

Stella let out a laugh that was so loud that Nessie was afraid it might wake up the entire neighborhood. "Lord, he's young enough to be my grandchild. Well, perhaps a very young son. But he's no relation. I really barely know him. But I think he's got something very special, a weapon."

"Queenie, you talk in circles, you know that? Around and around she goes and where she stops, nobody knows."

"I live in circles," Stella said thoughtfully.

"So tell me. What's the weapon for?"

Stella Swan stopped rocking in her chair. Tears had formed in her eyes. Nessie almost wanted to retract the question because of the shame she felt—shame from Stella, as if shame were a physical thing, and this warm shame was being passed over to Nessie like a torch. "A weapon to send a demon to Hell."

Nessie decided she had to be patient. This might take all night. Nessie was not a great believer in demons, but she respected other people's beliefs, and if Queenie was going to start talking sin and revivals, then that was okay with her if it helped whatever emotional pain was going on inside this woman. After a few minutes of silence, Nessie ventured, "Any demon in particular?"

"If I told you you'd think me insane. If I were to tell you, you would probably call a doctor yourself and have him put me in a rubber room."

"I got to be honest with you, Queenie. Ever since you moved into my place, I've had the sneaking suspicion you weren't playing with a full deck anyway."

"I admire honesty. Only someone like me who's lived her whole life as a liar and a cheat could see what truth is really worth."

"You do live in circles, don't you? So tell me about your demon, Queenie, I've had one or two myself—Cove over there was the last of them and now he's going to torture me to my last days, which might just take me to the end of this week. So who's your demon?"

"My daughter."

Stella Swan resumed rocking in her chair, beginning to unravel a thread she'd been stitching at for years on end.

8

"I was in my thirties when she was born, but what led up to her birth occurred when I was still a child, barely thirteen. I grew up in a little house near the ocean, and my mother and father were always away or, if at home, distant in their worlds of sophistication and glamour. I had no playmates—my family was thought odd in our community, and of course we were, although how do children know of such things? I created a half-dozen or more playmates. I pretended I was an orphan of European royalty whose current parents had kidnapped her from her rightful place on some foreign throne. I pretended to combat my loneliness. My older brother, Rudy, was one of the few people in the world outside of school who ever spoke kindly to me. My mother had been married before, and he was her only child from that marriage. He seemed wonderful and exotic to me. Girls flocked around him, starlets, girls really only a few years older than I was at the time. And I was a fat, little thirteen-year-old who knew deep in her heart that she was hideously ugly, so when Rudy, as worldly as he was, paid attention to me, well, it made me forget who I was. He had some sort of magic, you see.

"And when he raped me, the first time, I felt that I had encouraged him, that I had led him on. Yes, Nessie, rape, although we didn't call it that then, we called it, of all things, seduction, but I can tell you, I was not seduced, I was raped. My mother taught me something about men, that men were evil and good, all mixed together, and if a man had the morals of an alley cat it was usually because some woman had tempted him. So I thought that of myself: that I had made him do what he did to me. And sex, no matter what approach a man took, always seemed like rape to me, always seemed to be against someone's will. And Rudy loved me, I kept telling myself that, and I gradually began sinking into a fantasy world where Rudy and I weren't really related at all. I didn't really grow up, not the way other girls did. I mean, I *grew*, but inside I stayed a thirteen-year-old who had a twisted crush on her brother. I know you're shocked, and I apologize. These aren't the sort of things I would normally discuss over tea."

Nessie nodded, speaking solemnly. "Confession's good for the soul, they say."

"If that were true . . ." Stella began, but changed her mind and returned to her story. "Well, during certain interludes of my life, Rudy surfaced and we resumed our sordid relationship. I had begun another love affair, this time with opium, which Rudy always had plenty of, and then progressed to other available drugs not worth mentioning. I married and divorced—men who did not love me, but men who would take care of me and leave me alone at the same time. I make no excuses. I was selfish and emotionally cold, and I did not ever help another living soul. I led the life I wanted. And then, one night, Rudy returned to me. I had not seen him in almost ten years—since before the war ended. He had changed—the war had done that to him, not in the way it did it to other men because of the death and the horror, although those were factors with Rudy—he had changed in a terrible way: he found he loved the death, he loved the maimed bodies. He had transformed himself into someone I barely recognized. He confided to me that when he was in a battle he would choose one of his own soldiers to kill and he would carry it out in such a way that it seemed the Ger-

mans had done it. He would do it so that the young soldier would
know one of his most trusted buddies was going to kill him, slowly.
'Only six of them,' he told me. 'I was cautious, but if I had known
how easy it would be, well, Star, babydoll, I would've taken the
entire infantry.' "

"That," Nessie Wilcox said with disgust, "is the ugliest thing I
have ever heard, and yet when it comes to human beings, nothing
surprises me. The human mind is capable of absolute obscenity."

"Rudy was not really human. I had never thought that of him.
Another fantasy of mine, but he fueled that fantasy with his own
tales. Rudy claimed to have been sired by the Devil himself, and
spent his only studious moments collecting medieval texts on
witchcraft and black magic. He told me he consorted with demons
constantly and claimed to have learned how to raise twenty different spirits of Hell. I was fascinated by the sheer lunacy of it all—I
was a lair at heart, and I was certain that everyone else in the world
must be a liar, too. So where I had created a small fantasy world in
which to live, Rudy had made an entire universe stretching as high
as heaven and as low as hell.

"But, as I said, the war changed him. For the worse. He had
deserted in France, exchanging his identity for that of a young
man he had just murdered so that no one would come looking
for him, and traveled down into Italy, and it was there, in a castle in the Apennines, that he allowed himself to become possessed by a demon. He told me in detail how it had occurred,
how the castle was run by a nobleman, a supporter of Il Duce,
who had gathered together young men and women within his
castle walls for his satanic experiments. Do you believe in the
Devil, Mrs. W?"

Nessie shook her head. "If there's a devil who isn't a man or a
woman, he has yet to show himself to me."

"I believe that there can be . . . manifestations . . . perhaps not
part of some religious cosmology, but beings, spirits, if you will,
what might have once been considered *gods*, for lack of a better
term. Demons. Entities which exist in time and space and occasionally find their ways into our existence. I don't think anything
as noble or smart as the Devil, but demonic possession—a spirit
of some power finding its way into a human body like a parasite,
and then the human will becoming infected. Is it so different a

concept than, say, cancer? If every cell of an organism is being eaten away at, who's to say that a demon is not just another kind of cancer?"

"But your brother . . ."

"Rudy. Yes. He had invited this cancer, this demon, into his body. There was a young possessed girl which the Italian used for his pleasure—a girl who spoke with many tongues, who cursed all things holy, who performed bestial acts for the amusement of those around her. Rudy told me he took her to his bed and kept her there until he had drawn the demon into himself, he chained the girl to his bed for three months until she finally gave her own spirit up. But not before he had sent her soul to Hell.

"For Rudy had a taste for certain unusual . . . practices. He enjoyed . . . dead bodies . . . laying with them. Fondling them. He told me in detail how he had gone into an Italian town after a firing squad had killed . . . it's too horrible to tell . . . but the corpses, he would say, how beautiful, how still, how loving. And in his travels, he had come across one particularly beautiful corpse which he kept in the castle with the possessed girl. He spoke of the corpse being full of the disease of passage, of a state of a damaged soul still held within the body. He wanted to own the soul of the deceased, and so, day by day, he devoured the body.

"And when he had eaten all of it, he turned his full attention to the possessed girl. There was the blade. To him, not a weapon at all, but a path.

"You see, he brought home a souvenir from this sojourn. A dagger, which he called an athame, a ceremonial knife. It was ancient, he told me. Sanctified in unholy debaucheries. He believed in it. I do, as well.

"He told me that he cut her heart out as he raped her one final time. How he watched her eyes flutter as she realized what he was doing to her. Her body began burning even as he twisted the knife deeper into her. Her body blackened, flames licking at her from beneath her skin.

"The blade, he told me, was older than its hilt. It was a gift from the god of darkness to his first mistress, Lamia. Lamia was the goddess which Rudy worshipped. Lamia, the night, the corrupt, the eater of skin and drinker of blood, to whom countless human sacrifices were made centuries before her name was ever written.

Lamia, whose song is a demon howl, whose face is madness and suffering. He told me that when he . . . violated . . . the dead . . . that he was with her, with his demon lover. And so he would send her servants, handmaidens and slaves, as gifts. The soul he had eaten, the blood he had drunk, the girl he had set fire to with a twist of the knife. The dagger would be used in sacrifice, for men slaughtered with it would dwell eternally in the underworld. How he went on about Lamia, how he wrote her name across tiles with his own blood! The girl and the dead body had been part of his corruption. He said he had achieved ultimate union with his lover and her servants.

"He didn't return to find me until well after the war—I had prayed he had died, but he turned up in 1961, and his life was darker. He had eaten away at what little sanity had been left him, and then had only one driving thought: *to pass this madness into the world*. But something about his experience: it had aged him well beyond his normal years. He was a man in his forties then, but looked as if he were eighty. Stooped and bowed, infirm and gray and wrinkled and half-blind. I barely recognized him. Had it been the drugs, I asked. Had it been the war? But no, his body, you see, had died there in that castle. What I saw was decay. Not an eighty-year-old man, but a corpse which had not been attended to. I didn't believe a word he said; if I had, would I have not succeeded in the suicide attempt I made the same night he came home? I took what drugs he'd brought me—I was lost in my own world. I feared him, yes, but in those days I feared everything.

"Soon after this, one night, Rudy came to my bed as I knew he would, and lonely and feeble-minded woman that I was, I let him in.

"And then Rudy kissed me and I knew where this would end, this would end, this would end with me, like that poor girl, chained to his bed, begging for death, begging for a needle in my arm, begging for release from the nightmare my life had become.

"And suddenly, I didn't want that. I *knew* I didn't want what he had to offer me. Call it a life will, or survival instinct, but something bubbled up from deep within my soul, and every cell in my being wanted to fight those invisible chains which had held me so long.

"I took his knife. He kept it beneath his pillow. I knew, because

225

I would ask him why he kept it there, as we slept in the same bed. And he would say, God, his eyes wet with such an exciting thought, 'To kill you with.'

"I thought I would hurt him. When he came for me, I attacked him with his precious athame, slashing his right shoulder.

"I will never forget his face.

"It was barely a scratch on him, a small trickle of blood. Rudy screamed like I had murdered him. 'But you're already dead, you said so,' I reminded him. 'But my *soul*,' he cried out.

"The skin around the wound blackened, and the blackness spread out across his arm and chest and up to his neck. Sores began opening up like small volcanoes across his stomach—I thought for a moment I could see *inside* him, *right to his soul*. He began shaking violently, he tried to grab me, but I backed away. It was like watching someone step into their bath only to find a live wire there in the water. His skin crackled as it burned. From the inside. His blood, boiling. He was dripping with sweat as the blackness engulfed him.

"He was dead within seconds, and there, on his right shoulder, where the cut from the knife was, a flicker of light, of fire coming through. And then, the skin flaked, the bones crackled like paper, and ashes, he was ashes, he was nothing but ashes."

9

"Oh, Lord," Nessie Wilcox said. "You've got me believing it, I can practically *smell* him burning."

Stella sighed, huddling beneath her blanket on the rocker. "No one believes anything until it's too late. I am not lying."

Nessie nodded. "I believe *you* believe it, but, Queenie, if you were addicted to drugs . . ."

"You're right, of course, I lived most of my younger days in a haze, shut away from reality. But this was reality, Nessie, this was what I was running all my life from."

"What about your little girl? Not that I completely believe this rambling tale of yours, but hell, it's the most you've said in eleven months. So your child . . ."

"I thought you would've guessed."

"You mean, your brother. Natch. But it obviously didn't stop there. You had a daughter in what—sixty-two? Did you stop me, from doing myself in, in the bathroom—did you do it because you believe my soul would go to Hell for committing such a sin?"

Stella squinted her eyes and shook her head. "If I believed that, Nessie, I would've let you die. All the more company in the after-life for me. No, I stopped you because I knew *why* you were doing it."

"Cancer. Seemed like a good idea at the time."

Stella took a long breath, and was about to speak, but closed her mouth. When she opened it again, she seemed to have calmed down considerably from the old woman who had just sped through the story of her life. "Our universe, as mysterious as it is to me, seems to have its own logic, and there's always a balance, a yin and yang, a dual nature. Good and evil, even within the same person. My baby, growing inside me was cursed, I knew that, just as I was myself cursed. But my body changed in the months I carried her, and even after she was born I knew what I had acquired. A certain talent. Even my child, before I murdered all that was good within her, before . . . with these very hands . . ." Stella took deep breaths, her hands clutch-ing the upper corners of the blanket wrapped around her. "Even my little Wendy had good in her. But she had destruction in her glance, in her voice. She was the *daughter of obscenity.* I saw it all coming and tried to stop it from happening, but that was how I killed the girl I should have learned to love. And when I destroyed that part of her, the evil was allowed to take hold. Completely. Absolutely. No barriers."

"So you had a yin for her yang?"

"These elements. The evil she was capable of, it was like a power growing out of her, and she could cast it where she would, yet it would always come back to her. But I received something from her, something which she could not touch. A terrible good. I had—I still have—a certain gift for healing, limited, unpredictable. It comes in me, grows stronger, when *she* grows stronger. I had a vision of you in the bathtub, and the feeling inside me, my blood rushing like it hadn't for over a decade, and I knew that I was answering some call that could not be denied. It seems to make me stronger when it happens."

"So you think you can cure me? Is that it? Clean out my lungs? What if I was to tell you I don't want to be cured?"

Stella's voice softened to a whisper. "Then I'm sorry. Terribly."

"*You're* sorry, Queenie?"

"Yes, because it's too late."

"Too late to cure me, well, somehow I figured that would be the end to this story. You've been pulling my leg for an hour or more, and right now I'm wishing I was still soaking upstairs. Just happy Gretchen's still with me." She leaned forward to pet the Scotty, who rolled over sleepily.

"No, Nessie," Stella sighed. "I mean, it's too late for not wanting to be cured. That act is already done. *Fait accompli.*"

And Nessie Wilcox stopped scratching Gretchen's belly, realizing that since Queenie had brought her out of the bathtub, she hadn't been wheezing or coughing, and her arthritis wasn't half bad, either (although it was still there like wood splinters in her elbows and knees, so if Queenie were half the healer she claimed to be, she was as half-assed about that as she was about keeping her room tidy).

10

The purple hues of dawn were not long in coming. The two old women sat rocking in the twin chairs, chilled to the bone, but yapping away.

"We've been up all night," Stella said.

"I feel pretty good. Not great, but pretty good."

"It's just a healing, it's not as much of a miracle as it seems. I seriously doubt Sister Agnes Joseph would approve of a thief and forger making miracles. I can't control it. It just happens, between me and whoever needs it. But there's a price. Always a price. When it's stronger in me, that means *she's* stronger, too. And we've both been weak for a long, long time."

"I won't sign my will over to you, Queenie, but whatever's mine is yours for the asking."

"You do believe."

"All I know's the air's sweeter and cooler than I can remember, and when I let out a big old sigh, it comes out in a whisper and not a growl. I don't intend to run down to the dang hospital to get some X-ray to tell me I should or should not be suffering such delusions.

I say, when the goose lays you a gold one don't pass it around to your friends to tell you it's crap, pardon my French."

The sky was turning yellow-pink with the approaching sun, the mountains becoming a hazy purple.

"You must think me an awful woman."

"For what you did? Queenie, I think you're *blessed*."

"Not the healing. That's not *me*. *I'm* the one whose life has been a nightmare since it began."

"Maybe that's the price for a gift like you've got. Anyway, it's what's going on now that counts, it's what's happening day after tomorrow. Hell, I don't even remember half of what I did last week, and if you were to listen to half the stories in this house you'd think there's no hope for any of us if you based it on the past. No hope t'all." Nessie meant it, too, and in spite of Queenie's awful past, she knew that as long as they were both breathing there was hope. *It's all anyone needs*.

"I . . . don't think . . . there is. Hope? How can there be?" said Stella, who kept rocking faster and faster. "To tell you that I wanted to cure you is a lie. I don't care. I don't care anymore. It is just another addiction of mine that, when the pull is strong enough, I give in to."

Nessie shook her head, chuckling. "What kind of adversary are you, then? You're seventy if you're a day, you look just strong enough to pick up your fork at suppertime, good God, Queenie, a Santa Ana could send you flying. If this girl of yours sits out the next few years, there's a good chance you'll be dust. What kind of vengeance is that? I'll tell you what kind, the kind that life takes on every last one of us whether we go kicking and screaming or just taking it as it comes. It's like waiting for the bus. I've seen people go from bus stop to bus stop, walking between 'em as if that's going to make the bus come any faster, and folks like me just sit at one stop and wait, and some folks curse and others read their paperbacks. But the dang bus is going to come anyway, and if you miss it now you'll catch it later. So you live your life, and you can be afraid of your daughter or not, but death is going to come pick you up either way. What's to lose? Real estate? A couple of pairs of shoes and a purse? Ha! Now, slow down that rocking or you're liable to fly off the porch."

Stella stopped rocking. "I told you about my brother's transformation, his change. She wants me to be alive, Nessie, she wants to let me see her work, her change, her metamorphosis. I saw how the dragon inside her tried to assert itself. I *know* her. I watched what she can do. I told you I've tried to kill myself. For years, in every conceivable way. And it can't be done. She will not let me die. She wants me for herself."

"Well," Nessie said. "My mother always told me, if you're afraid of something, best to face it."

"I can never . . . face . . . that."

"Never," Nessie said, "say never."

11

Queenie Swan slept better that day than she had slept in years, and no dreams troubled her for once. Usually she would take one of her pills to keep the shadows off her bed, to put her out for a good ten hours, but it hadn't even occurred to her to take a pill as she plopped down on the mattress. She would sleep until seven that evening, and awaken feeling better than she had in over twenty years.

12

Nessie Wilcox, however, did not even consider sleep an option.

She was all-fired up. She felt that she'd gotten some kind of reprieve from the Almighty; it reaffirmed everything she had faith in and had been just about to lose. She took Gretchen for her morning mile walk around nine, stopping along the way to enjoy the fresh autumn air of the desert. To the west were the mountains rising up to meet the sapphire blue sky, and somewhere in the hills, above Yucca Valley, was the town Queenie had mentioned. Nessie remembered the headlines well, remembered the excitement and fear the entire population of the desert had felt rumble through it like an earthquake, the devastation, and the vast mystery that had surrounded that town.

"Gretchen," she told her dog, "we're going to find out what's up there, you know that? If Queenie can scratch out my black lungs and . . ." She remembered one of her favorite quotes from the Bible, " ' . . . *restoreth my soul*,' that's what she's done, she's restored it to me, she's given me my faith back, Gretchen, when I didn't even think it was missing. And somewhere up there in those hills, her soul is waiting to be restored, too. Two things," she said. "First we try to get a hold of these other people she mentioned. If she's too chicken to call this Peter whatever, then I'll put my head on the chopping block for her. She's got his address and everybody but *everybody* is in Information. And second"—she shaded her eyes from the sun with her right hand—"oh, the second thing'll be more difficult, but the Lord doesn't give us nothing we can't bear, and if it means driving up there with Queenie, well, then, Gretchen, so be it. So be it."

13

The only thing that disturbed Stella's sleep was a voice calling her from her lovely, empty dream.

She awoke to her daughter's call.

"I was your beginning," Stella whispered, sleepily, "I will be your end."

Chapter Thirty-one

Darkness

1

In the dark bowels of a cave, a creature felt the atmosphere change, felt the world turning, heard the whispers, *whatifwhatifwhatif*.

Remembered from what pain it had been born.

What howling pain.

2

From the tapes

"Why these children? What good are they?"

"Oh, witch doctor, you want me to tell you stories about how evil I am and how I wanted innocence to corrupt? I've gone through this before, centuries ago. They tortured some poor child and to tease them, I told the priests and judges about my host of devils and worshippers. I've made up good stories before. They burned me once in a woman's body and I gave them a show as they had never seen before."

"You've been alive how long?"

Pause.

"I am infinite."

"And yet, in 1980, you chose to—"

"I chose nothing. I was delivered into that tomb of a village, I was born in flesh and tormented there. Why shouldn't they serve as my nest? They deserved it."

"Your . . . nest?"

"And my beautiful boys, how I loved watching their young, fresh bodies thrust into the prison of flesh that held me. Sex is a torture for you animals. That's why they killed their families. They did it. Oh, yes, I gave them nudges, but it was all within them. But fertility and destruction are the same force. But you know that, don't you? You've always known that."

"You wished to bear their young?"

"Fuck you."

"Is that what you were after?"

The tape garbled as the creature occupying one of the teenagers began chanting Latin and Greek phrases over and over again. Later, the interviewer, Diego Correa, would translate two of them as: "It was in my mouth, sweet as honey: and as soon as I had eaten it, my belly was bitter . . ." and "Upon her forehead was a name written, Mystery, Babylon the Great, the Mother of Harlots and Abominations of the Earth."

BOOK FOUR

THEN, THE LAST OF PALMETTO, 1980

Chapter Thirty-two
Peter and Wendy

1

Peter Chandler/Confessions

Here's how it was, as best as I remember it. She wanted all of us. I didn't fully understand this when I was a teenager. She wanted both Charlie and me; others, too. She wanted all of us in a way that no woman—I should say, no creature—has wanted any of us since. I've often asked myself: why me? Why not any number of others in town? Why even our town? What distinguished it for her darkness?

I have no answer. All I know is I found myself in her embrace.

Wendy's embrace.

It had seemed like a series of hallucinations in the night, both horrific and sublime. When dawn came, I was alone in the truck. She had gone. I hoped she was gone. I won't try and second-guess the teenaged boy I once had been, but looking back, I felt fragmented into a waking life and a shadow life, and Wendy was the shadow. She was the drug, and I was an addict. I even experienced a joy in the feeling of the shadow-world. Lascivious and horny when I was in her presence, the feelings of lust died when I returned to my daily life at home in Palmetto.

Have you ever had a dark secret? One that you could tell no one? A secret between you and Creation? That's what this felt like—a secret between me and no one—a connection that was part of another life.

Let me draw you back with me, back to Then, that time, that place. I call tell you more about the history of Palmetto, and of its dark twin, Nitro, but this would be no more than the history of desert towns across the southwestern United States in 1980—and it would reveal nothing. We lived, we loved, some of us died, some of us moved on. One day the town burned. Shall I tell you about the burning? It was fast, and spread from one house to another as if the fire had the wings of angels. Children called out for their mothers, and husbands wept as they clung to their wives and knew that they could not escape the inferno. Yes, I was there, but it's not enough to say the town burned, and it's not enough to say that Palmetto no longer exists. It's still there, I suppose. It's still off Highway 4, but no one lives there; as Shirley Jackson might've said, what walks there, walks alone.

I live in the real world. I live in the world of Coca-Cola and McDonald's and presidential sex scandals and privacy issues on the Internet and "What's for dinner tonight?" and "Man, I really am tired of finding out that there's something in my drinking water so now I need to start buying bottled water at one to two dollars a cup." But even in that real world, places like Palmetto happen. I've read about them over the years, what little I could find. Magnificent galleons found empty in the Sargasso Sea, early American colonies empty of all traces of their inhabitants; lost cities, a civilization at its height, vanished; even the mystery of the Chicago fire with Mrs. O'Leary's mythic cow. These things do happen. I just didn't expect it to happen to me or to those I know. The media jumped on Palmetto, described it in several ways, as a madman's revenge, as fire from the sky, as a teen arsonist's wet dream, but no one knew but those of us who survived it. No one outside of us could explain where the bodies had gone. Not even a trace of human bone. Family members searched, investigators dug, but beyond the burnt cars and walls and foundations, it was as if everyone had just decided to move that day and then set the town aflame.

I never expected to look into the face of Mystery and know where the journey led.

And I'm telling you the end of things before you've begun to understand the beginning.

Let me take you there. I was in Sloan's truck, and an uncontrollable desire—a teen lust beyond all other teen lusts—had drawn me into Wendy's body. Without having ever felt that Alison would care for me beyond friendship, I had already cheated on her and felt as if I had destroyed any future I had with her. Yet my body had wanted to be absorbed into Wendy's, as if everything that I was at that age was for her, an offering. It was over. The physical bond broke between us like an invisible chain, clipped. My memory of sex with her is now only a memory of nightmare. Nightmare with pleasure. Nightmare without waking.

When it was over I was not merely empty. I was bereft. I was vacant. I was nowhere to be seen. I didn't even feel connected to my body.

I felt a shame I had never known existed as I got out of that truck, slammed its door, and felt the prickly heat of daylight along my back. I had been a virgin before she had taken me, and yes, I will say now: *she took me*, although then I thought I was a willing and eager disciple for sexual experience. I knew on some level that I loved Alison, that in a moment of weakness and stupidity—the kind that only other teenaged boys seem to truly understand—I had let my body venture into a woman's body without truly wanting that woman. Without truly wanting to ever connect with her; and yet, connect I did. The fears were foolish: that I would have to marry her now, that she would be pregnant, that I had destroyed any hope that Alison and I could ever be together. But the darker fears lurked: that there was something wrong with Wendy, that she was malignant, that my beer-induced hallucinations of her being some kind of oily, spindly creature, some subhuman race, was not as far off the mark as my sobered self would like to believe.

And now, she was gone—she had walked off somewhere, perhaps to get away from me. I was hungry. My shirt, torn, lay in the back of the truck. The rocky crags of No Man's Land rose not five yards from the truck, whereas Palmetto and Nitro seemed miles behind me.

I followed her footsteps in the dirt. She had gone into the cave of what had once been the entrance to the El Corazon Mine.

I had to follow her. I had to understand what my shame meant. What last night had meant.

What the unearthly visions I'd had meant.

I followed the daylight as far as it would go into the cave, and I called her name.

That's when I saw the flickering—that's the only word I have for it. It was like candlelight within the cave, a blue wave of pale light and a "glowance"—another word that sounds foolish, but might be the best I can come up with. A flickering and a glow— like an aura flashing—like soft strobe lights within the darkness of the El Corazon.

And then, I saw her.

She was no monster, no creature.

She was a girl just a few years older than me, lying there in a pool of her own blood.

I stood in that cave, shivering.

And then, she called to me. I realized in the dark of the bowels of the desert earth that she was not dead, and that it was not her own blood.

She was crouching over something, and when I saw the rabbit in her mouth, and the blood that flowed from her chin to her breasts—

But it was dark, and even the flickering changed, an unearthly lightning danced within the cave—

And she lay there, a girl again, a young woman, without blood, without a dead animal between her lips, without anything other than a look of longing and loneliness and now I know that just by having entered her body—partaking of her—I had stepped into the territory of demons.

But then, I went to her. She rose up, sleepily. "Was I dreaming?" she asked. "Was last night a dream?" I embraced her and dried her tears with kisses, and felt as if I were merely going insane. "I was born here," she said, but I did not understand. I walked with her into the burning light of day and drove her home.

Yes, this makes no sense. Yes, I know that I should've heeded the visions I'd had of her, of the light flickering around her in the cave, of the torn animal in her mouth, of the blood that was there but was not there in the next instant.

But it was a part of the world that made no sense, and so I didn't understand it. This is where the real world fails those of us who have stepped out of it. We can't understand the other world with its nonsense, with its unboundedness. Belief is the key. Belief is not part of the real world.

I thought it might have been all the beer from the previous night tormenting me with a hallucinatory hangover; or that it was family insanity within me, passed from my father into my blood. Or perhaps she was so inside me then that I accepted the momentary flashes of what her soul produced. I had spent my life pushing back the memories of a father who bullied and berated and beat me. Denial and quick burial of sights and sounds were nothing to me then, when I was nearly sixteen.

And so, to the flat light of the real world, I returned and put away childish things.

I had become a man, after all.

I walked tall and proud, for as pathetic as it may sound, getting laid was still one of the rituals of manhood, even in 1980, especially as a teenager. I felt shameful for it, too, for I had been raised to be a nice boy, not the wild kind who lays aggressive but comely lasses in trucks. I felt marked, as well, but it would be some days before I understood just how I'd been branded by that one act of nature that seemed, then, completely unnatural to me.

I had opened myself to monstrosity. But then, that summer, I thought I had opened myself to the normal mistakes of the world of men and women.

I saw Wendy every day after that.

I had to. She called, and I went to her.

2

We met like illicit lovers—in the cool of the evening. She would bring Sloan's truck around and I'd ritually ask where he was, and she would tell me one of several things in reply. She had no idea. Off with some woman. Drinking with his buddies. Sleeping off a drunk. Crying himself to sleep. Each time we met, I didn't plan on laying with her in the back of the truck under the stars, nor did I think of anyone other than Alison when I was with her, but she had gotten me addicted to her—Wendy had somehow drugged me with her very physicality, and when I closed my eyes, when I was in her full embrace, I was somewhere else. I was no longer the son of a bully, nor was I the guy who wasn't quite good enough at sports, not quite good enough at academics, not quite good enough socially. I was the king of the world when I was with Wendy. When I caught those glimpses of the Other inside her, the monster, the creature of dark and rotting caverns, it could not block out those other pleasures I felt.

And then, the inevitable occurred.

Sloan found us together.

Or rather, he came home.

3

I was in his bed, and she was with me. I felt as I always did afterward—confused and empty and angry. Like a wild beast pulled from mating, I wanted to lash out. I felt that she controlled my sex, she controlled how and when and where, and I was a victim to her. My inner rage grew with each meeting we had—each meeting that was a mating, also. Anger fueled anger. My father, of course, was my primary target, for hadn't he ruined us? Our lives? My mother's happiness? My sister's joy? My own life, as little as it seemed to matter? Joe Chandler was a man I would gladly bury alive under a ton of scorpions, just to watch his fear. He was my father, and I loved him, and I wanted to kill him, I told Wendy. She held me in the dark—it was a hot summer evening, and the trailer had but one fan whirring. Our sweat was like fire itself. My anger blossomed like red flowers in her arms.

"Let out what's inside you," she whispered, softly, like a loving mother to her son. "Let it all go. Release it. If you're ever going to be happy, unleash it."

Now, many years later, I can look back on those moments as the most terrifying of my life, for while I knew that what I was doing—this uncontrolled erotic lust for Wendy Swan—was somehow wrong, it was her control that frightened me the most. She always knew what to say, how to insinuate a thought into my mind, how to take a hacksaw and raggedly cut through whatever boundaries I had. And I felt less like a man, more like an animal, each time she called me to her side.

I was about to draw away from her, to reach for my clothes, ashamed of myself and furious at my need for her.

The small trailer door opened. Sloan dragged his ass in, drunk, a flop of his unruly hair covering most of his eyes, the brown stink of whiskey permeating his aura. He stood there pointing the same gun that he'd used to shoot his own dog.

I was just in my briefs, reaching for my shirt, when I felt the bullet. No, I was not hit. It was a feeling as if there were an earthquake just under the trailer, and my skin seemed to shake as the sound of the gun's firing burst around me. In memory, it seems as if it were all in slow motion—the shirt in my hand—Wendy's face in the shadow, almost a smile—Sloan's hand shaking with the Smith &

Wesson—a sound like whispering, the whispering of thousands of people, or perhaps it was of bats flying in a cave—for that's what I remember, even in the trailer in Nitro, it was as if everything about Wendy happened in a cave—

And then, I saw where the bullet had gone. It was as if Wendy's face was no more, and in its place a ripe melon had burst, its juice and seeds sprayed across a pillow above a woman's torso.

I remember nothing else from that night that makes sense. The world had become violent for me. I remember no more logic in life after that.

I was lost. I stood there, looking up at Sloan, thinking he would shoot me next.

Instead, he dropped the gun to the floor. Its clattering was muted by the memory-echo of the blast in my head. He had a funny look on his face. Not maniacal, not haunted. Just funny. Like he had opened a Christmas present expecting one thing and had found something he had not imagined. A moment later, he turned and ran, leaving me on the bed in my underwear, still holding the hand of a woman who had only moments before been in my arms.

I can write all this with complete coldness, for now I know what she was about. Now I understand her plan.

But then, the rage bloomed within me. Dressing quickly, I ran out into the night after him, grabbing up his gun, wanting to make him pay for this. People from nearby trailers had come running at the noise, but I pushed past them, allowing their shouts and screams to be drowned out by the deafening tide of fury that rose within me. The rage was beyond anything sensible or true. I had no tears for Wendy, and my shock just served to bury that personality known as "Peter Chandler" even further down within my brain. Something else emerged, something I can only call animal instinct, and all it knew was the kill.

I chased Sloan out into the Wash. My legs felt light, my body almost like the wind as I moved. I had begun to see better in the night, to smell things that I had never noticed before: the sage and mesquite, to hear the restless chirps of small birds nestled along an ocotillo cactus, to taste the dry air thick with dust. Sloan outran me fairly easily, but I found myself moving in a nearly liquid blur toward him—it felt like I moved as the wind. Finally, he slowed down as the night engulfed us both. Each breath felt as if it would ignite my lungs; my eyes blurred, unsure of what they could register. I could see the shiny yellow light of his eyes, and how somehow he had changed in the dark. His face had elongated, his eyes narrowed and moved more toward the side of his skull. Their yellow shine was a trick of the night and of my own vision, I was sure then. He looked as if he'd been beaten up, his jaw broken and hanging. Spittle flew from his lips as he shouted, with some difficulty, "Shoot me, Peter! Please just fuckin' shoot me! Look what she did to me! Look what she does! She ain't dead! She's a fuckin' monster!"

And then, he turned and ran again. I watched him go. I let him go. I sat down in the earth and covered my eyes with my hands, wanting to destroy the real world with my imagination. In days, my life had changed from boredom and family fucked-upedness to the world of murder and sexual slavery. I nearly laughed, then wept, at how insane it all felt. How I could not possibly have seen yellow eyes in Sloan's face, yellow eyes like an otherworldly snake, a jaw that had stretched, teeth that seemed canine . . . and then I opened my eyes to the world again. I lay back on the rocky earth, and looked up at the stars. They seemed so distant and beautiful, and I knew whatever lived on other planets did not care about one boy looking up at them from the desert. There was no end to the desert sky, but my world began and ended there that night. I began shivering. I stared at the stars and wished the world away.

I brushed off the dirt and stood. For a moment, I thought I saw a flash of light—a shooting star?—in the distance beyond the hills of No Man's Land. I took strange comfort from this, as if it were a sign from the universe that my life had been noticed. I suddenly felt overwhelming sorrow for Wendy. I was not good enough for anyone. My father had always been right. I was just not good enough for the world.

In this mood, I went back home. I blocked the rest. Oh yes, it comes back to me in bits and glimpses. But it's gone from me now. The police must've asked some questions. The neighbors must've mentioned that Sloan had the gun and most likely did the shooting. I probably lied and said I was there visiting. I probably told them that Sloan shot her. I was a believable nice boy; Sloan was not. There was not much discussion. My father, no doubt, beat the crap out of me for being involved with the white trash of Nitro. My mother probably wept and took her sleeping pills while my little sister rocked back and forth, staring at nothing. I kept the gun for protection, telling no one I had it.

But she was dead.

Yes, she was.

She had been killed.

I was there.

But that was just her beginning.

Chapter Thirty-three
The Death of Wendy Swan

1

"Peter, I've been having dreams for days. Nightmares. They're coming," Than said into the phone.

Peter hesitated. Then, "What are you talking about?"

"Demons. Bonyface was right. They're all here. I've seen something. Something I can't talk about on the phone. He comes into my room in my dreams. He has fishhooks in his mouth."

"Christ."

"It's a demon. But it's The Juicer. He's trying to warn me. And other things, too, man. I've been reading these books about how demons—"

Peter cut him off. "That's crazy."

"It is not. What's up with you? I thought we were friends."

A pause on the line.

"Than, look. We *are* friends. I can't talk right now."

"I used to be your best friend. As of like last week."

"You still are."

"No I'm not," Than said, hanging up the phone.

2

Than had checked out all the books he could find on demons and nightmares and such from the library in Yucca Valley; he had read them straight through and enjoyed the medieval woodblock prints in some of them. With titles like *Fallen Angels* and *Raising Hell*, the books seemed a treasure trove of all things demonic. Days passed; Than remained indoors, near the air conditioning, living off ham sandwiches and Cokes with the occasional half-pack of Oreos, poring over the books and making special notes whenever he saw anything about a Hand of Glory or a demon. One afternoon after getting his haircut, he wandered down Pinon Street and saw the Bone rooting through a garbage can. He wanted to say something to the old man, but Bonyface cackled a little too weirdly for his tastes. Another time, when Than was going through the dump behind Peter's house, he saw the Bone napping among the piles of tires. He went and stood over him, looking down at the gnarled face. When the Bone opened his eyes, Than almost shrieked.

"You been dreaming, heh, boy? You got something special. You got an understanding of demons," Bonyface said, but Than was already running down the narrow path between the old mattresses and the torn plastic trash bags.

When he next saw Bonyface, it was out among the mesquite, just off one of the side roads that led up into the hills. The sun was blazing hot, and the old man was gathering dried sticks from among the brush.

"Well, boy," the Bone said. "I see you come to find me again."

Than, covered head-to-toe with a sweat that seemed to soak into his bones, said, "I want to know about the demons. And that hand you had."

"If you do," the Bone cautioned, "there won't be any way for you to go back."

"Go back where?"

"Back to the world you call comfort. It changes you, boy. This and the demon juice. It gets in ya and it opens your—your freakin' eyes to all of it. But there ain't no going back."

Than nodded. "I've had nightmares."

"Ah," the Bone laughed. "He came for you."

"He?"

"The Juicer. It was his hand I showed you. The Hand of Glory. A murderer's hand! A man who had tasted the blood of innocence, and left his hand, filled to bustin' with demon juice." Bonyface nodded, passing his sticks to the boy. "Take these and come with me. We'll make a fire over there, in the caverns." He pointed to the hills. "I'll show you what this damn demon is so scared spitless about."

"It's too hot for a fire," Than said.

"It's too dark in this world not to have one," the Bone replied.

And so, Nathaniel Campus began his education into the nature of demons, with the help of the man who had once been known as Lucas Boniface.

3

The cavern had a low ceiling, and Bonyface used one of the sticks to bat away at the sleepy tarantulas and scurrying scorpions—tiny as these were, they scared the bejesus out of Than. The Bone led him to a small circle of stones at the edge of what seemed like a great well of darkness. The Bone could've used his breath to light the sticks, but instead resorted to a match. With a small fire begun, he took Than by the hand and told him, "I ain't her daddy, but I once knew her mama real good. She's the one brought demons into this place."

"What—what does she—what does Wendy have to do with this? She got killed. Something at the trailers." Than watched the fire-light dance across the cavern wall.

"Boy, she's why The Juicer come back," the Bone said, almost solemnly. "I got it in my blood she'd come on back one day. I knew it like I know my stink. But we have this." He raised the hand above the fire. "*The demon juice.*" He thrust the hand against his lips and began suckling one of the fingers.

Than watched in disgust, his lips curling. "That's so gross."

The Bone wiped his mouth of the last drops of the blood. He had a grin that was nearly a grimace. "It's the only way," he gasped, catching his breath. "You had the nightmares. It's already inside ya. You gotta drink."

"Please, no," Than said almost politely, his hands trembling. But something within him wanted to know what was happening: why he had his bad dreams, why Peter no longer spoke for more than a few minutes at a time to him, why he felt that he was somehow doomed. He took the hand, and pressed an edge of a finger to his lips.

It didn't taste the way he had expected. It was more like honey. "What happens now?" he asked.

"We prepare for the demon," the Bone said. "There's lotsa ways o' killin' a demon. Ceremonies. Rituals. All kindsa ways. Now, boy, in all my studies, I've only found one way to make damn sure that a demon don't return in the flesh. It's nasty. It's ugly. But it's gotta be done."

Then he told him.

And thus, Than Campusky's apprenticeship began. Bonyface gave him more books to read; taught him the place in the body where the most vital demon organ resided; told him the story of how the demon within Wendy Swan came to be, and how it was returned to her as the Bone himself had once foretold.

4

"You watch way too much TV, Ed," Alison Hunt said to her brother, who sat hunched over the small black-and-white Zenith that their father kept in his office. Ed Junior didn't look up from the TV, but made a *shushing* noise. She could hear Harv still over in the far garage bay banging and clanging at a bent fender; her father was out talking to one of the old farts from town who'd come in for a fill-up.

"Home." Ed Junior pointed to the small screen.

Alison glanced at the set. It was KCBS, the Los Angeles station. *What the hell were they doing in Nitro?* The camera panned back to reveal the Rattlesnake Wash against the sunset. "Ed, turn it up, turn it up."

Her brother, who was slow in all his movements, had trouble hitting the volume control right, but eventually the sound came up. The reporter said, "The alleged killer is still at large in this small desert community . . ."

"It's one of the trailer parks," Alison gasped. "Jesus. That truck blows up there two weeks ago and now this. No wonder they call it Nitro."

A husky woman in a muumuu was crying, although the reporter kept jabbing the microphone into her face.

Alison pivoted around and shouted, "Hey, Harv, you hear about this murder?" The clanging stopped, and Harv yelled back, "Yep. I even met the guy who did it twice. Worked on his truck. Friggin' unbelievable."

246

"She was pretty," Ed Junior said when he saw the picture of Wendy Swan flashed on the television screen. He shook his head. "Sad." He leaned forward and switched channels.

5

"Dad's at it again," Harv whispered to her when he came in to wash up. He didn't need to elaborate—it was code-talk for drinking, and Alison wondered if her father was going to come home again or just sleep it off at the Cantina or on the back porch. She looked out through the filthy office window, watching her father slap the guy he was talking with on the back, and then pick up his can of beer from where it rested on top of the gas pump.

"I hate this place." Alison shook her head. "I can't wait 'til I'm eighteen and can get out of here."

"Maybe I'll get out soon." Harv gave her a grin. "You can come sleep on my couch."

She snorted. "Your *floor* more likely."

"You talk to your friend?"

She almost blushed, and shook her head. "He's supposed to call."

"I thought you were more liberated than that."

She didn't dignify the stupid comment with a response. "Don't you get sick of it, Harv? Dad and Mom and pretending all the time. You're stuck running this place, but you don't even get paid."

"I get paid." Harv sounded hurt.

"You know what I mean. Paid the way you should. He's drunk every day and we never see him after eight and before noon, and I guess I can't even blame Mom for her . . ." She couldn't even say it: *afternoon delights*.

"Just shut up, Al, shut up." Harv shook his hands in the air to dry them, and then wiped them across his face. He stomped back out to the bays.

"Scissors rock paper," Ed Junior said, raising his eyebrows.

"I don't feel like playing right now." Alison calmed down enough to see the tear in Ed's eye. She felt bad as soon as the words were out of her mouth. She loved Ed Junior all the more since the car wreck that had caused his brain damage. He was older than she, but he would now forever be her little brother, never get beyond the age of five or six in his head, while his body aged.

The accident had sucked. That was the best she could think of it.

Alison closed her eyes. *Too intense. Too close. Think wall. Think wall. High yellow wall. Smooth plaster across wall. WALL.* But the wall couldn't hold: the memory came back to her again, like it was still happening, like she'd trapped it behind the wall so it would always remain fresh and perfect, always there waiting for her memory to be jogged. *Strapped into the backseat, staring out the big rear window of the station wagon, she'd been careful not to touch the metal platform around the vinyl seat because it was too HOT too HOT. She was six, and they had sat outside the Coyote Cantina for two hours in the heat, she and Ed Junior, who was twelve and restless.*

"I'm gonna go in there," he said.

Alison swiveled around in the seat.

"He tole us to stay put."

"It's taking for goddamn ever."

"Haugh," Alison gasped because of the naughty word.

"Well, he says it, so I can say it." Ed Junior crinkled up his face and looked nastier than she'd ever seen him. "I am sick of this, you know? He does this to me all the time."

"Daddy's just getting happy."

"Town drunk," Ed Junior muttered under his breath, "town drunk, town drunk."

"You be quiet about my daddy!" Alison shrieked. When she had calmed down, she said, "Hot. Hot hot hot."

"If you shut your mouth it gets cooler."

"I bet it's over a hunnerd degrease."

"I bet," Ed Junior said. "You wanta play scissors rock paper?"

"You cheat."

"If I don't cheat?"

Alison wished she could go back and tell him not to play, that it wasn't important for him to play that dumb game with her, that he didn't need to climb out of his seat belt, over the front and middle seats, to the back just to play that damned game, but the six-year-old with the blond hair didn't know to warn him. *Ed Junior, sweating, held out his hand.* Rock.

Alison's hand was flat. "Paper covers rock," she said.

"See? Didn't cheat, did I?"

"You let me win," she pouted.

You Come When I Call You

Ed Junior opened his fist, and inside was a stick of Juicy Fruit gum in its silver wrapper. She took it from him and unwrapped it like she was peeling a banana. Ed Junior, with his flattop and freckles, grinned in spite of the heat and the hassle and put his arm around her. "You done it all yourself, kiddo, now give your big brother a smackerooni and tell him he's the bravest, smartest, best guy in the whole world."

She pushed him away, giggling, "Gross, Ed, gross, not a kiss, oh, okay, you're the bravest." She cringed and giggled at the same time as he pretended to smooch at the top of her head. "Bravest— stop it—smartest guy—"

"You forgot best." He made farting noises with his mouth against her ear.

She squealed, "Bravest smartest best guy in the whole wide world."

He let her go, and sighed. "Okay. You're free. No kisses."

"Whew."

"Man oh man, I'm broiling up. If he don't come outta there in two—" Ed Junior stopped mid-sentence as Alison pointed. Their father walked out of the Cantina's doors into the flat afternoon sunlight, wiping his sweaty brow with a handkerchief. His shirt was unbuttoned and his belly hung over the front of his belt. His pants hung low, and his zipper was only halfway up the flagpole. He stumbled a little, leaning on the hoods of the cars as he made his way over to the Ford station wagon. He rapped on the window and waved to his son and daughter.

Only Alison waved back.

Ed Junior whispered, "Shithead."

Alison sucked in her breath as if it would make the nasty word go away. Ed stared out the back window. When their father got in, no one said a word. It took a while for their father to start the car up, and by then the wagon reeked of warm beer.

Alison began singing, "Buckle up for safety, buckle up."

Ed Junior moved closer to the back window. He tried to roll it down, but it was stuck. It always stuck in the heat.

"Didn't mean to take so long," her daddy said as he backed the car in a zigzag out of the parking place.

"Yeah, right," Ed Junior said under his breath.

"Got talking some business in there, ran into Mike Sawyer from

249

Twenty-nine Palms, and he was talking about maybe expanding his vending machine route out this way, and I was thinking, what if I carried his stuff at the station? I mean, we're talking M&M's and Life Savers, just like before, but Fritos, too, and maybe even some sandwiches like a mini-Automat, you know, so people on trips, they're always stopping, and they can get some good food. I mean, with this highway just expanding, and everybody's got to go through here if they want to get up to Victorville, or down from the mountains to Palm Springs, it just makes sense, I mean, the whole town is expanding, it's gonna grow, and I don't wanna miss the boat, I don't wanna just dry up when this town is ripe for development, and vending." And while her father jabbered away, Alison began humming, and Ed Junior tried to roll down the back window, and they hit a bump or pothole on the road (only it turned out to be a dog), and the car started spinning. The back end whirled; where Ed Junior sat seemed to be going in front of the car; and then Alison was trying to scream but her Juicy Fruit gum had gotten caught in the back of her throat. Glass broke, but she never heard Ed Junior make a sound, although she saw him flying through the back window. The absolute craziest thing was, though, that her father kept right on talking (or at least it was how she remembered it), talking about the town of Palmetto expanding and growing, the population explosion and the best of times for America and vending machines and gas prices.

Then she coughed the gum up from her throat.

She tried to see out the window to where Ed Junior had flown, but all she saw was the high yellow wall of the old house they called the Garden of Eden. Later, she heard the term "brain damage" for the first time. Much later, she heard the term "tardo," when other kids spoke of her brother, Ed Junior.

In those days, she learned how to build walls. Walls kept good things in and bad things out.

6

That was then, this is now, Alison repeated to herself, and began to see the wall in her mind again. Ed Junior seemed wrapped up in the cartoons he watched, and Harv continued to work on the Hughes' lemon of a Chevy. Her father gulped back another beer (number five) out at the gas pumps.

When work was done, she got in her rickety T-Bird—patched together by her brother Harv and able to run on a prayer and gas fumes—and drove away, ostensibly to get a Coke at Paco's Tacos; instead, she found herself attracted to Nitro and the trailers. It was after nine, the sun was mostly down over the far hills. A scattering of people were there, some in cars; a few of the residents still stood and gawked around the Sun Dial Trailer Park. The other parks seemed empty and dark, as if people were hiding.

Back on the highway, Alison drove down to the south in the tidal darkness as it spread across the land. *Get out, Al, while you can, get the hell out before somebody sets fire to you while you're napping through your life.* She covered her eyes with her left hand for a moment, and when she uncovered them, something darted out in front of her car. "Jesus!" She swerved out of the way and honked her horn. It had been some animal, a coyote, maybe a wolf. She pulled the car to the shoulder and parked. "God, don't scare me like that," she said aloud to her reflection in the rearview mirror.

Something leapt up from the ditch beside the road, pressing its face against the shotgun window.

A face, human, beast, like a man's face melted with a blowtorch until it's stretched and ridged. Reminded her of: pit bull. Reminded her of: a guy named Kevin Sloan who she'd only caught a glimpse of once or twice around town. Something about him and a pit bull. Melted skin. Eyes large and outlined in red. Like a comic book drawing. Shit, it looks like Sloan is a pitbull. Or a pitbull is Sloan. Her mind, in those few seconds, worked fast, but terror and shock create their own domains outside intelligence. The heart beats faster, the adrenaline pours, the ordinary way of seeing, of reversing images and then setting them right again as the image burns into the brain, all cut off the learned systems of logic and reason and rational thought.

Before Alison could react properly, the wall was there.

7

Sloan pressed his face to the window of the car.

Beautiful skin, smell meat.

The nights always began the same, with her call. What coursed through his blood had a language of its own, and the translation was: *hunger come hunt flesh taste infect spread harvest nest*. It awoke him with a stinging pain, and then the scent of his own sweat drove him mad. The stench, too, of the place where he stayed, the cave with its bat guano and lizard flesh, not the delicate perfume of human skin and pumping blood flowing beneath it like an underground stream searching for a well, for a fault, for a tunnel to burst out. Sloan's eyesight was keen in the dark, and he crawled on all fours through the corridor, sniffing the clean air of the outside world and the promise of humanity.

His own human feeling submerged, and even the dog feeling that had overtaken his bowed form was only there in his senses. His instinct was crushed in a blood obedience to her voice. *SHE'S IN MY FUCKING HEAD GET OUT OF MY HEAD, YOU CUNT, YOU ARE FUCKING DEAD, YOU GET OUT OF MY HEAD, I KILLED YOU*, the old voice roared. The call in his blood had sent him out on this night. He ran as if in a dream, as if she sat astride his back and reined him to the left and right, her bare heels like the sharpest spurs as they dug into his shanks, *prepare the way for my children to come*. He'd been heading for the trailers when he'd seen the car pulled to the side of the road. He felt her heat; heat was strong near the road, and the odor of blood and living tissue. He ran for it, and found her there. "Beautiful," he said, holding his claws up to the window. The girl seemed to freeze. She did not seem scared as much as she seemed blank, not there. *Smell tissue, blood, pumping furiously, the living animal flesh stretched taut across unpolluted meat*. Sloan's hunger was not one of feeding, but of passing. He needed to give her what he had. Needed to pass the demon into her, as he would others. *Prepare the way. Make ready*.

GET OUT OF MY HEAD! Something shrieked as it ricocheted through his brain. And then another car pulled up behind this one, and Sloan ducked down, out of the headlights.

8

Alison awoke abruptly, a flashlight shining in her eyes.

"You been drinking, young lady?" the man said.

She covered her eyes, blinded, and then the man leaning over into her half-opened window said, "Alison. Hey. Didn't know it was you."

When her vision adjusted, she recognized the man. Chip Grubb, deputy sheriff, on patrol in Palmetto. Grubb's sluggy face hung like a wheel of half-melted cheese over her. "You look like your mom, you know that?"

Alison tried to fight the image in her brain of this body on top of her mother's. *I wonder what my mother sees in you*, Alison thought. "I just pulled over to think," she lied, trying to send out whatever vibes she could to make him go away and leave her alone. Then she prayed he wouldn't ask to see her license, since she was just a month shy of sixteen and wasn't really supposed to be driving, anyway.

"My yes," Chip Grubb whispered, "just like your mama, pretty hair, and those eyes." He redirected the white beam of light to her eyes, and she turned to face forward.

"I have my father's eyes," Alison said.

9

After Alison Hunt had driven off back home, Deputy Sheriff Chip Grubb was about to get into his black-and-white Torino, when he thought he saw something, just a blur of movement, cannonballing toward him and he remembered the Nevilles, who had said a wolf had gotten into their backyard, not a coyote, a wolf, they insisted— and then the fragments of The Juicer they'd shoveled off the highway not far from this spot after some animal had torn into him—and fear didn't have much time to provoke a fight-or-flight response in the officer.

His hand automatically went for his gun, but the creature attacking him caught his hand before it touched metal.

10

Passing from Sloan's mouth, his spit, into the deep gouge of the wound, like snake's poison, through the epidermal layer down almost to the bone, cell invading cell, and slowly the walls would collapse and the new cells would take over, but none of this the dog-thing knew, only the demon consciousness knew as its feverish warmth spread from the hand to the wrist to the forearm to the elbow, on its path to the heart.

What Sloan knew: *taste of blood, passing pain out through teeth, warm, brief flash of strength with human blood.*

11

From Peter Chandler/Confessions

The day after Wendy's burial, I found the strength to go to her grave. Someone had come forward and bought her a little plot in the town boneyard on the other side of Nitro. I had been feeling a little sick, and I attributed this to many things, including the shock of Wendy's death.

It was the first week of July, and the town was decked out like a peacock in a hen house, with brightly painted flags and slogans and red, white, and blue crepe paper—Palmetto was going all out for the fourth and the Grubstake Days celebration. The local paper still ran a story about the family that had been attacked, apparently by a coyote, which was so unusual that coyote experts from as far away as Los Angeles were called upon for their opinions. But the family, named the Nevilles, were apparently unharmed by the animal, although Mr. Neville was bitten and had experienced some problems related to asthma or his heart or something. Others had seen the coyote, or wolf, or mountain lion, depending on who you talked to about it. A vigilante group was formed, and went on a search of the area, but didn't find it. Couldn't even find tracks. Sloan also was among the hunted, but the authorities believed he had run deeper into the hills, perhaps beyond Victorville.

Sloan had not gone far.

One night when I was taking the garbage cans out to the street, I felt someone's presence. It was late, and he startled me. He stood in the road, just out of the streetlight. My first reaction was to heft a rock at him, but I was shocked by his presence. I was sure he would've left town.

"Yeah?" I asked, trying my best to sound tough.

Sloan, half in shadow, looked haggard. The skin around his face seemed bloated as if he'd been drinking for two weeks straight. "Got-to-help," he said.

"You better get out of here, asshole," I snarled. "I told the cops it was you."

"Gonna-die-soon," he muttered to himself. "Callin', callin', callin'. Ya'allees come'n she callin'. In me, in you. Call out, she call, you come. Town-nest."

And then he moved from the shadows into the darkness, and was indistinguishable from it. I wasn't sure if he'd been there at all, or if I had hallucinated from the up-and-down fever I'd been having. Palmetto had gone crazy, or else I was seeing things crazy, and that was worse. I stood there a while longer, shivering, not from the cold or from seeing Sloan, but from a feeling in my body of bones and blood and tissue *aching*, and I wondered if I was going insane or if I was dying and just didn't know it. It was the beginning of feeling the turning, and I guess my body tried to resist it.

And then, I read the item about Wendy's funeral in the paper. It didn't mention her mother or father. All it had was her name and her birthdate.

My father was on the road for a week, on business, which I knew meant he was down in the flatlands chasing women and losing whatever money he had, but that was fine by me: a time of peace and quiet. I borrowed my mother's car. I had my learner's permit, and although it was against the rules to drive without a licensed driver sitting next to me, my mother understood my need to go alone.

Wendy had been buried in a small cemetery to the south of Pepe Alvarado's home, and just a few miles from the Coyote Cantina. It was the old Boniface Boneyard, as it was known around town. I went in the late afternoon, when it was getting cooler, and picked up some flowers at Connie's Florist. The grave was easy to find among the others: it was free from debris and plastic flowers.

As I stood, thinking about her, about Wendy, and that last day with her, I got the eerie feeling that I was being watched. I looked around, but saw no one.

And then, as if emerging from one of the graves in the far corner near the great stone wall surrounding the cemetery, a dark figure arose and began walking slowly, purposefully, toward me.

12

"You're the one who broke into my garden," the woman said. She wore a fairly smart, dark purple silk jacket and black pants. She had a multicolored scarf wrapped up in loops around her neck like a snake, and it finally curled around her head. "I knew you'd eventually show up here. I'm her mother. Call me Stella." Her manner was brusque and matter-of-fact.

"I never broke into anyone's yard," Peter said.

"Then who are you? You're the only one who's come here. Are you one of her lovers?"

"I was just a friend."

Stella smiled, and the smile was like a wild animal curling its lips back from its teeth. "My daughter had no *friends*."

"Look, I'm sorry she died. I was there that day."

Again, that hostile grin. She shook her head, and for a split second he caught the resemblance, saw a little bit of Wendy in that nose, in those cheekbones beneath the eyes, and then *gone*. "She's not dead." Stella pointed to the grave with her walking stick. "Oh, they may have buried her *flesh* there, and perhaps some useless bones, but I imagine she's already transformed by now. My brother told me how it would happen, you see, and my brother would know. Have you ever seen a caterpillar turn into a moth? It doesn't just change, you know, it has to close in on itself, and spin silk around itself. But moths are harmless, aren't they? Do you know about a certain kind of wasp that stings the grub and buries its eggs inside its body? And while the helpless grub lives on in a coma, the hatchlings begin devouring it from beneath its skin, until they finally emerge. These are all part of my daughter's transformation. It is a kind of evolution, even if the life that evolves must feed on the life that was. I am scaring you, aren't I?"

Peter shook his head. "I just think Wendy lived in a lot of pain."

The carnivorous smile faded, and something warm and compassionate overcame the old lady's face. "I suppose you're right, young man, I suppose you're right. You must think me a monster to say this about my own daughter, and that would also be the truth. Only a monster could breed a monster." She turned quickly and began walking away from him.

"I want to talk to you," he called after her.

She stopped. "You would be wiser to get in your car and drive home and help your mother and father pack and leave this place. But if you decide to stay . . ."

"I don't even know what you mean."

"I mean," the woman said, turning to face him again, "if you decide to stay, then I insist you come to my house. I can answer the questions you must have. But not here. Not by her grave."

"Who are you?"

"There's my home." She pointed her cane toward the Rattlesnake Wash. The high yellow walls of the Garden of Eden. "I'm the Beekeeper. Isn't that what you children call me?"

But Peter barely heard her words, for suddenly he felt a pain in his gut, and a feverstorm in his head, like the buzzing of thousands of flies, and his knees gave out. He remembered falling to the ground, and the light of day extinguishing all around him. Then, he was no longer in the graveyard with the woman, but raising a knife up and bringing it down into his father's left eye, only something pushed against the knife as it hit the skull, and the skin began to slough from his father's face. Something emerged from beneath it.

Wendy stood behind him in this dream—for he knew he was dreaming, knew that he was still in a graveyard with a woman who claimed to be Wendy's mother—he even had glimpses of the older woman helping him to her car, glimpses of a large gate opening to reveal a garden of many colors and the sound of bees—but Wendy was there in the waking dream, whispering that she would call him soon.

13

Beneath the grave, liquid forming liquid, Wendy felt the pleasure of movement in the confined space and wriggled through the abandoned bones and the seared flesh, and then the effort was tiring and all movement ceased, but the rejuvenating cells formed around her, taking over the surrounding thin wood, infiltrating each splinter; each fragment, until the wood and she and the bones and ash and the microscopic insects crawling across all of it, became her.

Peter Chandler opened his eyes and saw a white ceiling divided with thick, dark wooden beams.

The Garden of Eden. *She's brought me back.*

Stella's steel-gray hair and face were noticeably unmade-up, unbrushed, ungroomed—rumpled like the bed of a restless sleeper. Her eyes, as large and round as they were, seemed to recede into the skin around them.

"I know you want to leave," she said, "but, could you sit with me a bit?"

"I should get going."

"Oh. I see. You're feeling better?"

He nodded.

"Well, *if* you're all right."

"Tell me more about her."

"My daughter? All right. Do you know that she possesses demons? Not *possessed by* them, but *possesses*. And you've been infected," Stella said. She patted a cool hand towel across his forehead, and watched his eyelids flutter and close again.

"What time is it?" he asked, looking about the strange room. The light was dim, and he heard the beehive hum of an air conditioner. Stickiness of sweat around his neck and shoulders.

"Eight fifteen," Stella said as she tipped his head up so he could drink some water. She already has you. You walk in a dream. You don't even remember coming through my garden? Riding in my car? No. You were somewhere else, weren't you?"

"I need to get home." He tried to rise, but needle-prick pain jabbed at him all along his spine, and he lay back down.

"I don't keep much food in the house, but I think I've got something in the fridge—you must be very hungry."

"No." He bit his lower lip, and then nodded. "You said . . . I'm infected. By what?"

"Her. Wendy. I could feel it when I saw you there. I've seen it before, and to be honest, I'm surprised this town isn't completely infested. I'm not sure what she's waiting for. I only know so much about the turning, only what I've seen before. And I'm afraid there's nothing I can do to stop her."

"But she's dead," Peter whispered. "I was there."

"What she has," Stella said as if she were alone in the room and talking to the walls, "cannot die." And then she began telling him as much as she knew about her daughter.

15

Wendy tastes the seepage of night as it pours into the restless anthill above her, and her senses sharpen as activity in the nest grows with the dark. The ants tickle across the wood, and down inside it, for they are attracted to her odor. Sensations like violin strings plucked by delicate hands course through her as she reaches and they reach. They are caught in the amber of her skin, and she holds them, absorbing their energy, their small lives, breathing them in through her heaving thighs. Life. Tastes sweet to her, tastes like pure oxygen and orange blossoms, and as her breathing epidermis digests the insects, with their small puffs of vital smoke, her addiction grows stronger. Come, *her body shivers, and the ground around her moves; beneath her, the shockwaves of her turning move like an underground current, and there will be human beings who believe there is an earthquake, when it is just her vibrations. She sends them without even being aware, for she has no knowledge of her own consciousness. She has a drive that must be fulfilled, and so she waits for the coming of the brilliant color of life to pass through her and ease her torment. Her vibrations continue, and the tiny insects are absorbed, and a call is sent through the earth, an irresistible call.*

16

Stella set her face in a grim mask as she recounted her story. "About her birth I remember very little. It was not painful, or else I don't remember any pain. She seemed quite ordinary, in fact, and I was surprised, considering my anxiety. I had considered abortion—no moral dilemma there, you see, because I knew this child was cursed. But the most awful instinct imaginable arose in me, a disgusting reaction of chemicals and hormones and twisted nature.

"I believe it's called the maternal instinct. Months passed, and I moved to this house. The town was different then. Almost no one lived up here. The Urquarts had their ranch, and I had a lunatic ex-husband who would bother me at times, and some squatters living on the other side of the Wash where the trailers now sit. But it was an exquisite wasteland, and I was left fairly alone. I could dose myself up with killers—my painkillers and tranquilizers and booze—hoping that it would so misshape the child growing within me that there would be no hope of its survival outside the womb.

"When the day came, I decided that since I could not kill the child myself, I would have to set up a circumstance in which we both would die. I drove out to the caves in No Man's Land and crawled back as far as I could go into a particularly narrow cavern until I found a room of sorts. It had a small entrance—which I could barely squeeze through. I took some stones and piled them up, as if it were the most natural thing to do in the world. There was still some light that came through, but I assumed I would die in childbirth. She was born fine. I lived on lizards and large roaches, sometimes a bat if I was lucky enough to catch one. I was an animal. Truly. In my hallucinations, I believed I was eating the most elegant dinners.

"And my baby, my Wendy, began to seem beautiful to me, as she nursed, taking, not mother's milk from my breast, but blood.

"A few days after she started nursing, a vagrant heard my baby's weak cries, and we were rescued. I was so weak from loss of blood that I could not resist being taken from what I had once hoped would be my tomb. Oh, yes, and I tried murdering her a few times, but each time I did, there was some awful feeling—call it life, call it mothering, that kept me from accomplishing the deed.

"And the worst of it was: she was pretty and good and didn't seem like a demon at all.

"But I saw through that, I knew what she was, that she could be nothing else but the Lamia, the descendant of her bloodline, passed from the ancient world down through the possessed and the possessing, until finally she was born through me.

"Her eyes, you see, were glittering dark stones. They were her legacy. She was born with an outer eye, like a skin, that covers her real eyes. It is always through the eyes that we see to the soul, Peter, and her soul was all of darkness.

"You may think I hallucinated it all.

"But it was passed to me, got into my blood, and took me over for a time, too. In a strange way, Wendy saved me. Wendy was my scapegoat, for it was in her forming body within mine that the demon went, inhabiting the child, so that when she was born, it left my body completely. It is a parasite, and it will be attracted to whatever it can survive best within.

"And then I did something for which I cannot forgive myself, even when I think of what evil lay dormant within her then.

"I kept her locked away, in the cellar, like she was some animal. In darkness. I fed her, I brought her out occasionally, I was hoping, I suppose, that she would die.

"But she thrived. She *thrived*.

"And I knew then, I *knew* that she would avenge herself one day. But it is beyond that.

"Something I don't understand.

"There's something she wants this town for, something I'm afraid that is far beyond merely getting back at me.

"She needed her own physical death to begin the process, and I know that something will come out of that grave. And I intend to be ready for it."

17

"I don't believe you," Peter said when Stella Swan finished the story.

Stella reached into her purse and extracted a bottle of pills. She opened it and popped a couple of them, dry, into her mouth. "You think," she said, "I'm a hopeless middle-aged, drug-addicted witch who, because of guilt over the way she's treated her only daughter, has fabricated this tale which absolves her of all guilt of her monstrous mothering. But, Peter, you feel it, you have it. It's almost a disease, you know, and some people don't live through it. Most people. Some do, and they exhibit the classic signs of possession. Still others simply go insane. My brother Rudy told me of a man who had begun eating his own flesh because he wanted to rid himself of the demon. Wendy is not dead, I assure you, and this entire town, I'm afraid is doomed. And . . ." She swallowed a few more pills. "It's all my doing."

"I don't believe in demons," Peter said.

"Well, then," Stella said, leaning back on the couch, "that's all the worse for you."

Chapter Thirty-four
The Legend of Deadrats

1

This happened the night Charlie Urquart murdered his parents:

He wanted to cry out, not in fear, but in revulsion, as if it had finally sunk into him exactly what he had been touching all this time. What was taking him to that blind spot called the Big O. Not a girl with red hair and curved hips, but the thing he glimpsed in the dark, the thing that had recoiled from his match. The match burned his skin because he hadn't put it out; he'd forgotten about the flame burning. The skin of the creature—for he could think of no other *name* for it—*Jesus, it's got no name, nobody's ever seen something like this*—the skin was *glowing, Jesus, glowing like it was radioactive, flickering on and off like a firefly, but glowing only in the dark. Its mouth, dripping, its breasts, not Wendy.*

The creature hadn't even slapped the match from his fingers. It didn't mind being seen. The Deadrats side of Charlie couldn't even understand why it stayed still, watching him. As fascinated with his reaction as he himself was repulsed by the sight.

"Don't be scared, my Deadrats." It was Wendy's voice, and then the match burned the tips of his fingers, and when he lit another one, it was just Wendy standing before him. He passed the flame close to her face, and touched her skin with his other hand. Her skin was cold and rough. "I'm shedding."

In his fingers, bits of sloughed flesh, dry and flaky.

"It doesn't really hurt," she said.

"What I saw."

"It's an illusion of the dark."

"No. I saw."

"Do you believe everything you see?"

"What—what about now? How do I know this . . ." He touched

262

the side of her face, expecting warmth. It wasn't even cold, her skin, it was like touching a piece of paper.

"I have never lied to you, Charlie. Never."

"How do I know?"

"I told you from the first, what I wanted." Her voice faltered, and he saw a look of pain in her face for a moment, a cloud passing over.

"It hurts you, doesn't it?"

"Yes." She sounded ashamed.

"Why not stop it?"

From the chill darkness, she said, "it's not something I have control over. Once it's started . . . have you ever been sick?"

Charlie didn't answer.

"I have been sick since the day I was born, and the only thing that helps me is like a drug. When I don't have it, I am close to dying. I mean that. My skin tightens, hardens. I want to—just end. End. And then, there's this stuff. The dog, remember the dog? It had something in its blood, something that had been passed to it, something that has a will beyond human understanding. I can smell that kind of blood anywhere. And I drank the blood, and so have you, and so has this town."

"But it's not a drug."

"No. Something far older than herbs and medicines. Something that once flourished, Charlie, on the savannahs where mankind first walked erect. A vital fluid, Charlie, a liquid of the gods. In ancient legend, surely, you've heard of hybrids of man and beast, of demons that transform, of gods that turn into swans to mate with mortal women. This is the water of change."

"But I saw the demon."

"You saw what your mind can live with. It's all any of your kind sees. Until they change."

"Will I change?"

"You already have," she whispered, and then left him in the dark. That had been the night he had murdered his family.

2

The nights he could take.

The days were nothing but excruciating agony. Separation from her, from his beloved Wendy, was terror. The days from June to July had passed like kidney stones for Charlie Urquart, although his turning had happened so quickly he was barely aware of it. Something about having murdered his parents had helped push him further over the edge, until he couldn't even identify Charlie within himself, but only felt Deadrats there, out of its braincave, making the decisions, living on instinct. His father kept giving him marching orders, but Deadrats ignored his father, and using his claws, wrote Wendy's name over and over again across living room walls. He laughed at inner jokes, and spoke with his father and mother whenever they asked questions. But Deadrats was in total control.

Still, he felt lonely. And the meat from his parents' bodies could only go so far.

He tried calling Alison, hoping she would pick up the phone— *How delicious would that little piece be?* Deadrats thought. *All that pretty hair and those tits and the way her legs were swollen with blood. What a dainty dish that one would provide!* Alison never answered his call. In the night, he leapt from the second-story window and bounded across the back acreage, down into the arroyo, out into the caverns to meet his mistress. She made him watch her with the other boy.

He hated the other boy now. Hated like only Deadrats could hate: there was hunger in that hatred.

Peter My Next Dinner Chandler.

Wendy made him watch while they mated. That was the worst humiliation for Deadrats, to know that he wasn't good enough for her. To know that he wasn't the One. "I can do it," he begged her when the other boy had gone, and Deadrats could crawl out from the shadows of a cave, bat or ground squirrel in his jaws, dropped for her, just for her. "I want to. I need you to take me there. My head hurts so fucking much!"

But she was a bitch goddess to the extreme. She made him see things, she spun his mind with fire and fury, she made him want to go howl in the night and taste the FRESH MEAT of town. ALL THAT FRESH MEAT.

He wanted it.

"How long?" he moaned, the blood of animals on his lips. "How much longer?"

She gave no answer—her silence banged in his head like pots

and pans falling in a steel kitchen. GET IT OUT OF MY HEAD!
He raced the night, naked, blood on his face, out along the dark
mesas, to return to the house that had begun to stink of rotting
meat. Rolled-up newspapers covered the front porch, and the light
bulbs were beginning to go out.

Then he didn't hear from her for days. When he tired of waiting,
he called his buddies Billy and Terry over to the house for a pool
party to end all pool parties. July Fourth, he told them on the
phone, imitating Charlie Urquart's voice—Deadrats was so good
at sounding like that kid it astounded him—"Bring a friend if you
want, sure," he said.

Then Deadrats drew out some of his father's hunting traps from
the attic—the old bear trap would work nicely, he thought—and
got them ready for his friends.

Chapter Thirty-five
Digging Up the Demon

1

Than dreamed awake.

*The hand covered his mouth, and he wasn't afraid. He trusted
the Hand of Glory. The hand was covering his mouth for a reason.
The palm was like rough leather, with the smell of raw, drying
meat. The hand wanted him to be quiet because it would show him
something, something that would make him want to scream, but he
should not scream.*

There, in front of him, was the girl.

Wendy.

Down on all fours.

*He noticed her breasts first, dangling, he noticed the white curve
of her ass, he noticed her flared nostrils, and the wisps of hair
caught in her lips, her lips like drooping petals.*

*And then he saw the pulp of its white flesh, and what moved
beneath it like some other living thing in an encasing of skin. There*

*in the grave, she stretched and turned, and reached for him, buried
with her.*

Her kiss was rape.

The vision melted before his eyes. Than stood next to the Bone,
who pulled the Hand of Glory back from the boy's mouth.

2

"It's gonna protect you," the old man cackled. "It's like fightin' fire
with fire. She can't get in you if you build up your 'munity with the
juice, boy. And tonight, boy, we go out there and dig her up and
make sure we kill it before it gets out. Got to catch her while she's
shifting. And that's just what she's doin' down there, right now."

"Shifting?"

"Changing—you know, becomin' a full-fledged demon like in
the comical books."

"How do you know?"

"How do *I* know? How do *I* know. *You* know, dontcha? It's the
demon juice, you whelp, it puts you in touch with other demons. It
draws you to them and them to you."

"Wait a minute. You told me before you thought she's been dead
for years 'til I told you different. So how come you couldn't feel her
before you heard from me she was still around?"

"Didn't get a signal from her since that Southey boy cast the
demons outta her and into him so many years ago. Only, I felt it
again, like in headaches, killer headaches, comin' on this summer. It
was returning to her then. She musta been like a vaccuum for it, and
it eventually come back. The demon, ya see, ain't her, this Lamia
thing, but it sure as shit's drawn to her because in her it can survive,
hell, it had this incarnation in her, it was reborn in her skin. Can't
survive long in bad flesh, and from what I reckon, that Juicer was
getting more and more rotten for it, so it had to go home, back to the
girl. You always return to your first love, boy, ain't nobody ever told
you that? So I lied if I told you I didn't know it was back, 'cause I
did. Could feel it. Smell it, too. But I didn't know that girl was still
kickin' until you told me and then it all made sense. Now, we're
gonna go get that girl's bones out of that grave and make sure she
don't shift no more. I got me my family Bible in the backseat along
with a coupla shovels."

"A Bible? Are you gonna exorcise her or something?"

The old man laughed and swatted his scalp. "No, boy, it's the biggest damn Bible you ever saw, must weigh a ton, and we're gonna need it to hit her with if she starts to rise up."

3

It was almost midnight when Than and Bonyface arrived at the cemetery gate, a rusty shovel in the old man's arms. The gate to the boneyard was open and bent, for until this particular night, July third, there had never been any vandalism or shenanigans in the graveyard beyond local kids occasionally kicking over the stones.

The cemetery smelled like shitdust to Than. Old Bonyface was busy sniffing the wind. Than glanced about in the dark: the lights of town burned bright orange and yellow and white. "Wouldn't it be smarter to wait till tomorrow?"

"Eh? Boy?"

"You said demons don't come out in daylight."

"Tomorrow might be too late. You feel it?"

Than listened to the night. Cars drove by on the highway, and somewhere, a dog howled. He felt a prickly heat along the soles of his feet, and a tingling down his back. But he said nothing.

"You do feel it, son, and you ain't tellin' me on accounta you think it's your imagination in overdrive, but it's like fingers tickling you, ain't it?"

Than shrugged. "I feel something. But it could be anything."

"It's her. She's turning, boy, and now's the time to strike if there's anytime good. Here." Bonyface waved both hands in a circle over an area that covered five or six graves.

"There's a fresh one." Than pointed toward a pile of dirt. Sure enough, the marker read *Wendy Swan* when Lucas shined his flashlight beam on it.

The digging took forever. Than had never worked so hard in all his life. After the night went on without end, and the hole just got bigger and bigger, Than fully expected to hit the lid of a hard wood coffin, but, instead, the shovel went into something like mud, or perhaps even a lizard. It began vibrating in his hands, and Than dropped the shovel, scrambling out of the grave. He felt like he was going to have a heart attack from fear and overwork, and he wanted to shriek when he got up out of the hole, but was too winded to say much.

Bonyface, who had been sitting there perusing his enormous Bible, glanced down at the shovel. "Hit her, I 'xpect."

"It can't be the coffin. It's like . . . goo," Than said when he had caught his breath.

The Bone slid down into the small hole and popped the shovel out. Something shiny dripped from the tip. He wiped his finger across it, and then sniffed his fingers before licking them. "Yep, it's demon, all right."

"What are we gonna do?"

"Nathaniel?"

"I want to go home."

"You don't turn yeller on me, not now, not in a dang boneyard at the witchin' hour with me one foot set in the open grave of the demon in the middle of her shift." Bonyface wagged a finger in Than's face.

Lying there, beneath the dirt: Not a demon. But her body. Buried in the dirt. Whatever coffin that had been was gone, and there was a curious bed of gray ash beneath her.

"Look at her, Jesus, why's she like that?" Than asked. "I thought her head was shot off."

The beam from the flashlight illuminated the body. Wendy Swan lay there in the dirt and ash, skin white and healthy, hair red and thick, and a flush to her face as if she were more vital in death than in life.

"Ain't she bee-yootiful, son? She done got 'juvenated, at least part-way," Bonyface said. "Musta caught herself some bugs, boy, some *life*, even the wood, boy, even the wood is part of life, and Lamia's done taken the life and sewn herself back together, but she needs more life, boy, she needs the kinda blood we can give her, she's like a skeeter a little bit, boy, she only needs it when she's ready to lay, and she needs it bad, boy, c'mon, with me, help me do the deed before she wakes up and we get shifted into her just like we was folding eggs into batter." Bonyface held his hand out for the knife he'd told Than to bring along. Than reached into his backpack and withdrew it. Than could've been mistaken, but the blade seemed to shine in the moonlight.

He passed it to Bonyface, but as the man's hand closed around its hilt, Than pulled it back. "You sure this'll stop her? If we just cut this one thing—" He remembered what the old man had told him: *Demons can't be killed, boy, they can only be put somewhere safe 'til some damn fool lets 'em out again.*

But before Bonyface could answer, he gave out a shriek and fell to his knees into the grave, onto her body, sinking into her. He held onto Than's wrist, and Than almost fell into the shallow grave, but managed to stay at its rim. A gasp escaped Bonyface's lips, "She got me. Oh fuck," he said. Later, Than thought these were his exact words. His last words. Oh fuck.

Flesh fell in thick slabs off the sides of the old man's thighs— Than heard the sound of humming like a thousand locusts in the air, and the vibrations from the earth—before he dropped the flashlight, as he stood there shivering, Than saw Bonyface's skin along his face and neck and arms turn liquid and run like melting wax down his bones.

4

A hot, dry wind blew lightly across Than's face. The wind was like exhaust from some profound energy source, some engine converting fuel into movement, and then releasing this warmth, its waste product.

He tried to close his eyes, but fear seemed to be working against him. He had to watch. What was happening to Bonyface was fascinating, and even the terror Than felt gave him a warm feeling of being alive in a way he had never felt before. *No, don't look, don't, it's bad, it's evil.* He tried to move away from the edge of the grave, but the old man's hand still clutched his wrist, *glued* to his arm. *Don't look and it won't be happening, no demon, no demon, no skin falling, no blood pouring.*

He would not look. He would not look because to look would give it power. Fear, fear would give the demon power, he would not give it that, it could kill him, yeah, it could rip him to shreds, but he would not give it fear to eat.

This boy, Than Campusky, was often a coward in his lifetime, and he carried such epithets as "pig boy" and "thunder thighs" with some grace. However, this was a moment of truth, and he decided to be brave, after a few seconds, to stare the demon in the face and laugh.

So he looked.

The body in the grave pulsed a greenish-yellow glow. A network of tubes ran from beneath Bonyface's fallen clothes and skin, wrapped around the long bones of his legs, but then, Than realized they were fat and arteries, intertwined, interconnected to the liquid yellow neon of Wendy Swan's own legs. Pumping life from the old man to the young, dead girl, Bonyface dripped and pooled.

Bonyface's jaws parted and what seemed like a series of gasps came forth—as if the pleasure of being absorbed by her body was so intense he could not find the words to describe it. The warm wind spraying across Than's face was from the old man's mouth, the exhaust of being absorbed as the skin on his chest turned, opening and falling off so that the blood could pour more freely down to the power source. Finally, the pure wind of burning life died. The old man's face sucked in on itself, the eyes shriveled like raisins.

A glowing yellow liquid bubbled around Wendy's thighs, as Bonyface's skin fluttered down like a moth to cover the dead girl's nakedness.

His bones were the last to fall. They had been sucked clean. His skull fell first with its bit of tattered scalp, and then the ribcage with the spine, and then the rest.

The hand that clutched Than's wrist finally let go.

Wendy's body shimmered, wriggling almost imperceptibly.

Like a face breaking the surface of water as a drowning man might for one last gasp of air, the old man's face burst from her thighs, pulling at the skin of her belly as if trying to escape.

The surface of her skin was calm again.

From behind him, Than heard a dog growling.

Before him, Wendy Swan moved as if in a dream.

Above him, for a second, he thought he saw the beautiful stars, white and brilliant, and so far from his small corner of the world, and wondered why God wasn't there to lift him up. *Our Father who art in Heaven*, he began, but was not able to continue.

It's 'cause I drank the demon juice. Damn it, damn it, you screwed up Campusky, you went and drank it and now nobody's gonna save you. Bonyface was wrong, it doesn't make you immune, shit, it probably makes you taste *better.*

"I am your life now." Her voice came without movement from her lips. He felt something tickle the underside of his heart, as if she were stroking his chest from the inside, playing his veins like harp strings.

The growling died. *Kill me, just kill me now, do it quick*, he prayed.

The old man's words, *Ain't she beautiful, son? She done got 'juvenated, at least part-way.*

No, Than thought, *she got rejuvenated all the way. With you, Bonyface. Just like you said, must've caught some bugs, some life, even the wood of the coffin. Whatever had life in it, and then you, Bonyface, with one foot in her grave, near her thighs, absorbed, your life into hers. She drank you like a cool glass of water.*

Than didn't even scream when Wendy rose from the grave, her arms open to embrace him. Nerve endings jangled, and he felt a paralysis set in: first, his throat, and then the rest of his body. For a moment he thought she had the head of some kind of dog he had never seen, almost lizardlike, and her arms were snakes, even short antlers rose at her scalp, but then she was beautiful again, and he began an exquisite shivering, pee running down his legs, and he knew that his life would be over soon—he prayed it would come fast and furious—but she moved slowly at first, like a tarantula, and then so fast, scurrying toward him, the way the tiny, dark scorpions would run into the shadows from the front porch light of his house.

He waited for his fate to come to him.

5

But the landscape shifted, the sky blossomed with a streak of lightning that ripped apart the world within his vision. To Than Campusky. A beautiful woman, her cheeks flush with a peach glow, her eyes yearning, her hair sparkling in the white light of this dream reality that he had somehow entered. No shame in her nakedness as she drew herself to him.

"Nathaniel," she whispered as she pressed her lips to his neck. "Don't be afraid. Don't, my beloved, don't be afraid."

6

The night knew fear.

A family named Neville, who lived near the Wash—and had reported seeing a wild dog near their property for several nights—had gone to bed early. Lucy Neville sat up reading for a bit; her husband was already snoring by midnight. When she heard a noise in one of her children's rooms, she got up to see if Stevie had knocked over his lamp again, only what she saw instead was a young man standing before her, his face scarred and elongated as if he'd been tortured, and then her life was over; if you were to walk through the Nevilles' home a half hour later, you would see blood-spattered walls and what looked like a very messy butcher shop as Kevin Sloan satisfied what felt to him to be an insatiable hunger.

Deadrat—aka Charlie Urquart—raced across the mesas to the Ed and Inez Trailer Park, and managed to grab two girls he knew from school, and tore into them out on the edge of the Wash with mucho gusto—and as his heart beat rapidly, he howled, and felt the changes in his body as she took him over. She was there—he knew she was. She was there for him. She was giving him the power.

It was all he needed.

Feeling her inside him. With him.

She was back.

He danced out on the desert, feeling like some primal man, fresh from the kill, worshipping the source of his strength.

Before the first light of morning, Peter Chandler heard a scratching at his window. He sat up and looked out into the darkness.

He thought he saw Charlie Urquart, only he was naked and covered with blood. In his arms, a baby that was either sleeping or dead.

And then Charlie grinned, nodding to him. Behind him, Wendy stood.

It's a dream, Peter told himself. *It's a dream.*

But something else whispered, *She owns us now. We gave ourselves to her. She's part of us.*

Peter Chandler felt something that he could only think of as a magnetic pull draw him outside the house, out to where Charlie stood—*in a dream, it has to be a dream*—

The pavement and dirt were covered with small black scorpions, and the sky lightened with the beginning of day.

Peter stood by and watched as Wendy, her lips and chin drenched in red, reached for the offering in Charlie's hands, as the baby woke up from its brief sleep.

All the while, Wendy kept her eyes on Peter.

He felt a fever growing within his body. When he woke up, he found himself lying on the cold concrete of the front porch. The night and its dreams were through.

He shivered from fever, and went back to bed, but the visions of Wendy and Charlie and Sloan and even Than would not leave his burning dreams.

In his dreams, Than laughed at him and told him that it was all right, what he was going to do.

It's all right, Peter. We're all in this dream together. You, me, Charlie, and Wendy. We're hers now. We belong to her.

Chapter Thirty-six
The Last Day of Palmetto

1

Dawn broke like glass on the highway, all sharp and loud and ready to cut. July could get friggin' hot, that's what one cop thought as he got his day—and his ass—in gear, and wished. Friggin' hot and friggin' long and the damn celebration was tonight, he said to no one as he had a beer to cut off the bad taste in his mouth of the liquor from the night before. The coyote bite on his hand had got infected. He hated wild animals.

2

Women are like wild animals, the cop thought as he waited at the stoplight, watching the teenaged girl go by, wondering what color panties she was wearing. It was his hobby, for there was little else

273

to do in this town beyond stopping dogfights (when the mood suited him and he didn't have a bet going), and locking up town drunks (who sometimes happened to be married to the woman he was screwing on the side).

Officer Grubb, Chip to some, the Grubman to others, was about as fat as a man could get and still fit behind the steering wheel of a black-and-white Ford Torino, and if you had known him as a kid you'd've said he'd never make it to adulthood—he'd been the kind of bully everyone expected to get the shit beat out of him at one time or another by someone bigger and smarter and quicker. But somehow the Grubman had eluded the predicted fate and had made it to adulthood, and although there were other cops who cruised the strip of highway through Nitro and Palmetto, none of them questioned the Grubman's supreme authority in this territory. Not that a hell of a lot ever went on. *Hell, a fire in the Wash brings 'em out like flies in this pisspot. Some trailer trash whore gets shot and the whole friggin' town's acting like a tragedy happened.* Biggest thrill for the Grubman had been the television interview, shown on three LA stations, when The Juicer's body had been found out on the highway. In that interview, the Grubman had made the profound remark that, "We run a pretty tight ship up in Palmetto."

The Grubman wasn't known for his intellect, but for his unflagging libido. Like all ugly men, he had a need to constantly hear the kinds of lies you only hear in bed with someone who doesn't care for you: his flavor of the season was Jeanne Hunt, but she was getting too weird, too serious, it wasn't just fun and games anymore with her. She wasn't running a tight enough ship, she was letting real concerns in between the sheets. Her girl was a problem, getting sullen, giving accusing looks; her husband, Ed, that old piss artist, bothering her conscience. *It's just sex, for chrissakes, it's not like I'm taking something away from your family, woman.* Time to give her the old dump truck. *Least I still got my main squeeze, Jinx; who understands me.* His wife of twenty years, Jinx, had always given him his space, always made room for the fact that he was just more man than most women could handle. But Jeanne Hunt: she was like every other woman he'd ever encountered, she was beginning to act like some kind of friggin' *wife.* Women were like that, they only wanted to have fun so they could drag you into their little Whirlpools and then you were on a rinse cycle (*With gals like Jeanne it's more like a* menstrual *cycle*, he thought as he drove down to Trudy Virtue's Magnificent Diner for a coffee and sticky bun), and who knew which end was up once a woman got you going with *her* problems?

Today, the Grubman was going to meet Jeanne for what might be the last time, and it saddened him a little because she was a pretty good piece of tail even if she was slightly damaged goods, and that was hard to find in a town this small; he'd have to start doing his hunting up to Twenty-nine Palms or down in Yucca Valley. *'Course, I should've taken that Swan babe with the independent hips for a test drive before she got her head shot off.* He pulled his cruiser into the parking lot at the Majestic; the place was fairly packed for so early in the morning.

The Grubman looked up to the skies: a good day for partying, a bad day to dump a gal. His stomach rumbled, and he thought of breakfast, and then, later on in the day, that great chili that Jinx, his wife, always improved on at the annual cookoff. *Fill me up with chili and fart the night away.*

3

"This kind of weather don't bode well," he said to Trudy as he pushed his way into the diner and made room for himself at the counter. "Gonna be too hot for peppers. We're all gonna burn up."

Trudy filled up a cup of coffee for him, slapping it down on the counter. The Grubman knew she didn't like him, which was half the fun of coming in here for snacks four or five times a day. He could see it in her eyes, *Women are like wild animals, and Trudy's a big old grizzly.*

"Something sure smells good in here, Trudy, you start using deodorant?"

As she had been doing for nearly six years, she ignored him. She pushed the creamer in front of him. "How do you want it this morning, Officer, white or black?"

The Grubman grinned and said, "How about red, white, and blue, sweetheart?"

Trudy arched an eyebrow. "How about you just drink it and get out there and make sure we don't got no delinquents throwing no more rocks through my window?"

The Grubman craned his neck and saw the rectangle of card-board taped across the lower corner of the front window of the diner. "Coulda been the quake," he said. "Maybe the quake. I felt a quake. Little one. Probably from Indio."

"Mr. Policeman, you can't be telling me that no earthquake threw a rock from the ground through my window. No, it's those delinquents that run this town while you're eating your Twinkies."

"You want to come out and fill out a report, Trudy? Be happy to fix you up with some paperwork if it's what you want. You see these kids throw a rock?"

"Don't have to *see* things to know them," she grumbled.

Bristles like a cat. He sipped his coffee. "Could be some of the kids in town, Trudy, I won't deny that, but not much to do if we don't know for sure, you read me? Now how 'bout you slipping me one of those sticky buns over there? Not that little one on top, but that big old sticky bun down at the bottom of the pile—man needs food that sticks to his ribs, you know, I got a big day ahead, need all the energy I can get."

As he reached for the napkin dispenser, Trudy caught his hand.

The Grubman looked at the tear in his flesh as if it weren't even his own hand. Two deep gashes and four lighter indentations: something had bit him. But when? He remembered, vaguely, an animal. "Something nipped me a few days back."

"You got bit by an angry husband, maybe?" Trudy Virtue raised an eyebrow.

4

Palmetto and Nitro were twin aspects of the one true town, what used to be called Boniface Well, divided the way other towns were by railroad tracks, this one by the Rattlesnake Wash. Their alliance was an uneasy one, and one of the few visible signs of their connection, besides the telephone lines and the sewer system and the schools that all the children had been bused up to Twenty-nine Palms to, was happening this very day. The Fourth of July and Grubstakes Day had been plotted by a joint effort between the local American Legion Post, the Oddfellows, the Rebekahs and the Daughters of the Western Star. While every town in America was planning some kind of gala event, Palmetto had settled on a turn-of-the-century theme, its Grubstakes Days, since the original Boniface Well was founded in 1876 and therefore what was a national celebration also would have its own local resonance. The American Legion Post was halfway through a pancake breakfast, after which folks would drive down Highway 4 with the floats for the street parade. The Oddfellows and Rebekahs would host a luncheon at the Oddfellows Hall, and the Daughters of the Western Star, of which in Palmetto there were twenty-seven members, were taking over the home tour and the Western Star Dinner honoring the oldest resident of Palmetto, Mary McGee Joiner, who was born just fifteen years after the original town was founded. In spite of these planned festivities (involving endless committee meetings over the past two years), it was estimated that less than a third of the residents would be participating, since most would go down into Palm Springs, or over to Redlands, or up to Twenty-nine Palms, or even drive the two hours to Los Angeles for other, swankier celebrations.

They were the lucky ones.

5

The day is hot and long. Out on Highway 4, the lazy parade is passing, and it consists of a few cars and some children dressed as either Liberty or Patriots, with a kazoo band in back playing "Yankee Doodle Dandy." But the children are dragging their feet, and you might think it is from the heat, because it is a warmer than normal day—must be well into the hundreds.

The town has a ragged quality to it, as if it is just too tired to be up for a full-scale celebration of the Fourth. There've been reports of a mountain lion having come down from the hills, or of a child having gotten bitten by a mad dog—some citizen has taken it upon himself to tack up posters about it on the telephone pole, which Jeanne Hunt reads as she waits for the parade to go by.

Just because the town looks dead doesn't mean it *is* dead. July is the dead month for Palmetto. It is the dead month for much of the desert. Even the lizards stay out of the sun until the late afternoon. Tumbleweed gets caught beneath the Pinto and scrapes the road like fingernails as the car continues on down the empty highway.

A boy who calls himself Deadrats stands in the shadows of the oldest structure in town, the old meeting house. He thinks, *Teenaged wasteland.*

He smiles because he knows his thoughts travel to Her, his mistress, and, like radar, he feels this thought bounce against her skin.

The demon is passing, She responds, *through bites, through infection, and those who are weak will fall, and the strong will stay. I will spread my fingers across this parched land and it will be mine and for those who come after me.*

All this in one word, one thought he hears from her: *Lamia.*

He continues smiling, because he doesn't know that he is already in pain. He mistakes the curved needles hooked into his soul for a sensation of pleasure.

6

And then, the sun sets, and the whole town is there, and even Peter feels it, in his blood, the call, and he begins to not feel so much like a boy of fifteen named Peter Chandler but like a creature hankering for blood and feasting, and when his father comes home from some days down in the flatlands, Peter is waiting for him, and it's sunset, and something that might be fire seems to explode across Peter's vision as he takes his fists and pummels his father to death.

7

Or is it a dream? He can't tell anymore, he doesn't know in this moment of rage and power what is life and what is dream, and he goes with the dream and watches the blood begin to soak his shirt. He watches the blood, he watches the red scorpions crawling from the blood, dancing in some firelight, and he sees her—

—the girl of his dreams.

Wendy Swan is with him, and he's not killing his father— he's watching something else do it, some red creature like an angel tearing at his father, and then his mother walks into the room— she's screaming, and his sister, but Peter is no longer there, he's in a dark cave with Wendy and she whispers to him as she brings him into her body, "Come here, my lost boy, yes, Peter, yes, like that, just like that."

Peter Chandler/Confessions

So, here's the end of the road, as my father would say. If he had lived. Yes, I killed my father, and although I probably had enough justification for doing it from the various physical and mental tortures he'd put me through, I still feel the heaviness of a burden of guilt for that. And yes, I can blame a demon for it. I can even blame a demon for what Charlie did. What all of us did. Did I kill my mother, and my sister? I have no memory of those acts, although I suspect that yes, I must have. I must have, although there are no bodies and no blood and nothing other than a fire to indicate that anything had happened in Palmetto.

All of us did this, except for Alison, the one innocent in the bunch.

I would tell you that I was there for the barbecue of human flesh that got served up that day, that I remember the houses as they burned, and the people desperately trying to get out to their cars, trying to get away from the festivities of the Fourth of July, with Charlie and Sloan and Wendy there—

But whatever power the demon had, it took me over, and all I could do was watch as if from a sideline at a football game. My emotions were nowhere to be found; my will was gone. All I could do was watch and hope it was the dream.

I walked through a minefield of dead and dying bodies, a carnival of flesh tearing at itself, a curious steam rising as of energy being given off. Than stood among a pile of the dead, his face ragged, his eyes blurry with tears, his chin quivering.

Cutting through all my disbelief, I said, "Okay, so tell me what you know." I stepped over the wriggling body of the man who had been our mailman. My mind began a hammering sound, and then I heard what might've been the flight of a million locusts across the land, the sounds of plagues, I thought, the noises of the cursed.

"I drank this demon juice and it makes me see things, and I went with old Bonyface to dig up her grave—" And rather than interrupt him by shouting, "YOU WHAT?" I accepted all he tossed my way. I felt like I had looked upon the face of madness and nothing in the world would be the same. "And she had changed, Bonyface called it shifting, only he was one of them, and oh, shit, Peter, I think I am, too, now, I got it in me, and you . . . you must have it in you, too." His words slowed as he eyed me suspiciously. We got the keys to his mother's car, a Ford Country Squire. I didn't need to ask him if his family was dead. As far as I knew, everyone was dead.

"Are you one of them, Peter?" he asked me, passing me the keys.

"I don't think so. I've seen things, but . . . I don't think so."

"You might be lying."

"And so could you."

"Okay, look, I believe you. But she's done it. It was her demons that turned Sloan into his dog—"

As soon as he said it, I knew it was true. I remembered Sloan in the half-light of the streetlamp. His face had elongated, his body was stooped. *"Who weeps, Chandler?"* Sloan had asked.

"And she made him infect the town with what he's got. It's something like the juice I drank, only it kills some people and . . ."

"What about here! Is this some damn juice!" I shouted. The blood on my hands had driven me over the edge. Whose blood was it? Whose? My father's? My little sister's? One of my friends from school? Who had I butchered that day? Had it been me? Had it really been me?

These are the questions I ask myself to this day. I know I'm not insane. I know I'm not a killer. Yet I can distinctly remember the look on my father's face as he died beneath my fists.

"Look back there," I told Than.

Than turned and looked at the fire that grew downtown, with night and its dark cloth dropping behind the rising yellow and blue flames, and the wind blowing.

The town of Palmetto had become a funeral pyre.

"Alison," I said.

"She must be dead, too," he said.

"She can't be." I didn't know why I said this, other than a sixth sense, a feeling that Alison could not be dead, that something within my soul would not let her be dead, too, that she was somehow my future and I could not let that go the way of this nightmare.

The desert winds can blow a fire across a highway, from house to house, and if no one comes to put it out within the first half-hour, you can kiss a good ten-mile stretch of homes good-bye.

You Come When I Call You

I watched it burn in the rearview mirror as I pressed my foot on the brake. And then I had to laugh, because I had stopped at a red light and there was no reason. Who gave a fuck if I stopped at the lights? I laughed a little too heartily. I laughed a little too long.

At Alison's house, I smelled death, and resisted going inside.

Than began whimpering again, and then crying. I prefered dealing with whatever was in the house than with him, so I left him there with the engine idling and did a thorough search of the house. Nothing was touched, except in the dining room, where a vase was broken, as well as a china dish.

There was a whispering sound from one of the bedrooms, and I lost my courage. I think I even peed my pants. I began walking backward out of that house, and just as I was to the door, a voice like her mother's (although different, like a snarling animal) rasped, *"She's at the caves, Peter, they've taken her, tell her she must be home by eleven, we can't have her spreading her legs for every boy in town."*

I just lost it and ran out of there, jumped into the car. "Let's go, Than. They've got Alison in the caves, she's probably dead, but I don't give a shit, Campusky. Let's get the hell out of this place and drive!" I put the station wagon in reverse and gunned the engine; the car shrieked back down the driveway, to the street, in reverse all the way to the highway, and then we burned rubber as I put it in drive and slammed my foot on the accelerator.

We only got as far as the Rattlesnake Wash, though, because I saw something sitting down in the ditch with the motor still running: an old shitkicker Thunderbird. Her car.

I slammed on the brakes. Than's head almost slapped the windshield.

"You trying to kill me?"

"Campusky, you said you drank demon juice and you know all about them! If we go out there, to those caves, do you think we can save her?"

"Alison? I told you, I think she's dead already."

I pointed to the Thunderbird. "That's hers."

"You can't fight demons, Peter."

I looked at him strangely, wondering what else he knew about this stuff. "I may be one of them now. I may be just the one to fight them. Wendy wants me."

Than said, "There's only one way to stop what Wendy is. Bony-face taught me."

9

Than began shivering uncontrollably as Peter maneuvered the station wagon over the edge of the highway into the Wash, around the Thunderbird.

It was another twenty minutes, driving out across the hard, flat earth, before Than pointed back to the fire at the rim of the highway. "It's beautiful," he said. The comment didn't seem out of place. The hillside of houses and trailers was swept with a blur of fire. "Like a fire river. It's like the end of the world, huh? Maybe there're demons everywhere right now and every town is like this. Demonfire. God, I wonder if somebody's sitting on the can or waking up from a nap and they smell like smoke and the demons didn't get them, and . . ."

"This is the end, right? The end of everything." Peter looked straight ahead. The volcanic hills of No Man's Land were up there, and within them, caves and old mines. Somewhere to the east, the sun began its painful ascent.

And she was out there in the western hills, he knew.

He could sense her. Not Alison.

Wendy.

"Let's go find her and stop her before she gets in me again," he said. But he was lying—he could still feel the demonic within him.

"She'll be weak in the morning. At dawn, she's the weakest," Than said, the only person in the world that Peter knew had any knowledge of what Wendy truly was. "There's one way to stop her. That's what Bonyface told me. One way."

10

From the tapes

"All right, Peter. You say it was this demon and this demon juice and something taking you over. Because you slept with her."

"Yeah. I told you it was insane. It makes no sense. Even now I hear myself. It couldn't happen. I know. But I was there. I watched it all. It was like the town was vanishing and burning and melting—and everything and everyone was a phantom or something. But if you believe in demons, if you believe they can exist, then maybe it makes sense. I still don't know why she wanted us."

"She already told me why."

"Through Charlie?"

"Through you, Peter."

"I'm fucked. We stopped her but she still exists. You're bringing her back. No more interview. I'm out of here. It's over. And don't you ever come near Alison. I mean it. I've killed people before. There may be no evidence of it, but I've done it. And I will make sure you can't get near her ever again. It's you that's doing this. You and these interviews and hypnosis and shit. It's you. The demon is gone. We stopped it. And you want it to come back."

"Charlie, you'll be going to a psych hospital, but a good one."

"Cool."

"You'll get excellent care, I promise you."

"And the knife?"

"When you're released, you can have it. I would like to keep it longer. But I won't break my promise to you."

"Thanks."

"Now, who gave you the knife?"

"Wendy's mother. The woman who healed me."

"And where is she?"

"Beats me."

"Tell me one more thing about Palmetto, that night. The night of the Fourth of July. There was another boy, wasn't there? He was the one who knew what ritual to perform. What happened to him?"

"Ah. Yeah, Than Campusky. He thought he was protected from her. Some old desert rat convinced him he could get some kind of armor on if he drank this crap called demon juice. I guess it protected him for a little while. But that's the million-dollar question. What happened to Than? I guess she got him. As long as she doesn't have me, Pete, and Ali, I think she'll just stay put. I guess a looney bin's a good place for a guy who talks like me, ain't it?"

Douglas Clegg

* * *

"Who am I speaking with?"

"Wendy."

"What did they do to stop you?"

"If I tell you, it will ruin all the fun I'm having."

"Did they kill you?"

"You tell me. Am I dead?"

BOOK FIVE

THAT WAS THEN, THIS IS NOW
The mating of the past and present

"El corazon."
a día de los muertos card

PART ONE: RETURNING WHAT WAS ONLY BORROWED

Chapter Thirty-seven

Peter

1

Peter Chandler is in his thirties and looking at what he believes is his wife's blood on the wall of their apartment in California. He has come home from seeing a man named Diego Correa, who is supposedly helping his wife. It is October, even in his heart. He has listened to tapes of himself as a young boy; he has added to the older man's knowledge of the time by telling him the truth. About the town and its people and the girl of his dreams, the monster called Lamia or Wendy or, as Charlie Urquart would say, What-The-Fuck-Ever. He has called his wife's work and she hasn't been there all day. It is almost three o'clock in the afternoon. He has spent the day deliberating, not knowing that the time was quite as precious as it is.

As it has turned out to be.

Before he sees the blood on the wall, he thinks maybe it's time for the whole thing to come out. He has told the old man everything, but not what happened in the cave. Not what he found there; not what reached out and touched them all.

Perhaps he can even trust someone, an outsider. Perhaps Diego Correa. Enough to tell him about Alison's eleven months *after* the cave.

Now he is feeling more than a little feverish. A prickly heat rash on the back of his neck; the palms of his hands are sweaty; he is feeling weak and is wondering if this is the flu or if it's something far worse, something he's been trying to keep at bay within himself for more than a decade, something inside himself that he is *surprised* to have ever kept at bay. *But it's Her way of playing with me, it's Her way of showing me the extent of her power and of her damn eternal patience.*

The first thing he notices in the room is not the blood on the walls. The first thing he notices is his wife's purse. It is dumped in the middle of the beige carpet, all of her Kleenex, her extra tampon, her keys (although if he were to inspect it more closely, he would notice that the key to her car is missing), her half-eaten roll of cherry Life Savers, her Tic-Tacs, her wallet, all spread around. Then he sees the blood spread out like fingerpaints on the white wall just above the sleeper sofa, which also has blood on it. He doesn't for a moment think it is paint or theatrical blood; he has no doubt that it is human blood, but he stands there, stunned, hoping that it is not his wife's blood because there is a lot of it. It is smeared into loops and curlicues to read:

WHERE IS IT?
and, *SHE LIVES.*

He stands there, for a moment, thinking that time has stopped, thinking that the hours and minutes and days between that summer years ago and this moment have all been erased on some cosmic blackboard. He is wearing his white button-down shirt and his khaki slacks are hanging a bit loose on him because for the past six months he has been losing a little weight without really meaning to: it's the dreams, the dreams have taken away his appetite, particularly for meat. The world around him has just blinked off like a computer screen going down, and all he sees for the moment are those three words: WHERE IS IT?

The living room is completely torn apart, as if a storm has come through, or as if six thugs have come in looking for their stash, and living in Los Angeles, if this were anyone else, he would remember things like ordinary serial killers, people who murder for fun with no motive, who chainsaw and slice and poison and shoot, all random, all chance.

But this was no psycho coming in here, this was someone who had a purpose, who had a question that needed answering.

WHERE IS IT?

Peter Chandler, his dark blond hair already slick from sweat, his lips dry, his hands shaking almost imperceptibly, knows what *it* is.

He has spent his adult life trying to wash himself clean from the memory of *it*.

And then what he'd felt that morning, a feeling of being invaded, almost a feeling of *rape*, of something forcing its way beneath his skin. Coming over him again.

Standing there, wondering who or what had taken his wife, Peter Chandler knows without a shadow of a doubt that it has gotten into him, just a little of it, but that is enough. *Turning.*

He now has to face the fact that Wendy is—somehow—alive, that she is calling to him, that the only hope he has of rescuing Alison from her (if it isn't already too late) is to return to that ghost town and allow her to do to him what she must in retribution.

He has seen before what Wendy can do to men, what she is doing to him even from that distance.

If only we'd made sure, if only we hadn't been so goddamned scared and so goddamned relieved, if only we'd gone back to look, to see that she was completely destroyed. -

And then, he begins walking through a living dream.

2

"You must come," Wendy said. She had not aged since he'd last seen her in the flesh. She had that empty beauty that he remembered from his adolescence. She was wearing a dress sewn completely of human skin, faces stretched across her high, firm breasts, their curves and nipples giving the torn faces dimension, almost life. The skins clung to her, wrapped tight around her hips, and as she came toward him he was reminded of an old woodblock print he'd once seen of Beauty and Death meeting on a road, and this was it, Beauty and Death meeting in this one woman, her own skin and bones being the crossroads, her flesh and her skull mated together.

When she smiled, he saw that her lips were stained as if from eating berries.

As if from drinking blood.

Her eyes turned from dark onyx to deep red as the blood

flowed into them. Vampire, demon, shapeshifter, phantom—she was all.

He stood in the cool darkness of a cave, and from somewhere above him came the steady torture of dripping water.

Her mouth was like a small red rose blossoming.

Wet crimson petals bending backward, opening to him.

She said, "Turn with me, Peter, I forgive you for what you did to us. Turn with me."

"Where's Alison?"

The small red rose petals closed again, as if keeping a secret, but she couldn't hide a smug half-smile. She smoothed the front of her dress across her stomach, just below her stomach. She smoothed it over carefully until it stretched downward, clinging to her.

"What have you done with her?"

Peter saw what she was doing, he saw that this was her answer.

The face there, its forehead rising up to the curve of Wendy Swan's belly, the face she had brushed her hands across.

It was Alison's face, torn from her skull, eyes empty, dark holes, mouth ragged—the tanning of the skin had been rough, no time for delicacy.

But then, the eyes were there, opening, Alison's eyes filled with terror and pain and hurt, and the mouth widened into a scream, "IT HURTS, PETER, HELP IT HURTS."

And then Peter Chandler watched as the skin fell from his bones and he looked at his bleeding arms in wonder as something else emerged from his tissues.

3

Peter awoke, standing, staring at the blood on the wall of the apartment, and he knew where he must then go.

No Man's Land.

He reached for the phone and dialed Diego's office. The man on the other end answered. "Peter?"

"Too late. Alison's been . . . taken. Blood here. Going back," Peter said, and was in awe of how he was less shocked and surprised than he knew any normal human being would be.

But then, I'm no normal human being, he thought. *I'm infested.*

Diego said, "I'll be there in twenty minutes. We'll go out there, to that cave you spoke of, together."

4

Peter elected to drive against Diego's protests. "I need something to do, I can't just sit and watch the scenery," he said, and Diego saw the wild look there in his eyes and was a little scared. "I'm fine," Peter said. "I just want to drive. I can't just sit still."

They took Peter's car, an Oldsmobile on its last legs, but driveable, and followed the Ventura Freeway to the Pasadena Freeway to the San Bernardino Freeway until Diego thought the world was a blur of enormous highways and cloverleaf overpasses, and suburban communities like herds of sheep on the sides of yellow hills; the air was clean, owing to the Santa Ana winds coming through after the rains and sweeping the pollution back to Los Angeles from whence it had come. They did not talk at first. Diego was hesitant about asking any questions; he watched Peter to make sure he would do nothing reckless while driving, but Peter seemed a competent if speedy driver.

Diego wondered at the turns in the road life took: *Who would've thought when this man was just a boy, that their paths would again cross, that he would be going out to the desert, to the place of demons, together with Peter Chandler, who was so reticent to speak back in the eighties, and who was, now, willing to trust him on his journey.*

5

Peter began telling Diego the rest of the untold story. "We left Palmetto and I knew we'd be separated for a while. We were both minors and I knew if I put up a fight it would go worse for both of us and maybe people might try to keep us apart, and I didn't want that. I figured going to the papers was a good idea, because maybe, you know I was really stupid, but I thought maybe if we were upfront about a lot of it no one could touch us. I was wrong, and after that we all got it bad from the press—Charlie worse than me because he was such an easy target the way he babbled. Alison was in the hospital, and pretty much out of it and drugged up, and her grandmother got her pulled from there fast. Which was good. Her grandmother was one of those people who thought doctors were no improvement on God and Nature, so she got this legal care thing for Alison. She was kind of wealthy, this grandmother, and she hired a nurse there at the house in San Francisco, so Ali was okay for the time being. I got put in a group home near Pasadena, but I was out of there pretty fast. I had some relatives who got me emancipated minor status so I was pretty much a free agent, and I knew I had to go get Ali, because it was really going to hit the fan up at her gramma's."

"Because she was so sick?"

"Well, her grandmother was beginning to get suspicious about some things, and she believed Alison was a sinner doomed for hell. That kind of grandmother. And it was just going to get worse before it got better. The old lady hated me, thought it was all my fault, which I kind of felt at the time, too."

"And Alison had her hemorrhage during the fire."

"No. She was shellshocked and had nightmares like we all did, but she was pretty much okay. It was . . ." Peter hesitated.

Diego finished the sentence for him. "Later, the next year when she had the stroke."

"Cumulative effect, I guess."

"I talked to her grandmother before the book came out. To see if I could talk to Alison."

"I guess I knew that."

"She had a baby, didn't she?"

Peter kept his eyes on the road.

"Was it your baby, Peter?"

Peter sped up to seventy-five then to eighty.

"I guess it's not important."

"It is."

"There is no baby now, is that right?"

Peter shook his head. "Complications."

"It must've been very rough losing your baby at seventeen. It took its toll on her body, and it must've been hard on you, too. As parents, there must be a naturally protective feeling toward our children."

"I loved her," Peter said. "I love her."

"Did you love the baby?"

"The baby died."

"I'm sorry to hear it."

"No you're not. It's what you want to hear. But you want the rest, too, don't you? All right," Peter said. "I took Alison away and took care of her in the last months before she gave birth. And then when I saw it coming out of her—yes, I knew she might die, yes, I knew I might kill Alison just by keeping her away from doctors and hospitals. But I knew that it was not going to be a normal baby. I knew what it was going to be."

"It was a demon?"

Peter was silent for a moment. "It was a litter, Correa. Eels and scorpions and insects, covered with blood—delivered from her womb, a mass surrounding the creature and I took a large rock and I smashed into it and didn't stop until Alison started weeping, and I knew she was somehow back. And if you had seen its eyes . . ."

"Tell me," Diego gasped.

"There were hundreds of them, like a fly's, all over its malformed face. Black shiny eyes, tiny, all over the face, and the scorpions came from its mouth, and that's all she wrote," Peter said. "I believe the Biblical term is 'abomination.' I'd say that about sums it up. But at least it died. At least it had mortality."

6

"I've crossed a line, Correa, I know I've crossed it. So there's something I haven't told you or anybody, and I guess I'll come clean now. About Alison. And the caves. It wasn't just that we went in there and there was an explosion and the old mine caved in. We were in there awhile. I *saw* things. In the dark. Me and Than."

"What went on inside them." Diego nodded. "The great mystery of that time. What happened in those caves. If you recall, what you told me back then was the town was the place, the fires and the demons. But the caves. I knew they played into it. I knew from Alison that the heart of it was there. What was in those old mines?"

"It was a slaughterhouse," Peter said and the freeway seemed to go on forever before them, but in his mind he was still there. "We heard Alison screaming, so we ran toward that sound, and Than shines his flashlight up around the mouth of the cave, and there were things hanging there to dry, and he was the first to cry out. He dropped the flashlight before we could really see anything, so I grab it and flash it around and we see this room practically full of hanging body parts, arms, torsos, even a few people hanging upside down, but we can't tell who because their heads are cut off," Peter said. "I call out to Alison, and she screams back. It's her last scream. All we hear is that silence, for a minute. Maybe more. And then something's coming out of the caves at us. Moving toward us. We can feel its heat—heat and cold at the same time. The flashlight doesn't even help, because now there are thousands, hitting us, battering at us, and then out again into the night. Than is shouting they're demons, and I would've believed anything, but they're just bats. Cave bats, all over the place out there. Like a blizzard, and I get the wind knocked out of me from them. I fall down and hit my head on the rock, and it's dark 'cause Than lost the flashlight or it turned off or the battery died, I don't know. And Than is gone, completely gone. I call out to him, but he's not there. And when I try to stand, I feel those *things*."

Diego sat back, amazed, because Peter was driving automatically, even more cautiously than he had been moments before, but he wasn't here. *He's really there, in that cave, as if one half of him never got out.*

7

Then

Peter cried out, "Campusky! Where are you? Campusky!" But no answer came back to him. His head ached; he rubbed it, feeling the blood alongside his ear. The only sound from the cave now that the bats had scattered and had flown out into the desert was the sound of slowly dripping water. Peter's voice echoed back to him. "Alison!" he shouted, and heard it three more times as the shout wandered the caverns below. In the dark, brushing against him, a human leg dangled from rope; hands brushed his scalp as he moved through them, trying to crouch down low enough so that they wouldn't touch him.

His eyes began to adjust to the darkness. He saw a light coming from one of the three entrances into the mine. He kept his eyes on that distant, tiny light, swatting at the dangling arms and legs and heads like they were flies. The side of the cave dripped freezing water. He slid his left hand along the rock edge; tiny insects scuttled across the back of his hand, but he ignored them. *The light,* he thought. *Alison.* He had to crouch down lower as he went, because this particular chamber of the cave became smaller and smaller until he was on his hands and knees and crawled over the rough stones, hoping there would be no snakes to stop him.

"Alison?" he asked as he crawled, and the light up ahead wavered.

"*Peter.*" It was Than Campusky, his voice was high and weak. "*Be careful.*"

"Than?"

"*I fell down, it's a shaft, be careful, Jesus my leg hurts,*" Than whined.

Peter crawled on his elbows. Because of the light (which turned out to be Than's flashlight), he could see where the tunnel dropped. He leaned over its edge and gazed down into the blinding light. "What are you doing down there?"

"Hell if I know," Than said, almost laughing. Then he was silent for a few seconds. "Those things scared me. All those dive-bombing bats. Something grabbed my ankles and I crawled away and it wouldn't let go, so I kicked at it and moved back another inch and then, hey, here I am."

"Well, at least you held the flashlight."

"Yeah, my fat ass kept it from dropping," Than said, and then Peter heard a big sigh come from him. Than moved the flashlight around the walls of the shaft—it was made of rock and stone, but man-made, set perfectly together. *A well.* Then he turned the flashlight on himself so Peter could see how far down he was. Not as far as Peter had figured—maybe a hundred feet. Than's weight had actually saved him from falling the entire length of the shaft—he plugged it up.

"Just underneath me, Peter," Than said, and tears came to his eyes like he knew he was going to die any second, "*water.*"

"You're okay, Campusky, you're okay," Peter said.

"My leg hurts," Than whimpered, "the left one, it's crossed under me. I can feel the wind."

Wind? Peter wondered.

"It's like there's a bigger cavern down there," Than said. "Peter, *please*, help me, help me get out. I don't want to die, I don't want to die." Than began bawling like a baby, and after all they'd been through, Peter didn't blame him, not one bit.

"Don't," Peter whispered like a prayer, "don't cry, we'll be all right, we've got this far."

"I don't want to die," Than continued bawling and it was the saddest sound in the world.

"Look," Peter said, "I'll get some rope to pull you up."

"My leg," Than whined. "Hurts."

And then, from another part of the cave, a high, keening scream.

"Don't leave me!" Than shouted.

Echoing through the caves, *LEAVE ME!*

"Alison," Peter said, then leaned over the edge. "Look, Than, just stay put. You're safe here. You're not in danger of falling are you?"

But Than continued his whine. "Peter, please, please, please, don't you leave me here, I don't want to die."

"You're *not* gonna *die*, Campusky, you're gonna sit tight and I'll be back. Or—or try crawling up. Push your legs out and your elbows."

"It's gonna hurt."

"Just do it."

"Don't you leave me here," Than moaned.

Again, a girl's cry from the darkness.

Alison. Peter scraped his way back through the tunnel to the mouth of the cave.

8

"It's my one thought: Alison," Peter Chandler said to Diego as he drove the freeways of Southern California. They'd just passed Beaumont and Banning. The earth had begun turning from yellow-brown to white, and great empty mountains rose up. The desert. The traffic seemed to part before them. Diego attributed this to the speed at which Peter was going—eighty, although he barely kept up with some of the trucks.

"And you left your friend there?" Diego asked.

"Than?" Peter shrugged. "He was okay, he *really* was okay. Alison was *screaming*, it would've taken another twenty minutes maybe, if we were lucky, to get Than out of the well. I figured I'd just go get her. I mean, I had the gun. Sloan's gun. I had it and I could use it."

"A gun against a demon. I imagine others in Palmetto had tried it and found it hadn't worked."

"*No*," Peter almost shouted, slamming his fist down on the horn to try and get the slowpoke in front of him to move out of the fast lane.

"Please slow down, Peter," Diego Correa chuckled. "I want to live long enough to help her, your wife."

Peter went back down to seventy-five. "There was this old man in town, Bonyface, and he had convinced Than about all the magic and shit. He even got him to believe . . ." Peter's voice trailed off.

"Okay. So you go to rescue Alison."

Peter nodded. "It's like there's three corridors to the old El Corzaon Mine. The miners had really plowed through that cave. This area's larger than where Than's stuck, and it's got lots of chambers to it, and in each chamber, hidden from the rest by piles of rocks, the dead. Lots of them. People I only barely recognized from town, some with limbs cut off—I guess they were hanging at the entrance, you know—some scraping their flesh with their fingernails and eating it, the light was dim there, only a phosphorescence from the rocks, so most in shadow, scraping their flesh, and each other, and some even burying themselves in the piles of rocks that lay along the chambers' edges. I'm repeating the Twenty-third Psalm over and over, you know."

" 'Yea, though I walk through the valley of the shadow of death, I will fear no evil,' " Diego said.

Peter continued, "It's like a walk through hell, radioactive hell 'cause of the glowing, the demon shit was all shiny and gave off this weird light like a dimmed firefly or, I don't know, something atomic. The smell was pretty bad, too. It smelled—obviously— like the inside of someone. Something else, too. Something sweet, like melting chocolate or a pie sitting out on a windowsill to cool off. Disgusting and tempting at the same time. And I'm walking down this rock corridor and there's Grubb, the deputy from town, his feet missing, just crawling on his hands and knees, and something coming through his skin, something other than bone and muscle, the demon thing, the way it comes through, the bad part, the bad thing."

"What does it look like?" Diego asked.

Peter shook his head, shivering. "Unspeakable."

9

The thing coming through Officer Chip Grubb's skin began *absorbing* the discarded flesh and bones back *into* itself. Its ghostly yellow-green light flickered up like a lamp being turned on from a dimmer switch. Peter stood watching, fascinated and terrified. The glow of the rocks was strong all around it, and Peter could not take his eyes from the transformation. "*It doesn't hurt*," the thing rasped. "*It's turning, it's further evolving, it's beautiful, lovely, the next step, Peter, from the sea to the mud, boy, the churning clay of man to a higher form, you are moving backward, come forward with us, into the light.*" The voice was not the cop's voice, but a synthesis of all voices from the town that the demon in the cave had absorbed. "*Do not fear, boy, for our cells are in you, too, even now, we are all children of the same mother. Lamia, our mother of the caves. All hail our mother of the caves.*"

"*Her name is Babylon,*" someone whispered.

"*She is Mystery, Babylon the Great, the Mother of Harlots and Abominations of the Earth,*" another said.

"*Lamia, Mistress of the One Who Screams in the Night,*" still another voice said.

Peter stepped away from the rock chamber. The thing continued to move across the stones and sand of the floor slowly, absorbing even the pale insects that moved too slowly to escape its tread. As it went, it left a trial of yellow phosphorescence, revealing the litter of cracked and battered skulls, like broken eggs with their yolks sucked clean. Yet nothing attacked him, and he didn't understand why. Why she was waiting, why Wendy did not have these *things* destroy him?

It was like the demon voice in him, saying, *You* are *one of us.*

10

Now

As Peter took the old highway into the mountains, he said, "And so I kept asking myself then: why hadn't I turned? Why wasn't I killed, too? Why did Wendy let me live? I've been pondering that question for years, trying to work it out in my head, in my notebooks. Why?"

Diego looked out the window of the car, to the glorious sand-white mountains rising above the lower deserts and the cities and stretches of flatland below. *The wonders of creation, and the terror of it. How we've all stopped here, at the mountains, and never explored the caverns, the darkness.* "Perhaps it was the human part of Wendy. Maybe you were the one she cared for. Maybe in her own way, she loved you. She mated with you, after all."

Peter laughed. "I don't think there was anything human about her."

"A monster?"

Peter shook his head. "No, we were becoming the monsters, we were turning. Wendy controlled that, somewhere in her, the power of control. Like what was coming out of those dead bodies was a child's crude self-portrait with crayons. Like they were trying to make themselves over, but dying tissue wasn't good enough. Dying tissue only produced this *liquid* thing, this glow, this energy, it was only a waste product of what it could absorb, I guess. It couldn't go *beyond* its energy source, and I guess it died trying each time. Demons have a hard time in this world."

"The French philosopher, Andre Wandigaux, said, 'Our only will is to fertility, and in that we reflect the will of nature, and we recklessly pursue the means of propagation even if it leads to our own destruction.' Even this demon will," Diego said. "So you found Alison?"

"I swore I would protect her from this . . . this . . . memory. But I guess it doesn't matter. Maybe I protected her too well. I told you I passed the chambers, the dying voices, and I was careful in the cave, knowing that there might be holes and shafts. I kept near the wall and followed the light of the emerging bodies and those who were flickering out, like luminaria on the path through this long corridor of cavern. Then the light glowed brighter and brighter, and I heard the whispering."

"Whispering?" Diego asked.

"The wings of some large bat—or should I even say, demon? For there he was—not Wendy, but Sloan, a hellish creature with barely a human quality left, a pit bull jaw, and talons like an eagle, and the leathery wings of a bat. I saw the beast that Sloan had become, leaning over a girl who looked half-dead, her mouth gone slack. It was Alison. Sloan lapped at the side of her face, his body pressed down against hers. He was raping her. I reached for the gun. His gun. And you know what? He didn't attack me. Sloan didn't try to stop me. What was left of Sloan—what I could see in his eyes was still Sloan and not pit bull and not demon—just stood still, watching me. He said it was okay."

"To shoot him?"

Peter's mind slipped into the past for a split second. *Sloan growled, "Petey, I told you, I told you, but no, you wouldn't stop me before, but now you have to because if you don't, I'm gonna rip out her throat, I'm gonna eat her guts, oh, Petey, do it, just like I'm a tweetbird, just shoot, like into the trees, like I'm just a tweetbird in the trees, like I shot my dog, dear Jesus sweet savior, I want you to pull that trigger, please Petey, shoot me you son of a bitch before I* eat *her alive, you goddamn motherfucker, shoot me, I'm already dead, don't you get it, they're* eating *at me, can't you hear the chewing? Like a fuckin' leper, man, none of this skin's mine, it's all those things, Petey, 'member the dog? It had 'em in it, sweet baby dog of mine, she* put *them in Lammie, and she* put *them in me, and you got to kill me or I'm gonna eat your goddamn girlfriend before they eat me," and then Sloan brought his left claw up in the air, and Peter could see what was in it's path.*

Alison's throat.

And it was a dare, and before Peter pulled the trigger the first time, Sloan said, "Hey, tweet-tweet, hey, kinda funny, huh? Let's all sing like the birdies sing." And with the first and the second shot, Sloan continued laughing at his own joke.

In the car again, in the *Now*, Peter asked Diego to open the glove compartment and search around for the aspirin. Diego pulled out a bottle and handed a couple to Peter. "Four please," Peter said, and Diego complied. Then Peter swallowed them dry. "It took three shots and point-blank range, but finally he fell."

"And months later . . ." Diego said.

"It wasn't meant to be born," Peter said.

11

They did not speak for a time after this.

She's always with us. Peter remembered that line from the book, the one Diego had written, mainly because it had been a lie. "I told you, back then, she's always with us. Wendy. But that wasn't quite true. It's us always with her. In that place. In that time. Like I don't dream of the past, I dream of now. It's *then*. That's the reality. This is just what she lets us dream from that cave. We are actors in *her* dream."

"No," Diego said, his eyes scanning the terrain of the bumpy highway and the shapes of hills and shadows of mountains in the fading light. "I imagine even Wendy Swan is in the dream, too. I imagine that if she's here, in any real sense, then she's as much a victim as your wife, as you, as any of the other survivors."

They drove up the highway to the winding hills leading to Joshua Tree and Yucca Valley, only another half hour or so to Palmetto, only another thirty minutes and twenty years to go back.

"I don't know," Peter said. "We must look like ants in her demon mind. We're easy enough to step on and kick out of our nests. If we're tied to her, why in God's name is she so tied to *us?*"

Strong gusts of wind sprayed dust across his windshield; his car rocked side to side, the steering wheel tugged at his hands; tumbleweed and litter scattered across the potholed road that snaked upward into the darkening hills.

Chapter Thirty-eight
Alison Wonderland

1

It hurts, Peter, help, it hurts, my neck, God, please . . . Alison Chandler thought for a second that it was her husband, Peter, who stood over her. Was she finally waking from this horrible dream? Were her eyelids fluttering open, would she be back in her bed this morning, Peter standing over her, asking her if she was ready for coffee?

But it wasn't Peter.

And it didn't *feel* like a dream.

Feels too damn real.

Cold, her back hurt—pebbles and jagged stones beneath her. She was lying in a shallow ditch, and it smelled like chalk. Her breathing was difficult. Neck was sore. Tried lifting her head up, but the effort sent darting pains into her head, and she was afraid she'd black out again. *I think therefore I am. If only I could think clearly . . .* Tried working her jaw, but again the pain stabbed at her; painful swallowing; easier to just lie still. *It hurts every-fucking-where on my body.* Dark—but light enough to see *him*, her abductor. His face like a hellish green-yellow mask; no mask at all, but *him*. She couldn't even associate this man with the boy she had known, the boy she remembered. Standing above her, gazing down at her, his drool hitting her on her forehead,

She'd been out for a while, she knew that much, all the pain she felt after he'd curled his fingers around her throat, her thought before her mind faded: *Let there be a God.*

But if she'd had the energy, she'd laugh at that thought now. For God, if He existed, had left her to this.

The drooling creature held a shovel up for her to see.

She blinked—a clod of dirt fell across her face.

How long had it been since she'd last been conscious?

How many hours? Days

This human monster had opened his own veins with a razor and smeared blood across her face, and she'd hit the wall so hard that she had no energy. Life seemed to pour out every time she breathed. His blood had been everywhere, he'd written words across the walls, and she'd read the words first when she entered the apartment: WHERE IS IT? But it meant nothing, what could it mean? After his interrogation, the long ride out, Where are we going?

Don't you remember?

Who are you?

Don't you remember?

And then, after the memories had come back to her, not flooding back to her, but burning through her, burning out the wall she'd built up around her memory, especially the last memory

when she saw the torn bodies of her brothers and her father and her mother, burning across her eyes, and leaving the whole world a blackened field, and in the middle of the field, this man, this monster.

She'd thought at first the monster was named Charlie Urquart. But she'd been mistaken.

This monster in the jeans and hooded sweatshirt, this monster who was going to torture her and kill her, had the name of someone she thought was long dead.

Nathaniel Campus.

Than Campusky.

His face, now gaunt and drawn, skin peeled back from his forehead, and on his fingers the cold stone smell of dripping death.

"Than," she whispered, using all her energy to spit the words out. "Your . . . friend . . . please."

"A name from a dead boy's grave," he said. "I am the Angel of the Desolation, and I don't hear you because you are already dead." The man standing over her was shoveling dirt across her face, and she could barely breathe anyway because of the way he'd tried to strangle her until she'd begun to black out.

Please let me wake up, please don't let this happen.

She tried to move, but her hands were numb and tied behind her back, her feet were similiarly tied.

"Please," she whispered. Alison turned her head to the left, trying to look away and keep the dirt from getting in her eyes.

What she saw there made her open her mouth to scream.

A skull lay on its side, facing her. It was yellowed and cracked almost down the middle, with dried leathery skin attached around the scalp, a few hairs sprouting there.

The skull crawled with large red ants.

Fire ants like a lava river flowing into the eye sockets.

Flowing toward her.

She felt the first sting on her neck, a bite really, from the ants and she shut her eyes, hoping it would block them all out, but she remembered her mother telling her not to run barefoot in the yard in summer because of the fire ants. *"Honey,"* her mother said, *"they sting worse than a bee and it's usually more than one doing the stinging."* Above her she heard the whispering, *whatifwhatifwhatifwhatif*, and she remembered.

Douglas Clegg

2

(*I'm a teenager, wearing jeans, wearing a white blouse and my gold chain*) coming home from a boring Fourth of July town picnic, having hoped to see Peter, but catching no sight of him whatsoever. Then, seeing Charlie at the dinner table, another shocker, and that wild look on his face, as if he was scared in a strange way just like Peter. She wondered what the hell was going on. "What are you doing here?" she asked him, and her mother (*oh God, Mom, I forgot all about you, I couldn't remember what you looked like, you're so beautiful*) said, "That's no way to talk to a friend, Alison. Charlie's just been entertaining us with stories about the championship game last year against Grove High. Fascinating."

"What's going on?" Alison asked Charlie directly.

"I wanted to apologize for what I did before."

"Isn't that gentlemanly," her mother said. Her mother wore one of Alison's own skirts and a sea-blue blouse that showed off her breasts nicely. *She's flirting with him*, Alison marveled.

"I was really faced. I mean, drunk," Charlie grinned, and Alison was having trouble reading any of this. She looked from Charlie to her mother and then back.

Harv sat at one end of the table, and Ed Junior next to him. *I've missed you guys*, Alison thought as she watched herself take a place, uncomfortably, next to Charlie at the table.

"Hey, Al," Harv began.

"Alison," her mother corrected, obviously annoyed.

"Ali*son*, what do you think of going to one of the car auctions in LA—see if I can pick up a Porsche or something. I was thinking maybe after the Fourth we could drive into Hollywood and look into them."

"That would be great," Alison said, but was still watching her mother and Charlie, who were smiling at each other. *Jesus, he's acting like Eddie Haskell on* Leave It To Beaver.

Ed Junior said, "Scissors rock paper?"

"Maybe later," Alison said.

Her mother smiled knives. "You've been out letting that boy finger you?"

Alison wasn't sure she'd heard it right. "Mom?"

"Dear?" Her mother.

"What if she did?" Harv muttered, "Jeez, Mom, like no one's ever done it to you, huh. We all know you been getting plenty down at the police station, like we all don't have eyes."

Charlie laughed. But no one else was laughing.

"What if I do?" her mother huffed.

Ed Junior said, "What if what if what if what if."

Alison looked from face to face. "What the hell—"

"Your mom said it was okay that I peed on the porch," Charlie whispered to her, reaching up to stroke her hair. Alison pulled away from his touch.

"Boys will be boys," her mother smiled. She set her glass of wine down and began coughing. "Went—down—the—wrong," her mother said between coughs.

"You like it when boys touch you? Huh, Alison?" Charlie asked.

"What the hell is going on here? Harv, what is it with everybody?" Alison stood up so fast her chair fell down behind her.

"Oh," her mother said, still hacking away. "Just look what a mess—"

Alison didn't scream until Harv's hand fell off into his soup, and what had pushed its way out of the exposed bone of his wrist, like a crocus coming up through hard winter earth, dripped an almost clear, yellowish fluid. Skin began unraveling from her mother's face as she kept on coughing, and with each cough, another layer of skin, but no blood, just skin upon skin. Harv said, "What if you get bit by like a dog or something, or even eat something kind of gross not knowing that it's there." He looked down at his soup. "Say, *in your clam chowder*, and it gets into you and takes you over, you know, cell by cell, I mean, what if that goes down?"

Ed Junior chanted, "What if what if what if."

Charlie's arm snaked around Alison's waist, holding her tighter than she thought any boy could. "Lookit," he said in a voice that sounded less like Charlie Urquart's than some animal's. "Watch how they come through, the demons, man, they just eat at all the soft parts, just like when you unscrew an Oreo, you know, Alison Cunt? You eat the hard part last, but the soft parts—look how your brother's shedding his skin, like a snake, ain't it cool, huh? Tell me that's not totally cool."

But Alison was feeling sick, and she wondered if it were a bad dream, so she looked up at the wall behind the dinner table, the high yellow wall right behind her mother. She heard Charlie's voice like a gnat in her ear: "She's gonna pop, Al, I've seen this before, she's gonna pop like a zit. It happens, babe, it happens when the cooties can't quite absorb the body right. Here we go, it's a shooter, man, ten-nine-eight-seven—"

Alison was fading, and her eyesight darkened and all she saw was yellow wall, and then something bright red sprayed across it, and Charlie shouted, "Yee-hah! Just like a cherry tomato, thar she blows!"

And then in darkness, she heard the *whatifwhatifwhatif*, but it was the whispering of the darkwings, fluttering, moths brushing their dust along her face, and a dog over her, and she was screaming in the dark again, and something touched her, at the center of her body, and it wasn't the boy she was in love with.

"Don't ever take me back there," she whispered to the darkness. "Peter, don't ever, ever, ever . . ."

She awoke one day, over a year later, and the first thing she said to Peter was, "Promise me. Never. Never go back there. Never take me back."

But one day a man who called himself the Angel of the Desolation would take her back, and she would awaken to

3

soft earth raining down on her. Rain like rose petals on her skin. Rose petals on her skin. A hand, above her, wiping away the dirt around her mouth and eyes. A sound like an animal snarling. Above her, *what?* She couldn't see clearly, but it was a girl, a girl just like she'd been, and for a moment she thought that it was her teen self burying her adult self. Above her, *the girl? creature? monster?* growling at something, long stands of hair almost reaching her face. The small hand, smelling of cold and rose petals, spread a cool taste of water across her lips. *Good. Thirsty.*

And then the thing above her moved away, and another face looked down at her.

Angel of the Desolation. He held a piece of paper over her face, showing her. But she could not read it—what did it say? And then she saw for a moment: it was a human face. Skinned back. A mask. And the Angel brought it down and set it over her own face.

She smelled his foul breath and felt the press of his lips against her own, through the mask. Crimson ants kissed her along her arms and legs, along her ribs, her chin, her ear, her scalp, her eyelids, and as their liquid fire burned through her skin, she saw the patterns emerging, the wallpaper of existence scraped back and beneath it a blood red insect whose feelers brushed her face, it pincers opening to her skin, her eyes seeing red red red.

And then a distant light, like a glowworm measuring inches across a fiery red rose petal, moving closer, closer, to the center of the flower.

Hurts, Peter, it hurts like—

4

"Friend," the Angel of the Desolation said, reaching inside the front pocket of his sweatshirt. He leaned against his shovel as he withdrew a pasty-gray lump that looked like a dried sweet potato. The Juicer's hand. He brought it up to his nose, sniffing its gnarled fingertips, kissed it, scratched his chin with it thoughtfully, took a quick lick on the back of the hand and nibbled on the corkscrew fingernails that had grown long again. He pressed it back in his pocket.

He tried not to look at the woman because she had said something from that dead boy's life, *Than*, and Than was buried, too, somewhere around here. There was only the Angel of the Desolation, Nathaniel, and there was Lamia, his mistress. But the woman disturbed him, for he remembered her clearly from before. *She's one of them.* He had shaken her own memory back into her, the memory of her crime, her bloodguilt, but along with the remembering, he'd seen that teenaged boy in her eyes.

Fat pig boy.

She was ordinary. What power would this weak vessel have over him? Why did she show him the fat pig boy in her eyes? The boy was dead, long live the Angel!

"Friend," he repeated. The word she'd used.

Alison was not his friend. She was a friend of the fat pig boy. The Angel of the Desolation would scorch her with his divine breath; he would grasp her in his talons, this woman Alison and the other sinners and take them to the highest peak and smash them open on the boulders below.

Friend.

"My friends," he said, squatting down suddenly beside the woman. She'd passed out, her eyes were swollen shut. But her very skin seemed to be alive and crawling. The fire ants. He picked one from her chin—lifted it up by its pincers. He laughed as it tried to bite him. He brought the insect up to his face, getting a closer look. Its blood-red body was translucent. He felt he could see its insides working. The ant's abdomen was bloated. Nathaniel let the ant run up onto his right thumbnail while he brought his left thumb up to it, and popped the ant's abdomen into the back of his throat.

It tasted like honey, and he grabbed a few more ants and drank their juices.

"My friends," he said, slurping back their small, drained bodies. Their honey painted his tongue amber.

5

Between the fire ants and having buried the woman halfway in the ditch at the entrance to the cave, and also her weakness (because sinners were always weak, particularly in the face of Judgment and Damnation, which went hand-in-hand), Nathaniel knew she would be no trouble. Her face was red and swollen from bites, and possibly her arm and legs, too, but finally he'd had to start stomping on the fire ants, smashing the shovel down on a thick trail of them, cutting off their route back to their nest. When he was satisfied that Alison was still breathing, he went on with his business.

First, he gathered up the human skulls from his collection.

6

The Angel of the Desolation began his trek back down into the canyon, because, truly, to get to Hell you may not need a detailed map, but you've got to at least have some road signs. He would post those signs.

He dragged the sack behind him in the dirt, reaching in for the first skull when he was at the entrance to the cave. The skulls seemed smaller than the people they'd belonged to.

These are my friends, the welcoming committee for the big homecoming.

The skull said, "They'll be coming 'round the mountain when they come, when they come." Nathaniel opened his eyes. The skull had said nothing. It was Her power, growing. Growing because they were on their way: the one who tried to stop Her, his goddess; the unfaithful servant who had betrayed Her; and the witch who had created Her and now wished only to destroy Her.

"All my good old friends," he giggled, dropping another skull along the narrow path up to the cave.

7

Alison, in pain (*perhaps I'm dying*) thought she heard a baby crying, but the yellow glow was getting closer, and the red ants tickled her forehead.

The crying sound changed into a shrieking howl.

8

Down a corridor of the caverns, beneath a low rock ceiling, a creature drank from a pool of water. When it was satisfied, it grabbed a pale lizard that rested, too, by the pool. The lizard was unaware that it was being stalked, for the creature that grabbed it had no scent beyond the scent of the sandstone and crystal and dust of the cave.

Then the creature let out a mournful howl.

Chapter Thirty-nine
Stella and Nessie

1

Nessie Wilcox slammed the phone down, and the whole contraption went sprawling onto the kitchen floor. *Damn that Mr. Chandler for not being there to answer the phone, now that Queenie'd gotten herself in such a tizzy wanting to go up into the mountains tonight.*

Gretchen, her Scotty, snapped at her heels like she knew something was up; her boarders, Cleo and that masher Mr. Evans, whispered together whenever Nessie came in the living room because of the strange alliance they'd noticed already between her and Queenie. What would they do if Nessie told them she was cured of lung cancer by Queenie herself, that Queenie was a drug addict who had been raped by her devil-worshipping brother who had given her not just a daughter, but a possessed daughter who was out for blood? *Let the old farts gossip that we're just two senile old bitches who race each other on the front porch rockers all night long. Let 'em think we're going up to the desert to die and feed the vultures.*

"You seem to be full of beans today," her ex-husband, Cove Wilcox, said as he came in the front door, free-as-you-please. "I heard you and the Queen Mother into the wee hours, but it was your voice booming into my bedroom window."

"Old man," Nessie said as she crossed to the staircase, "you're not staying for dinner, and I won't have you taking any more of my Pepperidge Farm Distinctive Champagne Assortment cookies now that I know you found my hiding place in the cabinets, you common thief, and if you don't walk right back out that door this minute I'll make you fix the garbage disposal because of all those eggshells—" But before she was finished, Cove had turned around and was gone again, the front door swinging shut behind him.

It's Queenie's got me this nervous. Nessie took the steps two at a time, and then paused on the landing.

I feel like I'm twenty.

The weight of the cancer was gone. Only a smidgeon of her arthritis remained, and she felt like she had boundless energy.

Lord, I do owe Queenie the world at this point, if not for a miracle, then for making me think I got a miracle put over on me.

2

"I'm already too late," Stella said as she hurriedly tossed her last bottle of pills into her enormous sacklike purse. "She'll have them with her, I can feel it. Out there." She nodded to the dark window. "What time is it?"

"Almost five, can't we wait 'til tomorrow, or at least after supper?"

"Five-six-seven," Stella counted the hours. "He may already be there. I am such a vain, selfish woman. Oh, why couldn't I see what she had planned? Why didn't I know?"

"Queenie, what in heaven's name are you babbling about?"

Stella plopped on the edge of the bed, feeling nearly exhausted. "She wants it back, what they took. Each one of them is a piece of her puzzle."

3

"What the heck's a Lamia?"

They were in the station wagon, heading out on the flatland desert that would shortly leap into mountains. The sky was indigo, stars flickering across the sky as if God hadn't paid his bill to the electric company. Nessie drove ("Because it's my car, unless you've forgotten."). Nessie assumed that whatever waited for Queenie up in the high desert, in those hills, would only keep them occupied for a few hours and then they would just turn the car around and go home. Her heart had been heavy when she tied Gretchen, her Scotty, up in the kitchen and told one of her boarders to only let the dog off the leash when she and Queenie had gotten the wagon going; but then when they came to the first stoplight, there was Gretchen in the rearview mirror, trotting down the road after them. So now Gretchen lay sleeping between the two women. Ordinarily, Gretchen would beg to be put up against one of the windows; Nessie would crack it slightly so that a breeze would come in, and Gretchen would press her cold wet nose against the breeze and roll her eyes up in some semblance of canine nirvana. But Gretchen sensed the foreboding, and she pressed her head up against Queenie's lap as if trying to comfort and calm her.

"You hear me, Queenie? What's this 'Lamia' business?"

"It's the only name I have for the demon, for the *essence* of whatever came through my brother to me. It must have been wonderful in the dark ages to be able to give names to evil, because once you have named something you can separate yourself from it," Stella said. "What have the years given me? Good Lord, they've stripped me of sense, and they've weakened my heart. Why am I not wise? Why am I not an old wise woman? If one must live long, why must it be in pain?"

Stella's voice was a monotonelike rain splashing on the windshield with the wipers going. "I never told you the rest, about how

I tried to *cure* my daughter. I never told you about *after* she was born, what I tried to do to her. What I *did* to her."

Nessie reached over and patted her arm, and then slipped her hand down to give Gretchen a scritch behind her ears. Gretchen practically purred her approval. "Well, it's a good bet it'll take an hour to get up there, so I guess you got yourself a captive audience here. So, shoot."

If Nessie Wilcox had said any other word in the English language she might not have reacted as strongly as she did. But when she said *shoot*, there was a violent explosion from somewhere around her station wagon, and she screamed at the top of her lungs, and Gretchen leapt up into her lap and started barking.

4

And Nessie would've had an accident right then and there, if she hadn't had the good sense to realize that it was only a blowout. "Pardon the hysterics," Nessie said, signaling to get in the right lane, slowing down to fifty, then forty, and finally twenty-five and a full stop on the right shoulder. "The tires are all as bald as my ex, and I should know to expect this kind of thing. Everytime I go out in this old jalopy I pray for no flats and I guess I just had my mind on other things this time. The road just reached up and got me for forgetting my prayers."

"I . . . I don't know how to change a tire," Stella said.

Nessie laughed. "You make it sound like fixing O-rings on the space shuttle. You just take the old one off and put the spare on and fiddle with it a little. If there's no spare, we just stick out our thumbs and hope some good Samaritan's driving by."

"What if—what if some crazy person stops?"

"Queenie, Queenie, Queenie." Nessie shook her head. "If we meet up with some psycho out here I do believe between you and me he'll have met his match."

5

"Keep pumping, Queenie," Nessie said as she rolled the spare tire around on the gravel.

Stella glanced up, pausing in her labor. She was hunched over the jack, bringing all her weight down. It was the front right tire that had flattened, and was still warm from burning rubber. The car had only risen slightly since Nessie had shown her how to insert the jack. Her back was killing her, little electric shocks running up and down her spine and between her shoulder blades each time she pressed down on the metal bar.

"I'll bet you've never worked this hard in your life. Okay, I think it's high enough, so now you just stand aside and watch the mistress of tire changing do her stuff, Queenie."

"I really don't enjoy being called 'Queenie.'" It was cold and she wanted to get up into the mountains, she wanted to *be* there already, she had to prevent anything further. She still saw Peter as a boy, just as she still saw Wendy as a young woman: *all victims of some nameless evil*.

"Okay, okay, no more Queenie. From here on in, it'll be Stella, *or perhaps I should call you 'Star'*?" And the woman who had moments before been Nessie Wilcox, had melted like a smouldering wax figure into her brother Rudy, dressed as he had been when Stella had cut him with the knife, but looking healthier than she'd ever seen him.

From inside the car, Gretchen began barking frantically, scratching her front paws up against the glass of the window.

6

No longer on the freeway's shoulder almost to the turnoff up to the high desert, just beyond Desert Hot Springs, Stella opened her eyes to nightmare. This was new geography, and Stella wondered if she were in Hell itself.

Torches had been set up along the dripping walls of a cavern; a shallow underground stream ran over Stella's feet, now bare, the water sluicing between her toes. Red water, a river of blood. It ran the entire length of the cavern floor. Beneath her feet, soft, spongy mosses grew. The cavern walls rose up to a bat-encrusted ceiling. She would've been frightened by the bats, but her brother seemed the more terrifying prospect.

Rudy approached her, and she found she couldn't move. She smelled his breath: like sour milk on a dead baby's lips. He ran his fingers over her breasts, and she felt something horrible stirring

313

inside her, a sensation, a spark she tried to douse with her blood, but the feeling just became warmer and warmer the more she tried to kill it. He smiled at her torment. His lips were bright crimson, like clown lipstick. When they parted they revealed teeth that shimmered. As he spoke, she wondered at first why his teeth seemed to move, some of them uprooting themselves, dropping back in his throat. Crawling under his tongue.

Not teeth, but maggots.

"It's too late, Star," he said, and his hands squeezed her nipples through her blouse. He leaned forward to kiss her; she tried to draw back; his breath was again that sour milk on a baby's lips—she remembered that moment: clutching Wendy when she was barely a year old, screaming at her to "BREATHE! DAMN YOU, BREATHE!" And her baby had answered her prayers then in the worst way, for she had begun breathing again, after her mother had tried to strangle her to death and had almost succeeded. Always remember that smell, baby's breath, sour milk, and the tugging of life, whatever life force there was not wanting to let one so young die, and maybe something else, too, some other life inside the baby, sharing space like uncomfortable roommates, some other creature who was trying not to die, also, trying to bring oxygen into the baby's lungs because as long as the baby lived, It would live, too. The baby was Its hope.

Rudy kissed her, his lips wriggling into her mouth. Stella heard a ripping sound, and felt something slither into the back of her throat and without wanting to, she swallowed.

Rudy stepped back. She could not have known he was grinning except from his eyes. His mouth was torn away, dangling tendons of red muscle, pink, swollen gums going all the way to his chin. The jaws opened, and he said, "You have my lips, Star my love, and now you must take my heart," and he tore his shirt open and grabbed her right hand in his left. He traced her fingers over his nipple, and as he pressed her palm to a place just below it, a place where his flesh was like a damp, full sponge, she began squeezing her fingers, searching for the thumping heart beneath.

And then, another voice, from so far away she barely recognized it, said, "Queenie? Stella? Stella? You okay?"

Nessie caught her as she fell, and both women landed on the gravel.

"I thought you were having a heart attack," Nessie said. "The way you were clawing at your mouth and at your chest, I thought you were going into cardiac overdrive. And who knows what Gretchen thought was going on." Nessie nodded toward the car. The Scotty sat up at the window, head turning from side to side in confusion, alternating between growling and wagging her tail. "It was like boom-boom-boom, you grabbed the car, you started hitting yourself or something, then you started to keel over. I was thinking, 'next stop, country morgue.'"

Stella readjusted to her surroundings: a strong wind blew dust across the road, and in the distance came the call of a distant train. Every joint in her body ached. "I thought I saw something."

"Can't have you hurting yourself. Look, just sit here and relax and I'll finish this job off, although I'll need a little help steadying the spare, I am just an old feeble lady," Nessie said. She rose, dusting her jeans off, and then squatted over the spare tire, hugging it against her chest, lifting it up and over onto the car. "You gonna make it?"

Stella nodded, drawing her knees up—her bones felt like breaking twigs, and even this simple action hurt. "It seems colder now."

Nessie shrugged. "Dropped a few degrees. I've got a blanket in the back, it stinks a little . . ."

"No, thanks, I'll be fine. Here, I can help with that—"

"Don't hurt yourself."

"What's another hurt added onto the heap?"

"I'll remember that line when I deal with my ex. Now, tell me again about this lamb thing. Take my mind off the pain I'm feeling in my hindquarters right about now."

"Lam*ia*. It was in my body for several months, but I managed to get rid of it, most of it, in my baby. But I didn't understand, even then, that she was still my baby, she still was a part of me, even if she had the Lamia in her, too, she was still my child."

8

"But your healing power." Nessie had finished putting the spare on the wagon. She checked the lug nuts, tightening them.

"Why couldn't you stop its course? Just like my lungs . . ."

"My healing power," Stella laughed cynically, "didn't come until some years later. *Lex talionis*, an eye for an eye. When you vacuum, the machine sucks dust in through the metal cylinder, and you watch that, that's the part of the vacuum that seems important, it gets the job done. But remember, remember that the other end of the machine is giving off exhaust, hot air, when you put something into another thing, that other thing then must *lose* something itself."

"You got me confused." Nessie brought the car down, disassembled the jack, and walked around to the back of the wagon.

"I spent ten years cursing her, cursing myself. Rudy, in spite of his death, still came to me, still raped me, in my dreams. I kept his urn beneath my bed and in with his ashes I kept some jewels and the knife. If I heard a strange noise in the night, I reached for the athame. If Wendy tried to come for me, I was going to use the knife on her. And she was, you know, possessed, but not in the classical sense, not some little girl blaspheming and floating above her bed, but she was, other children knew it. I kept her away from the world. Away from other children. Away from everything."

"I've got hives, Quee—Stella. Cheese and crackers, I haven't had hives since I don't remember, goose bumps, and I don't think it's from the cold," Nessie said as she went around to the driver's side door. "You just get in and we'll try and figure out something pleasant to talk about for the rest of the trip. I know you've been through hell most of your life, and I know I asked you to talk this out, but it's making me think about how ugly the world is, and not just this world, but maybe the next, too, and I've just got to remember some of the good old days."

"Yes." Stella opened the door and got in her side, nodding. "The good old days."

9

The climb up into the hills was touch and go: the old station wagon was not good for much other than getting back and forth to the Mini-Mart and down to the Queen of Heaven Catholic Church. The engine made strange rumblings, and each time the car hit a pothole (which it did frequently), the entire frame of the car seemed to leap and dive. Gretchen, who had moved to the back-seat, growled correspondingly. "Back when Cove and I were married, we used to come up here for the Joshua trees, in the spring, and all the yucca blossoming, it was beautiful, and practically nobody up here." Nessie pointed to the suburban sprawl of the high desert, acres of houses where once there had been wild country. "Back then, only old families and crazies lived up here, now every commuter from San Berdoo and even Los Angeles stakes a claim. Wish the Santa Anas would just blow'em all over the hills."

"Like Palmetto." Stella gazed out the window at the lights of Yucca Valley.

"It was like that with Palmetto, wasn't it? I drove up to see it, after that, think it was about 'eighty-two, and I still couldn't believe it, still couldn't believe what happened to it, but in a secret way I was glad what happened because it was going to be uninhabitable for a while. Those kinds of things, stories like what happened there, all those news stories, well, they bring gawkers and crazies in with cameras and such, but they do tend to keep the populations to zero. Sometimes I think," Nessie said, gesturing with her right hand to the houses and stores and gas stations and mini-malls of Yucca Valley, "I think, if only it had happened on a grander scale—not the deaths—but just that nature had been allowed to take this whole area over again, just let it be wilderness, let it be a patch of earth without damn real estate."

They drove in silence, with Gretchen's occasional whines, and the squeal of the brakes whenever they came to a stoplight.

At the stoplight, Nessie noticed the sign to Highway 4. It was spray painted over. Local hooligans had gotten to the sign.

NARANJA CANYON—15 MILES

PALMETTO—17 MILES

The spray paint, which ran the length of the sign, read:

PREPARE TO DIE

As if continuing a conversation that had stopped several miles back, Nessie said, "Okay, Stella Swan, give it to me straight. You cleaned up my lungs, but you can't clean up your baby. So what's it got to do with a vacuum cleaner?"

When the light turned green, when Stella began talking again, Nessie turned up the road that used to be paved, that used to be a popular turnoff, almost a shortcut up to Twenty-nine Palms and

Landers, but that was now torn by the elements over the last twenty years, a road used now only by teenagers on dares and by crazies with cameras, and by two elderly women who were headed for something that might just be the end of them.

PREPARE TO DIE

The small print beneath that had been unreadable to Nessie. Some joker had scribbled: *or is you dead already?*

PART TWO:
THE CAVE-DWELLERS

Chapter Forty
The Gathering

1

Diego Correa and Peter Chandler arrived in Palmetto just as the sun was setting over the hills of No Man's Land.

The land was dark where Palmetto had once risen. A few house-fronts still stood, a few chimneys, but the town dump had spread like a fungus from the valley in back of the Chandlers' house all the way to the last standing walls of the Alhambra. Peter felt a sweat break out along his back, and he hoped it was only from exhaustion and fear. As if something were being revealed to him like a cloth coming off some toy from childhood, he said, "I shouldn't have come."

"You had to," Diego said.

"Something about this place, the desert, she said it once, Wendy said it, the intersection of the past and the future, the *idea* of no man's land." Could Correa tell that he was breathing more rapidly, that he might hyperventilate at any moment as he felt fingers pumping his lungs, and the insects crawling up his back? "The turning's happening. Right now, *look*." Peter held up his arm and it was flaking dust from his wrist to his elbow like he'd been in the sun too long.

Diego reached over to touch the skin, but Peter flinched and drew back, turning the wheel sharply to the left. The car began a slow spin, and he pressed his foot down on the brake, but *I must be confused, Jesus* because his foot was missing the brake and hitting the accelerator, and the car spun out of control—

And did not come to rest until it had skidded all the way to the left and went careening over the edge of the highway into the Rattlesnake Wash.

2

Peter dragged himself out from the Oldsmobile. He limped across the Wash. He waited there, just beneath one of the few standing walls of the Garden of Eden, and watched to see if Correa would get out of the car alive. *Can't help you now, Correa. Thought I'd end up killing you as it was with the call getting so strong in me.*

Diego shouted after him. "Peter! Come back, it's okay, I'm okay, come back!"

He knew the old man would try and come for him, and Peter didn't want that. Didn't want the old man to get infested, either. Who knew the full power of the demon? When he finally came to one edge of a rise, he hid there. Thought he was going to vomit. *Is my nose bleeding? Jesus, is my nose bleeding?* He wiped at his face, afraid that he might pull his lips off, or his nose, or that his eyes might drool down across his cheeks. His hands were blackened with thick blood. *Correa would be fine if he just stayed away. Shit, why did you bring him out here, anyway?* A headache was coming on, hard, like a locomotive running in between the right and left hemispheres of his brain, and his thoughts jumbled. To reassert himself, to make sense again, he said, "My name is Peter Chandler, and I am going to protect Alison no matter what." Down the Rattlesnake Wash, Diego Correa had stopped calling; Peter hoped the old man would just give up and leave him to his fate.

3

Diego's right arm was banged up from being pushed against the dashboard when the car had gone down the embankment, but it had saved his head from smashing against the windshield. He felt exhilarated from the spin and crash. It had made him feel like a kid again. Most people felt the journey in life was toward meaning, but Diego believed it was for moments like this, the out-of-control spinning, of experiencing for a minute *life* and feeling every cell in your body act and react without thought, without pattern. Spontaneous propulsion into a mystery of existence. "Oh, Peter." Diego sat on the hood of the car and looked out across the wasteland that had once been the intersection of desert and town. "You have it in your hand. In your hand."

Several minutes passed and he listened for the yipping of coyotes, or the sounds of night birds, but this acreage of the desert was silent. The night smelled of nothing. Diego saw headlights approaching from the other end of the highway, and was less startled by them than by what they revealed in their beams: objects strewn around the road, not carelessly, but in neat rows. He did not want to assume they were human skulls even though that was his first guess.

4

Nessie Wilcox turned her station wagon up Highway 4—the pavement seemed to have been eaten off, revealing stretches of dirt and gravel that shot up and hit the windshield as she floored it in an effort to just get up the damn hill. From the backseat came the occasional whine of Gretchen, who was used to smoother rides than this. Nessie tried to keep her eyes on the road, to avoid tumbleweed and fallen branches, the trash someone had dumped, even a tire that had been discarded for some odd reason in the center of the already-narrow road. Nessie *tried* to keep her eyes on the road, but as Stella began talking, unraveling yet another thread of her story, Nessie found her eyes glazing over, found her imagination clouding her vision, and at times she knew she was in her car driving up to Palmetto—

And at other moments, like the flickering lights of the dark valley below them, she was seeing the inside of a dusty tent, seeing the faces of a hundred or more strangers, seeing a younger Stella with her child standing before a boy-preacher who raised his hand to slap the girl.

Stella kept talking. "I'd taken her to doctors, to psychiatrists, to all charlatans of Los Angeles, to priests—the list was endless. The tent revival was something of a lark. I believed that God was truly dead and that if there were a will behind the universe it was the will of an imbecile, and survival in the world must be at any cost. The boy was making a name for himself, a preacher's son who had the healing gift himself. Michael Southey. He was on the television one night telling the world that he could raise the dead and cast out demons and heal the sick. The Second Coming. But he was unprepared for what I brought before him. Wendy. I took her before him and I told the whole circus crowd that she was possessed of a demon. He made me confess my sins, and it was a three-ringed circus, and the show I gave them, Nessie! I lied and lied, I painted a picture of myself as the best mother in the world, humble, a victim, and a penitent before the altar of God. Then he made Wendy confess, too, and I saw in my little girl's eyes her fear, all her fear caught up in her eyes, and I watched it turn to anger. I watched her unleash something within herself, something that had been under control. A little girl. All her childhood, completely taken over with self-control, and now she was losing it, she was *willing* it gone. And the boy began slapping her, his hand coming up to praise the Lord, and then again and again and again and again. Until she was bleeding." Stella fell silent.

She looked out her window, and Nessie saw again what she'd witnessed before with Stella—the woman wasn't really looking *out* her window, but was looking back *into* herself. *Locked inside herself and the key is somewhere up here.*

"So he didn't cast out her demon," Nessie said.

"He got more than he bargained for with her." Stella crossed her arms over her chest. "I told you about the vacuum: it sucks in dirt, but also blows out air. Well, the demon left Wendy, left her, but that young man slapped it right into himself, probably without even knowing it. The boy hadn't lied—he really *could* cast out demons, and I soon discovered he'd once been able to heal the sick."

"Once?"

"It was the air blowing out when the dust got sucked in. He was holding my hand, he was slapping her, squeezing my hand, Nessie, hard, very hard. Scratches all up and down my hand. It was like he was trying to squeeze the juice out of me, but it was *his* juice I got, I got that gift, that imbecilic gift that heals when it wants, but not always, and not with everyone. He got the dust, but I got the air. And the fire . . . all around us. Explosions, lightning, all the energy that boy had drawn from her, from my girl, it caused a short circuit, it caused some kind of *wire* to melt, the whole place went up, and only a handful of us got out of there with not much more than a charred arm."

Stella began rolling the sleeve of her sweater up, and the blouse beneath it, rolling it up and exposing pink mottled skin.

Nessie glanced over, slowing the car down to a full stop. She turned on the inside light of the car.

"I can't even heal it myself, it's a burn that never heals."

"The fingerprints," Nessie said, finally looking back to the road. "What the hell—"

"Hers. Wendy's. Where she grabbed me, where she held on to me. Always there. Always with me. It never heals." Stella's voice was weary, and she clutched her left arm with her right hand. "I've spent years just trying to scrape it away with razor blades, but it only made the scar worse." Then Stella said, "There's where Naranja Canyon used to be."

But where she pointed was just an empty mesa.

"I wonder if Peter is here at all. I wonder if it isn't a mad dream I've had. Wendy. The Lamia."

Nessie took her foot off the brake and the car shuddered forward. "If there's a route to madness, this is definitely the end of the line. Looks to me like I just entered that dream of yours."

Nessie Wilcox couldn't believe that she had gotten it together enough to acknowledge what she saw just a few feet ahead in the road.

"You see those skulls?"

Stella was not listening to her, but to something else: a howling animal.

A dark figure scrambled from the desert to the side of the road, and for just a second, Nessie thought it was some kind of demon from Stella's past.

But it was only a man waving his hands in the path of the car's headlights.

5

Diego Correa waved the car down, and the station wagon pulled over near him. Inside were two old ladies, *older than even me*, he chuckled, and they had locked their doors and rolled up their windows as if he were a thief or worse. He smiled his best smile, and one of the women, the one driving, rolled down her window and shouted, "Oh, hell, he doesn't look like a demon to *me*."

And the other woman, whose face Diego could not see clearly, said in a very loud voice, "You've never seen one. You don't know."

Diego leaned over to get a good look at the woman on the passenger's side. She was a beautiful old woman, and even though the wrinkles had got her in their grip, she had that thing in her eyes, that spark. She had what people who had gone through this kind of experience had: a fire of life that could not been doused. Hell just might be worth going through for that. "You must be her mother," he said. "How do you do. I've wanted to meet you for a long, long time."

6

The lights blinded Peter—*What in god's name kind of lights are those? Lasers?* The twin beams of light seemed to bleach the darkness of night away, and with it, the landscape of Nitro and Palmetto. The light had found every crack and crevice, it obliterated the contours of the rises and canyons out across the desert. A flatland of night. He shut his eyes because the pain was too intense, like a pounding headache, but pressing from the *outside* of his head, someone punching him in the eyes.

And that noise, that *howl*.

He was sweating, and when he looked at his hands again, they looked just like his good old hands. Not the claws of a demon.

The light down the road was no longer a magnificently hurting light.

Just headlights.

Headache was gone.

Car headlights.

The headlights down the road: would they belong to someone who could help him? Would it be Stella? Were they already her victims? Would they be, like he himself was, afraid he was becoming one of her own? Would her disease be taking them over, too?

Peter glanced around from the hill behind the last standing walls of the Garden of Eden. Few traces of the community stood. These walls around him had been gutted by the fires in eighty, and like the few remaining walls that stood on distant mesas like gravestones, these were blackened and crumbling. The town had, for the most part, been cheaply made. All but the oldest houses had gone up like the dried summer grass that surrounded them. Skeletal hulls of fast-food joints were barely visible down the highway. The plateau above the wash, on either side, was a junkyard of used home appliances, old refrigerators in a stubby field, a rusted-out car along the highway's shoulder, a massacred piano propped between the standing walls of an old stone house. It had become a dumping ground for people who had never lived there. It was where they went to lose the things that their county or city waste management wouldn't allow. A large mound of trash bags, set in a pyramid, rose from a gulley near where the Majestic Diner had been. This small footprint in the high desert had become something unwanted, unloved, untended. So, even the man who tossed the first old broken-down mattress off the back of his truck, thinking he was getting away with something—even he had known, beyond the wild legend of Palmetto and Nitro, even he had smelled it: this region was poisonous.

Should carry a government warning: TOXIC WASTE DUMP, KEEP OUT.

The wilderness had not reasserted itself too much, either. Palmetto and Nitro would never again be in anyone's guidebook to the wildflowers of the desert. The vegetation that had come up, mangled Joshua trees and thrusting scrub brush, had not conquered the plain that had been the town; instead, they were dwarfed by these trash bombs thrown from car windows, tossed out the back of trucks, brought by someone tired of seeing the old Westinghouse taking up space in the garage, or the old Ford Pinto rusted out from floor to roof. *"Hey, I got an idea," a guy would say to his wife. "I'll borrow the neighbor's pickup and lug it off up the hill and just bury it standing up in that place in the hills. Nobody gives a crap about that old shithole, and anyway, everybody else is dumping up there, why not us?"*

"Why not us?" Peter said aloud, trying to ignore the fever that burned up and down his arms and legs. He leaned against the wall and thought he was hallucinating. There, among the adobe brick rubble of the Garden of Eden, interspersed with trash and mattress springs and the silhouettes of a couple of old cars, was a grove of beautiful flowers, with a slight shine to them as if there was a light coming from their center. Roses, mainly, growing as he had remembered them growing there when he had been a boy and had seen over the wall, perfectly cut, blooming this evening just as they bloomed then, on the rough desert. He went over and sat down near them, smelling them. They smelled delicious, and their petals held tiny pearls of dew.

"All these years," he said, shaking his head.

Something moved from among the roses, a thin shadow. The only impression he had of it was that it was some kind of animal, like an antelope, which seemed absurd.

But then it was gone.

Peter heard a rustling among the trash bags, and his heart again skipped a beat.

"Peter," someone said from the shadows. "You're here too. Guess I should've counted on that." The man had been there all along, inside one of the junked cars, sitting up in the driver's seat. He must have been sitting incredibly still, and it was only his voice and a slight movement of his head that clued Peter in to the fact that this was more than just a trash bag bunched up on the front seat. Peter's head was pounding like crazy and they both heard it again, a howl out in the desert.

Something stung Peter's hand, and he looked down at it. He'd been touching the wet edge of one of the rose petals, and some small insect scampered across his forefinger. Like a ringing in his ears, sound *shifted* for a second, and he heard Alison's voice, *Hurts, Peter, it hurts, my skin, crawling . . .*

The man in shadows said, "Hey, Peter? You okay? It's me, it's Charlie, remember? I been sitting here watching her. Or it. You okay?"

Alison's voice, transmitted through the insect and the rose, to Peter, *Peter, hurts, help me, warm, warm . . .*

7

Alison could barely open her eyes: the lids were heavy and swollen almost shut.

Above her, she could make out Nathaniel's face, and she felt drool hit her cheek. His face had been picked at, like an adolescent who wanted to pop all his pimples, and in so doing had left gouges and scar pockets around his chin and beneath his eyes.

"She wants you to come to her now," he said, and she felt his hands, scraping at the dirt-bed he'd stuck her in, tugging at her and everywhere he touched her she felt shooting pains like cold, hollow, dull needles thrusting into her skin.

8

Twelves hours before, when Charlie Urquart had entered the town in early morning, his first thought had been: *ghost town.*

That was what the newspapers and television reporters had called it the second week of July, when most of Palmetto and Nitro had been gutted by fire. What hadn't been charred had died of fear.

"I'm one of the ghosts now," he said as he drove his cab through a quick tour of the junkpile that Palmetto had become. He couldn't bring himself to see all of the town. Some of the memories were too painful. He didn't associate the sixteen-year-old Charlie with himself. Not much, anyway. It was as if he'd been asleep until July 4, 1980, and then someone had awakened him.

What am I waiting for? he wondered, as he circled back through the hollows of town, the spaces in the dirt where he could vaguely remember houses and stores and hamburger stands. The cab was finally, after three days of almost constant travel, beginning to overheat. He smelled burning rubber as he approached the Rattlesnake Wash.

"Giving up on me, are you?" He patted the steering wheel. "Well, you and me both. Knew I couldn't run too far from what I was."

He was tired, felt a heaviness in his head as if it were filled with marbles. *Been losing a few on this highway.*

As he sat there in his cab, staring aimlessly out the window, he thought he saw something shining in the wash, but it was only the glint of a plastic trash bag. "Getting spooked," he said. The wind was strong that morning, and much of the garbage blew like tumbleweeds across the bumpy stretch of road. *She's not even here anymore. I'm just brain-damaged. What I'm afraid to face is that I'm insane. I should be undergoing some kind of therapy—is that what Paula back in New York was leading up to? Study the lab rat and then a little shock treatment to get his chemistry going in the right direction. Might've been a good thing.*

His throat was dry and the spreading odor of burning rubber filled his nostrils.

Douglas Clegg

"Don't die on me yet," he prayed to the god of taxicabs, and turned up to the driveway of the Garden of Eden. He drove across its lawn, and his foot hit the break as soon as he'd gotten around an old refrigerator. He had expected nightmares to resurface and the dead to walk.

But he hadn't expected this.

"Jesus," he gasped, turning the key off in the ignition.

Wildly growing rosebushes all up and down the main courtyard and what could mildly be termed the lawn—all the colors of the spectrum, just as they had been when he was a boy, only now there were more, and they grew around much of the trash; they rose in thin creeping vines up the sides of the burnt walls of the house. As he investigated further, getting out of his cab, not bothering to shut the door, the roses even grew in the old foundation, pushing up from beneath the cracks in the concrete, twisting together with the grillwork of a rusted-out old Hudson Hornet. The roses had blended, even, with the car's wheels, so they appeared to be blooming all along the underside of the Hudson. It was not a mess, but seemed perfectly ordered, as if it were meant by nature to please the human eye. Charlie wondered at the miracle of the Earth, how it took over even the most chaotic places and set them in order. As if a cosmic gardener had come through for the past decade and woven a tapestry of flowers amid this burnt heap. Charlie walked around the car, looking at the flowers growing inside it.

And saw something that made him believe he was walking through one of his waking nightmares. He was ready to see his father, or an enormous Deadrats sitting there behind the wheel.

Sitting upright in the passenger's seat, a small human skeleton. A child's bones. Some madman had put a baseball cap on the skull, and Jockey shorts around its pelvis.

Each bone in the skeleton had been tied together with small bits of string or wire, threaded through holes in the bone which had been bored through or chipped at. Whoever had done it had taken his time, a craftsman from hell, perhaps, for each bone was delicately sewn piece by piece, with not one out of place. Around the skeleton's neck was a thin gold chain, and on the end of the chain, a small watch.

Something about the watch caught his eye, and, without wanting to, Charlie leaned through the window to get a closer look at it. He heard a buzzing, and glanced in the back seat—there was some kind of beehive built into a hole that had been torn along the vinyl. Every few seconds a small bee crawled out of it and flew out through the glassless back window. Charlie touched the watch with his fingertips. It was running, but it was not a battery-operated watch. It had been wound by someone.

He lifted it up, closer to his face. On the back was etched, *To my son, Charles.* "I am walking through a dream," Charlie said, almost laughing. "Dad, that watch you gave me, way back in, what was it, 'seventy-two? The last nice thing you did for me. About the same time you started cutting me up and jabbing me big time, huh? Well, if you're listening, Dad, you know what? It sounds crazy, but I forgive you. You were one fucked-up-son of a bitch, and who knows what demons drove you, but you're dust now, and I forgive you. Hope you and Mom can forgive me." Charlie shook his head, smiling at the absurdity of his existence. "A watch. To keep track of time with. All I've got of you, Dad. You were never there, not really, it was just some bad piece of you. And now, just time."

There was a crack running across the crystal of the watch, and for a moment, Charlie almost forgot how that had happened, and then he remembered. *Holding Wendy, feeling her warmth, how she led him out of the braincave for just a respite, and the feeling of her body as she wrapped her legs around his waist and he entered her with most of his clothes still on, his pants down around his ankles, and his shirt only partially unbuttoned. How she had reached for him, and held him by the wrists while she took him even higher into the realms of the Big O, and then something bad happened. She had felt it, too, something different, and for a second or two, she lost control in fluttering gasps and heaves, and her hips had rocked, and he had been there then, his mind not shot out into some cosmic well of forgetfulness, but right there with her and instead of a demon he had held a woman and bad thought: she's human, too, she's not just what's inside her, but flesh and blood, and in a panic, she had almost crushed the watch on his right hand, scratching at him desperately in that moment of self-recognition and vulnerability.*

The scratch on the watch. Still ticking beneath that scratch. The realm of time. Someone had kept winding the watch, keeping it going, and it smelled to him like memory.

But it's a stupid, mean joke. She's done this. Put this in this old car with this little pile of bones to show me up. Because she's conquered time. The bones dry, and the clock ticks. She means to put me in this car, too, and the bees'll fly right through the gaps in my ribs and collect pollen and the watch will keep perfect damn time. "Well, it ain't gonna fly, sister!" Charlie yelled out into the clear sky. "Who the hell am I talking to? Hey, I'm here for the taking. Just cut through my brain and have yourself a good old sandwich."

Morning was ending, and a warmth spread across the land. For the first time in years, Charlie lay down among the roses and went to sleep. *Just an hour at the outside*, he thought, wearily. He wasn't even certain that he *would* fall asleep, only that he would close his eyes for a moment and then figure out what he was going to do. *Besides*, he thought, drifting into the warm, gray, fuzzy blanket of rest, *I know you, Wendy, you're a sundown kind o' girl. And I'll be up before nightfall.*

But he was wrong.

When he awoke, with a start, it was because someone was touching his face.

He opened his eyes, and thought for a second he saw Wendy, and then it was just a darkening night. A shadow creature crouched down at his side, tugging at his closed fist. He opened his hand as he sat up, and the creature grabbed the watch from his hand, and then fled.

Or so he thought.

"Hey!" he said, but he only heard a rustling of plastic bags and a movement of the bushes.

And then he scrambled over to his cab, got inside, slammed the door. Tried to start the car up, but it was no go. He checked to see if his cigar box was there, beneath the seat. It was. Just because of a nagging suspicion, he lifted the lid.

What he thought he would see would be an ancient ceremonial knife. What he saw instead was a dead lizard, unusual in its lack of pigmentation. It looked like some throwback to some older species of lizard, and he knew it was, in a way. *From the caverns. In No Man's Land.*

And then, in the twilight, he saw the creature, rising up among the roses, and it was just a shadow, but Charlie had the unmistakable feeling that it was Wendy. He had seen her in so many of his waking dreams that this did not surprise him. It also did not surprise him that he didn't act the way he had done in those dreams in the past. Normally, in the dream, he would attack her. Then he would awaken to find he was beating up an old man on the street, or sometimes even a lamppost. But he would not attack this shadow figure, because this time, she had it.

The athame.

It was the only weapon he knew that she was afraid of.

It was the only weapon that he thought might subdue her.

And now, it was in her hands.

The creature didn't seem to notice him, though. She had risen with the sound of squealing brakes out on the highway, and let out a keening howl to wake the dead.

9

". . . and I think she *can* wake the dead, too," Charlie said to Peter, telling of his arrival at the Garden of Eden. "I was scared shitless there for a while and stayed still. But she—or it— didn't attack either one of us."

Peter hadn't said anything for the brief duration of Charlie's story. He'd been feeling shooting pains through his arms and legs and gut, and somehow, Alison's voice, like a pained whisper. All this was too much—the creature in shadows that had howled and run, the garden of roses, the sound of Alison's voice, and Charlie Urquart. *Charlie fucking Urquart, a kid I would be happy to see dead, grown into this man. And I don't even hate your guts, Irk.* "I guess," he said finally, "I should say I'm glad to see you're still alive. Last time I saw you—"

"I know. I was crap," Charlie laughed, getting out of his cab. "I was a blithering idiot with the police and the shrinks and juvenile hall and the funny farm and that professor who wanted to ask me all about the demons. Well, I figured out how to play the game their way. Guess you did, too."

"No, wasn't thinking about then. I was thinking about after that day, when we . . . With that thing in your hands."

Charlie nodded, grimly. "The Awful Thing."

"That's what Than called it."

Silence between them, as they both tried to block the memory from their minds.

They heard the sound of the car, and the doors slamming, just beyond Eden's wall. Charlie said, "Hey, looks like there's more of us. I wonder . . ."

Peter ignored the headlights that flashed across the garden. "I don't think it was her. Wendy." He nodded in the direction that the creature had run. "May be just some scavenger. This place must have lots of scavengers."

"Stole my," Charlie was about to say *watch* and *knife*, but as he approached Peter to shake his hand, maybe even reminisce in some awkward way, Peter hauled off with his fist and tried to slug Charlie. Charlie stepped out of the way, and Peter fell to the ground. "Peter?"

"*Oh, God,*" Peter gasped, "*isn't it happening to you, too?*"

Charlie kneeled down and patted him on the shoulders. "You sick?"

Peter shook his head. "*Turning.*"

The itch of fever heat.

Flickering.

Peter clawed at his shirt, for it was hard to breathe. Her voice, *Wendy*, seemed so close, and then the headlights from the car. And his nausea. His limbs were heavy, weighted with an absurd gravity. His every movement seemed ponderous; when would he ever scrape his damn shirt off? *So sick, so weak . . .*

He looked down at his fingers—they tore at his own shirt, against his will. They had grown long, opaque—nope, they were definitely talons. He opened his mouth to scream and a strangled howl emerged from his throat as he felt the pain of his vocal cords shifting.

Peter Chandler raked his newly formed nails across his bared chest, leaving five thin trails of blood behind. The flickering lights came up stronger, not headlights, not lightning, but the flickering of his life.

10

And it was gone.

The demon shifting in him had been part of a nightmare.

It was all a nightmare.

Peter Chandler awoke on the couch in the living room of the apartment he shared with his wife, Alison.

Alison started to say something, but he felt a curious emotion overwhelm him and it left him momentarily deaf. It was almost relief, and an incredible feeling of love, love of simple things like home, and family, and good health.

Alison held up a square of white paper. "That crazy old woman again."

Peter wiped the sleep and tears from his eyes. God, she was beautiful with that thinly hidden smile beneath the smirk, the way her lips curved like that. "Stella?"

Alison nodded, plopping herself down next to him as he curled his feet back to give her room. "This one says: *Peter, I need you.* Kind of warped, huh?"

He felt her hand tickling his bare feet. A vague thought crossed his mind: *too good to be true.*

But he brushed it back into a corner of his brain. He could smell the clean, fresh smell of soap when he leaned nearer his wife, and chocolate chip cookies, the crumbs still around her lips. "I hope you didn't eat all of them."

She grinned. "Not all. There's still some I've been saving. We can both eat them later. You think maybe you should call her?" Alison passed him the telegram. She had long, almost elegant fingers.

He held the telegram up to the flickering bulb of the lamp. "I suspect she's going to call us and then I guess I'll have to tell her to leave us alone. She's been through hell, you can't blame her for being off her rocker."

He had trouble making out the words on the telegram.

As he tried to read the words, he pulled Alison to him. He kissed her cheek, hugging her tight.

She pushed him away, slightly. "Peter, it hurts, it's hurting me, please . . ."

His eyes, through the tears of happiness, finally focused on the words of the telegram. It said: *WELCOME HOME, PETER. LOVE DAD.*

His brain began short-circuiting, and for a moment he felt like he had become a radio receiver picking up voices. "*It is Peter, don't shine it on his face, he looks—*"

"*What's the matter with him? Is it a seizure?*"

"*In a dream, she's causing it.*"

"Isn't there anything we can do? Oh, dear Lord, he looks like he's dying."

". . . have to until he comes out of . . ."

Static on the line, a party line in his head, and Wendy's voice cut through the overheard conversations, *"No matter where you are, you are always here, with me."*

A moaning, weak voice responded, *"Peter, oh, God help me, I hear them coming, they crawl, they crawl . . ."*

Alison?

11

Flickering like the source of his light was going out, like he was *dying*.

The white-hot pain shot like a lightning bolt down Peter's spine; his ribs stuck him beneath the skin like knives trying to poke their way out; his knees seemed to have caved in. He crawled across the ground, trying to press himself down into the dirt—he barely felt the burs and spiny stalks of stiff grass scratching at his skin.

A light pursued him, smaller than the headlights out on the road. But the physical hurt he felt overpowered him, and at last he sank completely down, unable to move.

"Don't come near me," Peter gasped, finding it hard to breathe. His words had come out sounding like a cry for help. *These people—why did they torture him with their light*? It burned in his forehead. "Just get away."

"Peter? It's you?"

Stella? Stella?

A numbing icicle thrust through his ear, spiking his brain, coming out the other side. He screeched with the sensation; the world went from black to white to a smoky yellow; Peter felt himself shoot out of his own body and stand outside it, looking at himself.

What he saw was the same beast that Kevin Sloan had become years ago, the legacy that had been left him.

The wild creature that was Peter looked down at itself, and began tearing into its own stomach with its talons. The feeling was like being tickled, and looking at his hands he saw they were hands, and then they were hairy, with black nails, and then again just his hands, and he wasn't *turning. Hallucination. Bad acid flashback*, he thought with a sick humor, *only without the benefit of having ever dropped acid*.

As he came to, *flickering* on again like a light, a tremendous sense of loss chilled his bones. As if someone close to him had just died. He was covered with a blanket, bundled up against the old wall. Two old women, one scroungy-looking guy, a tattered-looking older one, and a small black dog were watching him as if at any moment they would have to kill him.

Chapter Forty-one
The Fear-Eaters

1

Peter felt as if he were breathing through molasses. His reaction time was slow, the very air surrounding him seemed to press against him, smothering him. Between that last *flickering* inside him and this moment, some dark moon had eclipsed him, something had been pushed aside just as surely as if he'd received a concussion from a fall.

I'm still human, he thought, *not like Sloan. Not yet. But in another couple of hours. Or, hey, maybe in the next twenty minutes*.

His eyes didn't quite register the four people surrounding him; a sputtering campfire had sprung up before him, and now he only vaguely remembered lying there when the woman he recognized as Stella covered him in a blanket, and one of the others who now stood before him had gathered up some of the litter and started a fire. A man crouched down in front of the fire; he raised his eyebrows as if in a toast to Peter and said, "Glad you made it back, even if this ain't exactly heaven on earth."

It was like being outrageously drunk and having friends forcing coffee and cold showers on him. *Just let me go back to sleep*, he thought. Something was in the cold night air of the desert, something that was heavy and thick, weighting him down. *We've all been drawn here, reeled in like fish caught and struggling to break free, but the line is strong,* Her *line is made of steel and Her hook is so far under our skins we can't wrench free.*

But I'm still human, and with that thought came something that Peter Chandler didn't know he even still possessed: *hope.*

Thank God I haven't turned yet. He was more ashamed than surprised that he was surrounded by this small and eccentric-looking band. He had known that others would be called besides himself. It was as inevitable as the tides: Wendy could draw them in with a magnetic force that was beyond imagining. He felt ashamed because he knew they must've heard him. Watched while he flickered in and out, while the demon nature with which She'd infected him tried to assert its control. *It's because I'm back. She's stronger up here. It's her territory—no wonder Palmetto's remained a wasteland. She's poisoned it.*

"The blanket's from my wagon," one of the old women said—her voice was like a knife slicing into stale bread. Peter was just happy to hear the *human* quality of it. He felt a warmth spread through him that had nothing to do with the tartan wool blanket they'd wrapped around his shoulders. Beneath the blanket, his shirt was in shreds, and he could feel the soreness in his chest and stomach where he'd scratched himself. "The name's Nessie Wilcox, and I'm a friend of Stella, here, who I guess you already know, and the shy one—that's her, some call her dog, but she's named Gretchen, only she takes a bit of warming up to."

Peter didn't glance at the small dog that was studying him carefully from a slight distance. He was stunned, and a dozen half-formed thoughts floated through his mind at once. "And then there's—" Nessie turned to the man who was leaning against an old gas range that had been dumped right in the middle of Eden's ruins.

"Hey, Chandler," the scraggly-looking guy said, and Peter needed no introduction. "Thought you were a goner for a second."

"Charlie Urquart," he said with some wonder. "It's *really* you. I was beginning to think I dreamed you."

"Your old worst nightmare." Charlie grinned, although his smile was drawn downward as if he had trouble making his facial muscles pull up in a look of happiness. It was a *grim* smile, a weary look, that told Peter that Charlie had been paying for his part in the events of 1980. *So it doesn't matter whether she's called us back or whether we've come here out of the badness of our hearts. We've got to be here. It's the intersection of our lives, and Wendy might just be our compass to show the way.* Peter nodded to Stella, but an itchy silence overcame all of them, as if just acknowledging each other were enough, as if words were not just irrelevant but too painful because of the memories they might dredge up. *Charlie, you've been a murderer. Stella, you've been one, too, and I guess I've got to join that club, too. He who lives by the sword, dies by the sword. We're just here for Judgment Day, and our god is a demon in a dark cave into whose hand we've played. Life's a bitch and then you die.*

Diego Correa came over to Peter's side of the campfire and squatted down next to him. The old man looked from one person to another, and Peter could practically read his thoughts: *He must feel like he's in heaven, here are three of the four people he's been trying to get together for more than a decade to tell the whole story.*

Stella was the first to break the uncomfortable quiet. "As opposed to your *new* worst nightmare. All of us here together. We're all practically strangers," she said, mainly for Diego's benefit. "And yet we've got something in common. We survived what was not supposed to be survived."

"Why do you think you survived?" Diego asked. "What kept you alive when others died?"

"I know what it was that kept me alive. It was her." Charlie nodded in Stella's direction. And then he told them his story.

2

The death of deadrats

"I had been shoved aside, taken possession of, if you will, by a rage I'd been nursing from a young age. The rage had a name and a face. It called itself Deadrats, and Wendy found a way to let it out of its cage and to keep me in it. It was like being a split personality because even though the rage had leaked out before, it had never stayed out and kept the real me locked up. So I did . . . some things which will, ha ha, put me in hell in the afterlife. Sometimes I pray the atheists are right so I won't have to worry about it. At the age of sixteen I helped murder some people. I still . . . can't . . . talk . . .

337

"Well, it was this part of me. This lunatic twin living inside my flesh. When it took over, it was like watching a horror movie in feelyvision. Smells, tastes, the sounds of screaming. And then, on that last day, the Fourth, this Deadrats got to go hog-wild. I watched while he . . ."

"It wasn't you, Charlie," Diego said. "It was the demon. It was beyond your control."

"If only I could believe that. So, anyway, I was doing what kids do, right? On the Fourth of July. I was setting off fireworks, sort of. I was running around town that night of the chili cook-off, after doing things . . ." Charlie remembered what Deadrats had done to Alison and her family. How he had watched Alison, in shock, walk calmly out to her Thunderbird and drive out to the Wash.

Not knowing that Sloan waited, crouched, in the backseat of her car. Ready to take her out to the cave.

"And so I had one more job, something Wendy wanted me to do especially for her."

Stella piped up, dry humor in her gravelly voice. "Kill me."

"Not just kill, Stella, send you to Hell, do not pass Go, do not collect two hundred dollars."

3

Then/1980

Deadrats smelled the fire as it leapt house-to-house, and as cars exploded in driveways, and knew it was good. It was a hell of day, a fine night for setting the whole goddamn planet on fire. The Majestic Diner lit up red and yellow in the night, with Roman candles shooting out of its roof as the fire grew. It was so incredifuckingbeautiful, man, it was like the Big O . . . it was like, well, *the fucking Fourth of July!* He'd driven the Mustang from Alison's house, setting a few fires of his own, shooting off a bottle rocket here and there, tossing a pipe bomb he'd made for just such an occasion as this. When he arrived at the Garden of Eden, his last mission before going back out to be with Wendy, the gates to the driveway were open wide.

The old lady was standing there in her nightgown, her tits sagging like two sandbags, her face drooping. She was fucking watering her rosebushes for Christ's sakes! *What a looney.* All around her, the bees—those damned bees she kept like watchdogs to keep kids out. He had been in there once, in her basement, he and Campusky when they were both little squirts, and that was when he'd seen the thing in the basement,

the thing with wings, and leathery skin, scales along its stomach—

It came to him now, like lightning across his face:

it had been Wendy, little girl Wendy, chained in the basement of that beekeeping bitch's house!

"I know you mean to kill me," Stella Swan said. "Someone stole the athame. I suppose it was you." The bees flew about, but were subdued by the smoke that drifted across the garden wall from the street. The woman stood there, her hands working at the snippers, not in a move toward defending herself, but against the roses, cutting each bud.

As if waiting for him to come to her.

Daring him.

"No shit," Deadrats said, grinning. "I'm gonna eat your soul, bitch. Yep, that's just what I'm gonna do. After I torture you awhile."

The broad continued snipping at roses, and sprinkling the water from her tin can across the ones that had not yet bloomed. She turned her back to him. "All I ask is you do it quickly."

"No last requests, sweetheart," Deadrats snarled.

"You know, I have never understood why she can't do this herself. Is she scared of me?"

"Look, Beekeeper, she's a fucking *god*, she's not gonna be scared of some hag like you. She owns this place, she owns it and everything in it, bitch, so don't think you can—"

"My, my," Stella said, turning to face him again. "You're quite a talker. I think you should kill me so I don't have to listen to you jabber anymore."

"Oh, shit, that's it, you cunt." Deadrats pointed the knife blade at her. "You know what this is? Huh, dead woman? Do ya?"

He noticed, in her hand, a drop of blood.

A small perfect rose, its thorn imbedded in the skin of her palm.

No small amount of fear crossed the woman's face, and even in the semidarkness, she could not hide the trembling of her chin. "I know about that blade, because it was given to me. It is an instrument for the surgery of the soul. It was forged in the fires of Hell, and its power is immense. I have only known of its use twice. Once, on my brother, Rudy. I pricked his skin with it, and watched him burn. Previous to that, a woman was killed with it. It is a knife of return, according to its inscription. The name on it is the name of the demon which is the driving force behind my daughter's life. I know what it means to be stabbed with it."

Deadrats shambled over to her, holding the knife heart-level. He reached out and boldly touched the old woman's right breast through the thin material of her nightgown. "Been a long time since a guy's done that, huh?"

Then he got what he wanted out of her: absolute fear. Her face wrinkled up completely, and he hoped she would start crying. He was sick of all this shock and delayed-reaction bullshit he'd been getting from people. She looked like a lamb about to be slaughtered, and he was certain she would begin bleating any moment. "She calls you her reservoir," he said. "But now she don't need you no more. What you got she can do without."

"What is it I've got?" Stella whimpered, her head hanging down.

"Fuck if I know," Deadrats muttered, and found that in the excitement and expectation of a truly primo kill he was getting hard. *Savor the moment, Deadrats, it don't get much better than this.* "Maybe we can open you up and find out what you got before I kill you. Little open-heart surgery." He stroked his fingers down her breast, to the place just above her heart. He felt the delicious beating, the racing, the blood-pumping terror. He scratched his fingernails through the nightgown and felt the shivering warmth of her skin.

And then, he dropped the knife.

"What the fuck are you doing to me, you goddamn—" Deadrats growled, feeling a sucking wind, like a cyclone, pulling at him, and then the sound of metal scraping metal, of a door opening, a refrigerator door opening and closing, and he felt himself being shoved— and observed the sensations in his mind as a cage door was closed on him somewhere in the braincave in his head.

It was like being born, that's the only way he could describe it, like being born into a whole other world, as if breaking through the womb; the liquid that kept Deadrats going, now dry.

You Come When I Call You

Charlie Urquart could not stop screaming when he came to, with the fire growing all around him and the old lady holding him tight, the old lady whom he thought he had just killed, but who was, instead, making sure that he didn't die.

4

Now

Charlie finished his story. "So she healed me. Or at least, that part called Deadrats. I still lost my ability to sleep or to distinguish between hallucination and reality—there was always Deadrats just lingering, or maybe it was Wendy, herself, I don't know. And then, to make a long story short, I went mad. For many years. I guess my mind couldn't deal with the kinds of things this body had done. I knew I was still infected, too, never completely healed. And in Manhattan, just a week ago, I got another visit from Deadrats and was sure I'd murdered someone. I didn't. But it was, you know, just like old times. You know what I mean, don't you, Peter? Turning." Charlie's lopsided grin disappeared. "Yeah, for a second I thought your skin would drop off. I'm willing to bet we've all *turned* just a little, in our own ways. She's given me a run for my money for quite a while now."

Diego Correa, who had been fairly silent, added, "I've seen demonic possession among the Yanimatees on the Amazon, and it is similar. Yet, the Lamia's possession can reach across time and space and touch you. It's like telepathy."

Peter shivered, looking into the fire. "But it's stronger up here. I've felt it before, but I thought I was crazy. After a while it's like none of this ever happened. But here, it's happening, just like with Sloan. These are her stomping grounds. It's just like Wendy said, when she called . . ." Peter's thoughts raced ahead of his words, and he suddenly felt an overwhelming need to begin *panting*.

"And you did the one thing that I thought would stop her."

"Yep," Charlie said, glancing at Peter. "All of us did. Alison, me, Pete, and Than."

Nessie glanced one to the other. "And what was that?"

"We ate her heart," Peter said.

Charlie laughed. "Shit, you said it so straight, Peter. Christ, I've never even said it out loud. But we did, we ate her fuckin' heart. Oh, Christ." He began weeping and laughing at the same time.

"Why in heaven's name did you do something like that?" Nessie asked as if they had just said they ate a pie that was cooling on a windowsill.

Peter looked at Charlie and felt a chill go through him.

"Than said it was the only way. Charlie wanted to send her to Hell with the knife, but Than said that wouldn't do it. He told us we had to eat her heart."

"And how," Diego asked, "did you get it from her?"

"That was the easy part," Charlie said. "By dawn she was just a girl again. She was easy to hold down. The night gave her strength. At dawn, she was just a girl. Christ, Peter, tell me we didn't really do it."

Peter glanced around the group, feeling as if the darkest secret of his life were about to be revealed. "Oh, yeah, we did."

"But," Diego asked, "how did any of you *get* her heart?"

Peter said, "She slept in the cave. It was dawn. I guess even the Devil sleeps after a big night. Than told us dawn was her weakest moment. She was asleep. That's all. I doubt now that she really slept. But I wanted to do anything I could . . . anything . . . to stop her. She looked just like a sleeping girl."

"And beautiful," Charlie added, wiping his eyes, "don't forget that."

"She was." Peter nodded. "She didn't look like a demon. And Than, he said that we had to cut out her heart, it was best done with our hands. I couldn't do it."

Charlie shrugged, apparently reconciled with the memory. "I could. Me and Campusky, both of us. Her flesh was soft. It was like she was a vampire or something, because I used this rock to dig into her, but when I did, there wasn't any blood, or anything. And she opened her eyes."

"That's right, she opened her eyes, and Than shrieked and you made a grab, right into where you cut—"

"Knew right where it was—I spent half my childhood looking at the pictures in *Gray's Anatomy*, just so I'd know where people's soft spots were—" Charlie rubbed his face with his hands, as if trying to clean himself of the memory. "I ate the biggest part, but everybody had to share. Than, Alison, me, and then . . ."

"And me. I had to eat it, too. We all agreed. We promised we'd never talk about it. When Alison lost her memory, I promised myself never to tell her what she'd been part of," Peter said.

"You really ate a human heart?" Nessie asked. When both men nodded, she shivered. Then, she had to ask: "It taste like chicken?"

6

The silence grew intense. Peter closed his eyes. Wished the world away. Tried not to see with his mind's eye that moment in his life when a demon had been within him, when he had dug with some fury into a sleeping girl's breast, and had watched Wendy's eyes open wide in terror as he brought the bloody beating heart from her, and had passed it around—Alison, Charlie, Than, and himself.

And each had partaken of the communion.

The sacrament of the sacred heart.

7

Nessie Wilcox said, "I didn't believe Stella here when she told me her stories, but now that we're all here together, well, I guess you can count me in as a convert." Even though she looked ancient, she seemed spry and fit, plopping down on a chunk of wall. Her Scotty hopped up onto her lap.

"All these years," Charlie said, "I've been running, hoping I'd never bump into any of you. *Ever.*"

Stella nodded, sadly.

Peter fumbled with thoughts that he couldn't put into words. What was he forgetting? Why did it feel like in that last flickering, something had eaten away part of his brain, something had done sloppy surgery on part of his memory?

"Diarrhea of the mouth and constipation of the brain," Nessie said. "You folks are here by God's graces so you can get in and do your business and you're going to sit here and jabber until kingdom come. My father used to say you got to eat fear for breakfast."

"Must you be so energetic, Nessie?" Stella asked.

The other woman nodded. "You got it, Stella, you gave me the healing and now you expect me to take it like an old mule ready for the glue factory?"

"We're all in the funny farm." Charlie grinned. "It almost feels *better* to know it's not just me, that I'm not the only one. I knew it a little back then because I knew I wasn't clever enough to make it all up." He laughed, and then noticed the others were staring at him. "Sorry, but it's such a goddamn *relief*. I thought I'd come here and I'd end up wandering in some waking dream for the rest of my days and the birds would get my carcass and the sun would bleach my bones. I guess I shouldn't rule that out. Really. I got as far away from this town as I could, well, maybe not to Australia, but to Manhattan, and that's as foreign a country as you can imagine. And *even there*, she got me. It's just funny. You healed me, Stella, but Wendy kept part of me here, always here, with her." He snorted a laugh, shaking his head.

"See?" Nessie said. "Charlie here's eatin' his fear. It's okay to laugh while you eat. So if Stella healed you, Charlie, what kind of disease did you have?"

Charlie shrugged. "Something in my brain that I couldn't control. Anger. Hatred. Maybe a little bit of a human monster that most people can keep under lock and key. But Wendy had the key, and she let it out. Living with what I did . . ." He turned his face away from them for a moment, and when he turned back, it was tense with determination. "If I lived in the past I'd've strung myself up by now. Even tried a few times. But I knew if I did, I would be damned. One thing Wendy did for me was she made me a *believer* in the afterlife, and eternal damnation seems to be just around the corner sometimes. So I keep hoping for, you know, some way to *redeem* myself. Maybe there's no way. Jesus, it's cold." He took a few steps away from the small fire until Peter couldn't see his face anymore, just a silhouette.

Stella's voice was warm and soft when she spoke, turning back to Charlie, her hand out to bring him back to the fire. "It wasn't *you*, Charlie, it was a demon mind. And all my healing did was make you strong to fight it. And you did. Once and for all."

Charlie looked off to the hills of No Man's Land. All darkness, with that aura of moonlight sketching the outlines of vegetation and boulders and slopes. "Wish I could say that was true, but I don't believe it is. I fought it, and maybe, with your help, put it away, but it's always been there in me."

"No, it's gone, Charlie," Stella said, her eyes bright in the firelight. "It's gone."

From the dark silhouette of Charlie Urquart came a whimper. "*You.* You did this to them, *you.*"

8

Charlie Urquart pointed to Wendy, who stood there, leaning against the wall of the Garden of Eden. "You," he said.

The firelight sputtered multiple shadows about her. She turned from the work with which she'd been occupied; as she faced him, he saw first the slick swatch of flesh between her teeth, which she gulped back. Then he saw what she held in her hand.

"She can't heal you now," Wendy said after she swallowed.

In her hand she was clutching long silver-white hairs that tangled as they descended to the scalp; the woman's eyes had been sewn shut, her lips had been nailed together, and Charlie recognized Stella even with these alterations. "Give me what is mine, that's all I ask, Charlie, give me what you took from me."

Wendy plucked one of the nails from Stella's lips, and then another, and another, ripping the edge of Stella's mouth. The mouth sagged open, *and Stella moaned, "Charlie, stop, what are you—*"

"No!" he cried, clapping his hands over his ears. "I know what you're doing!"

There, in Wendy's hand, a red rose, blooming,

and then, not a rose, but a beating human heart,

and then not a heart, but a swarm of red ants.

Even covering his ears, he heard Stella crying out, "It's all right, we're here, we're with you, we can—"

He felt invisible hands raking at his back, at his arms; looking down, he was covered with large red ants, swarming across his shoes, crawling in an undulating army up his pants legs, up his crotch, up his stomach, across his chest. The more he plucked at them, the tighter they latched onto him until they'd made steel bridges of their bodies, and they were a part of him. The Stella-face in Wendy's fist said, "PETER, HELP ME, HURTS, WEAK."

Charlie began shuddering as the ants began biting him from his feet to his neck. *"Get them off me!"* He managed to flick several off him, and those that fell down on the ground began rising up in a crawling heap; the more he scraped off him, the more the pile of red motion grew, until the ants in the heap before him began crackling and sputtering; climbing one on top of the other they rose up and fell, rose and fell in cresting waves of red; and then it was no longer a heap of ants, but a fire spouting out of the earth; Wendy dropped the head into the middle of the fire, and Stella screamed, *"Charlie!"* just as the flesh on her face began blistering and splitting, bubbling liquid running from between the fire cracks, and Charlie reached into the ant fire to bring the head out, but the fire crawled from her head up his fingers, his hand, his arm, his shoulder, and he could see each flame-burst ant scampering up toward his face.

9

Diego socked Charlie Urquart in the jaw, and Charlie stepped clumsily back a few paces, weaving, almost falling, but Diego went to him and kept him from sprawling out in the dirt. Instinctively, Charlie pushed the old man back, and twisted on his ankle, falling down on his rear; the world seemed to vibrate as he touched earth; he bit down on his tongue hard; he saw a flash of light and then he knew where he was. The ruins of the great house, like the shell of a bombed-out cathedral. The others there with him. Not Wendy holding Stella's head, but Stella with her body and head attached the way they should be. *Christ, the waking dream is stronger here. In New York I had a chance to see through it, but* here, *it seems more real than* this.

"You could've *killed* yourself," Diego said. He bent over and grabbed Charlie's right arm, holding it in front of his face.

Charlie looked down at his own hand and barely recognized it.

It was red-blistered, and skin bubbles had erupted around his knuckles.

Nessie nodded toward the campfire. "You stuck it in there and if you'd left it in there for more than a second who knows what would be left."

"Wendy," Charlie said, looking at the fire. "Alison. I heard Alison. I know it's her. Oh, God, Peter, what we did—she wants it back! Oh, Christ, don't you know what that means? Oh, Jesus."

"Alison," Peter said, his face impassive. He looked like a man who knew what must be done and had finally decided that now was the time to do it. "We'll be dead by morning if we don't get going now. She won't need to kill us, we'll do it to ourselves." He turned to Nessie. "Can we use your car?

"Nessie," Stella said. "There's no reason for you to be involved in this at all. None of us has a choice. None of us, that is, except you and Diego."

"No choice here." Nessie nodded as if confirming something in her own mind. "Not after what you did for me. Owe you at least this much. All of you started eating your fears by just coming here. I can eat a few fears myself. Besides, key's in the car, and we can all fit."

"I'm in, too," Diego said. "I've been searching for this all my life. Whatever Wendy is. Demon, spirit, hallucination."

None of them spoke again until they were halfway to the station wagon.

Charlie brought a pack of cigarettes out of his pocket and plucked one out. "I guess it won't matter if I smoke a few more of these."

Nessie fixed him with a stern look. "Not in my car you don't."

Chapter Forty-two
Flickering

1

Again, that light switch going on and off, faulty circuitry inside him. Peter slowed down as they walked toward the station wagon. Charlie kept talking but stepped a little ahead of him, and Peter allowed him to. Nessie and Stella, with the dog at their heels, were almost to the car. Diego kept up with the ladies, looking like a kid in a candy store.

This must be the old man's dream, to answer his questions, to hope for what he had called an *illumination*.

Peter glanced up at the stars. They were also flickering in and out. *Like me*, he thought. *What am I to them? In a thousand years, who's going to care what we do now?* A pain shot through his arms as if he'd banged his elbows against hard rock; his left hand twitched.

He thought he saw a lightning bolt rip down through the sky, and its white-hot light cut into the darkness, ripping the night sky in two.

Then it was gone. Then others hadn't noticed it.

Part of me.

We're like cattle, just like the ghost herd they used to talk about up here. We're that herd and we're being rounded up for the final slaughter.

An old dream came back to him, one in which Wendy showed him skinned animals hanging upside down, their blood dripping into silver buckets, and now Peter knew what the dream meant. *It's us. We're those animals.*

He saw them: *Stella tied by her ankles, life not completely gone from her as wounds drained. Charlie, whose face had elongated into a rat's muzzle, his gray, matted fur burst in sections where blood blisters erupted. And Sloan's dog, Lammie, the midnight-black pit bull with its hindquarters drawn up by a meathook, and it was not a dog but Peter himself hanging there. She had turned him and then sacrificed him.*

Wendy lifted her face to him; dried blood in a mask across her skin.

Not Wendy.

Alison.

What was in Wendy, what Stella called the Lamia, the demon, the dark adversary of his youth, had taken Alison over.

A voice inside him: *And you, Peter, She will turn you and hang you there for what you did to Her.*

He slowed to a stop. Nessie was just opening the door to her car, dropping her dog in the backseat, helping Stella into the shotgun seat. Charlie was almost to the wagon, too; he had not looked back to see if Peter was keeping up.

The distance between Peter and the car seemed like an enormous chasm.

If I ran?

They'd get in the car and come after me.

But if I took the car. If I took the car away from them, they'd be here. At least they'd be safe for a while. Maybe in that time I could stop Her. Or maybe in that time I would turn *and come after them.*

But, hell, it would be time.

They'd have a chance, and maybe I'd have a chance, maybe Alison is still safe. The Big What If has to work my way sometime. There's always the chance I can stop whatever turning She's doing to Alison. Always the chance.

Stella was having some trouble getting in the car; she glanced back at Peter and turned to say something to Nessie, who also turned to look at Peter.

Flickering.

Charlie, as if in slow motion, crooked his neck around, his eyes growing wide.

Flickering, Peter felt the fever and pain coming on and he knew what he must do before the beast in himself had complete control.

Car—out into the wash—out to Her—to Alison—to Lamia—to stop what—once it's started it can't be stopped— but there was a chance—buried her once—bury again—

Peter, the muscles beneath his skin contracting in uncontrollable spasms, bounded to the wagon, and leapt in the driver's side, swiftly turning the key in the ignition, slamming his foot down on the accelerator and as the car sprung to life, he sped over the side of the road, down into a cloud of dust that came up from the Rattlesnake Wash as he went.

2

Charlie ran down the edge of the Wash, but the station wagon was going too fast out into the desert.

Up on the road, Nessie turned to Stella and whispered, "I hope to God Gretchen gets through this okay."

3

Flickering as Peter drove, his eyes blurry, trying to keep his eyes on the trail, studded as it was with rocks and trash heaped up like sentries, and a phosphorescence that emanated from something he could not quite identify. He tried not to glance down at his hands (*talons*), trying to swallow the strangling feeling in his throat, trying not to run his tongue across his teeth, because they seemed sharper than usual.

Without wanting to, he glanced in the rearview mirror. He saw the dust cloud his driving had raised, and the shadows of the others back on the ridge. "You're *safe*," he whispered as if it were a prayer for them. And then he saw himself in the mirror, and it didn't look like an animal, it looked like Peter Chandler. He was *human*. It was a fight, a struggle, his blood against the invader, against the parasite that had invaded him years ago and had patiently waited for the moment when it would be activated by *Her* call.

But if I can get to go Her before I turn completely, maybe Nessie was right, maybe I can turn *on Her. Got to be a way, got to be some way.*

Just having left them back on the road at the mouth of the Wash, he felt they'd already been saved, that if they didn't try and follow him they might get out of this nightmare alive.

When he heard the sound of barking in the car he slammed his foot down on the brake and the station wagon spun a 360 in the dirt, crashing over brush and cactus, finally resting against a newly smashed Joshua tree.

"Shit!" Peter cried out, and saw that Nessie's dog wagged her tail in the backseat, and continued barking until he reached back to pet her.

His hands had not changed. He had not turned.

But still, he felt that switch inside him, a finger on a trigger about to be pulled.

4

"It's Wendy," Stella said. "She made him do that, because of me. I can feel something here."

"Excuse me, but I think we *all* feel something here," Charlie said.

"I mean something different. When you take two magnets with the same charge, positive or negative, you can never put them together. There'll be an overwhelming repulsion between the two of them. She and I are like that."

Nessie clucked her tongue. "But you've got the positive power, and she has the negative."

Stella shook her head. "I wish it were that easy. It's the same power, only different uses, and I suppose that makes it bad whether or not it's used to destroy or to heal. The only difference is my daughter has more of it than I do, or than any of us has."

Charlie shook his head. "So Peter and I just got radiation poisoning under our fingernails from working in the factory. *She's* the nuclear reactor."

"Right," Nessie said, "just like I been telling you, we got to go in there and fight fire with fire."

"We tried that once here, already," Charlie said, grimly. "Out here, you can't fight fire with fire. It's got fuel out here, it eats up the night."

Stella looked at her dark companions, and then out to the place where the station wagon had gone. "She doesn't want me out there, but she wants me here, like she wants all of us here. It can't just be for revenge. It must be because we may be the only living creatures who have in us what it will take to destroy her."

"Yeah, only we're hunting Dracula here without a stake," Charlie said. "Look, we can stand here talking all night, but my cab gave up the ghost this afternoon and I seriously doubt anyone can resurrect it. So we can either start a twenty-mile hike or make bets as to whether or not Peter left his keys in his car. I lay my money on the keys. So I'm going up the highway and when I find the car I'll be back."

Diego said, "I'll go with you."

Charlie looked at Diego the way he had when he was a boy and the old man had interviewed him six months after he'd been put in juvenile hall. It was a look that carried equal parts suspicion and confusion, as if he were sorting something out in his head.

5

Charlie hadn't wanted to tell them the real reason he needed to get away from them: he was beginning to feel the world slant and the color of the night go from indigo to a sulfurous yellow. Just when he blinked, and not completely, but he didn't want to wake up again with his left arm burned up to the elbow this time. Or with his fingers around Stella's neck.

351

He felt like a tired soldier at the close of a long war. The cold night felt good because it made him shiver, and shivering, he knew he was just a regular guy. Even the guilt he'd been carrying practically from birth was good. He had spent just about half his life being a bully, an asshole, a juvenile delinquent, someone who other kids ran from, and then the other half of his life had been in repentance and introspection. *Guilt just comes with the territory.*

He thought about what God was as he walked, but only a little—the idea of a God didn't quite figure in this part of the world, there'd been some line of demarcation over which he'd crossed, and if there *was* a God, He was the God of people outside this circle. This was a Members Only club and even God hadn't applied for membership. "Although," Charlie said, looking up to the stars, "you could be my guest for the day, God, and I'd get you in for brunch on Sunday and a friendly game of golf if you wouldn't mind coming early, like maybe tonight."

The stars were oddly square in their flickering light, and for a moment Charlie Urquart though he could see *through* them into a vast whiteness beyond, but it was just his eyes tearing up. "Always bringing God out whenever I need something badly, and then hiding from Him the rest of the time. All I ask is, you know, like an old Coke bottle, just redeem me. Even if it's just for chump change."

Then he heard a voice, within him, like a divine fire in his loins, in his stomach, bubbling through his chest and he was racked with pain.

The voice said, *Charlie, I am your god, through me your soul will be redeemed, through me you will find your way to the place wherein I dwell. Come.*

It was the voice of Deadrats. The rusty bars of a cage slid open, and a gibbering creature crawled out from a dark corner of memory.

He let Diego catch up to him.

6

An hour later, Peter slowed the station wagon, finally stopping it completely where two boulders stood like sentinels to the El Corazon Mine. Gretchen curled comfortably in his lap. He petted her, rubbing behind her ears. The fever was strong—the backs of his hands were soaked in sweat—but the flickering was less pronounced. And he wasn't turning completely. *Hey, I still got my sanity. A shred, anyway.*

He killed the headlights.

Through the boulders he saw a thin shaft of yellow light.

Demonfire. *Toxic waste of the gods, right here, the lighthouse of hell shining its path my way.*

"Good-bye, pup." He gave the Scotty one last pat on the head. There were a couple of flashlights on the backseat; he reached around and grabbed one, testing it. The light was strong. He got out of the car, shutting the dog inside, windows down. "They'll come get you and you'll be fine. Me, on the other hand . . ."

He almost fell down when he stepped away from the car. His stomach twisted. Peter balanced his hands on his knees as he bent forward to vomit, but nothing came out. He wanted to open his guts and just pour out whatever had been polluting them for so long. *But you don't have the guts,* he thought wryly.

Last time you were here you were running like crazy to get away, and now look at you, you're just aching to get in there.

He straightened himself up, trying to ignore the pain in his joints, and the fever on his skin. He also ignored the dog's barking as it sat in the dirt beside the car.

He walked up the path to the cave's mouth.

His one thought: *Alison.*

Chapter Forty-three
The Sacrament of the Sacred Heart

1

Stella

When Diego followed Charlie to revive Peter's car, Stella pulled Nessie back. "You don't have to go out there with us. Charlie said the athame was stolen; we don't even have a real weapon anymore."

Nessie opened her purse and withdrew a small handgun. "It was my papa's. It's got a few bullets in it. I carry it with me everywhere."

"I wish bullets worked. She's beyond death and life. But you're not, and I wish you'd wait here. Who knows what'll happen at those caves?" Nessie gently eased the gun back into her purse and covered it with Kleenex. They walked together through the rubble and the Garden of Eden, toward the old highway. They could hear Charlie cussing while he and Diego tried to start the car down the side of the Wash. "You saved my life, Queenie."

"Only to lose it here."

"Funny thing about that. I was all prepared 'til this morning to die, either in some sad hospital bed or in my bathtub. But you cleaned out more than my lungs this morning, Queenie, you scrubbed something that's been needing an overhaul for a long time. My soul. You know that line in the Bible? 'He restoreth my soul.' Well, you did that. I was all ready to die, but glad I got a change of plan—at least I didn't want to die from anything as mindless as cancer, and now, maybe not even from old age. I don't mind dying so long as it's for something, not just because I was sitting someplace and time and biology finally kicked in."

Stella crossed her arms in front of her, almost wistfully. "I wish I was that brave."

"Or foolish," Nessie added. "But I'm going under the assumption that none of us is going to die tonight. Because if this Lamia is what you say she is, dying's not going to be like a twenty-four hour labor with a baby at the end to make it all worthwhile. It'll be a real pain in the keester. I guess the word *agony* comes to mind. Don't think I'm so brave when every ounce of me is yelling to jump off the edge of a cliff and roll back down to the civilized world where nobody believes in this stuff anymore. Only one thing I still don't get, though."

"Only one?"

"Yep. With that other fellow, Peter. If you can cure me, and you put Charlie's bad side back somewhere, why can't you cure Peter?"

When Stella spoke again she sounded ashamed. "I can't control it. It's like a lightning bolt shoots through my fingers. But only sometimes. It's not like I can direct it. It's like this power surge."

"I figured as much. But there's a little speck of hope, then. You told me that what's in your daughter is like nuclear power. But nuclear power can get harnessed just like anything else. In fact, without people to make sure the nuclear reactor functions, there's no use for the power. It just sits and waits. So maybe we go out to that old mine and we jiggle with the machinery and just maybe we get it so it either works right or we just shut it off."

"Or," Stella added, "we have a meltdown. Remember Three Mile Island? Chernobyl?"

"Yes, Queenie, I do. But I also remember what life was like before nuclear power was in use. And I don't care what any damn kids say, they weren't *there*, they don't *know*, but life seems a lot better now with a bit of *energy* behind us."

They fell silent as they watched the headlights move along the Rattlesnake Wash. Charlie and Diego had gotten the car going again.

When they were all in the car, with Charlie driving, Nessie sat up front, trying to see through the darkness, but clouds had moved across the scant moonlight and the desert seemed like a vast crater in the dark of the moon.

"Sure hope your friend Peter is nice to Gretchen," Nessie said.

Charlie turned to her and smiled, and for a second Stella thought he growled at her, but it wasn't Charlie at all.

It was Rudy. His eyes were torn out and in their place were shiny stones. "Star, my baby, you will join me soon, yes? We will enjoy the pleasure of each other's company again, I hope. The feeling between your thighs, as old as they are, still sets my juices flowing, makes me thirsty, baby, for your blood. You still bleed, don't you?"

When the scream burst out of her throat, Stella realized that it was another hallucination. The others were staring at her. Charlie had pulled the car to the side of the road. *Rudy is gone.*

She wiped the tears from her eyes and tried to calm the heart that beat rapidly within her. "Getting hysterical. I don't know if I can really go out there. The things I did . . ."

Diego, sitting next to her, slid closer and put his arm around her to comfort her, but she saw a strange look come over his face.

2

Diego

Diego felt something from touching her, a *sucking*, like a fire in a house sucking all the air into itself. Or a vacuum cleaner. "You've got so much power in you." He tried to hide the astonishment in his voice. *Nothing should astonish you anymore, viego. Yet, this does.* His arthritis flared a little along his wrist and fingers where he'd felt the pull from her. "I've only seen it once before, in a shaman in the mountains in Chihuahua. He took herbs and homegrown narcotics to keep from being in a constant state of pain—human nerves, he told me, could be played raw by the healing gift. You're on medication?"

Nessie chimed in. "Until last night she was stoned, since, what, Queenie—oops, I mean Stella—1960 or so? But when she's on, she's like a generator that can light up the desert. I felt it."

Stella, still shaking from whatever she had seen, seemed embarrassed. She swallowed, wiping her hand across her mouth as she spoke. "I threw the last pill out this morning. God, I wish I had something."

"Maybe it's just as well you don't," Diego said. He reached over and patted her back—the pulling feeling was gone. "My friend the shaman was narcotic-free when it was time for one of his grand rituals. Apparently, the pain was a necessary part of releasing his energies."

Charlie had been fairly quiet as he drove, and Diego had just been wondering what he was thinking about when he said, "We're almost here. You guys ever wonder what we're gonna do when we get inside there?"

Nessie patted her purse. "We're going to stop her. And then we're all going to my place for some whiskey."

Stella glanced out the window. She noticed that the moon had come out from behind the clouds, and a veiled white light spread from its shine across the bumpy land. "Charlie," she began to say, but realized that it might be smarter to say nothing because Nessie was sitting next to him in the front seat. It was something she noticed, something that seemed to be getting stronger the closer they got to the caves. She smelled that animal odor, the one she'd smelled on him when she'd healed him. *It got out, again. Because she's stronger here. She's stronger than she's ever been. And now, we don't even have the athame to protect ourselves. Nessie with her gun in her purse—as if that's going to help any of us against the Lamia.*

You Come When I Call You

3

Peter

Skulls smeared with the glowing amber of demon juice lit his way up to the mouth of the cave. He hadn't seen that juice for a long time, and he wondered if, spread across the bone like that, it was somehow alive or if it had been merely touched by the Lamia. The cave was still covered over with rubble and rocks, and he remembered *carrying Alison out, thinking he would come back for Than, who was still there, with Wendy . . . Charlie had already run off with the athame . . . her heart was within each of them . . . and then the vibrations began, and something was following behind him. Something was moving with the earth toward him as he crouched down, listening to Alison's moans in his ear, and Than screeching, "OH, GOD, IT'S COMING FOR ME PETER, DON'T LEAVE ME, DON'T LET ME DIE! OH, GOD!" And the beams of wood that buttressed some parts of the old mine cracked and began falling. Some stones hit him on the head, and he went blind for the longest second before he realized it was blood dripping across his eyes, and he wiped it away. Almost to the outside, he'd thought. He whispered to Alison, "It's okay, we're out," and then it was the truth as he pulled her out of the caves, and then heard a final scream from Than Campusky as the vibrations turned into an earthquake and the mouth of the cave collapsed, and he ran with her in his arms to what he thought was safety.*

But it was only a stay of execution.

To face her.

There was a gap in the rocks that formed the only entrance in to the cave. It was big enough for a child to squeeze through. Peter scraped away at other rocks and brushed pebbles off to the side.

He began shivering like he'd been locked into a walk-in freezer and knew he would not be able to get out. He leaned down, squeezing his head and part of his shoulder through the opening. The air was dusty and damp. *Like an old cave,* he thought, swallowing the urge to laugh. He felt beneath him for solid ground, and then pulled himself through the rest of the way.

Someone on the other side grabbed his arms and helped him.

4

Stella

"You keep patting your purse," Charlie said when he pulled the car along the thin path between the rocks that led to the entrance of the cave. The station wagon was parked several yards away. Peter had left the headlights on. The Scotty sat by the back tire of the wagon, as if she'd just been waiting for them to arrive. She leapt through the open window, and ran for Nessie, who called out the dog's name.

"Gonna run my battery down, damn it." Nessie reached for the door handle to get out, but Charlie tugged on the sleeve of her sweater.

"You got a weapon in that purse?"

"My papa's gun; I been using it since I was twelve."

Charlie grabbed the purse from Nessie's lap. Stella leaned forward, reaching over to Charlie, but Charlie lunged against his door, opening it and getting out quickly before she touched him.

He leaned back into the car. "Uh-uh, lady, you ain't gonna do it twice in this life, I been locked up for too long. I know what your miracles do." It was the snarling voice of Deadrats coming through Charlie's mouth. Foam bubbled up from between his lips. "No old farts're gonna try to get to my Wendy, no fuckin' way." He reached into the purse, tossing out Kleenex and lipstick, until finally he'd found the gun. It was a small pistol. It would do the trick. He withdrew it, letting the purse drop. "I'm not so good myself at target practice, Nessie, so I'm afraid I'm gonna have to take you each out at point-blank range. Say hey to the return of Deadrats."

Gretchen sensed danger, or else she smelled what was inside the man, and she darted toward him barking and yipping.

5

Peter

The cave walls were smeared with the glowing light. *Demonfire*, Peter thought, *like firefly butts mixed with Day-Glo*. A dark figure stood before him, holding him at the shoulders.

"You remember me?"

Peter said, "Who are you?"

When the man opened his mouth it was like an old refrigerator opening, and inside, rotten meat. "I was the fat pig boy, before I died," he sniggered. "Remember?"

Peter felt it in him, and he wanted to cry out, *not now, not now,* but it was the call, her call, coming through, what had been passed to him in a dark ritual. The sacrament.

His temperature was rising rapidly. He knew it, he could feel himself go hot and cold suddenly, the salty taste of sweat across his lips.

Behind the dark figure, shadows flickered and danced against the glowing light of demonfire.

"Welcome home, son," his father said in the sweetest tones he remembered him ever using. "Good to see you, Peter."

"You're one of us now," the dark figure said, the creature that had stolen Alison from their apartment, *fat pig boy.*

Than Campusky.

"Help me, Jesus. Please help me." Peter's limbs felt like they were about to bust through his skin.

"Help me," Than Campusky imitated his impassioned voice. "You're good at this, Peter, let me tell you. Help me. The fat pig boy spent several hours saying that."

And then his old friend, and the other dark ones, fell upon him.

6

Alison

Alison was barely conscious where she lay, but she tried opening her eyes when she felt the vibrations in the earth, and heard the sounds, *whatifwhatifwhatif,* moving in a wave with the vibration toward her.

Then she thought she heard her older brother, Ed Junior, say, "Scissors cut paper, scissors cut paper."

And she could not scream, for when she tried to part her lips, something covered them tightly.

The fear that crawled within her made the pain more intense, and now she felt them—like tiny cactus needles pricking her face and her shoulders, some beneath the earth where she was partially buried. It might've been her circulation, and it might've even been the fire ants stinging her, but she knew it was something else, knew it because her nerve endings began sending electrical signals to her brain.

Her skin was shedding from her, and she imagined herself for one horrible moment as a snake giving up its old scales, and beneath it . . . *what?*

7

Peter

He saw their faces, half in the pulsating yellow-green light, and he recognized none of them, although they had all lived in Palmetto. They dragged him across rocks, and he felt the knifelike pains of their fingers in his flesh. Phantoms? Can the dead rise with demon-fire along their bodies? Of course they could. He had always known that one day he would be back among those the demon had taken. He was one of them, after all.

Then there was one face among them, which, when they set him down, was so familiar and yet so foreign for a moment.

"Dad," he gasped.

Joe Chandler stood there, his eyeless face grinning, "Peter, where have you been all these years?"

"Don't cry. You killed him. But the demon brought him back," Than Campusky said, glancing at the glowing figure of Peter's father, pulling the hood from his sweatshirt to show Peter the face that had been born beneath his first face.

"Jesus, Than," Peter whimpered, "what—"

"My name is Nathaniel, and I am the Angel of the Desolation. Fat pig boy is gone. Fat pig boy got left behind and you went to rescue your girlfriend. The pig boy screamed until he had no more voice left, and then he saw a light coming for him, and he thought it was his best friend come back just like he told him he would, or even another rescue party, but it was something else, Peter. Can you guess what it was? What's green and yellow and slides down a well? Do you know? Huh? Time's up, Petesy. You lose. It was the blood of the demon, it has a mind of its own, you see, it feels every movement of life and seeks it out, and it slid like, oh, what shall I say? Boogers, I think. Slimy boogers flowing down the stones, but flashing with light so I could see it coming. But Pete, I'd already had me some demon juice, remember? I drank some of Old Bony-face's stash, so the demon and me were friends. It spat across my face, and then like a thousand tiny inchworms, measured the space across my nostrils and then crept into them, up into my head. Up through my BRAIN, MOTHERFUCKER!" His voice echoed down the passage. When he calmed down, he began again. "It was—oh, how do I put this delicately—it was like a tickling at first, my nosehairs, and then it hurt a little but I couldn't scream because I was having trouble breathing. But no blood was spilled, no, not a drop, for the little boogers drank it as they punctured each membrane, as they flowed up through the passageways, melting bone to their liking as they went, and then into the oatmeal that my brain had become at that point. Imagine hearing chewing in your head, like a bee had crawled into your ear and was buzzing so loud—you know that feeling? It's what it was like—the demon was eating out my brain to build a little nest there. You see, the Lamia had picked our town, our little home area, Peter, because she had a tough time surviving for the past three thousand years on this hostile planet. The air is difficult for it to breathe, and the cells it invades normally die—animal cells, especially. Tissue becomes unglued for the most part. That is, unless the animal and the demon have mated, and then the offspring, say five out of fifty million times, can live, at least for a period. But the demon has spent the past thousand years moving like, well, molasses, if you will. It kept mostly to the less demanding life forms, more perfectly made than human flesh, the wild grasses, the worms that fed upon those grasses, and then, when it had spread sufficiently, it grew into the sap of a tree that was rested upon by a flea and through that flea and its descendants, passed throughout an entire continent, oh, near nine hundred years ago. And then humans became more the raw material, for Lamia taught them how she could be extracted and injected or swallowed, *passed*, if you will. Seducing teenaged boys in the middle of nothingness was easy. She came back here to spawn. This is her breeding ground. Here, in this wasteland, she was born again, and the incarnation held. She is wisdom beyond knowing." He breathed in through his nostrils. "She taught me how to absorb life, how blood was the wine of gods. She can make the dead live, and she can transform dying tissue into the most *beautiful, wondrous . . ."*

Peter's delirium made him giggle, and he thought: *I'm finally insane, and even this, around me, may not be happening. My brain is leaking. I'm turning. I'm more demon now.* His father, face sliding halfway off its skull, leaned near him and began stroking his hair.

"Alison lived. She fucked the eternal, Peter, and she lived. Do you know how few people ever do that?"

"Shut up."

"She lived longer than other flesh has with the demon inside it. I'm alive. Jesus, even *you're* alive." Than smiled. "Wendy's alive. Again. With you here." Than Campsuky leaned over and whispered in his ear, "All flesh dies. Even you, Peter, even here. Show me your pain of dying, Peter, and I'll always be your closest friend. There are others who have been waiting here for you, too, Peter. They want to share your death, will you do that for them? Will you let them watch? And after you die, Peter, oh, you will be reborn as the most beautiful creature the world has ever seen, and your number shall be the number of Man."

"Oh, my boy," Peter's father murmured, "I forgive you for killing me. You showed me the light, Peter. You showed me how blood and the stink of death is pleasure. You showed me good."

8

Diego

Charlie began laughing as the Scotty came at him with its teeth bared. He grasped it by the scruff of its neck and shook it. "I hate little yappy dogs," he said, putting the gun up to the back of the Scotty's head.

"Oh, you just put that poor dog down," Nessie warned, her arms crossed in front of her. "Imagine, someone as big as you threatening a dog."

"Nessie," Stella whispered. "It's in him again. It's not Charlie."

"You're darn tootin' oh great mother of us all," Charlie said sarcastically. He dropped the dog, which squealed and then leapt up into Nessie's lap. Nessie held Gretchen tightly to her bosom. "And now there ain't no way you're gonna cure me, and Correa, you should've done some of those drugs with your shaman buddy, might've saved your ass from coming here. Hate to knock you off, I enjoyed reading the lies the Urquart kid gave you back then for your book. Wish I'd been a free rat then, you would've gotten the whole enchilada. I think I killed about ten or twelve of my closest friends and relatives before the old bitch sent me back into the fuckin' braincave."

"How did you get out?" Diego asked. "I thought she locked you up for good."

"Oh, yeah, right, man, like I'm really gonna tell you so you can just put me back there. Well, it ain't fuckin' gonna happen. Old Widow Electrolux here ain't coming within five feet of me."

Diego thought of that sensation of touching Stella when he'd put his arm around her. *Electrolux. Why does a vacuum seem right? That sucking wind—what is it, what is it about a healing, or a casting out?* He snuck his hand over to Stella and rested it on her knee. Again, he felt it. It was a vibration, a movement. He had seen countless medicine men and shaman, and very few of them had actually generated this kind of power. *A generator. That's what Nessie had called it. She called Stella a generator. A power source. But what could be done to turn that power on when it was needed?*

And then he knew.

It had to be switched on. There had to be a switch. Something that could release the healing energy, and cast Deadrats out of Charlie. Diego tried to think hard about this as he cautiously stepped out of the car. The barrel of the handgun never left any of them; Deadrats turned it from one to the other every second as if he would shoot at random with any sudden movement.

"What we're gonna play," Deadrats said as he lined them all up, side by side, "is called slow death. I'm gonna shoot each one of you in, oh, let's say the leg, and then I'm gonna shoot one of you in the shoulder and another in the stomach, and maybe you, old man, in the balls. Hey, death is where you'll be in the next four, five years anyway, right? Your lives are over, so this ain't really gonna be a sin, now is it? I want to make sure you go with a bang. Get it? A bang? How come none of you's laughing?"

"Because it's not funny," Nessie said, clutching Gretchen up under her chin; the dog nuzzled and whined. "It's okay, Gretch, don't you worry about a thing."

Deadrats spoke with a delicious quiver. "You seem pretty fuckin' relaxed for someone so close to death."

"I am," Nessie stated, looking him in the eye.

And then, Diego turned to Stella and whispered, "You need to let it go. Push it out."

Deadrats took aim and fired the first bullet into Diego's left leg, and the old man fell to the ground, holding his knee.

It caused less pain than he'd expected: it was like an electric shock, and then just an ice-cold feeling. If Diego hadn't seen the blood dripping through his fingers as he held his hand over his knee, he wouldn't have even been sure the bullet had gone in.

Let this be the switch. Let her turn it on. "Let it go," he whispered, looking up to Stella, whose eyes were closed. *Good*, he thought, *keep your eyes closed and let it go, turn up the volume, don't keep it on low, let it out.*

He heard another bullet rip through the air, and it was meant for Nessie, but she ducked and rolled on the ground, dropping Gretchen. The dog went charging for Deadrats, and he pointed it at the approaching dog when suddenly Diego saw a chance. He remembered Stella's hysteria in the car and that feeling—as if by touching her, he was touching a live wire—and he knew he had to push that button. "DO IT! DO IT! FOR THE LOVE OF GOD, WOMAN, JUST—" And before the final shout was out of his mouth, he saw the white-blue sparks of electricity playing along the edges of Stella's fingers. He thought, at first, it was an hallucination from his own pain; later, no one could convince him it was anything less than a miracle.

Deadrats cried out, "Aw, shit!" Turning his attention to her, he aimed the gun for her midsection, but the dog was at his feet now tugging at his pants leg. He was trying to kick the thing off him and aim for the old woman at the same time. Nessie was up, too, and threw a rock at him, missed, so he turned the gun on her and fired, and this time hit her. Deadrats turned the gun on Stella and cocked the trigger back, but Diego managed to crawl on his belly toward Deadrats, who then turned the gun on him and shot him in the shoulder. Diego saw a white flash across his vision, like a neutron bomb going off, and then he looked up.

"Don't do it," he said to what he hoped was some semblance of Charlie Urquart behind this face curled in a foaming snarl.

Deadrats had the gun pointed at Stella. "Have to kill you guys a little faster than I thought." His thumb pulled back on the trigger.

Click.

Diego thought: *Thank you, Nessie, for only having four bullets in your father's gun.*

And then Stella reached over, barely even touching the young man, and he shrieked like he was being burned alive. Diego heard the popping and sputtering of a live wire.

9

Charlie

After the smell of seared flesh had stung his nostrils, Charlie came to, looking down at the gun in his hand. The last sparks of electric fire played out along his fingertips, which Stella had held for the barest moment. His hand was blackened from fire.

Charlie thought he saw some animal run out from his pants leg and scurry off, burning, into the underbrush, but it might have been a waking dream.

But Deadrats had finally deserted him completely, and he was left with the shame and the self-hatred as he had been when he was a boy. "NO!" His shout echoed through the canyon. He shoved Stella out of the way and ran up the narrow trail toward the old caves.

He was going to find Wendy and destroy her for what she had done to his life, for what she made him do to others.

10

Stella

"I can heal you." Stella knelt down beside Diego and ran her hands along his shoulders.

"I think Nessie needs you more. I'm okay for now."

"I'm afraid I can't do that, Diego. I can only heal things. I can't raise the dead."

Diego heard Gretchen whining near where Nessie had fallen. "Are you scared?" he asked.

"Not for the first time. But also, for the first time, I'll do like Nessie told us. I'll eat my fear. If Peter and Alison are in there, I helped put them there. And my daughter. There's something I've got that even she's scared of. I don't think it's the healing, but I think it may be the source of where the healing gift comes from." She felt the warmth of her electric field pass from her hands through Diego's shoulder, and watched the healing process speed up, the wound drying, the new skin growing over it. "Now, let's look at that knee," she said.

11

Charlie

Charlie saw something in the shadows after he crawled through the entrance to the mine. There, by the phosphorescent rock . . . he could smell the festering-wound odor of the demon—stronger even than it had been when they'd passed through the town.

A human figure, a girl, in silhouette.

"Wendy," he said.

The girl made a lowing noise, and pushed herself up against the rock wall.

She's scared of me.

He sniffed the air, and he didn't smell the demon from her.

Just filth.

He took a step toward her and almost tripped over some object. He looked down for a second. He could barely make out what it was: a flashlight. Peter's. Charlie bent down and picked it up. Still squatting, he shined it over at the shadow girl.

She was naked, but stood there with no shame. He thought for a moment that it was Wendy, but there was something different about her. This girl had long, reddish-brown hair, and the pale skin that Wendy had, but her face was arranged slightly differently, and she was a little shorter than Wendy Swan had been. "You're the one I saw out there, at the house," he said. "In the garden. You took the knife, didn't you? Knife?"

"*Nyeii*—" She tried to imitate the word.

But then, after the flashlight's beam had hit her, she shrieked as if she were burned by it. She tried to brush it off her face and neck, and, failing to do that, stooped over and sprinted through a low opening farther up the path. The mine itself had changed since he'd been there—it had been the cave-in that had done it, because the mines that had been dug into the three hearts of the cave had become narrow, and only the one that the girl had run off into was large enough to walk down. He would have to crawl through the others.

He went in the direction she'd taken.

Charlie thought he had lost the girl, and realized she'd led him into a poorly lit area. He was about to turn and go back when suddenly an arm shot out and grabbed him. It was the girl—she had blended like a chameleon into the side of the cave.

She sat him down, signaling with her hands for him to keep silent by covering her mouth and motioning to him. Then she brought out what looked like a rotted jewelry box. She lifted the lid, holding up what he took to be an earring. She passed it to him and he set it on his knee. Then she drew out something in her hand as if it were a small bird that she had to be gentle with. She passed it into his hands, which he cupped beneath hers.

When Charlie looked down at what she had given him, he said, "How did you get this?" It was his watch.

She didn't seem to understand his words.

"My father gave this to me. It's old." There was something about this girl that seemed familiar, beyond her resemblance to Wendy Swan. She reminded him a little of his mother, and the memory frightened him.

And then she brought another object from the box.

In her hand, she held the athame.

He shined the flashlight's beam across the dagger's hilt. The word *lamia* gleamed there.

"Careful," he said.

She brought the edge of the knife's blade to his outstretched palm.

The ceremonial knife that might be the only weapon against the demon.

The girl handed him the dagger. She murmured an unintelligible sound.

"It was you in the garden," Charlie said, "and you played in the car with the bones and the watch. If you could only speak."

Something startled the girl. She leapt up and ran farther down into the darkness. He thought that it had been his voice, but then he heard the scraping against the rocks, and turned to see something that should've stopped his heart, but *damn it, I'm still alive, my heart's still beating, and now I've got to make up for my miserable life.*

12

Peter

"Don't resist the turning," Joe Chandler said as he comforted his son, wiping his sticky hand across his forehead, "my baby, my child." Than had dragged him down the passage, through a corridor smeared with the yellow light as if by a mad child in a playroom, and then down a shaft into a cavern strung with stalactites.

He's not really your father, you heard what happened to your father. The demon in you killed him. This is the work of Wendy. This is a phantom, a dream. He shook his head. *I bet, Peter, you could just reach up with your hands and stick your fingers in her eyes.* He tried to muster the strength it would take to do it, but he could barely move his arm, let alone lift it. He tried curling his hand into a fist, but his fingers weren't even working right. Other faces, hovering above him, and he recognized Alison's father, his big, jowly face nodding in a series of silent burps, but not a word. Just a hissing sound like thousands of leaking balloons, all floating and bobbing above him.

And there, among all the faces, he thought he saw Wendy Swan. She was more beautiful than ever, and she smiled as if they had a secret between them.

He watched as her eyes seemed to draw apart from their eyelids, across the whites, and then the whites themselves pulling back like a curtain, the way he had seen the inner eyelids of cats draw back, until he saw something even his mind could not comprehend—it was like a light that gave off no light, a cold shininess, a brilliant darkness, her eyes. "You will become as one of the gods," she said, and her voice had lost none of its delicacy, its soft intonation, its seduction. She had remained young, in this cave, and she had waited just for him. And then he saw he was mistaken: it was just the eyeless face of a girl watching him, not Wendy at all, but someone he had never known from a dead town.

His father grinned toothlessly, lips drawing back over milky, drippy gums. "We all like it here," Joe Chandler said. "We're all part of her, we've all been absorbed. It's heaven."

And then, of all the horrifying things that had happened in Peter Chandler's brief existence, as far as he was concerned the worst thing of all happened when he looked up into those empty holes where his father's eyes should've been.

They got to him. He just wanted it all to be over. He wanted to be nothingness.

He lay there, shivering with fever, weeping as if he would never stop while phantoms of townspeople he hadn't even known cooed and gasped all around.

To his left, Than Campusky: his sweatshirt hood once again drawn over his head. "Turning is good," Than said, his hands gesticulating wildly about the small crowd. "These never turned, they never became. They were only good for absorption. The juice was in them, and it harvested their souls, their personalities, their lives. But you, Peter, you are one of the chosen few. Your will has been strong, but now you do not need to resist anymore. You have been called, and you have come to back to us."

His father combed his gummy fingers through his sweat-soaked scalp. "I am so proud of you, Peter, so very, very proud."

13

Stella

Stella had healed Diego too well: he told her he felt like he was fifty, and wouldn't it be great if she could bottle what she had in her, but she knew differently. They got up to the cave and, after a good twenty minutes of pushing and pulling, got inside.

"Bright as day," Stella gasped.

Diego was about to touch the rock walls with the glowing, but Stella grabbed him by the wrist. "It's residue," she warned him. "It might still be able to infect."

As if he'd been about to stick his hand into acid, Diego dropped his arms to his sides. "Guess I won't touch anything if I can help it."

"Curious." Stella crouched down as the cave narrowed. She began sniffing the cave. "I can smell her. She has a strong smell here, although I would never have recognized it before. I would know that odor anywhere. I thought she would be gone. Oh, God, I don't think I can . . ."

Diego put his hand beneath her elbow in support. "We have to."

"It's a human smell." Stella turned her face against Diego's shoulder. "It's not just the demon here, it's her human self, too. My baby."

"And in here, too," Diego whispered, "the others."

Stella didn't tell him what she thought, because she was sure he wouldn't care, this man. This man who wanted to witness some mystic experience, or a vision of the eternal. What he would get would be a flesh-eating demon that illuminated nothing while it bled them all.

What she did not tell him was: she felt a drain. Like a power surge and then a break.

Whatever healing power she had was losing strength.

It had been the only weapon she'd thought there was left.

The closer she got to Wendy, the weaker she became.

And one other thing I can't tell you, Diego.

I smell something other than my daughter here.

I smell death like I've never smelled it before.

Like a charnel house.

14

Charlie

There, among the glowing rocks, something dark moved, and Charlie hit it with a flashlight beam to see it better.

"*Charlie.*" The voice. Wendy's. Struggling to form the sound of the name.

In the light, he saw it was her. Only different. Her face seemed pinched and too unmoving, her hair wild, her body like a photograph. Her eyes were the twin obsidians he had seen so many years before, her real eyes, *demon eyes*. And she still was beautiful, her breasts were full and round, her lips accomodating, her legs long and well-formed. He saw scars running the length of her body, and as he got closer, trembling in his shoes, he realized they weren't scars at all.

"*Come,*" she rasped, and he noticed that her lips were not moving.

She moved her right hand, and in that action, he heard a tearing. Then he saw how she'd been put together, like a patchwork, her skin divided and then resewn together as if by some demented seamstress. Her face, her wrists, her breasts, all had the seams showing where the skin had been torn and then restitched. She did not sit there like a queen on a throne, but like a snake lounging by its pool. As her skin slipped like silk from her wrist, and off her breasts, she shivered, and her face began sliding down from her forehead. As it went, another pulsating skin revealed itself, glowing, not with the sickly yellow of the demon disease, but with milky liquid.

He did not want to scream, he had taught himself not to scream over scary things, but this . . . the word that came to his mind: *unspeakable,* and the scream escaped from between his lips before his mind knew madness.

15

Stella

"It was Charlie," Stella gasped. "My God, she has him."

"I can't tell which direction . . ." Diego said.

"This way." Stella pointed down one of the narrow corridors, following what she knew was whatever her daughter had become. For the closer she moved toward Wendy, the weaker she felt.

16

Peter

A howl crept up the back of Peter's throat, until he could no longer keep his mouth shut, and he let it escape. He couldn't believe it came from him as he listened to the last of its echo through the mine. He felt a tightness around his face, and along his arms and back, and then he rubbed his body against the rough stone floor. He felt a tremendous itching, as of ants biting him everywhere, and he began rubbing his skin harder and harder against the rocks, rolling around while the creatures stood back. Something, like a scarf, brushed across his lips, and he found the energy that he had lacked only moments before, to reach up and wipe it from his face.

Douglas Clegg

When he did, he looked at his fingers and saw, not only a thin layer of skin peeling back from them as if his fingers were breaking free of a glove, but also, the scarf that had brushed his face flaked into a million motes of dust in his hand.

But before it did, he saw that it was a perfect epidermal layer of skin from his face. "What's happening to me," he whispered, watching the dust that had been his flesh float lazily through the glowing air.

"Turning," Than said. "You will shed first the outer skin, layer by layer as if the finest razor is shaving it away, until you are pared down to muscle and fat and tissue and blood and bone. And then the demon will resurrect from your corrupted flesh. And you will become as a god, Peter, and drink life as one of us, and we will spread like blood across the land."

Peter inhaled the acrid scent of necrotic tissue, and realized it was his own skin, rotting, and yet rejuvenating as it died. "Oh, God help me."

Peter's father dribbled cool foam across his lips as he spoke. "Remember that trash friend of yours? The boy who killed his dog? He became a dog, too, remember? It's because on the inside he already *was* a dog, and so it just came out through his skin."

"Just look at yourself, Peter," Than gloated. "Just look. What you really are inside is gonna come out. Do you know what you look like on the inside? This is what I looked like on the inside, Peter, and you, friend, how you will look interests me a great deal."

From somewhere nearby, Peter heard a slow, steady drip of water.

Jesus, is that my blood?

"Does it hurt?" asked Than Campusky, Angel of the Desolation, as he bent down close to Peter. "It does, doesn't it? *Oh*, very good, I watch pain, for she is there, in pain, Lamia, Lamia, come into him." Than brought his face down to Peter's, and Peter saw the holes and scars like acne pockmarks along his cheeks and across his chin. The rotting stink of his breath formed a mist in the air, a steam from Than's gut rose up, a curious heat. Than brought his lips down to Peter's cheek and kissed him. "Tell me, friend, about your pain. Is it not like small, dull knives sawing slowly and unceasingly across nerve endings until they splinter and small hooks fly up their wires to your brain, to your stomach, to your balls and dig deep, deep, deep until there's pain upon blessed pain, hurt upon hurt, sore rubbing sore rubbing sore? Until pain, friend, becomes an end in itself, a friction between flesh and bone, a boil that swells around a barb that one longs to draw in and out and swirl for that . . ." Than gasped as if feeling the most exquisite pleasure. "That one moment of explosion."

My father is dead, all these people are dead, even Than probably is, too, so maybe this is an hallucination, but jeez is it like Dad said? You believe something you can't see, boy? You believe in Santa Claus? You believe in the boogey man? In demons and demonfire and demon juice and girls with stone eyes and boys who turn, turn, turn?

And in spite of the intense shooting pains that seemed to follow the course of Than Campusky's sadistic description, Peter thought: *Yeah. I do believe in what you can't see. Like love. Like brotherhood. Like good triumphant. Like hope. My will has been strong. My will is strong. I am my will. I will resist. I will fight. I will not,* and he had to resist giving into the humor of despair, *fall apart.*

And then he heard it, and it sounded like hope.

A woman moaned from somewhere nearby, not a word, but the sound was so distinctly human and helpless when compared with those of the people surrounding him, that he *knew.*

Alison. You're alive.

17

Alison

Someone stood over her, but she barely felt the presence for the pain was so intense—it was as if she were on fire and the fuel was in her bone marrow.

Alison was able to open her eyes and see a girl with beautiful shiny eyes, her face so close Alison felt she could feel the girl's breath. Alison had only ever seen Wendy Swan two, perhaps three times in her life, but she was sure this was her, although there was something different about her. She was young, she looked like a teenager with her pale white complexion and perfect skin. The girl said, "Freh."

The girl held a large leaf in her hand, and wiped it across Alison's lips. Droplets of water from the leaf tasted rusty and cold and delicious.

Alison suddenly was more terrified by the lack of pain than the pain itself. She was numb, and she thought, *I must be going into shock, I must be dying now.* Gradually, she felt the needles-and-pins of feeling coming into her arms and legs.

The girl crawled back a few feet and grabbed something. She scootched back with a dead lizard dangling from between her teeth like a cat holding a mouse.

Again, the trembling of the earth, and the whispering sounds, *whatifwhatifwhatif.* The girl dropped the lizard on Alison's neck, and turned to shoo away whatever creatures were coming forward.

The girl returned her attentions to Alison, looking at her face in a kind of awe as if it were so different than any face she'd seen before.

And then, when she touched Alison's wet face, an electrical shock shot through her like she was being poked at with a live wire, sputtering sparks across her vision until she finally had to pass out. Just before she lost consciousness, Alison thought it was no longer a teenaged girl near her, but a creature that had great leathery wings and eyes like burning candles.

18

Charlie

As the skin of Wendy's face slipped down her neck, Charlie saw what she had become. He remembered the pale lizards of the caves. This face was like that, pumping with milky fluid beneath its transparent skin, almost Wendy's face. *Almost.* Its cheekbones perfectly formed along canine jaws, the shape of its eyes, the curve of the smile. The hair growing wild from the scalp, but more like a mane of a wild animal than of a human being. Scales down her muscular arms; and she was growing larger, her neck lengthening.

Showing her true form.

"My God," Charlie said. Wings grew from her shoulders, and something burst out from her back—a long swaying whip of a tail—a stinger at its tip. Like a scorpion. *No, it's a waking dream. You're back in the dream again. Wake up! Wake up!*

What she looked like—

a dragon.

"You stare," the thing said, but its jaws did not move—instead, he saw its gullet moving as if it were swallowing something in a gentle peristaltic action. The sound of its voice came from there, below its chin. Eyes staring at him, shiny black stones. Its form elongated like a lizard's, and he could see her internal organs through the skin. Across her waist, a sheet of skin remained. As he watched it, he saw it crawled with movement. She noticed him watching. He could feel her inside his head, picking through his thoughts. She brought her hand down and brushed through the sheet—and a good part of it came off in her hand and crawled along her fingers.

Ants. Fire ants. Scorpions, too.

He felt something brush by his ankle. He looked down, shining the flashlight.

It was his father's face, lying in the dirt, staring up at him. The face moved by its scalp, which crawled with hair feelers to his shoe, leaving a trail of liquid yellow. "That's one, now, son, you hear me? That's one, and I want you to be a good boy, do we understand each other?"

Charlie tried to kick the thing off him, but his father's face opened its obscene mouth and clamped its teeth into Charlie's left leg just below the calf.

The Lamia crawled toward him as he tried to pull the face off of his ankle, and even though he had dropped the flashlight, Charlie could see through the dark and the pain to her jaws, which were open and dripping with digestive juices. The voice in her gullet said, "My lover, my Deadrats, your seed so sweet," and Charlie was blacking out, his vision becoming smaller and smaller as whorls of darkness surrounded him, and as he did, something fell from his face onto the ground in front of him, and the crazy thought went through him on his way to his braincave: *shit, it's my lips, my lips are dropping, I lost my lips . . .*

"Come to me, my love," she said, and he felt warm saliva hit the side of his face and burn like acid. He was sure she would bite a chunk of his face off next, but instead, she pressed her lips against the edge of his scalp. He knew it would be something worse than merely being devoured by this demon. He tried to fight her, but he

375

was weak, and the more he kicked at the thing attached to his leg, and tried to shove her away from his face, the more he broke through her, into a clear jelly, a wall of jelly surrounding him, and it was her body.

She was in the process of *absorbing* him.

He felt the sting of her juices working against his flesh and bone.

He brought the athame up and jabbed it into her throat, hacking away into the jelly. *Go to Hell. Go to Hell. Go to fucking Hell.*

19

But nothing happened.

We were wrong, you hear that, Peter? Ain't no weapon. Maybe on flesh, maybe if it really was still Wendy in human skin, but you can't fucking send a demon to Hell, to darkness eternal, 'cause it's already there! It would be like sending a dog home and thinking it was punishment! WE WERE WRONG!

And then he knew, in his last moments of life, why the Lamia needed to infect human beings, what she had been preparing for by spreading her demon juice through the town those many years ago.

Like passing resistance to allergies from a nursing mother to her baby, through milk, the demon spread itself through blood to prepare the flesh . . . her heart. We did the worst thing, the Awful Thing, Than lied, he lied, and it's too late, and we can't be saved, no one can . . . Charlie Urquart's thought processes cut off as her skin absorbed his scalp, then the melting skull, to get to his succulent brain.

And finally, a bit of heart that had been so long denied this creature returned home.

20

Stella and Diego

"Listen," Diego said as he entered the chamber of the cave. He smoothed the air with his hands as if trying to isolate the noise. "Whispering. Must be bats."

Stella prayed quietly to herself. She must not tell him how her body felt like it was barely holding itself together. *I am too old for this. I should've died already.*

Stella followed behind, keeping her hand to Diego's shoulder as if to let go of it would mean falling off the edge of a cliff.

They both heard it, barely audible. *Whatifwhatifwhatif.*

Stella let out a shriek, and then covered her own mouth. "I stepped on something," she whispered. "It moved."

Diego directed the flashlight beam downward, and scanned it across an enormous cavern, and a garden of sorts, white and yellow roses growing alongside indigo pools. And among the roses, other things were planted.

Human beings lying in heaps together. "From town?" Diego asked.

Stella was shivering so badly she could not speak. It had been the boy who once upon a time delivered her copy of the *Los Angeles Times* that she had stepped on. His face had felt like jelly. He looked up at her, and she could not tell if he was dead. She was sure his lips were moving. The imprint of her shoe was still on his nose and cheek.

Stella finally whispered, "I've seen all of them. There's Trudy Virtue." She pointed to a large woman lying in the dirt, her eyes open and fluttering.

whatifwhatifwhatif

"Are they dead?" Stella asked.

Diego walked among the roses and bundles of human flesh like he was wading through a river. "I don't know. Look—their eyes. Some are open, and there's movement, and some are closed. Their lips."

"Moving," Stella said.

A shadowy movement at the far end of the cavern caught Diego's eye; he flashed his light toward it.

The man standing there looked like a living corpse. "This is my Garden of Eden, which has been untended too long," he said. "Welcome, one and all."

Stella noticed that Peter Chandler was there, too, only he was partially buried in the dirt, and his face was blank, as if he had seen or felt something so terrifying that his mind had leaked from him as a survival mechanism. *If I can just get to him. Touch him. To bring him back from turning.*

377

She tried to remember how Diego had driven the power into her fingertips outside when she'd cast Deadrats out of Charlie. But she trembled, feeling the power flickering as if she were no longer a generator, or even an Electrolux, but just an old sixty-watt bulb that had been in the socket too long. *It's the field, the electromagnetic field between us, when we get close to each other, we both weaken.*

At least, I hope she's weakening. I hope to hell she doesn't draw strength from my weakness.

21

Alison

Alison awoke to find herself in the underground hall, pressed against other bodies, all of which seemed to be breathing. Although she was too distant to see Stella and Diego as they stepped through the cavern, she thought she heard the sound of Peter's voice, and it chilled her.

He was howling.

The girl still crouched over her, and put her fingers to her lips.

Alison experienced a strange sensation: her limbs still felt heavy, and there were shooting pains along her ribcage.

22

Stella

"I am Nathaniel, Angel of the Desolation," the man said as Diego approached him.

In the light, crawling laboriously behind Than, were small creatures.

"Demons," Stella said.

"*Children!*" Than raged. "Her children!"

They resembled small hairless kittens, their eyes large and charcoal black, and they moved on their bellies in a rippling, coiling motion like worms. Something about their faces remained undeveloped, as if they were almost formed—as if some sculptor had yet to put the finishing touches to them.

Than nodded, waving his hands out to reveal more of the creatures pouring from the walls. "She is the great goddess, she contains multitudes within her. She only needed to mate at the fertile time, just before the death of the human flesh. Welcome to her nest." The wriggling creatures whispered among themselves, *whatifwhatifwhatifwhatif*, it was the sound of their developing hearts beating like wings against a cage.

23

Peter

Lightning across black eyes, searing heart of yellow green flame, see it, see it, SEE THE PARASITE EATING DEMON CELLS, PREPARE THE WAY OF THE LAMIA, HER NEST, HER CHILDREN, A TOWN FOR FOOD, A PERFECT PLACE TO SETTLE DOWN, PALMETTO HAS RIPE FLESH AND NO ONE CARES FOR IT, SCORPION WITH ITS YOUNG ON ITS BACK CRAWLING, Peter felt the turning pain like branding irons sizzling, tickling his belly, his chest, ripping flesh like jelly with pincers.

24

Than Campusky watched Peter writhe on the ground. "The father was one of us, Peter. You, I, or Charlie. We were the seeds in her garden. And only one mistake, only one freak. And the rest, these beautiful children. See how they grow."

"But *they're* freaks," Stella said, her demeanor changing from one of fear to one of anger and authority. "My daughter is the mother of . . . of . . ."

"Demons?" Than giggled. "Like you?"

"No, I'll never believe that. Part of her was human."

"*Was*? She lives still, here, she is mother of us all."

"She can't be," Peter said. "The demon was in her. It destroys flesh."

Than said, "It loves the flesh, Peter, it *caresses* the flesh. Look," and Than pulled the hood of his sweatshirt down and showed Diego where his scalp had been opened up and bored into. "Still in me, giving me pleasure, so much pleasure, Peter, and in you, too, and in Alison. Demon juice. Even Charlie tasted it before he was absorbed. He died in love, drunk and in love. The wine of the gods."

Stella said, "And Alison—what have you done to her?"

"YOU GODDAMN BITCH!" Than spat, his rage turning his skin yellow. "YOU SHOULD DIE FOR YOUR UNNATURAL CRIMES! AND PETER, YOU BETRAYED ME, YOU LEFT ME TO DIE, AND NOW YOU COME BACK, ALL OF YOU, AND WE ARE ONE FLESH! I SHOULD LET ALISON DIE THE MOST PAINFUL DEATH AND LET YOU WATCH!" Then his voice quieted. "But she is being harvested. Lamia needs her, needs you, too, Peter, for the harvest."

Diego asked, "Are you harvesting blood?"

Than shook his head. "You are mistaken. I myself have developed a taste for blood, but Lamia's children are *in* the blood. Passed through the blood."

"Then what does Alison have?"

"She is turning, and turning successfully, and so is my friend Peter. Lamia's children need her cells, because as you see, for all their beauty, they do not live long, my little ones, they feed." He pointed to one of the things as it attached its lips to the forehead of Alison's brother Harv. "They regenerate the skin and the blood of the dead, but they can't live off their own creations, just as you could not live long on your own vomit."

"You said there was a freak here," Diego said, feeling bold.

Than hissed, "Stupid monkey child, immune to Lamia, she is a mutation. Her brothers and sisters will not even drink her blood. She will die like any mortal. She has nothing but weakness."

And another child stepped out from the dark of the cave, but this was a human child standing about five feet, four inches tall, with a sallow complexion, and long red hair. She scurried over and crouched down beside Than, who petted the top of her head. "Too much of Charlie, I'm afraid. See her eyes, how they are ordinary and human."

"She looks the way my daughter did," Stella said, "once upon a time." Stella watched the girl leapfrog across the garden of bodies, to where Peter writhed in his turning agony.

"She is useless," Than growled. "She is a different . . . *frequency*. . . ."

380

The girl crouched beside Peter and looked at the others as if she wanted them to explain why this man writhed so in the dust.

25

Peter

He was only dimly aware of the animal bent over him, but he smelled his flesh where her touch burned him.

My will to resist, the thought seemed to come from nowhere, and with it a strength.

26

Something moved through one of the tunnels into the cavern, into the smear of yellow light, and as it came, it said, "Mother, you've come to me."

27

She was beautiful. Her skin shone like porcelain, her hair was radiant, her eyes the darkest stone. A smile played at the edge of her lips. "Life tastes so beautiful," Wendy said. She wore a dress of human skin, faces all strung together, their lips and eyes sewn shut. "Charlie Urquart had a vibrant will, a pulse that burned when you tasted it. His life has rejuvenated my flesh. He took good care of my heart."

"I see through you," Diego said.

"Stupid old man. Of course you do. I am everything you've dreamed of knowing. I am your Mystery."

"You're something that lives beneath rocks," Diego spat. "You hide in darkness because the light will show you for what you are. You're not even a demon, are you? You're some throwback, an intermediate stage in our evolution. Our flesh is stronger than yours, it lives beyond your short life."

"I am your life, dying man, I eat your life and turn it into something beautiful."

"No, you're just a snake, a worm, a crawling stomach with eyes and a mouth, and reproductive organs. You absorb, but you don't generate."

"Come here, and I will show you what I can do."

"All right," Diego grabbed Stella's hand.

"*Please,*" Stella whispered, "*it's gone. The healing. All I feel is some wavelength passing through me, like static, with no signal.*"

28

Peter found his strength and began to rise. Only later would he realize what had cured him, what had stopped the turning.

29

Stella let go of Diego's hand as she stepped so close to her daughter that she could almost touch her.

30

Than ran over and grabbed Alison by the wrist. He shouted, "Lamia, absorb this one. She is turning, she will give you the strength."

Wendy Swan, or what had rejuvenated the skin and hair and bones of Wendy Swan from the energies of the dead, glanced over at her Desolation Angel and the girl he held.

And in that moment, Stella grabbed Wendy's wrist.

31

Peter lunged for Than, knocking him onto the ground. Alison stepped back; hands from the earth grabbed her ankles and began pulling her down; she lost her balance and fell into the open arms of her dead brother, Ed Junior, who whispered in her ear, "what if what if what if what if."

32

The Lamia's true form reasserted itself through the skin and dress of Wendy Swan. Milky fluid pumped through the open wounds of its transparent skin. "You think you can heal me, Mother?" She writhed beneath Stella's grasp. The older woman had the sensation of holding a live eel in her hands. The demon was wild, it was made up of all things it had once been. Diego reached forward and grasped Stella's free hand, and the feeling was passed to him: *lamia was fluid from steamy swamps, trapped in fossils a million years before, released in an upheaval of the earth, moving through a soup of organisms, from the simplest to the most complex, but always remaining in the dark, beneath rocks, in the shade, always feeding from the dying, trying to reproduce, to spray itself into anything that would bear fruit, until finally a depraved animal walking on two feet learned to pass lamia, to cultivate and worship lamia, to call it god, then demon, when all it was was some parasitic cells combining and recombining to imitate the life it took. And something even deeper buried in its makeup, a spark of life that was almost identifiable, and Diego's only word for it was spirit, or perhaps, illumination.* He let go of Stella's hand when it got too hot.

33

"You gonna kill me again?" Than spat at Peter.

Peter slammed him against a rock. "Don't you ever touch Alison."

"Know what time it is?" Than asked, wiping the blood from his lips. "Time to die." He swung out at Peter, catching him behind the left ear with his fist, and then getting him in a headlock. Peter struggled in the iron grip. "I'm gonna juice you, Peter, it's what I've dreamed of doing. I've juiced a lot of people, but I bet your blood's gonna be sweet. You ever taste blood, Pete? It's so *sweet*, it's so *sweet*."

And just when Peter Chandler thought he was going to feel the blood burst like a zit out of the back of his head, Campusky started screeching at the top of his lungs.

34

Stella said, "You're terrified of me, aren't you? It was what had gotten into my blood that kept your flesh alive."

"I stopped needing your sustenance years ago. At the first death. And I know how you lose your energy when we are together. I suck it from you. You being alive has given me strength. You don't even understand, stupid human."

"And now, I will come to you, my baby," Stella moved closer, almost touching the thing that was quickly losing all its human characteristics. "Absorb me, Wendy." Stella pressed herself into the digesting skin of the Lamia. She felt the sting of digestive juices as the jelly of skin folded around her forearm.

35

Than Campusky let go of Peter, and stopped screaming as a flame shot out of his mouth.

Peter watched as Than's body began burning. Red and yellow fires burned along his scalp like a halo; and then his skin blackened.

He didn't understand, until he saw Wendy Swan's daughter standing over Than with a dagger in her hands and a wild look on her face. The athame—the girl had it. She dropped it at his feet.

He heard Alison cussing, and got up to go help her.

But above all this shouting and screaming, he heard a remembered voice.

Wendy Swan cried out to him, "*Peter, you are always here with me. We are joined forever.*"

36

Diego cried out, "NO!" He tried to pull Stella back, but it was too late, the absorption had begun.

Stella, hiding the pain she was just beginning to feel, gasped, "Do you feel it yet, Wendy?"

The creature eyed her suspiciously. "I feel nothing."

Stella had a grin of triumph. She mouthed the words, "Get out, get them out," to Diego, who still tried to draw her from the demon, "she dies with me."

Then Diego felt it from her.

And knew that the demon had been correct in its assessment.

I feel nothing, it had said.

Diego had felt it, too, touching Stella. The nothing of that electrical wavelength, the static, the emptiness.

Like the meeting of matter and antimatter, his thoughts raced ahead of his actions. He wanted to thank Stella for what she was doing, but he knew he had to get the others out of the cavern, out of the mine, and they had no time.

Matter can never combine with antimatter. Where they coexist, there is nothing, there can be nothing.

As the demon, halfway through its absorption of Stella, began to feel its own mortality, it sent vibrations through the cave that spread like water, and the earth began trembling violently.

"*Peter,*" Stella gasped, as if inside his head.

37

Peter

Wendy stood before him, young and beautiful. Her hips beckoned; her eyes flashed; her red hair flickered with some electrical energy. No one else seemed to be there; a yellow smoke surrounded them. She was naked, and beautiful, and covered with blood as if someone had sliced razors along her lovely, pale skin.

"Please, Peter," she said, tears in her eyes, "I need it back. It's the only thing that will release me from this . . . this torment."

His body betrayed him; he felt an erection straining against his pants; he felt, again, like a sixteen-year-old, horny, lusting, longing, wanting to be wrapped in those arms, wanting to enfold himself into her angel's wings, to feel that warmth and the surge of power . . .

And then he felt the call, her call, and he knew that he would be turning, he would become the creature the demon blood had destined him to be.

"Peter," she said.

It's a waking dream. She's a monster. She's fucking with my mind.

38

Waking dream

He pressed his talons—for he had turned, and he was like her, demon, and whether it was a waking dream or reality, he knew his fate was sealed—he pressed the sharp nails into the flesh, just where his heart would be—

And withdrew a beating fragment—she had been there all along, within him, in this dream, her heart buried in his body like a seed planted in a garden.

The blood as it dripped on the heart seemed to fill its crevices, and the heart began to grow, and beat, until it was like a small red bird, a dove soaked in blood, cupped in his hand.

"It's mine," she said, her breath warm on his face as she reached her hand out for the red dove. "The sacrament of the sacred heart."

He lifted the bird up to her, and held it, felt its beating, in his hand. He knelt down with the bird in the one hand, an offering.

"Peter, you shall be my lover," Wendy said. "I have loved you all these years. I have given you my heart. Bring it to me. Join with me."

Kneeling, he saw the torn skin beneath her breast.

The flesh nest where the red bird would be caged.

He felt in the dirt.

He found what he needed.

Something like a beast seemed to beat against his head, from within his own skull, a wild animal trying to take him over.

As he passed her the red dove, her hands encircling it,

He found the blade, the athame, and he prayed and believed in its power like he never had before, remembering Charlie and Than and Alison and Sloan, the way they had been, and their families for all the pain, it was worse not having them, the childhoods that had been stolen by this creature.

Even the true Wendy he remembered, and how her life had been taken over by this monster.

She's weak now, while she's absorbing me, Stella's voice came into his head.

Do it. I've weakened her. I've broken through her power. Now is the moment.

The dream burst apart, and the world of the cave was half-dream, half-real . . . Peter brought the blade up against Wendy's hands, against the red dove, the beating heart forming even as the trace of flame grew from its center with the knife digging into it.

To send it back home.

To send it to Hell.

And as the red dove burst into a shower of sparks, and Wendy's eyes melted from human to dark stone,

he heard the silence within him, the silence of his own mind, and there was no beast there, no other voice, no call.

The cave began to shake violently, rocks falling from the cavern ceiling. Peter's one thought now was: *Alison.*

Peter ran along along the trembling rock floor, and through the billowing smoke, he found Alison entangled in the grip of the demon larvae. He lifted Alison up in his arms, pulling her free of the grasping phantoms that were dying even as they were born.

Epilogue
Legacy of the Demon

1

Peter Chandler/Confessions

Diego escaped, as did Alison and I, and Wendy's daughter, too, running faster than the wind out of the mine. We were greeted by Gretchen, barking and leaping, leaving her dead mistress's body briefly to greet us.

The old El Corazon Mine fell again—one of its many cave-ins since it was first created. Earthquakes and temblors are no strangers to the high desert, and perhaps it was nature, or perhaps it was the Lamia, but it came down in dust and smoke and ash. It was a tomb now, for what Wendy had become, the creature known to us as the Lamia, the stealer of children and the drinker of blood by legend; or a synthesis of one species with another, perhaps of this world, perhaps of another. But it seemed to me then that it was Wendy and Stella, and Charlie and Kevin Sloan and Than Campusky and all our parents, all there, within that geologic monument, an entire town's energy unleashed for the purpose of changing one form of life into another. A spawning ground of some infinite creature. And, like all creatures, its will was to breed, to find a way to survive in a hostile environment, to go forth and multiply. Later, Diego would tell me that when the Lamia had absorbed Stella, the demon and the healer, coming together as one body, had been enough to destroy it. Or perhaps my waking dream of destroying that part of her heart that I had taken from her—perhaps that had stopped the demon. The vibrations were from that, although we would hear on the news that an earthquake was reported up in Twenty-nine Palms that morning.

But I believe it was Wendy's heart that destroyed the monster. A heart we all carried with us for all those years.

The mine burned by some internal fuel.

It was like fireworks.

It went up like the Fourth of July.

Morning. We came out into the warm desert sun, not knowing until then that the night had passed. Survivors of the infinite, of the unknowable. Of demons. Of shadows. Of our own youth, we had survived, Alison, and I, through the terror and memory and lies, somehow we had stopped the beast. And the world had continued revolving.

"The athame," I said, "it's in there. What if one of . . . those . . . offspring . . . survive."

Diego managed a smile and said, "Ah, that is the big What If, Peter. Perhaps we will be fighting all over again one day. But now, it's time to rest."

And it was: I felt as if I might die from exhaustion at any moment, as if in sending what Wendy had become to Hell had taken all but the last drop of life from me. Alison slept in my arms, in the station wagon, the windows down, and a gentle breeze from the hills. I did not sleep—I watched the mine, afraid that it had all been an hallucination, that in fact the progeny would come crawling through the cracks in the hill, and with them, their mother, stronger, her voice calling us to come to her now, come and be part of her . . .

Diego sat up, too, on a pile of rocks near the car. He wiped his brow with a cloth, and watched the mine. His eyes didn't seem to register fear, only a kind of amazement. I had not liked this man before, I had not thought he was anything other than a graverobber. I knew differently now. I asked him, "So did you find it? The illumination you were looking for?"

The old man shrugged his shoulders and looked at me like I was still too young to know. "We never find what we look for, Peter. That would mean death. The journey never ends. But I found something more important. I found a reason to believe. I had almost lost that. I almost lost it."

"Me, too," I said, cradling Alison, closing my eyes, finding something within me, another voice, not Wendy's, not even mine, but a voice that was there all the time, a voice that has no name, but calls us to our fate, our journey.

Perhaps that area of the high desert, what has been named Boniface Well, Palmetto, Naranja Canyon, and Nitro will always remain a blank spot on the map, a place for refuse, a place to be avoided by human beings. A place that will always be No Man's Land. We've got the whole human race rushing to make toxic waste dumps for its mistakes, for the things that men have created that have gotten a little too out of control. Nobody wants toxic waste in their backyard, and so places like Palmetto and its hills become ideal dumping grounds.

No energy is wasted. This is true. Maybe absorbed, but never wasted. What had been in Wendy Swan, and The Juicer, and who knows how many tormented souls before that, what we called the Lamia, was toxic waste, perhaps fallout from the beginning of the earth's history, something that could not be destroyed, could not be undone, the exhaust from some primordial fuel, but fuel for very human evil, for vengeance and murder and hatred and cruelty. It was a vital fluid that could sweep through the blood and take it over, but in its exhaust lay a deadly poison. If we became beasts, or worse, beneath the Lamia's gaze, it was because we humans have beasts in us just waiting for release, waiting to break through the bars of our soul-cages. And the demon disease was stronger in us than in others, as was our ability to resist. Can the fires of Hell really burn out such poison?

Another Big What If: What if she is still in us? In Alison, in me. Stella healed Charlie, too, and his dark side came out through his skin again. When will the call come again? When will that splinter that's gotten under our skins work its way to our hearts? Have we defeated the dragon only to take its place? Or is it sleeping there in our cells, waiting for the password that will awaken it and open its prison?

Stella's last words, "She dies with me."

She dies with me.

Did she at last find the cage within herself to lock the demon in, to make it go down whatever dark and mysterious road her consciousness took as it left her body? Could she draw the Lamia out of this earthly sphere and take it to whatever idiot wavelength exists beyond the material world we know?

I hope.

I guess that's the best I can do. And I hope that they had the strength to keep the demon caged on the journey. No, that I don't hope. That I know. Whatever world exists beyond this one, whatever frequencies our souls will ride when our flesh dies, that world must be one of justice and mercy and redemption, it must be a finer place for all those who, in the name of friendship and love and what is right, are used so cruelly by the toxic waste of this landscape. No energy is wasted, Charlie and Stella, so I know you've tamed that beast in the cage. Than and Sloan, my friends. And even Wendy, and perhaps even that sliver of humanity in her, together, perhaps, where the mother and child are not made strangers by the vulnerability of flesh and damaged spirit.

I once had a friend who asked me to kill him, and I once betrayed a friend, I once murdered my father. It seems to me that I have never had a friend but that I somehow let him down. Once Kevin Sloan asked me: "Who weeps?"

And I will finally confess that I do, and I would hazard a guess that there is not one person who enters the wasteland and does not.

Alison wonders about Hell, wonders about Wendy and Stella and the others who went ahead of them. But it seems to both of us that Charlie and Wendy and Stella may already have lived in Hell before they left this world, that if there is an afterlife, then it has to be one of peace for those who have been so tormented.

We covered the small space at the El Corazon's entrance with rocks to help discourage those who will come later. Gaps, too, all around the mine—we filled them with stones, patched them with pebbles. Perhaps we'll come back with cement and seal it further. But the creatures are not in the cave, they are in the world, in us, but we will seal this place like a holy tomb. We covered Nessie's body with a blanket, and will have to deal with the authorities sometime this evening. There is another world out there, what some people call the real world, but which enough of us know is not real enough. And then, there's Wendy's daughter.

"It's done," Peter says as he places the last stone at the entrance to the cave; but he wonders if it will ever be done. It has been a long and arduous task, but Alison has matched him rock for rock, and it is still daylight. There are thin fumes escaping from the cracks between the rocks.

"All those years, she waited," Alison had said when she had rolled the first stone in front of the cave. *"Maybe we're only buying time, but we might be able to make it longer this time if we do it right. If there's a chance something is still in there . . ."*

And now, six hours later, there are only small cracks through the rocks. The cave entrance is filled.

The girl, Wendy's daughter, stands off to the side, watching them. Sniffing them. Diego sleeps in the back of the car as old men must do when they've been through such ordeals, and Nessie's dog stays near her mistress's blanket-covered body at the car.

"Charlie," Peter tells the rocks he has just set up to the entrance, "your daughter is wild and born out of nightmares. But she is beautiful."

Alison looks at Peter, and she doesn't even have to ask, because they now seem to communicate without words between each other. *What are we going to do with her?*

Peter does not even have to say it aloud, what he is thinking, and Alison nods, understanding.

"It's going to be difficult," Alison says. "What if she can't live in our world?"

Peter watches the girl as she crouches down near a rock. Around her wrist she wears a watch. She holds the watch up to her ear, listening to the ticking. *Time*, Peter thinks. "Diego will help us, I think. And she's mostly human, isn't she?" But it is hard to believe—she looks so much like her mother—the red hair, the pale white skin, the way she stands. She clutches the tartan blanket they gave her around her shoulders.

But her eyes.

The truth of her, through those eyes.

Not the dark onyx beneath the outer eyes that Wendy had.

But her father's eyes: blue and clear and human. *I will try to be*

391

as good a father as you might've been, Charlie, Peter thinks, *and I will not abandon her.*

Alison turns to him, reading his thoughts, and even with the welts on her arms and her neck, and the swollen skin on her face and the cuts and bruises and burns, he thinks she is more beautiful than any creature on the face of the earth and he feels a surge of joy within him even in the midst of this tragedy. Peter takes a deep breath and the air is cool and fresh, and he can feel the sun on his scalp. His hands and arms hurt from all the night and day's labor. Peter Chandler takes Alison's hands in his and he feels something he has never known before although he doesn't know a word for it, a sense of peace, of having come through the wasteland to the higher ground. Being alive, breathing, feeling her warmth in his hands, like a strong current going through him, getting stronger.

He draws her to him and holds her and she feels what he feels, and it is only the feeling of desert sun and light wind. And something entirely human, too, something that can only exist between flesh and blood and bone, something that has no name, although the closest word Peter can come up with is: *grace*.

For a moment, the man and the woman forget their wounds from the past and turn toward the child, who is watching them with something approaching wonder.

3

The tapes, interview in 1980

"You want to give birth."

"I have given birth. I want more than that."

"Tell me."

"I'll tell you now, old man. But one day, when we meet face to face, you'll see for yourself. And we will meet. My will is strong. I will watch each of you suffer before me for what has been done. What they did to me. What they still do to me, even now. How I brought them into the world of the gods, and how they turned their backs on creation."

"What more do you want from these boys and this girl?"

"I will never leave them," the creature says, speaking through the mouth of the boy named Peter. "They believe they have performed some ritual to keep me in darkness. But I will grow in each of them, like a heart growing within their own hearts, until they will not be able to resist my call."

"And then?"

"My children will walk in the sun. Why should I only live in darkness, or in other's flesh?" the creature asks, and then the creature goes silent within the boy.

The man turns off the tape machine.

NIGHTMARE CHRONICLES

DOUGLAS CLEGG

It begins in an old tenement with a horrifying crime. It continues after midnight, when a young boy, held captive in a basement, is filled with unearthly visions of fantastic and frightening worlds. How could his kidnappers know that the ransom would be their own souls? For as the hours pass, the boy's nightmares invade his captors like parasites—and soon, they become real. Thirteen nightmares unfold: A young man searches for his dead wife among the crumbling buildings of Manhattan... A journalist seeks the ultimate evil in a plague-ridden outpost of India... Ancient rituals begin anew with the mystery of a teenage girl's disappearance... In a hospital for the criminally insane, there is only one doorway to salvation... But the night is not yet over, and the real nightmare has just begun. Thirteen chilling tales of terror from one of the masters of the horror story.

___4580-X $5.50 US/$6.50 CAN

Dorchester Publishing Co., Inc.
P.O. Box 6640
Wayne, PA 19087-8640

Please add $1.75 for shipping and handling for the first book and $.50 for each book thereafter. NY, NYC, and PA residents, please add appropriate sales tax. No cash, stamps, or C.O.D.s. All orders shipped within 6 weeks via postal service book rate. Canadian orders require $2.00 extra postage and must be paid in U.S. dollars through a U.S. banking facility.

Name_____
Address_____
City_____State_____Zip_____
I have enclosed $_____ in payment for the checked book(s).
Payment <u>must</u> accompany all orders. ❑ Please send a free catalog.
CHECK OUT OUR WEBSITE! www.dorchesterpub.com

DOUGLAS

HALLOWEEN THE

MAN

CLEGG

The New England coastal town of Stonehaven has a history of nightmares—and dark secrets. When Stony Crawford becomes a pawn in a game of horror and darkness, he finds that he alone holds the key to the mystery of Stonehaven, and to the power of the unspeakable creature trapped within a summer mansion.

___4439-0 $5.50 US/$6.50 CAN

Dorchester Publishing Co., Inc.
P.O. Box 6640
Wayne, PA 19087-8640

Please add $1.75 for shipping and handling for the first book and $.50 for each book thereafter. NY, NYC, and PA residents, please add appropriate sales tax. No cash, stamps, or C.O.D.s. All orders shipped within 6 weeks via postal service book rate. Canadian orders require $2.00 extra postage and must be paid in U.S. dollars through a U.S. banking facility.

Name_____
Address_____
City_____State_____Zip_____
I have enclosed $_____ in payment for the checked book(s).
Payment <u>must</u> accompany all orders. ☐ Please send a free catalog.
CHECK OUT OUR WEBSITE! www.dorchesterpub.com

BLACK RIVER FALLS
ED GORMAN

"Gorman's writing is strong, fast and sleek as a
bullet. He's one of the best."
—Dean Koontz

Who would want to kill a beautiful young woman like
Alison...and why? But whatever happens, nineteen-year-old
Ben Tyler swears that he will protect her. It hasn't been easy
for Ben—the boy the other kids always picked on. But then
Ben finds Alison and at last things are going his way...Until
one day he learns a secret so ugly that his entire life is
changed forever. A secret that threatens to destroy everyone
he loves. A secret as dark and dangerous as the tumbling
waters of Black River Falls.

"Gorman has a way of getting into his characters and
they have a way of getting into you."
—Robert Block, author of *Psycho*

——4265-7 $4.99 US/$5.99 CAN

Cold Blue Midnight

Ed Gorman

In Indiana the condemned die at midnight—killers like Peter Tapley, a twisted man who lives in his mother's shadow and takes his hatred out on trusting young women. Six years after Tapley's execution, his ex-wife Jill is trying to live down his crimes. But somewhere in the chilly nights someone won't let her forget. Someone who still blames her for her husband's hideous deeds. Someone who plans to make her pay . . . in blood.

___4417-X $4.99 US/$5.99 CAN

Elizabeth Massie
Sineater

According to legend, the sineater is a dark and mysterious figure of the night, condemned to live alone in the woods, who devours food from the chests of the dead to absorb their sins into his own soul. To look upon the face of the sineater is to see the face of all the evil he has eaten. But in a small Virginia town, the order is broken. With the violated taboo comes a rash of horrifying events. But does the evil emanate from the sineater...or from an even darker force?

___4407-2 $5.99 US/$6.99 CAN

DRAWN TO THE GRAVE — MARY ANN MITCHELL

"A tight, taut dark fantasy with surprising plot twists and a lot of spooky atmosphere."
—Ed Gorman

Beverly thinks that she has found something special with Carl, until she realizes that he has stolen from her. But he doesn't just steal her money and her property—he steals her very life. Suddenly she is helpless and alone, able only to watch in growing despair as her flesh begins to decay and each day transforms her more and more into a corpse—a corpse without the release of death.

But Beverly is not truly alone, for Carl is always nearby, watching her and waiting. He knows that soon he will need another unknowing victim, another beautiful woman he can seduce...and destroy. And when lovely young Megan walks into his web, he knows he has found his next lover. For what can possibly go wrong with his plan, a plan he has practiced to perfection so many times before?

___4290-8 $4.99 US/$5.99 CAN

Dorchester Publishing Co., Inc.
P.O. Box 6640
Wayne, PA 19087-8640

Please add $1.75 for shipping and handling for the first book and $.50 for each book thereafter. NY, NYC, and PA residents, please add appropriate sales tax. No cash, stamps, or C.O.D.s. All orders shipped within 6 weeks via postal service book rate. Canadian orders require $2.00 extra postage and must be paid in U.S. dollars through a U.S. banking facility.

Name_____
Address_____
City_____ State_____ Zip_____
I have enclosed $_____ in payment for the checked book(s).
Payment <u>must</u> accompany all orders. ❑ Please send a free catalog.